THE
ICARUS
JOB

THE ICARUS JOB

TIMOTHY ZAHN

A Baen Books Original

Baen Publishing Enterprises
P.O. Box 1403
Riverdale, NY 10471
www.baen.com

ISBN: 978-1-9821-9325-6

Cover art by Dave Seeley

First printing, March 2024

Distributed by Simon & Schuster
1230 Avenue of the Americas
New York, NY 10020

Library of Congress Cataloging-in-Publication Data

Names: Zahn, Timothy, author.
Title: The Icarus job / Timothy Zahn.
Description: Riverdale, NY : Baen Publishing Enterprises, 2024. | Series: The Icarus saga ; 3
Identifiers: LCCN 2023048253 (print) | LCCN 2023048254 (ebook) | ISBN 9781982193256 (hardcover) | ISBN 9781625799517 (ebook)
Subjects: LCSH: Interstellar travel—Fiction. | Life on other planets—Fiction. | Assassins—Fiction. | LCGFT: Science fiction. | Thrillers (Fiction) | Novels.
Classification: LCC PS3576.A33 I285 2024 (print) | LCC PS3576.A33 (ebook) | DDC 813/.54—dc23/eng/20231016
LC record available at https://lccn.loc.gov/2023048253
LC ebook record available at https://lccn.loc.gov/2023048254

Printed in the United States of America

10 9 8 7 6 5 4 3 2 1

THE
ICARUS
JOB

CHAPTER ONE

As my father used to say, *The best strategy in a barroom fight is to stay completely out of it.* I'd always considered that wise advice.

Of course, as he also used to say, *That probably won't work if you're the one who started it.*

Which technically I hadn't. All I'd done was show up in the same taverno as a man named Oberon, bounty hunter and all-around nasty person, who typically came here for his evening pick-me-up. I hadn't even had to remind him why he was nurturing a long and simmering grudge against me. He'd picked up on that all by himself.

"We don't have to do this," I protested as I backed slowly but steadily across the taverno floor, hoping that I wasn't about to back into a chair.

Or, worse, into a person. If Oberon had friends in here watching the show, the whole thing could quickly degenerate into very unfavorable odds.

Still, I figured that was unlikely. It was true that bounty hunters as a group tended to stick together against the hard and uncaring Spiral, and while I once again had my license I was mostly retired from the business. Given there were probably at least a couple more hunters in a place like this, that mutual support attitude might lead to trouble.

But Oberon's lovely little niche market of organizing slave-on-slave and prisoner-on-prisoner death battles to amuse the more degenerate of the wealthy class hadn't exactly endeared him to the general hunter population. It was a good bet that anyone in here who knew him well enough to stick their neck out for him probably wouldn't bother. More likely they would settle back and enjoy the show.

Still, as my father used to say, *The only sure bet is the second letter of the Hebrew alphabet.* If I didn't wrap this up quickly, I could still end up unpleasantly surprised.

"Oh, yeah, we gotta do this," Oberon snarled back, half turning and throwing a roundhouse kick at me that I was just barely able to dodge. "You cost me a good two hundred thousand commarks back on Pinnkus, and I'm going to take it out of your skin."

"I think you have to be a media celebrity for your body to be worth that much," I corrected. "Or maybe you have to be a couple of Ulkomaal slaves."

His hand had been drifting toward the Golden 6mm belted at his waist. Now, abruptly, the hand came back up to personal combat position. At a guess, he'd started wondering whether it would be less trouble to just shoot me, but the dig about his lost Ulkomaals had repersuaded him that he really, *really* wanted to kill me with his own hands.

As my father used to say, *Never make someone madder at you than they already are unless it's already working in your favor.*

Still, I was the one backing up in the face of his attack, and at the speed I was going I'd run out of floor in another twenty seconds. I passed a couple of burly freight-handler types who were watching us with idle interest—apparently fights weren't all that uncommon here—and then a pleasant-looking young man gazing down into his drink like he was hoping to find the meaning of life in there. A couple more steps and I'd be right beside a group of rowdies who had looked like they might be inclined to join in the fun if the opportunity presented itself.

And as I deflected a straight-in punch, the pleasant-looking loner slipped out of his chair, moved silently up behind Oberon, and did a quick double kick into the backs of his knees that sent him crashing to the floor. Oberon bellowed, twisting around onto his back, and grabbed for his holstered Golden.

His hand stopped short of its goal, the fingers just touching the weapon's grip, the glare he'd started to direct at his attacker now transferred to the black Libra 3mm pointed steadily down at him. "I wouldn't," the gun's owner said mildly. In his free hand, held high for everyone in the taverno to see, was a bounty hunter ID. "Sebastian Trent, licensed bounty hunter," he called, just in case anyone was still unclear on the whole thing. "This man is officially in my custody."

He slipped the ID back into his pocket, his gun never wavering from Oberon's face. "Hands on your head, please," he said lowering his volume to a more conversational level. "Then over onto your stomach."

For a long moment I thought Oberon might decide he'd rather have his face splattered across the floor than suffer the humiliation of getting caught. A lot of the criminal types I'd run into over the years seemed to have ego where they needed brains. But he took another look into his attacker's eyes, and with reluctance and impotent fury he complied. Trent glanced at me, as if wondering if he should offer to let me do the honors, then crouched down, pulled Oberon's arms one by one from his head down to the small of his back, and used a set of quick-cuffs to secure his wrists. Only then did he holster his Libra and give me a satisfied nod. "Nicely done, Roarke," he said, his voice as pleasant as his face. "Thanks for the assist. I think the Spiral will rest easier with this one off the streets."

"Actually, I doubt most of the Spiral even knows he exists," I said. "But you're welcome. So what now?"

"Now my colleagues take him to the badgemen—ah," he interrupted himself as two large men strode through the door. "Package for delivery, gentlemen," he called, beckoning them over. "Tell the station chief I'll be there shortly to collect the arrest documentation." He smiled at me. "My new colleague and I first have another matter or two to discuss."

I cocked an eyebrow at that. I did indeed have another few questions to ask him, and in fact had been wondering how I was going to talk him into having a celebratory drink with me. Apparently, he had an agenda of his own.

Which could either be very helpful or very ominous.

He and I stood together and watched as the two men got Oberon back on his feet and hauled him out into the night. Then, Trent gestured to the server at the bar. "A puff adder for me, my good woman, and a—?"

"Small Dewar's," I supplied.

"Large Dewar's for my friend," Trent corrected. He sent me a small and slightly lopsided grin. "I'm the generous type, and I'm buying. Come on, let's sit."

"There's a nicely private spot over there," I said, pointing to an isolated table near the side wall.

"You expect a need for privacy for our little chat?" he asked.

"Don't you?"

He smiled in a friendly sort of way that I suspected most people would foolishly take at face value. But I could see the subtle contradiction between lips and eyes. Trent was definitely not a man to take lightly. "Touché," he said. "Lead on, Macduff."

Whoever Macduff was. I led the way across to the table. The rest of the patrons, I noted, had gone back to their drinks and conversation. Apparently, like a stray barroom fight or two, a bounty hunter popping in to nail a target was just another Tuesday here.

"First things first," he said, digging into his pocket as we sat down. "The five hundred commarks I promised for your assistance."

"I'm glad we could make it work," I said, taking the five bills he handed across the table. "Just out of curiosity, who finally got tired enough of Oberon to put a bounty on him?"

"Ah-ah-ah," he said, wagging a finger reprovingly. "You know we're not supposed to kiss and tell."

"Just curious," I said. Confidentiality was indeed a major part of bounty hunters' protocol, but we'd been known to bend the rules on occasion. "He must have led you on a merry chase, though."

"Oh, that he did," Trent said, shaking his head in memory. "Two days ago we both came in from Niskea—nearly nailed him there, but he ducked out early. Before that was Bardeenia, before that was Hopstead, before that was Kelsim, before that—well, you get the picture."

"But now you've got him," I said, tucking the four planetary names into my memory for future reference.

The server appeared at Trent's side, set our glasses in front of us, and smiled thanks as he put a hundred-commark bill on her tray and waved away her offer of change.

"Some days I'm a millionaire," he explained, taking a sip of his drink as he watched her head back to the bar. "Millionaires tip well, I'm told."

"Well, if they don't they should," I agreed. "Wait a minute.

Oberon was on *Kelsim*? I'd have thought an Ihmis world would be a terrible place for a human to try to hide."

"Maybe he wasn't hiding," Trent said, his voice and expression changing subtly. "Maybe he was doing a job. I assume you heard about the ship hijacking there a few weeks ago."

"No, actually, I hadn't," I said, frowning. Hijackings—successful ones, anyway—were pretty rare birds, which should have made such a thing the talk of the Spiral, at least for the ancient rule of fifteen minutes. "Who got hit?"

"The ship was Saffnic registry, but there were no details on who had cargoes aboard," Trent said. "You ever hear of Oberon going in for that sort of thing?"

I shook my head. "Far as I know, he stuck with hunting and his sordid little death matches."

"Oh, this was a death match, all right," Trent said grimly. "They left thirty dead behind them."

I stared at him. "*Thirty?* What the hell did they do, roll a bunch of hellspawns down the corridors?"

"No, they just came in with a team and shot everyone in sight," Trent growled. "Funny, really."

"I'd hardly put that in the *funny* category."

"No, I mean I'd actually been thinking about trying to find a hijack crew for a job when I heard about this one."

I frowned at him. "Seriously?"

"Seriously," he assured me. "A good job, great pay, and no less than four solid bounties to split up afterward. Whoever came up with the Kelsim plan would be perfect to lead it."

"Not if his endgame usually comes down to mass murder," I said. A hijacking with thirty dead—why the hell *hadn't* I heard about this?

"That part may not have been his idea," Trent said. "I mostly put that down to having a few trigger-happy psychopaths in his crew. But the planner himself..." He shrugged.

"Yeah, maybe," I said. "But as my father used to say, *If your boss's Plan A involves death, your Plan A should be to find a new boss.*"

"I suppose," Trent said. "Pity, really. I guess now I'll just have to nail the four of them one at a time. So much less efficient." He cocked an eyebrow. "I don't suppose you'd be interested in joining me. Like I said, great pay."

"I appreciate the offer," I said. "But like I told you before, I mostly work as a crockett these days."

"Money's not nearly as good," he pointed out.

"Neither are the chances of getting shot at."

"There is that," he conceded. "Well, I appreciate you coming out of retirement long enough to help me out here. Moving on someone with Oberon's reputation is a lot easier if he's busy looking somewhere else." He looked at his watch. "Speaking of moving, I'd better. Don't want the badgemen deciding Oberon wandered into the station all by himself and figuring they can split the bounty. See you around, Roarke." He stood up, gave me a final friendly smile, and left the taverno.

I gave him a count of sixty, just to make sure he wasn't coming back. Then, picking up my drink, I crossed to the white-haired woman sitting quietly at a table by the door. "Did you enjoy the show?" I asked.

The delicate features of Kadolian faces didn't lend themselves to emotional expression nearly as well as human faces did. But the pupils of Selene's deep-set gray cat's eyes more than made up for it. Right now, they were showing a nice mix of relief and dry humor. "I still don't know why you agreed to decoy Oberon like that in the first place," she said. "We could have found another way to talk to Trent."

"But it wouldn't have been nearly so entertaining," I pointed out.

"Or as dangerous."

"Or as productive," I said. "You saw how reserved he was earlier tonight. I've seen men like that get positively chatty once the job's finished and the tension's gone."

"He certainly seemed to be relieved," she agreed. "You say your talk was productive?"

"Very," I said. "The four worlds he most recently visited were, in order, Niskea, Bardeenia, Hopstead, and Kelsim. The server interrupted before he could go any further back, and then he was on to another topic."

"That should be more than enough," Selene said, her pupils going thoughtful. "The portal scent was faint enough. It couldn't have been on him more than a few weeks."

I scowled down at my drink. The outer hulls of the alien star portals that our Icarus Group bosses were so hot to locate and acquire gave off a faint but distinctive scent, a subtle marker that would be picked up by anyone who touched one or was even in reasonably close proximity. Unfortunately, not even the finest sensing devices on the market could pick up on anything that faint.

Fortunately, the hypersensitive Kadolian sense of smell could.

"What about the two bruisers who carried out the garbage?" I asked. "Anything from them?"

Selene shook her head. "There was a vague hint, but that was probably just from casual contact with Trent."

"Or from the commarks he paid them in," I said, nodding. "I assume you didn't smell any significant or guilty-conscience changes when he ran down his list of planets?"

"Actually, there *was* something," Selene said, her pupils now showing a sort of vague dread. "But it wasn't . . . it was anger, Gregory. Anger and suspicion and . . . it was almost a bloodlust."

"Really," I said, frowning. "Are you sure you weren't misreading him? I mean, we only had, what, three hours with him for you to establish his baseline."

"It's possible," Selene said. But her pupils still held quiet fear. "But there was definitely something there. I'm thinking we should take the long way back to the *Ruth* in case he has something planned for us along the way."

I looked over at the table where Trent and I had been sitting a few minutes ago. I'd picked that table specifically because the taverno's gentle airflow would send our scents directly toward Selene. Even with my pathetically limited human senses I could smell the bourbon in the puff adder he'd abandoned. With that kind of information flowing across her nose and eyelashes, Selene could match our moods to our scents half asleep and with her eyes closed.

Still, without a really good baseline to work from there was always the chance she might misread one emotion for another.

"Actually," she added reluctantly, "I almost wish . . ." The words faded away.

"You wish I'd drugged him?" I prompted gently.

She lowered her eyes to the table, but not before I saw the embarrassment in her pupils. "Yes," she admitted.

I looked at the other table again, this time focusing on the abandoned glass. I'd lost my left arm below the elbow during our final official bounty hunt six years ago, and when I got my artificial replacement I'd made room for a couple of hidden compartments. One of those, the one at the inner wrist, was just the right size for half a dozen knockout pills, a secret cache I'd found useful many times in the years since then. A full set of the pills was nestled in there right now, which I could have easily and invisibly introduced into Trent's drink.

But aside from Selene's subjective and admittedly vague impressions, I had no real justification for drugging the man. Not now, certainly not then. And if he didn't hate me before, leaving him passed out and helpless in a marginal place like this would have certainly advanced me to that lofty position.

Still, as my father used to say, *Never bet against someone who's been right ten times in a row unless he's running a pyramid scam.*

"The long way back it is," I agreed. "Actually, we should head over to the StarrComm center before we leave anyway. The admiral loves getting new data to feed his minions."

I stood up and offered her my hand. "And given the usual wait for a booth, even if Trent's waiting at the *Ruth* there's a good chance he'll get bored and go home."

In my admittedly limited experience I'd seldom found Admiral Sir Graym-Barker, the head of the Icarus Group, to be happy with anything in life. Still, he seemed pleased enough with the four new system names I'd gotten from Trent and promised to look into them. I could tell that Selene was waiting for me to mention that Trent also might be wanting to kill me, but I didn't see any point to that. As my father used to say, *Don't bother stirring the soup until you're sure there's an actual fire going beneath the pot.* We said our good-byes, and I called my Xathru mail drop to see if there were any new messages.

To my surprise, there was.

"This is Floyd, Roarke," the familiar voice came from the screen. "I need to talk to you about a special business deal. Can you meet me on Xathru in six days? If you can't get there, message me with where you are right now, and I'll see if there's somewhere else that'll work. This thing is time-sensitive, so don't drag your feet."

The message ended, and for a moment Selene and I looked at each other. "I thought we were done with him forever," she said, her pupils showing distaste and reluctance.

"So did I," I said, feeling a pretty good level of reluctance myself. Floyd was one of the top enforcers for the criminal organization that economic realities had once forced Selene and me to work for. Those days were thankfully over and done with, but though Floyd and I had parted on reasonably good terms, that wasn't to say I wanted to renew acquaintances. I certainly wasn't interested in hearing about any deal he wanted to pitch.

But he and his colleagues had had a chance to kill us—actually, I was pretty sure he'd had specific orders to do so—and he hadn't. I supposed that bought him at least the courtesy of a hearing.

"*Forever* apparently isn't as long as it used to be," I continued, checking the timestamp on Floyd's message. Thirty-two hours ago, about the time Selene and I had arrived here on Nua Corcaigh. And yes, we could make it to Xathru in time for his proposed meeting. "But Floyd's the persistent type. If we ignore him, he'll just pop up again somewhere else."

"The admiral might not like us meeting with him," Selene warned.

"There's that," I conceded. A severe understatement—the admiral had been furious that I'd let Floyd and his friends off Fidelio without letting him read the riot act to them as to what would happen if they talked to anyone about the Gemini portal we'd dug out of the Erymant Temple grounds.

Though knowing the sort of people Floyd worked for, I doubted even the admiral's impressive repertoire of threats would have made much of an impact on him.

"But what the admiral doesn't know won't hurt him," I said, pulling out some bills to feed into the slot. "We'll meet, we'll listen to his proposal, we'll say good-bye, and that'll be the end of it."

"We thought it was the end of it last time."

"Yes, we did," I conceded. "And we'll keep saying it until it comes true. So where exactly would you suggest we invite him?"

There were half a dozen restaurants Selene and I liked to patronize whenever we were on Xathru, along with about a dozen tavernos. We settled on one of the latter, a place that had a large selection of spirits and some of the best barbequed ribs and baked-bread pizza I'd ever found.

Floyd was right on time, strolling in with a casual air that nicely masked his panther-like global awareness of his surroundings. I waved him over, and as he neared the table I stood up and offered him my seat, the one against the wall with a clear view of the patrons, servers, and doors. As my father used to say, *Never disrespect the other fellow's paranoia, especially when the other fellow is armed.*

"I appreciate you meeting me like this," Floyd said. "I know that friend of yours—McKell?—wasn't exactly happy with us running off without getting to deliver whatever threats he had on tap."

"He got over it," I said. Actually, knowing Jordan McKell, he probably hadn't. "How was your own homecoming?"

"You mean to Huihuang?" He shrugged. "I have to tell you, I was a little concerned about going to Mr. Gaheen and telling him Cole, Mottola, and I had had orders to kill him."

"You *told* him about that?" I asked, staring. "I'd have thought that was something better dropped into a deep hole under a *no death, no foul* sign."

"We thought about doing that," he said. "But there were others who knew. Mr. Gaheen appreciates honesty, especially when the honesty gets to him before the rumors."

"I guess that makes sense," I conceded. "I gather you're not working directly under him at the moment?"

He eyed me closely. "Why do you say that?"

"Because Huihuang isn't within six days of Xathru," I said. "That means you must have called from somewhere else, and the time-sensitive aspect of this proposed deal suggests you called from wherever you were at the time."

His lips twitched in a small smile. "Not bad," he said. "Yes, Mr. Gaheen has sent me to work temporarily with Mr. Cherno, one of his regional lieutenants. He's the one making the proposal on Mr. Gaheen's behalf."

"I assume Mr. Gaheen knows all about it?" I asked.

Floyd frowned. "Of course," he said, as if that was obvious.

"Right," I said, suppressing a sigh. *Meet, listen, say good-bye.* "Silly of me. I don't think Mr. Varsi ever mentioned Mr. Cherno."

"Why would he?" Floyd said, frowning some more. "You weren't exactly high up in the organization."

"No, of course not."

"But if you had been, you'd have heard plenty about him," Floyd continued. "Been with us for a long time, working his way up through the ranks. Don't worry, he knows what he's doing. Mr. Gaheen wouldn't have put him on this if he didn't."

"Well, that makes me feel better," I said. "So what exactly is this offer?"

"It's pretty simple," Floyd said. "Mr. Cherno has a passenger he wants you to take from one planet to another. Unspecified for now, but shouldn't be anything drastic. Single person, no contraband, nothing illegal about it."

I looked at Selene, sitting quietly and sifting through Floyd's scent. We'd spent enough time with him that if he started lying, she'd know it. "Does Mr. Cherno not realize there are public and chartered transports that can do that job?"

"Sure," Floyd said. "But none of them would be interested in the payment he's offering."

He paused, giving the taverno a slow, careful visual scan. "Mr. Cherno's found something," he continued, lowering his voice to a volume barely above a whisper. "One of those things from Fidelio."

I stared at him, my earlier reluctance to this conversation abruptly vanishing. "You mean a *portal*?"

"Yeah, a portal," he said. "You take his passenger where she needs to go, and it's yours."

CHAPTER TWO

"No," the admiral said flatly. "This has to be some kind of trick."

"Maybe, but why?" I countered. "To what end? Draw me out into the open? I'm already here. Get me to lead them to one of your other portals? Pointless, since I haven't the foggiest idea where any of them are. Get me to lead them to McKell or Tera? Equally pointless, for the same reason."

"No," he said again. "I simply don't believe it. How could he possibly have stumbled across another portal?"

"How did *you* stumble across the original *Icarus*?" I countered.

"That's classified," he said tartly.

Tartly *and* reflexively. It was a variant of the same question I'd asked at least half a dozen times in the past year, and it had gotten me the same dead-end answer each time. Even with the upgraded status Selene and I had talked the admiral into giving us there were apparently some things we still weren't allowed to know.

"Anyway, it's not quite as good a deal as it looks," I went on. "From the launch module pictures Floyd showed me I'm pretty sure it's another Gemini dyad like the pair we got from Popanilla and Fidelio, not a full-range portal like Icarus or Alpha. That makes it valuable, but not ridiculously so."

"The Path would still pay a great deal for it."

"The Patth have their own Gemini," I reminded him.

Which I probably shouldn't have, I realized as his expression went a little stonier. The fact that the Patth had sneaked a portal right out from under our noses was clearly still a sore spot with him.

"The point is that right now Cherno is offering it to us," I continued hurriedly. "If we turn him down, as you say, the Patth would be happy to open their wallets."

"There's one other point I think we should consider," Selene spoke up quietly. "I presume you've been reluctant to take apart any of your portals, concerned that you might not be able to put it back together again."

"In fact, I'd guess it's less *concerned* than *terrified*," I said, seeing where she was going with this. "But if you had a *second* set of dyads to play with . . . ?"

The admiral's expression didn't crack. But I could see he'd been so focused on Cherno's possible treachery that he hadn't yet considered the larger implications of the man's offer. As my father used to say, *People who can't see the forest for the trees probably also can't see the value of the lumber.* "So you think we should take Mr. Cherno up on his offer?" he asked.

"Only if you want us to," I said with a shrug. "If you're not interested, there's a nice group of planets northwest of the Bonvere Cluster we haven't yet checked out—"

"Yes, I'm sure there is," the admiral cut me off tartly. "I assume Cherno's portal is dormant?"

"It looked that way in Floyd's pictures," I said. "I assume you'll want us to activate it?"

"Why would I want you to do that?"

I frowned. "I don't know," I said, trying not to sound too sarcastic. "Maybe to make sure it *works*?"

He shook his head. "We can sort that out once we've secured it. I don't want random people out there knowing how to activate portals, and there's really no way you can keep Cherno or anyone else from spying on you while you turn it on."

"Understood," I said. Actually, that was a good point. "All right, then. Selene and I are the hired help, and we don't know anything. That work for you?"

"Yes, it does," the admiral said. "It also has the virtue of being essentially true." His eyes narrowed. "Just make sure you keep me informed every step of the way. If there's something else going on, I want to know about it. Preferably before you fall over some hidden tripwire."

"I'm sure we'll be fine," I said.

"Yes," he murmured. Probably thinking about how well we'd eluded tripwires and other general trouble on previous occasions. "Something about this still feels wrong."

"I'm not crazy about it myself," I admitted. "As my father used to say, *Looking a gift horse in the mouth puts you in a perfect position to get bit.* But I think the offer's worth following up on. If for no other reason than to find out which part of the bait has the hook in it."

The admiral rumbled something under his breath. "I assume you'll be flying the *Ruth* to this meeting with Cherno?"

"Actually, Floyd's taking us on one of Cherno's personal yachts."

The admiral grunted. "Which we can't track and can't get backup aboard."

"We'll be fine," I said again. "After all, Floyd owes me. So does Mr. Gaheen."

"And Cherno?"

"I'm sure he'll warm to us in time."

"As so many of your acquaintances have," the admiral said with more than a hint of sarcasm. "Well. Good luck." He reached for the control, paused. "And try to come back alive," he added. Without waiting for a response he finished his reach for the control and the screen blanked.

"We love you, too," I said, pulling out more bills and feeding them into the slot. "The old softy."

"Who are we calling now?" Selene asked.

"No one," I told her, punching in the number for my mail drop. "Just wanted to check for messages."

To my mild surprise, there was indeed a new text message in my mail drop. To my even greater surprise, it was from Trent.

That hijacking job I mentioned on Nua Corcaigh is starting to come together. Not too late for you to join in on the planning. Fifty thousand up front, one-quarter share of four major bounties afterward. Reply as soon as you can if you're interested or have other questions.

"Interesting," I commented, gesturing to the message. "What do you think?"

I watched her eyes, saw puzzlement drift into her pupils as she read through Trent's note. "He's certainly persistent," she said slowly. "He also seems... Does he seem a little wordy to you?"

"Indeed he does," I agreed. "The typical bounty hunter would have whittled that down to *Hijacking job still on. Join in? Fifty thousand, share of four bounties. Reply ASAP.* That's a third of the words."

"And a third of the cost," Selene said, her pupils going thoughtful. "Either he's been very successful lately, or else he's spending someone else's money."

"My guess is the latter," I agreed. "So who has money who also might have put him in contact with a portal?"

"The Patth and Cherno are the obvious possibilities," Selene said. "But it could certainly be someone else."

"Yes," I murmured, her last sentence bouncing me in a new direction. "Tell me, did you happen to smell any portal metal on Floyd?"

"No," Selene said, her pupils frowning at the question. "Should I have?"

"Well, Cherno says he has one, and Floyd works for him," I said. "He also has pictures of the launch module."

"I assumed they were taken by someone else and just sent to him," Selene said. "If Cherno is keeping the portal's location a secret, he might not want Floyd to know exactly where it is."

"Lest he be snatched and the secret wormed out of him?"

"Or lest he take that information to a higher bidder."

"Maybe," I said doubtfully. "But Floyd's always struck me as being the loyal type."

"When he's working for someone who deserves it."

"There's that," I conceded. "So try this one. Let's say it's Trent, or Trent's boss, who actually has the portal. In that scenario Cherno may be trying to hire us, not with the patently ridiculous story of wanting us to cart someone across the Spiral, but in hopes that we'll find the portal and figure out how to steal it for him."

"I suppose that's possible," Selene said slowly. "But it also works just as well the other way. Trent has already said he wants to hire us for a hijacking. Could the plan be to steal Cherno's portal?"

I shook my head. "Trent already has portal scent on him."

"Maybe he's got the other half of Cherno's Gemini."

I stared at the message still hovering on the StarrComm

display. That one hadn't even occurred to me. "Oh, now wouldn't *that* be a treat and a half?" I murmured. "Cherno and Trent fighting over the same Gemini. Bonus amusement points if neither of them knows they have the two ends of the same portal. So why pick on us?"

"Floyd will have told Gaheen about Fidelio, who will have told Cherno," Selene said.

"And Trent?"

"Maybe he has a spy in Gaheen's organization." She hesitated. "Or, as you suggested earlier, maybe he's working with the Patth."

I huffed out a sigh. "Would it really unbalance the universe for us to someday fall in with people who *didn't* wish the worst for us?"

"Well, there *is* the Icarus Group."

"Yeah. Like I said." I stuck a data stick into the jack, copied Trent's message, then blanked the screen. "Fine. Let's get out of here, then call Floyd, then get back to the *Ruth* and grab whatever we'll need for this little jaunt. I'm guessing we won't be back for a while."

The last time Selene and I had been given an upper-class ride it had been aboard the *Odinn*, Sub-Director Nask's private Patth transport. It had been impressively luxurious, but given we'd been his prisoners at the time we didn't get to see very much of the ship. Floyd's yacht was smaller and not nearly as impressive, but at least here we had more or less the run of the place.

Except for the cockpit, of course. And the nav station, engine room, security stations, armory, Floyd's private stateroom, and a couple of additional compartments that came with no specific designations but plenty of veiled warnings. But at least we could walk through the corridors and stretch our legs.

The food was good, too.

It was a nine-day flight, and for the last six hours of it Selene and I were confined to our stateroom with the viewports opaqued. We landed and emerged from the yacht to find ourselves on a single-pad landing field in the middle of a forest of blue-green conifers. We got to look around for only the couple of minutes it took to cover a hundred meters at a brisk walk before Floyd hustled us into a waiting four-person aircar. He got us settled in the back seat and climbed in beside the pilot, and as the repulsors lifted us off the ground he reached over to the control panel and opaqued all the windows except the windscreen. Given that the only thing Selene and I could see in that direction from our angle was sky, I was cleverly able to deduce that our destination world had a blue sky and occasional clouds. Apparently, Cherno didn't want us getting even a hint of where we were or how we'd gotten here.

Given the unique value of his prize, I couldn't really blame him.

The aircar ride lasted about an hour. We landed again, this time in a private hangar, Floyd waiting until the retractable roof had closed above us before escorting us to a van with the by-now-familiar opaqued windows. We started this final leg of the trip with the noises and stop-go pattern of city traffic, which faded into a quiet and steady drive after about fifteen minutes. Wherever we'd landed, we'd apparently been somewhere near the outskirts of town.

Of course, there was caution and there was paranoia, and in my private opinion this level of security had already overshot that line. There were dozens of habitable worlds out there, and so many different locales, climates, cultures, towns, and peoples on each of them that I'm pretty sure I could have stared out the window the whole way and still not had a clue as to where we were.

But it could have been worse. Floyd could have made us wear bags over our heads.

We came at last to the end of our journey in a windowless garage that had room for at least ten vans like ours, half again as many regular cars, or probably eight multi-passenger aircars. The place was empty except for our van—again, our host eliminating any clues as to where we were—and we were led through a door and up a short staircase to a large and nicely furnished ground-floor foyer. There we were met by three other bodyguard types, who gave Floyd respectful nods and Selene and me the quick once-over that men in their position learned in order to check for hidden weapons.

In this case, a waste of time. At Floyd's insistence we'd left all our weapons aboard the *Ruth* before we boarded his yacht.

We passed the guards and Floyd herded us up to the next floor, this time via an elaborate open curved staircase that led to a balcony overlooking the floor we'd just left.

The wall behind the balcony had three doors. Floyd steered

us to the middle one and knocked. There was a muted reply from inside, and he opened the door and gestured us through.

Inside, seated in one of the chairs of a conversation circle set beside a floor-to-ceiling window with a panoramic view of forests and distant snow-capped mountains, was Cherno.

I'd never seen any pictures, and Floyd hadn't given us any descriptions. But even so there was no doubt in my mind as to who he was. Even seated comfortably in an overstuffed chair with a drink in his hand and a relaxed body language the look in his eyes was that of a calculating, ruthless, soulless predator.

Our former boss, Luko Varsi, had had much that same look. Mr. Gaheen, Varsi's successor and Cherno's boss, had a lot of the same cunning, though my single meeting with him had left me with the impression that he had at least a partial soul left.

As my father used to say, *There's a fine line between ambition and maniacal insatiability, and it's frighteningly easy to cross that line without noticing.*

Briefly, I wondered which side of the line Cherno was on.

"Good afternoon, Mr. Roarke; Ms. Selene," he greeted us as we walked into the room. His voice was measured and urbane, as calculating and soulless as his eyes. "I'm Mr. Cherno. I trust you had a pleasant journey?"

"Quite pleasant," I assured him. "Though air and car trips do get a bit tedious when all there is to look at are your fellow passengers."

I'd wondered if the mild criticism would get any kind of pushback from him. But he merely gave me an easy smile. "I imagine so," he agreed. "Though certainly Ms. Selene is easy enough on the eyes. I'm sure you understand the need for absolute secrecy in this matter."

"Of course, sir," I said, ducking my head in an abbreviated bow. Varsi would have been annoyed by my comment, possibly dangerously so, and would have made no effort to hide it. Cherno's less irritated response put him at least a step above my former boss in the walking-on-eggs department.

Still, now that I'd performed my test, it was time to back off. Just because Cherno was less volatile than Varsi didn't mean it would be safe for me to cross him. "Especially since those precautions will also have stymied any attempt to keep track of me personally."

"*Are* there people trying to keep track of you?" Cherno asked, his smile slipping just a bit. "Aside from the obvious, of course?"

For a split second I considered asking him who he thought these mysterious stalkers were. But Floyd would have told him about McKell and Nask, and playing innocent at this point would probably be a bad idea, as well as being pointless. As my father used to say, *Playing coy usually only works if you're a large goldfish.* "Aside from the obvious, not that I know of," I said. "But one never knows when a new player is going to pop out of the woodwork."

"Indeed one doesn't," Cherno agreed. He eyed me a moment, then gestured to two of the conversation circle chairs across from him. "Please."

"Thank you." I walked to one of the chairs, reflexively noting the various ventilation grilles and doing a quick evaluation of the room's air flow. Neither of the seats he'd indicated would be ideal, but one was clearly situated better than the other. I picked the less useful one and let Selene settle into the other. Floyd, I noted, stayed back by the door where he could oversee the scene.

"So tell me, Mr. Roarke," Cherno said as we settled into our seats. "How exactly did you get into all of this?"

"As Mr. Floyd may have told you, I used to be a bounty hunter," I said. "When I lost my arm, Selene and I joined the Association of Planetary Trailblazers and have been crocketts ever since. As to the portals..." I shrugged. "Actually, we fell into it mostly by accident."

"*Mostly?*"

"Well, it was accident on our part, anyway," I said. "But I'm sure your time is valuable, Mr. Cherno. Mr. Floyd's thumbnail description of your proposal was quite intriguing. I'd like to hear more."

"Certainly," Cherno said. "You take my passenger where she needs to go, and the portal is yours."

I waited a couple of heartbeats. Apparently, that was all he was prepared to say. "Understood," I said. "Nice and succinct. Also pretty much what Mr. Floyd already told us on Xathru. I was hoping for a few more details."

"Such as?"

"Such as who this passenger is," I said, ticking off fingers. "Where she is now, where she needs to go, where the portal is, when we get possession of it." I lowered my fingers. "And why us."

He took a sip from his glass. "You're an oddly curious sort, Mr. Roarke," he said. "I'd think that one being so handsomely paid for his time and effort would be content to work within certain restrictions."

"Ah, but you see, *I'm* not actually getting paid," I pointed out. "It's the people I'm working with who'll get the portal. All Selene and I get out of this is, as you say, the chance to put in some time and a lot of effort. More importantly, I'd kind of like to know what the chances are that this project will involve us getting shot at."

Cherno raised his eyebrows slightly. "Really? *That's* your big concern?" His eyes flicked to Floyd. "Floyd didn't mention that you were the squeamish type. How in the Spiral did you survive as a bounty hunter?"

"I almost didn't," I said, wincing a little as the ghost of that memory briefly overshadowed the room. "Which is the point. I don't mind a little gunplay on occasion, but I like to know the odds of it going in. Especially since our recent history of taking on passengers hasn't exactly been smooth sailing."

"I see." Cherno took another sip of his drink. "Very well. To your questions. I can't as yet give you the name of your passenger, but she shouldn't be a burden to you. I can definitely assure you no one's likely to draw down on her. You'll be picking her up on Balmoral; the drop-off point is as yet undetermined, and your colleagues will be able to take possession of the portal as soon as your part of the bargain is completed. As to why you, I believe Floyd already explained that you're the only people who would be interested in such a trade."

"So he did," I said, the mental image of Nask and his presumably galactic-sized budget hovering in front of my eyes.

"As to where it is . . ." He took one last sip and stood up. "Let's go take a look."

CHAPTER THREE

We left the office, Cherno in front, Floyd at the rear, Selene and me sandwiched between them. Cherno led us to an unobtrusive elevator discreetly tucked away in one of the hallways near his office. We went down an undisclosed distance to an underground tunnel, rather like the secret passage that led to Gaheen's own mansion headquarters on Huihuang.

Back when we'd used that one, Floyd's fellow enforcer Mottola had suggested that the tunnel might be a leftover from some previous owner, and that Gaheen might not even know about it. Now, with a second secret tunnel connected to a different local boss's headquarters, I was beginning to wonder if whoever first started this organization had simply liked secret tunnels.

If so, he'd had a much bigger budget to work with on Huihuang than he had here. Instead of leading to a hidden entrance with an elaborate opening mechanism, this tunnel merely took us to a narrow flight of steps, up through a trapdoor, and into a huge, windowless, warehouse-sized building.

There, looming high over our heads, were the conjoined spheres of a Gemini portal.

The things were monstrously huge, bigger than anything I'd ever seen that wasn't a space station, a Class X freighter, or a ground-side building. The larger sphere, the receiver module, was a good twenty meters across, while the smaller sphere, the launch module, was slightly smaller at fifteen meters and was attached to the receiver's side like a mismatched cell starting to undergo mitosis. Five wide, thick bundles that looked rather like bales of hay nestled close to the sides of the spheres, which puzzled me until I realized they were the rolled-up ends of cargo straps that the portal was resting on, probably what Cherno had used to bring the portal here. The structure around us was just barely big enough to contain it, with no more than a couple of meters' clearance around the ends of the portal and a slightly less claustrophobic ten meters on the end that housed our trapdoor. It was, I thought as Cherno led the way toward the portal, almost as if the place had been built specifically to house it.

In fact, it had. I peered down at the flooring as we walked and spotted the mismatch in the tile pattern. There'd once been a much smaller building here, possibly a panic room or a hangar for an emergency aircar, which had been torn down and this warehouse thing put up in its place.

"The hatch is over here," Cherno said, leading the way toward the left side of the receiver module, where the edge of a dark rectangular opening was visible at the sphere's curve. "So far only the portal's gravitational field is operating." He looked over his shoulder at me. "I presume you know how to turn it on?"

"Sorry," I said. "I'm afraid we can't do that. But I don't think—"

Cherno stopped short and turned to face us. "Excuse me?" he asked, his voice suddenly gone very quiet.

I stopped, too, a dozen warning bells going off in the back of my mind. "I said we can't activate it," I said, choosing my words carefully. "But I've already been informed that my associates don't need to see that it's fully functional."

"I don't care if your bosses want to see it work," Cherno said in that same voice. "*I* want to see it work."

"I'm sorry," I said again, trying to kick my brain into gear. Floyd was somewhere behind us, but I couldn't tell how close he was without turning to look.

Not that that mattered. He was armed, and I wasn't. I had my handful of knockout pills in my left wrist's secret compartment, but unless I could persuade Cherno to take high tea with us they weren't going to be of any use.

Still, back when Floyd had first pitched this deal Selene hadn't

detected any deception from him. That suggested Cherno hadn't
shared any of these new plans with him. Did that put Floyd on
our side?

Probably not. Just because Cherno was suddenly taking an
unanticipated left-hand turn on this deal was no reason for Floyd
to not stick by his boss.

"It's not that we're unwilling," I continued earnestly, stalling
for time. "It's that we simply can't."

"Because it's the wrong one," Selene spoke up.

Long and sometimes painful experience had taught me to
never show surprise unless it was part of the story or the plan. In
this case, Selene's statement was neither. What in hell's name—?

"This portal is half of a dyad," she continued. "What we call a
Gemini. You can activate the pair together out of a dormant state,
but only from the dominant one, the one called the master." She
gestured to the spheres filling the room. "This one's the slave."

"How do you know?" Cherno demanded suspiciously. "And
why didn't you tell me this earlier?"

"Because you didn't tell us you wanted a demonstration," I
said, hoping I was picking up correctly on Selene's play. Whatever it was. "You said you were going to trade this for passenger
transport. It didn't matter to our associates whether it was the
master or the slave."

For a long moment Cherno just stared at us, his eyes flicking
between our faces. Once, his gaze went over my shoulder, presumably to Floyd. "Very convenient for them," he growled at last.

"Not as convenient as you might think," I said. "Now they'll
have to figure out where the master is and dig it out before they
can do anything with this one."

Cherno's gaze went over my shoulder again. "Floyd?" he asked,
the word a mix of question, demand, and accusation.

"I didn't see their other portal being activated, sir," Floyd
said. "That was done before we arrived."

"And you're sure this is the slave?" Cherno demanded, shifting
his glare back to me and ramping up the shrivel power.

"Very sure," I said.

"There's an easy way to tell if we go inside," Selene offered.
She looked at me. "The triangles."

"Right," I said, clamping down on my surprise for the second
time in this same edgy minute. Her pupils were registering a tense

agitation way beyond even the danger we were currently in the middle of. Something about the portal had figuratively kicked her in the teeth, and I had no idea what it was. "There's a row of small triangles etched into the master portal's status board between the oxygen readout and grav-status panels."

"About midway from the hatch to the extension arm," Selene added. "They're..." She broke off, waving her hands helplessly.

"They're easier to point to than describe," I told Cherno. "Let's go in and look, okay? If they're there, then we obviously misread which dyad this is and we'll start it for you. No drama, no foul."

Once again Cherno gave us a hard look. "Fine," he said, his voice heavy with suspicion. "Floyd, keep your gun on them. If they even look like they're trying to pull something..." He pointed at Selene. "Shoot her in the leg. After you, Mr. Roarke."

The receiver module's hatchway was positioned about a meter above the warehouse floor at one end of the portal. I walked over to it, noting that from that position I could see the other rolled-up end of the nearest cargo strap, and stuck my head and torso inside. For a moment I felt the usual disorientation as the local gravity suddenly pointed my inner ear toward the portal's inside hull. I waited until that had passed, then pushed myself in far enough to swivel up into a sitting position on the edge of the opening. "Okay, I'm in," I called, standing up and backing away. "Come on."

Floyd was next, his lack of experience making his entrance a bit awkward. Or maybe it was the Skripka 4mm gripped in his hand that hampered his movements. After him came Selene, and finally Cherno. The boss's entrance was nearly as good as Selene's and mine—clearly, he'd practiced going in and out while Floyd was busy flying us here. "All right," Cherno said when we were once again assembled. "Show us."

"Fingers crossed," I said. "This way. Watch your step."

I led the way around the receiver module to the open hatchway that led into the launch module. I kept an eye on Cherno the whole way, watching for the vertigo that initiates invariably suffered. But there was none. He'd definitely spent time in here. We reached the hatchway, and I lay down beside the opening and rolled through into the smaller sphere's competing grav field. Once again I stood back while I waited for the others.

And as Floyd, Selene, and Cherno each took their turns, I

gave the space around me a quick but careful survey. As far as I could tell, it was identical to the Gemini portals we'd pulled from Popanilla and Fidelio, except that the loose mesh that covered much of the inside surface had been cut away in a few places to expose the wires and cables lying there.

"All right, we're here," Cherno growled when we were once again together. "Where are these oxygen and grappling panels?"

"Oxygen and grav panels," I corrected, starting toward the black-and-silver-striped extension arm stretching toward the center from the other side of the module. "They're over here."

The panels I'd described were exactly where they were supposed to be: Two long rectangular sets of button lights that would be colored blue, red, and orange if the portal was fully active. I hadn't the foggiest idea what they actually indicated, of course, but for purposes of our story I figured oxygen and gravity were good enough.

And of course, there were no triangles etched into the hull between them.

"Right here," I continued, squatting down and pushing aside the mesh. "Here's where they would be, right here on the hull between the panels. They're faint and hard to see unless you're right on top of them...but no. No triangles here."

Cherno stared down at the deck, his face set in stone, and for a long moment the module was filled with a brittle silence. Then, finally, he stirred. "So. You can find this master portal, I assume?"

I stood upright again, swallowing against the sudden lump in my throat. "I don't know," I said. "As far as I know, there's nothing in either the master or slave that points toward the other one. Even if this one was active, which it isn't."

"What about the range?" Cherno persisted. "Do you know how far they can operate?"

"As far as I know, no one's ever put a limit on it," I said. "The master could be anywhere in the Spiral. Possibly anywhere in the universe."

"That's...unfortunate," Cherno said, his voice gone deadly quiet. "In that case..."

"But there may be a way to narrow the search," I cut in hastily. "The Erymant Temple where we found one of the other Gemini portals has a distinct and unique alien architecture. That may—*may*—be a pattern that points to where others are located. If you can get your organization's information sources busy looking for similar styles elsewhere in the Spiral, we may be able to get a leg up on the search."

"There isn't anything else like the Erymant Temple," Floyd said suspiciously. "I looked it up."

"Because that one's mostly intact," I said. "What we're looking for are ruins that show some of that same architecture but might not be immediately recognizable as following the Erymant style."

Cherno snorted. "You're talking years' worth of searching," he said. "We've got—" He clenched his teeth, his eyes gone distant as he seemed to work out some calculation. "Six weeks."

I blinked at him. "Six *weeks*?"

"I told you this was time-sensitive," Floyd reminded me.

"So you did," I acknowledged, trying to think. The Icarus Group might have additional data, but I didn't dare drag them any further into this. Especially not with Floyd or Cherno looking over my shoulder. "But it's not as bad as it sounds. Most alien ruins on the Spiral's inhabited planets have been at least catalogued, and I presume Mr. Gaheen has people everywhere who can sift through their own local data and forward anything that sounds promising."

"Mr. Gaheen's people have more important things to do than read small-town legends and research reports," Cherno bit out.

I braced myself. "In that case, you're right," I said as calmly as I could. "It probably *will* take years."

Cherno looked at Floyd, and I had the uncomfortable feeling that he was wondering if a little torture or a few judiciously placed gunshots would jog my imagination a little. "Fortunately, as soon as we have some leads, Selene and I can narrow the field considerably," I added in hopes of swaying any such decisions. "Once we're on the ground, there are a few specific tags we can look for. Nothing we can teach your own investigators, unfortunately."

"*Can't? Or won't?*"

"Can't," I said. "It comes down to more of a gut feeling than anything else."

He rumbled deep in his throat. "Convenient."

I waved my hands in a helpless gesture. "I'm afraid that's just how it works."

Cherno looked at Selene, his eyes tracing her alien features, perhaps wondering if she was the one with the sensitive gut and I was more expendable. "And once you've found it, you *can* activate it?" he asked.

"Absolutely," I assured him.

For another few seconds he continued to stare at me. But this time, I had the distinct impression his mind was spinning elsewhere and I just happened to be in the direction his eyes were pointed. "I need to make some StarrComm calls," he said at last.

We made our way back through the receiver module to the warehouse. "Floyd, escort them to the guest suite and make sure the dispensary is properly stocked with refreshments," Cherno ordered. "I'll be back in a couple of hours."

"Yes, sir," Floyd said. "Shall I have the beds made up for them?"

"Not yet," Cherno said. Brushing past me, he headed for the stairs. "As I said, this may only take a few hours." He paused at the trapdoor and looked back. "Or it may take a few days," he added. "I'll let you know."

With that, he headed down. "A few *days*?" I murmured to Floyd.

"Probably not." Floyd considered. "Hopefully not. After you."

Cherno's guest suite consisted of two bedrooms, a sitting/conversation room, a bathroom with a complete spa setup, a large balcony, and a kitchen nook with an extensive food and beverage dispensary.

I wasn't really hungry, and I could tell Selene wasn't either, but both of us availed ourselves of the nook's selection. As my father used to say, *Never pass up an opportunity to eat, drink, or sleep. Bathroom breaks are good, too.*

The spa bathroom was also very nice.

Aside from the waiting itself, the most maddening part of the whole exercise was that I couldn't ask Selene what was with the master/slave fabrication she'd spun for Cherno. Nice though our quarters might be, we were in the home of a criminal boss, and I had zero doubt that the room was loaded with enough hidden cameras and microphones to supply a news center for months. So we ate and drank, chatted a bit about frothy topics, and occasionally rested on the contour couches. Floyd had insisted we leave all our electronics aboard the yacht, which also limited our entertainment options.

I was bracing myself for the few days that Cherno had threatened us with when, four hours later according to the elaborate wall clock, the master of the house reappeared.

"It's all set," he said, talking mostly to Floyd but the information clearly intended for all three of us. "You'll take them back to Xathru and their ship, then proceed to Balmoral to pick up the passenger."

"This early?" Floyd asked, frowning. "She wasn't supposed to—"

"Of course she wasn't," Cherno cut him off brusquely. "But the situation has changed. Fortunately, she was able to make this new schedule." He looked across the room at Selene and me. "When Mr. Roarke finds the other portal—*when*, Mr. Roarke, not *if*—we won't want to risk the need to add additional travel delays to the schedule."

"Understood, sir," Floyd said.

"In the meantime," Cherno added, "we'll have our people make up that list of alien ruins you wanted." His expression went stiffer. "I trust that will prove sufficient."

"Let's all trust that," I agreed.

"Good," Cherno said. "All right, Floyd. Get them out of here."

The trip back to Floyd's yacht was very quiet. Selene didn't seem inclined to talk, and we'd run out of innocuous subjects during our forced relaxation. Anyway, I wasn't much in the mood for conversation, either. Floyd, for his part, gave occasional instructions to the drivers, but otherwise also maintained the overall silence.

Selene mostly kept her face turned away from me as we traveled. But occasionally I caught a glimpse of the brooding dread in her pupils. Something was going on in there, something beyond simply the situation we were in. But it was clear it wasn't something she wanted to talk about, at least not with other people listening in.

So I sat quietly beside her, cultivated my patience, and wondered what the hell we were going to do.

We were back on Floyd's yacht, and I was settling down in my sleeping nook in our suite, when the moment finally came. Selene slipped into my room, climbed into bed alongside me, and pressed her lips to my ear. "I need to talk to you," she whispered.

I found her hand and gently squeezed it in silent acknowledgment. We'd used this trick once before, back when we were aboard Nask's ship and knew there were multiple cameras and microphones trained on us. If Floyd or the yacht's crew were monitoring us right now, they would probably just assume that Selene and I were taking advantage of our presumed privacy to get cozy with each other and not consider that we might merely be talking. "The portal?"

"Yes," she said. "Gregory, that's not . . . when we were standing outside I thought I smelled . . . and then when we went inside . . ."

She paused and I felt her brace herself. "Gregory, Sub-Director Nask's scent is in there."

I felt my breath catch in my throat. What the *hell*? "Are you sure?"

"I'm positive," she said. "That wasn't some portal Cherno found somewhere. It's the one the Patth took from Fidelio.

"Cherno stole it from the Patth."

For a few seconds I lay silently beside her, staring up into the darkness, my brain spinning. No—that was impossible. The Patth had dug it out of the ground, hauled it into space, presumably transferred it to one of their massive freighters, and disappeared into the eternal night. How could it have ended up in a warehouse outside Cherno's mansion?

With a great deal of effort, of course. And, knowing the Patth, probably a great deal of blood and death.

"Were there any other Patth scents in there?" I whispered.

"There were several others in the area," Selene said. "Probably on the hull, possibly inside. With the hatch open so long all of it was mixed together."

"What about Floyd? No—never mind Floyd," I interrupted myself. With Floyd standing right beside us she wouldn't be able to sort out whether or not he'd been in there earlier. "Forget Floyd. What about Trent?"

I could visualize her pupils forming a frown. "Trent?"

"Trent," I repeated. "Remember the hijacking on Kelsim he was talking about?"

"I thought he said that was Oberon."

"He *implied* it was Oberon," I corrected. "I'm wondering if Trent pitched it to us backward. That *he* was the one who masterminded that attack."

I felt warm air on my ear as she huffed out a sudden breath.

"The second hijacking. The one he wants you in on. You think he's going after the other portal?"

"It's the logical conclusion," I said. "Which doesn't necessary mean it's the *right* conclusion."

"What are we going to do?"

Idly, I brushed my fingertips across her hair. Human hair was soft and silky; the Kadolian version was even more so. "Top of the list is to drop this whole mess in the admiral's lap as soon as possible," I said. "Nice stalling tactic with the Gemini master/slave thing, by the way. Keeps Cherno from pressuring us to get him the activation instructions. On the other hand, nine days is a hell of a long time to hang fire. Maybe I can persuade Floyd to stop somewhere near a StarrComm center."

"Maybe you can frame it as getting the admiral to start looking for the other end of the Gemini, too."

"Good idea," I said. "And then, once we've got Icarus in the loop, I'm thinking we should touch base with Trent."

"Are you going to take him up on his offer?"

"Probably not, but I at least want to find out what he knows and what exactly his plans are," I said. "If he knows where the other end is and is readying an attack, we play it one way. If he's still searching for it and is just getting his personnel ducks lined up, that requires an entirely different approach."

Selene pondered that a moment. "If he's searching, then we're back to who's funding him," she said. "If he has better resources than Cherno, he's likely to get there first. If he doesn't, we may be able to beat him to it."

"Good point," I agreed. "Especially when you throw the Icarus Group's resources in on our side."

"*If* we can get them fast enough."

I scowled. "Yeah," I said. "I'll get to work on Floyd first thing in the morning."

Because as my father used to say, *Most people only want to know how a deal will benefit them now. A handful of others want to know how the deal will benefit their future.*

I was pretty sure I'd find Floyd in that second category.

My guess on that one was dead on. Unfortunately, for once that foresight not only didn't work to my advantage but instead worked against me.

"I agree we should get your people on top of this," he said, eyeing me over his second cup of coffee of the morning. He would down at least five more cups of the stuff before the day was over, if the trip out from Xathru was any indicator. I hadn't noticed that much of a caffeine addiction the last time we traveled together, but then I hadn't spent much time with him on that occasion. "But stopping along the way will delay our arrival on Xathru and our subsequent trip to Balmoral. Your passenger will be there within twelve hours of our current projected landing time, and we don't want to keep her waiting." He raised his eyebrows. "*You* don't want to keep her waiting. Trust me."

"I'm sorry, but I'm confused," I said. "There have to be fueling stops within a few hours of whatever vector we're on. We head over to one of them, I make a quick StarrComm call—"

"Along our present vector, you said?"

"Yes," I said, feeling a whisper of growing irritation. Why was Floyd being so resistant to the idea? "Why, were you thinking of wandering across the Spiral until we found a place with good barbeque—?"

I broke off. He was just looking at me, his expression that of a teacher facing down a particularly dim student.

And then, belatedly, I got it. "You don't want me to know the direction we took after we left Xathru, do you?"

He favored me with a thin smile. "Not only don't *I* want it, but neither do Mr. Gaheen and Mr. Cherno."

"Of course they don't," I said with a sigh. "And they're more concerned about that than they are the six-week countdown?"

Floyd shrugged. "If it makes you feel any better, I've told the captain to jump our speed to plus-ten. That's the best we can do without having to stop along the way for fuel."

"Which we *could* still safely do," I pointed out. "As long as you keep Selene and me in our stateroom during the fueling stop, you can land wherever you want. In fact, with full tanks you could probably jump our speed to plus-thirty, get to Xathru that much earlier, and get my people on this even faster. We'd have to double-time it to Balmoral to make our connection, but it should be doable."

He shook his head. "Orders," he told me. "Even if you don't know where we are, someone out there might tag the ship while we're on the ground." He drained his coffee cup and refilled it from the carafe beside it. "Of course, none of this would be a problem if you'd been able to turn on the damn portal."

"It would have saved us a lot of grief, all right," I agreed. "But the best laid plans of mice and men, and all that." I cocked my head. "Speaking of plans, can you give us *any* idea what our end of the deal is about? Who is this mysterious passenger, why does Mr. Cherno need us to cart her around, and what's the endgame to all this?"

For a long moment he gazed at me, clearly pondering the question. I waited, just as silently, wondering if the flexibility he'd had with previous orders would extend into whatever his boundaries were here.

Then, to my disappointment, he shook his head. "Sorry," he said. "I'd like to, but my orders are clear on this. You're not supposed to know what's happening until after the passenger is aboard and you're on your way to wherever she wants you to go." He paused. "I *will* tell you this much, though. You're not going to like it. Not a bit."

"Great," I muttered. "Yes, that kind of anticipation makes things so much better. Thanks."

"At least you won't be completely blindsided when you find out." He took a last sip from his cup and set it down. "I need to work on some logistics files. I'll see you later."

For a few seconds after he left I sat there staring at his empty mug and the coffee carafe. If I dropped one of my knockout pills in there...

Ridiculous. I had six pills; there were eight crew aboard plus Floyd himself. And while the yacht wouldn't have the kind of pilot-implanted systems that made Patth ships impossible for anyone else to fly, there were bound to be passcodes and bioscans to make sure that unauthorized personnel kept their hands off the controls.

Which left me the choice of relaxing during the rest of our trip back to the *Ruth*, or being tense and frustrated the whole time.

And as my father used to say, *Worrying is just like planning, except that it doesn't get you anywhere and keeps you awake nights.*

CHAPTER FOUR

At long last, we reached Xathru.

"All fueled up?" Floyd asked, leaning over my shoulder as I ran the *Ruth*'s preflight checks.

"Fueled, docking fees paid, and Balmoral programmed into the helm," I confirmed. "I also laid in a supply of the coffee you drank aboard the yacht."

"Very observant," Floyd complimented me. "Too bad it'll be for nothing. I'm getting off at Balmoral, and I have no idea whether your passenger likes that blend."

"Really?" I asked, frowning. I'd assumed that Floyd would be on hand the whole way to ride herd on us, the passenger, or both. "We *can* sleep four in a pinch, you know."

"Pretty tight pinch," Floyd said. "No, I already checked. You've got new bioprobes in both of your bays. That must have set you back a bit. Or set McKell back."

"Mm," I said noncommittally. Floyd didn't seem all that concerned as to who we were working for, but he had McKell's name and occasionally liked to prod me with it, probably just to see if anything shook loose. "So tell me. Balmoral's only about fifteen hours from here, so why didn't you arrange for her to meet us here instead of there?"

"You're a clever boy," he said in a half serious, half mocking tone. "You tell me."

I sighed. As my father used to say, *Playing stupid gives the other guy a chance to show off how much smarter he is and how much more he knows.* Unfortunately, Floyd wasn't the type who needed to pump up his ego, and he already knew how smart I was. "Like you said when I asked about stopping along the way, someone might recognize Mr. Cherno's yacht. This way, the only connection between you and our passenger is the *Ruth*, which no one in their right mind would bother to keep track of."

Which wasn't exactly true, of course. Sub-Director Nask, for one, was probably keeping loose tabs on us, and there were also a few people from our bounty hunter days who wouldn't mind knowing where I was at any given time. Especially if they could run into me when I wasn't armed.

"Very good," Floyd said approvingly. "If you ever get tired of working for McKell and his friends, give me a call. I'm sure we could find a spot for you."

"Thanks, but I'll pass," I said. "My deep-rooted dislike of getting shot at, remember?"

"Right. I'd forgotten. Pity." Floyd yawned. "Well, you seem to have things in hand here. I'm going to take a quick nap in the dayroom. Let me know when we get to Balmoral."

"You'll be the first."

We put down on a bustling landing field at the edge of the capital city, New Aberdeen. I arranged for the fuelers to top off the *Ruth*'s tanks, and as Floyd grabbed a runaround and headed across the field to wherever he was meeting our passenger, Selene and I got our own vehicle and headed for the nearby StarrComm center.

I was prepared for the admiral to be his usual eloquently unhappy self. But I'd underestimated the extent to which the sheer shock value of our news would affect the man's vocabulary. For a solid three seconds after I'd finished he just sat there and stared at us, which was probably the average person's equivalent of a two-week coma.

"You're certain?" he asked at last. "You're absolutely certain?"

"Selene is," I said, nodding sideways at Selene. As usual, she'd let me carry the ball on this one, only speaking up when there was a small detail I'd forgotten to mention. "Unless you think the Patth have more than one Gemini and that Nask has been inside all of them."

"I would think that highly unlikely," the admiral murmured. His eyes were unfocused, his brain undoubtedly running the situation through the full sand-sifter. "If we could snatch the Patth Gemini out from under them..."

"Bear in mind we have no idea whatsoever where it is," I reminded him.

"Somewhere nine days' flight from Xathru," he reminded me back.

"Or not," I said. "Floyd could have circled us through hyperspace for eight and a half days and then landed somewhere within spitting distance of where we started."

"And then went through the same charade on the way back to Xathru?" he countered. "You think he would deliberately waste those extra days even with the window of opportunity for whatever Cherno has in mind steadily closing?"

I shrugged. "Depends on whether Cherno's more worried about the tightness of his timing or that you and Icarus will find him and sneak the portal out of his backyard."

The admiral grunted. "I suppose that makes sense. And speaking of his backyard...?"

"The hangar we landed in had a mix of fir trees and Vyssiluyan pampas grass nearby," Selene said. "There was also water in the area, and the smell of algae, so probably a pond or lake instead of a river. The nearest inhabitants were humans, Doolies, and Mastanni, with other fainter scents in the distance. Cherno's mansion had hyacinth and masala chai, and his garage had Craean lubricating oil for his cars."

"There was a forest outside his office window with a mountain range in the distance," I added, plugging in my data stick. "I drew a sketch from memory, but of course it's only a rough rendition."

"And from a single point of reference, too," the admiral said, his eyes flicking to the side as the picture I'd drawn came through. "Well, I suppose it's something. I'll get our analysts on it right away."

"There's one other thing," Selene said hesitantly. "I don't have a good baseline for Cherno, but he reacted very strongly to the news that we couldn't activate his portal."

"Oh, definitely," I agreed tightly.

"No, I don't mean just that he was angry," Selene said. "He *was* angry, but I think there was also fear and maybe even some desperation mixed in. He needs the portal to be functional, and he needs it that way within his six-week time limit."

"Any ideas as to why?" the admiral asked.

Selene looked at me, and I could see the frustration in her pupils. Even with her extraordinary senses she sometimes had to fall back on gut instinct, and she hated that. "I'm sure it has something to do with our passenger," she said. "But how everything fits together ... I don't know."

"But we should have another clue soon," I put in. "Floyd's bringing her to the *Ruth*, and once we know who she is we may be able to figure out what Cherno's got in mind."

"Whatever it is, it's not likely to be wholesome or civicminded," the admiral growled. "I've got half a mind to pull you out of this right now, and to hell with the portal."

"I don't think that would be a good idea," I warned. "Whatever Cherno's planning, I doubt us disappearing from the scene will stop it. Not being able to use the portal might, but I somehow doubt that he doesn't have a Plan B ready in the wings."

"And he would be very unhappy with us," Selene said with a shiver.

"To put it mildly," I agreed. "Besides, if we bail now we'll never find out who our passenger was going to be. Aren't you at least a little bit intrigued?"

"You'd be well advised to rein in your more impulsive instincts," the admiral warned. "There's a saying about curiosity and cats, you know."

"I prefer my father's version," I said. "As he used to say, *Curiosity is what distinguishes us from the lower animals, and why we eat shellfish.*"

"I'm sure he did," the admiral said. "Very well, go and be curious. But keep us informed."

"We will," I promised. "One more thing. I told you that Cherno's got his people looking for ruins that might be similar to the Erymant Temple. I presume you've already connected those dots and have done the same search?"

"We're working on it," he said, his eyes narrowed slightly. "There are a lot of worlds out there. I presume you're asking for our list?"

"That would be highly appreciated," I said. "My thought was that we can see what Cherno comes up with, then compare it to yours. Wherever they dovetail will be where we start our investigations."

"That's reasonable," the admiral murmured. "Or we could let Cherno come up with his list and do our comparison then."

I frowned. "So that's a no on your list?"

"That's a no," he confirmed. "For now."

"They're just ruins, you know," I reminded him. "Archeologists make lists of them all the time. One more isn't going to raise any eyebrows."

"Certainly not if no one sees it," the admiral agreed. "Is there anything else?"

I glared at him. After Fidelio I'd made the case to Ixil that Selene and I needed better and faster access to Icarus Group's information, and he'd promised to bring the request to the admiral's attention. Apparently, it hadn't gotten as much traction as I'd hoped. "No, I guess that's it," I said. "For now."

"Then good luck," he said, nodding to each of us in turn. "Oh, and let's keep this bit about Cherno's portal being Nask's between ourselves for now."

"You mean except for McKell if we happen to run into him?" I asked.

"I mean except for no one," he said firmly. "Until I decide who and when to tell. Understood?"

I nodded. "Understood."

"Good," he said. "Check in again when you can. And be safe."

The screen blanked. "Nice to know that our safety comes second to regular field reports," I said, collecting my change. "A quick check for messages, then we'll be off. I doubt Floyd likes to be kept waiting."

"What about Trent?"

"Trent will just have to wait," I said, keying for my mail drop. "We've got plenty on our plate already."

Floyd and a tall woman were waiting at the foot of the *Ruth*'s ramp when we arrived.

At least, I assumed his companion was a woman. She was dressed in a loose black-and-dark-green wrap, belted at the waist and extending to mid-calf, with tall black boots and a matching narrow-brim black hat and gloves. Her figure beneath it all was a bit vague, but it showed enough of the usual feminine shape.

A chin-length veil attached to the sides of the hat was wrapped around her lower face, leaving only her eyes and a narrow band of skin visible. The overall impression was that of style, comfort, and complete anonymity.

Floyd had avoided telling us anything about our passenger before now. Apparently, that coyness was going to extend into the trip itself.

"I trust we're not late," I said as Selene and I joined them.

"Not at all," the woman said, her voice smooth and precise. "Mr. Floyd was just telling me about the *Ruth*. Interesting name."

"We like it," I said, turning to Floyd. "So this is where you leave us?"

"Yes," he said, digging out a data stick and handing it to me. "Here's the preliminary information you requested from Mr. Cherno. There may be additional entries over the next few days or weeks. They'll be forwarded to your mail drop."

"Excellent," I said, dropping the data stick into my pocket. The admiral had wanted me to send him Cherno's list of possible portal sites, and for a moment I considered asking for an additional hour and heading back to the StarrComm center.

But while our passenger seemed calm enough, I had the sense that she was impatient to get going. For once, the admiral could just wait. "I'm Roarke; this is Selene," I continued, looking back at the woman. "And you are...?"

"Call me Piper," she said, looking up at the *Ruth*. "The ship is acceptable. I'll let you begin prepping it for flight while I go and get my luggage."

I felt my eyes narrow. I'd have thought she would have everything with her already. "Do you need help carrying any of it?" I asked.

"No," she said. "From either of you," she added, looking at Floyd.

"Whatever you say," he said. "Roarke, good luck."

"Do I get to know where we're going?" I asked.

"Piper will give you your destination once she's aboard," Floyd said. "She has a few stops to make before we get to Mr. Cherno's job."

"We'll begin with Vesperin," Piper said. "Not too far from Balmoral, and it will give me time to decide on our next port."

"Ah," I said, my eyes narrowing a bit more. "If I may suggest, it might be simpler for all of us to just wait here until you've decided. I guarantee you'll be a lot more comfortable in a hotel than aboard the *Ruth*."

"I appreciate your concern," she said. "But I like to travel. We'll start with Vesperin."

"Vesperin it is," I said, conceding the point. "Though depending on where we're ultimately going, there may be other intermediate points closer to your destination."

"I'm not in any hurry." Her eyes flicked to Floyd. "Am I?"

"Not right now," he told her, a slight crease in his forehead. Either there was something he was deliberately not saying, or else he was confused himself by the delay. "We're hoping that will change." He locked eyes with me. "Soon."

"We'll all hope that," I agreed. "Ah . . . if I may ask, what sort of business will we be doing on these other worlds?"

Floyd gave a sort of warning grunt. "That's none of your—"

"It's all right, Mr. Floyd," Piper cut him off calmly. "They'll have to know eventually. We might as well be up front about it."

She paused, and from the way her veil creased I had the impression she was giving me a tight smile. "I'm a professional assassin, Mr. Roarke. Mr. Gaheen has hired me to kill someone for him."

Distantly, through the stunned silence filling my head, I heard Floyd's voice: "I *said* you wouldn't like it."

I was on the bridge, running the preflight and keeping one eye on the entryway monitor, when Piper returned.

Given that Cherno had implied his job wouldn't happen for six weeks—closer to five weeks now, of course—I'd expected to see her hauling a fair amount of luggage. To my surprise, she had only two bags: one large and rolling beside her, the other a duffel slung over her shoulder. "She's here," I called down the corridor to Selene. "Is my cabin ready for her?"

"As ready as it can be," Selene called back. "I've moved some clothing and your personal effects to the dayroom."

Where I would be bedding down as long as Piper was aboard. I wasn't crazy about giving up my cabin, but there were only two of them on the *Ruth* and I wasn't about to ask Selene to give up hers. "Thank you," I called. "Would you go let her in?"

"All right," Selene said. "That was fast."

"I doubt the art of sauntering is anywhere in her job description."

Selene didn't answer. I gave the displays a final look, confirmed that the diagnostics were proceeding correctly, then turned my attention to the display where I'd pulled up Floyd's planetary data.

Despite my current opinion of Cherno, which after the revelation of this new employee was somewhere down in the seventh circle of hell, I had to admit that his people had done a terrific job of data sifting. They'd worked up a list of thirty ruins that had at least vague similarities to the Erymant Temple, ranked from most to least promising.

Of course, the fact that the experts gave the highest-rated ruins, on Niskea, only a six percent similarity to Erymant didn't exactly fill me with confidence. Still, unless and until I could get the admiral to loosen up and feed me the Icarus Group's data, it was all we had.

Our lift slot was three minutes away when Selene appeared on the bridge. "She all settled in?" I asked, glancing over my shoulder at her.

"Yes," Selene said, an odd tone to her voice.

I turned back for a closer look. There was a strange sort of confusion in her pupils. "Trouble? Let me guess—she doesn't like my cabin."

"No, she says the cabin is fine," Selene said. "She looks very nice in that outfit, don't you think?"

"Nice enough," I said. "Though the fact that she kills people for a living takes a lot of the shine off her natural charm and attractiveness. Whatever attractiveness she's hiding under that veil, anyway."

"Yes; the veil," Selene said, lowering herself carefully into the plotting table seat. "Very convenient."

I looked at the countdown timer. Ninety seconds until the landing pad repulsor boost lifted us off the ground and into range of the perimeter grav beams. "Whatever you're getting at, Selene," I said, "get to it now, or else sit on it until we're on our way."

"I'll get to it now," she said. "That woman—the person unpacking her things in your cabin—isn't the woman Floyd introduced us to."

I swiveled fully around in my chair, feeling my mouth drop open, my right hand dropping reflexively to the Fafnir plasmic belted at my side. "What do you mean, she's not the same woman?" I demanded. "Who is she?"

Selene shook her head, looking furtively down the corridor. "I don't know," she said, lowering her voice. "She looks like her, at least from what I can see. Same height, same hair and eye color, and her voice is either identical or very close. But her smell is entirely different."

"And she's wearing the same outfit."

"*Exactly* the same outfit," Selene said. "Her clothing also carries the scent of the first woman."

I looked back at the timer, my stomach churning with indecision. I had about twenty seconds to call the tower and abort, or we were leaving the planet. "Were there any tears in the outfit?" I asked Selene. "Was it rumpled or dirty?"

"No," she said. "And it wouldn't take much to tear that veil if you were struggling not to give it up. The scents of both women were on the luggage, too."

"First woman's scent might have just been left over."

"Yes, it might."

Ten seconds. It was clear that there was some kind of con game going on.

But on whom? Selene and me? Ridiculous. We had no idea who either woman was. There was no reason to pull a swap unless someone just wanted the practice.

Floyd, then? He'd certainly seemed to know the woman he'd introduced us to. Swapping after he was gone would leave him fully convinced that we'd left with Piper.

And if the women were conning Floyd, they were probably conning Gaheen, too.

I came to a decision. Our passenger wanted us to believe she was Piper, and I saw no gain in blowing the whistle on her here and now. Actually, for all I knew, *Piper* was a joint alias for a whole group of assassins. Stranger things than that went on in the Spiral's darker corners.

"What do we do?" Selene asked.

"We go as planned," I said, turning back around to my board. "Strap in."

Two seconds later, the *Ruth* rocked gently as the repulsors lifted us off the pad. Five seconds after that, the grav beams lanced out from their towers and pulled us up. I was ready, cutting in the *Ruth*'s thrusters as soon as it was safe and legal to do so, and we were off.

Twenty minutes later, with the haze of Balmoral's atmosphere faded into the starry black of space, I activated the cutter array and we were on our way to Vesperin—Selene, me, and a mysterious passenger trying to conceal her identity who made her living killing people.

As my father used to say. *Where there's smoke there may be fire, but there's almost certainly somebody trying to hide something.*

CHAPTER FIVE

Dinner that night was our special official first-night meal that we always provided for our passengers.

Or at least, that was what I told Piper. In reality, most of our recent fellow travelers had been unfriendly toward us to one degree or another, while back in our bounty hunter days any spare bodies aboard the *Ruth* were in restraints and a long ways south of unfriendly.

But inventing a special occasion would give us an excuse to spend some time with our guest, and hopefully let us learn more about her.

Hopefully, it wouldn't also get her angry and get us shot.

I'd frankly expected Piper to decline my invitation and instead insist on eating her meals alone in her cabin, where she could keep her face permanently out of our sight. To my mild surprise, she accepted without hesitation. She arrived in the dayroom on schedule dressed in a casual jumpsuit, all smiles and cheerful conversation, her veil nowhere to be seen.

As my father used to say, *When an otherwise secretive person voluntarily shares something with you, it's either of no value or it's a trap.* Either she didn't expect us to recognize her face, or she was deliberately putting it on display in order to see if we knew her and to gauge our reactions.

Something of a gamble, probably, for a person in her profession. But in this case, the house paid out the bet. I didn't have the foggiest idea who she was, and I could tell from Selene's pupils that she didn't, either.

Not that Piper was reticent about her profession. On the contrary, she was strangely, even disturbingly, open about it.

"Mr. Floyd tells me you're crocketts when you're not transporting killers around the Spiral," she said, as she took another spoonful of Selene's chicken tetrazzini onto her plate. "From what I've read, that's a pretty dangerous job."

"I suppose," I said, sipping at my drink. I usually had a little wine with this type of meal, but I'd sworn off all such indulgences for the duration of Piper's stay. Alcohol didn't usually affect me very much, but I had no intention of opening myself up to even the smallest lapse of judgment or thinking. "But every job has its downsides."

"And of course bounty hunting is even worse," she said, slicing off a bit of chicken with the edge of her fork. "I did that for a while myself before I switched to my current job."

"Ah," I said, my brilliantly inventive way of verbally stalling while I tried to figure out whether she was baiting us or merely chatting. "Was hunting easier, or harder, do you think?"

"It was pretty similar," she said, popping the chicken into her mouth and chewing carefully. "Same prep work. Much the same leg work." She paused, considering. "About the same risk of getting shot at. You don't approve of what I do, do you?"

For some inexplicable reason, I hadn't been prepared for that question. "Pardon?" I asked.

"You don't like professional assassins," she clarified. "Actually, Floyd tells me you're not big on killing of any sort."

"It's not my favorite thing in the Spiral," I admitted. "I figure you have fewer ghosts haunting your dreams when most of those spirits are still attached to their bodies."

"Even if those united bodies and spirits get out of prison someday and come after you?"

I shrugged. "The people I hunted usually had a lot of names on their vengeance lists ahead of mine," I said. "It's also a lot harder to track down a hunter than someone who's more settled in their ways and habits."

"Especially when those hunters have become crocketts?"

"Especially then."

"Mm," she said, nodding thoughtfully. "It's not illegal to be an assassin, you know."

"It is in most of the places we travel," Selene spoke up quietly.

Piper shifted her attention to her. "Never seen your type before," she commented, looking Selene up and down. "May I ask?"

"Kadolian," Selene said.

"Never heard of you, either," Piper said, scooping up another bite. "Interesting. But you're misinformed. *Murder* is illegal most places, as you say. Being an assassin isn't."

"Isn't that a distinction without a difference?" I asked.

"Depends on where you are," Piper said. "Take me, for instance. I'm registered on one of the handful of planets that allow professional assassins, the same way most of the Spiral allows professional bounty hunters. On all the other worlds, as long as I don't actually kill someone on their soil they more or less tolerate my presence."

"So you can be an assassin as long as you don't actually do your job?" I asked.

"More or less," she said. "But it's less an oxymoron than it sounds. While my job is technically illegal in most places, there are a surprising number of governments—local *and* planetary— that turn a blind eye to my activities as long as my targets are criminals."

"Or political figures they consider a threat to their own interests?" Selene asked pointedly.

"One of the many definitions of *criminal*," Piper said with more than a hint of irony. "There are also officials who directly hire me—*very* informally, of course—to eliminate their opponents."

"And you're all right with that?" Selene asked, a hard edge of challenge in her tone.

Piper was silent a moment. "Did you ever hear of a man named Ajagavakar on Golden Bough? He was governor of Brach-nell Province."

"Name's not ringing any bells," I said, searching my memory. "Selene?"

She had her info pad out and was running the name. "He's not in the general personnel listing."

"No reason why he should be," Piper said. "Minor planet, small province, highly forgettable man. You'd have to dig deep into that sector's archives to find even a mention of him. He'd been governor for a year and a half when a mysterious explosion killed him, his wife, his four children, and six workers on the floor of the hotel where they were staying."

My stomach tightened into a painful knot. "That was you?"

"No," Piper said, the word wrapped in anger, her face stiff with contempt. "Absolutely not. If I'd been hired for the job, his family and the others would still be alive. I would have taken out the target, and *only* the target."

"Unless you missed," Selene murmured, her pupils roiling with contempt.

"I never miss," Piper said flatly. "Ever. Political and business killings will always happen, Roarke, whether or not there are people like me in the business. My point is that many of those killings are handled by butchers. I'm a surgeon."

"Congratulations," I said, swallowing back as much of my own revulsion as I could. She was still our passenger, she was still our responsibility, and I had no evidence besides her own word that she had ever killed anyone. There was nothing I should do, or indeed nothing I could do.

Not to mention that she was a killer and was undoubtedly armed.

But not even all my skill at self-control could fully suppress my emotion. "You don't like me," Piper said. She took a final bite of tetrazzini, then laid her fork at the side of the plate. "That's all right. I don't ask for acceptance or even understanding. I've chosen this path, and whether my reasons are valid or not is my burden to bear. Thank you for your hospitality, and I'll be out of your lives as soon as I can." She stood up, nodded to each of us, and walked to the dayroom hatchway.

"Why Vesperin?" Selene called after her.

"As I said earlier, it's close and convenient," Piper reminded her. "We can also see if there's any news—"

"Why Vesperin?" Selene repeated.

For a moment Piper stood there, silent and motionless. "There are one or two things I need to look into," she said at last. "Nothing either of you need concern yourselves with."

She turned her head just far enough to put me in her peripheral vision. "I should also mention that there's one other reason some governments allow me on their soil. They give me free rein in hopes that I'll slip, they'll catch me in the act, and they can then take me out of circulation for good. If that soothes your cynicism toward our dedicated governmental leaders any."

"Not really," I said. "But to be honest, Ms. Piper, you're only a small part of that cynicism anyway."

"I'm sorry to hear that," she said. "Life is much brighter when you look on it with calm eyes."

"So we've heard," Selene murmured.

"Yes." Piper seemed to hesitate, as if working through a decision. "And *Ms. Piper* is far too formal for our current situation. Call me Nikki."

"Okay," I said. "Good night, Nikki."

She gave me a half flash of a half smile, then walked through the hatchway and disappeared down the corridor toward her stateroom.

I turned to Selene—

"Are you going to order me to be polite to her?" she asked stiffly before I could say anything.

"No one's ordering you to do anything," I assured her, frowning at the emotional intensity in her pupils. She'd been more than a little pushy toward Nikki during dinner, but I'd had no idea that whatever the problem was went that deep. "In fact, you don't have to deal with her at all if you don't want to. You can stay out of her way and let me handle everything."

She looked down at her plate. "No, that's all right," she said. "I can't let you carry this by yourself."

"If you're sure," I said, standing up. "Why don't you go and relax for a while? I can clear the table."

"I can help," she said, standing up as well and starting to stack the plates. "Gregory . . . do you think she's going after someone on Vesperin?"

I winced. "Could be," I conceded. "I doubt she's going handbag shopping."

"You realize that if we're giving her transport we'll be accessories after the fact if she kills someone."

"Possibly," I said. "Though that'll depend on how Vesperin law is written. Actually, there are enough autonomous regions on the planet that it'll probably depend on exactly where it happens."

"I meant morally, not legally."

"Yeah. Probably."

"Yes," Selene murmured. "I just thought I should mention it."

We worked in silence for another minute, Selene loading the plates and flatware into the cleaner, me sealing up the leftover tetrazzini and putting it away. "Tell you what," I said as I wiped the table. "When we land, you stay here and handle the refueling paperwork while I follow her and see what she's up to. How does that sound?"

"It sounds dangerous," she said, the private brooding in her pupils now taking on an edge of concern. "I don't think she'd want you watching her work."

"I'll make sure she doesn't see me, then," I said. "Okay. I'm going to do a quick status check, then settle down for the evening. I'll probably crash out a bit early, actually, so if you want anything from in here you should get it now."

She shook her head. "I'm fine. Sleep well."

Three hours later, I was still reading everything on my info pad about Vesperin, its people, and its laws when I finally fell asleep on the dayroom foldout.

Vesperin was one of the more unusual colony worlds in that it had been started by a joint consortium of three different alien groups—Ulkomaals, Yavanni, and k'Tra—for the express purpose of inviting other interested species to come in and set up their own enclaves and trading centers. The call had been enthusiastically answered, and while Vesperin had started out somewhat off of the main travel lines, the presence of so many other groups had spun off other nearby colonies, some of them single-species, others following the consortium's original vision and building coalitions, to the point where traffic had ended up bending toward it and turned Vesperin into a substantial hub for that part of the Spiral.

Of course, the subsequent arrival of the Path and their superfast Talariac Drive hadn't hurt Vesperin's rise any.

Nikki had specified which spaceport I was to land at, which turned out to be one of the seven fields in and around the sprawling city of Mikilias. From my earlier research I knew Mikilias was largely a k'Tra city, though it had sizeable minorities of other species. More interesting was the fact that it bordered on both a human and an Ihmis enclave. I called Planetary Control, was assigned a slot, and dropped us smoothly onto our landing cradle.

I'd barely gotten the engines shut down and the rest of the systems on their way to standby when Nikki was gone.

"I was running the thruster diagnostic when she left," Selene said, her pupils showing a mix of anger and embarrassment. "I'm sorry—I never expected her to get out so quickly."

"That's all right," I assured her, punching up a city map on my info pad. "I'll catch up with her."

"You don't even know where she went," she retorted. She paused, and I saw her brace herself. "I'd better come with you."

It was the logical approach, of course, given that Selene's incredible sense of smell could track Nikki's fresh scent even through a crowded alien city. But given her feelings toward the assassin... "Thanks, but I can handle it," I told her. "Anyway, I'm pretty sure I *do* know where she's going. Be sure to lock up behind me."

I grabbed my phone and plasmic, hurried through the entryway and down the ramp, and headed into the spaceport traffic.

Nikki was a human. We'd landed in a city bordering a human enclave, and in fact had taken a slot in the spaceport closest to the crossover point to that enclave. What little I knew about professional assassins suggested that they, like bounty hunters, tended to target members of their own species, if for no other reason than that it was more difficult for members of one species to positively distinguish between the members of another. In addition, someone going undercover naturally wanted to be able to blend in as much as possible, which again meant sticking with one's own species. Taking all of those together, rolling them into a loaf and baking in a medium cooker, you ended up with the obvious conclusion that Nikki was heading for the human section.

But Nikki didn't strike me as the obvious type. More than that, all those indicators were *so* one-sided that I didn't buy the logical conclusion for a second. So instead of heading toward the HUMAN signpost hovering ten meters above the streets that marked the entrance to the human enclave, I turned toward the IHMIS one.

I *did* expect Nikki to at least follow the blending-in part, which included the dictum to travel at the average traffic speed. I made sure to keep my pace a bit higher than that, and kept my eyes open.

Sure enough, ten minutes later I spotted her striding along a block ahead of me.

I dropped back a little, slowing to match her speed, trying

not to be too conspicuous among the nonhumans crowding the walkways. She was dressed in the same identity-concealing outfit she'd been wearing back on Balmoral, and had the satchel she'd brought aboard the *Ruth* slung over her shoulder.

In theory, tailing someone through a bustling crowd was relatively easy. Here, though, the practice was a bit trickier. The local k'Tra, as was typical with their species, had a tendency to form instant clumps in the traffic flow as two or more of them spotted acquaintances or business associates and stopped dead in the middle of the walkways to chat. Such instant roadblocks presented a hazard to navigation, especially when your eyes were mainly focused a block away.

Nikki, with no such split attention, was always able to maneuver gracefully around the obstacles without bumping into them. More interesting was that as I watched her I realized she wasn't just seeing the clumps forming ahead of her, but sometimes seemed to actually anticipate them. That suggested that not only was she scanning a ways ahead of her, but was reading the k'Tra facial and body cues before the aliens stopped for their conversations.

The woman was smart, knowledgeable, and nimble. And, given the presence of the satchel on her shoulder, she was also undoubtedly armed.

And here I was, following her on a clandestine job, with no one knowing exactly where I was.

As my father used to say, *Recipes for disaster also come in quick-mix versions.* Strolling along behind someone on the street was about as quick-mix as you could get.

But I was here, and Nikki was here, and Selene's comment about accessories after the fact was nagging at the back of my mind. And so, trying not to think about what Floyd and Cherno and Gaheen would say if I got their hired assassin arrested, I kept going.

We'd been walking for about fifteen minutes when Nikki suddenly turned left into a partially completed ten-story building, stepping over the low line of flapping warning tape across the open entrance.

I scowled, my throat tightening. I could see no sign of workers anywhere through the many openings in the half-finished walls, which suggested the place was abandoned, at least for the moment. It was a perfect place to set up an ambush, and as I approached the entrance I found my hand resting on my holstered plasmic. I walked past without stopping, with a half-formed plan of pretending she and I had merely and coincidentally been walking along the same street if I was challenged.

But no one called to me or, more importantly, shot at me as I walked past the taped-off entrance. In fact, as I sent a sideways glance through the opening I spotted her walking toward a construction elevator near the middle of the building.

I continued past the opening, not breaking stride. When I was once again shielded from view by the walls, I reversed direction and headed back to the edge of the entrance. I paused there, gave my left thumbnail the gentle double stroke that turned it into a mirror, and eased it around the corner. I was just in time to see Nikki slide the elevator door closed and start upward.

I glanced around, confirmed that no one seemed to be paying any particular attention to me, and stepped over the tape and into the building.

Even if I could get the elevator to return to the ground floor after Nikki got wherever she was going, it would be beyond even my level of ridiculous optimism to assume she wouldn't notice the clank as the car started back down. Fortunately, from the entryway I could see three open stairways. Picking the nearest one, I started up.

I stepped carefully, not just out of concerns that Nikki might hear me but also because the wooden stairs seemed rickety beneath my feet and the single railing looked nearly as unsafe as the stairs felt. I made my way to the next floor, easing my head cautiously up as I reached the level of the underflooring, looking first for the elevator car and then for Nikki's shadowy figure.

She wasn't on the second floor, or the third, or the fourth. I continued up, feeling my tension rising with each successive level. Had she spotted me and used a combination of the elevator and stairs to slip past while I was working my way up? If she was trying to lose me, such a gambit would be trivial to pull off, and while it would be preferable to shooting me outright it would be a rather annoying slight on my personal pride as a former bounty hunter. I reached the open hole that led onto the roof.

And there she was.

She was at the northern edge of the roof, kneeling behind the low parapet, looking at something in that direction with her back to me. I couldn't see her hands, but from the way her elbows were bent I guessed she was holding something. A camera? A phone? A gun?

The smart thing to do would be to turn around, head back down the stairs, and return to the ship. Whatever Nikki was doing, it really wasn't any of my business—

"If you're looking to stop me, Roarke," she called, "you're going to have to get a lot closer." She half turned, giving me a profile of her veiled face. "Or were you planning to shoot me in the back?"

Abruptly, I realized my hand was once again resting on the grip of my plasmic. "No," I assured her, opening my hand and lifting it away from the weapon. "Neither, actually. I was just curious as to where you were going."

"Selene put you up to this?"

"Like I said, I was just curious."

Her head twitched with what was probably an unheard snort. "You know what they say about curiosity."

"Yes," I said. "Everyone seems to feel I need reminding about that."

"That should tell you something." She waved me toward her. "Come on. Join the party."

Clenching my teeth, wondering briefly how much it would hurt to instead throw myself backward down the stairs out of target range, I walked across the roof toward her. "Here," she said, waving at a spot beside her. "You might want to get down, too."

I did as ordered, lowering myself into a crouch behind the parapet. In her other hand, I saw, she was holding the targeting scope of a sniper rifle, the rest of the rifle lying disassembled on the roof between the parapet and her knees.

"Over there," she said, pointing past a group of lower buildings to another unfinished structure a block away. "You see two Ihmisits, a k'Tra, and four Yavanni gathered around a human holding an oversized info pad?"

"Yes," I said. Actually, only the Ihmisits and k'Tra were standing close to the human. The four Yavanni were spread out in a classic containment box formation, their eyes and attention focused outward. "Which ones are the Yavanni guarding?"

Her head turned to me, and I saw a hint of approval in her eyes. "Very good," she said. "I don't think one hunter out of a hundred would have spotted that so quickly."

"Long practice," I said shortly. "Which one's your target?"

"As it happens, none of them," she said, offering me the targeting scope. "Take a look at the human. You recognize him?"

I took the scope and put it to my eye, my senses kicking into instant overdrive. Calm conversation, a casual denial, and a shiny-object distraction—it was tailor-made for an attack on the unsuspecting idiot who'd blundered into her job. This would be the moment where she would stab me, shoot me, or just roll me over the parapet and send me crashing to the street below.

Only she didn't do any of those things. She just knelt there patiently, waiting for me to ratchet down my nervous anticipation and focus on the man I was supposed to look at.

He was an older man, though with his sun-wrinkled face and pure white hair he probably looked older than he really was. He was gesturing to points on his info pad, his mouth moving with quick conversation, his stance that of a man fully in control of himself, his sales pitch, and his future.

"Nope," I said, passing the scope back. Still no attempt to kill me. "Never seen him before."

"No reason why you should have," Nikki said. Shifting back and forth between knees, she moved half a meter back from the parapet and started putting the pieces of her rifle back into her satchel. "He's Horace Markelly, a big land developer from Randaire. Clawed his way up to his current exalted position, squashing everyone who got in his way. One of the people currently on his to-squash list decided to move first, and asked me to handle the job."

I frowned. "And?"

Nikki shrugged. "I have a rule. Just one, really, but it's important to me." She paused in her packing to turn those intense eyes on me again. "I don't take contracts on people who've previously hired me."

For a moment we locked eyes while I ran that totally unexpected statement through my mind a couple of times. It didn't sound any more believable the third time around than it had the first. "Excuse me?" I asked carefully.

She shrugged again and returned to her packing. "It's pretty self-explanatory. Markelly once hired me to eliminate one of his rivals. Therefore, I won't take a contract on him."

"Ah," I said. Still didn't make any sense. "So no matter how bad someone is, all he has to do is hire you and he's forever untouchable?"

"You got it." She looked up at me again. "And that's not hiring me to paint his house or something. He has to hire me for my professional services."

I looked back across at the distant rooftop. "I can think of a lot of people I've dealt with through the years who would have paid good money to get on a list like that."

"*Very* good money," she agreed. "My fee starts at half a million commarks."

I gave a low whistle. "So only the very rich can afford to stay out of your sights."

"Yes." She finished packing away her gun and zipped the bag closed. "But then, most people aren't worth that much money to have killed. It balances out."

"Ah." Offhand, I couldn't see how, exactly. But it didn't seem the right time to launch into a philosophical discussion. "So what now?"

She stood up and slung the bag over her shoulder. "I go to the StarrComm center and tell my prospective client I'm not taking the contract. You head back to the *Ruth*, and I'll meet you there. Or do some shopping. Whatever you want."

"And then?"

"According to Floyd, Cherno's contract is hanging fire and you and Selene are the ones who need to do something about that," she said. "So I guess you two get to say where we go next." Her eyes narrowed a bit in thought. "Though if you can't figure it out, I've got a couple of other places that could be more useful than just sitting around somewhere doing nothing."

"I'm sure there are," I said. "I guess we part ways, then."

"For now," she agreed. She took one last look across at Markelly, then turned and started back toward the elevator. "You joining me? The car has room for two."

"Thanks," I said. "I like the stairs."

She shrugged. "Suit yourself. I'll see you back at the ship."

The stairs were just as rickety and unsafe feeling on the way down as they'd been on the way up. Still, they were preferable company to the alternate I'd been offered.

I was halfway down, and the sound of the descending elevator had stopped, when it occurred to me to wonder why work on this building had been abandoned and how Nikki had known it would be a good place to set up for a kill.

But really, those were questions of barely idle interest. The only reason for my brain to focus on them at all was to crowd out all the other thoughts swirling like banshees through my mind.

It wasn't Nikki's calm viciousness, or even the almost urbane casing wrapped around it. I'd known plenty of other people like that, and usually tried to steer clear of them as much as I could. It was, rather, the bizarre self-imposed limitation on who she would kill and who she wouldn't.

Had she come up with that on her own? Had it been suggested by someone else? Had she been faced with a contract on someone she liked or respected, declined the job, then decided to make that refusal a permanent part of her life?

Preoccupied with questions I couldn't answer, I'd made it three blocks before I realized I was being followed.

CHAPTER SIX

My first thought was that Nikki had reconsidered her decision to let me go and had come back to remedy that mistake. But a bit of judicious window-shopping, along with the use of my thumbnail mirror, showed that my new would-be playmate was an Ihmisit, and furthermore that his outfit was in line with those of the rest of the pedestrians around us. A local, then, or someone who'd at least been here long enough to learn how to blend in. Possibly someone who'd seen my exit and was wondering what I'd been doing in an abandoned building; more likely someone who was fully aware of why I'd been there and wanted to have words of a very different sort.

People who knew me sometimes labeled me as overly talkative. But after my conversation with Nikki, I decided I was done with social activities for the day.

Which didn't mean I didn't want to know who this was and what the hell he wanted.

More questions. But at least here I had a chance of finding answers for them. Assuming the Ihmisit back there was a local, he had the advantage of knowing the city and the people far better than I did. But I had determination, a modicum of innate cunning, and maybe a trick or two he hadn't seen.

First on my list was to pick up a few props. Two storefronts

ahead was a place with a selection of small gifts and knickknacks
in its window. I walked in, bought an item of the proper size,
and asked for it to be gift-wrapped. I then sent the proprietor
into the back to look for an item I was pretty sure he didn't
have, and while he was gone I used my knife to carve a hole
in the bottom of the gift box that was just the right size to fit
my plasmic. When the proprietor returned, empty-handed and
apologetic, I thanked him for his efforts and left, the box and
hidden plasmic balanced on my right hand while I stabilized the
package with my left.

My tail was still there, maybe half a block closer, pretending
to window-shop as he waited for me to reappear. I resumed my
path back toward the main city and the *Ruth*; he resumed his
path behind me.

Earlier, when I was following Nikki, I'd spotted a couple of
likely-looking service alleys along my current route and filed
them away for possible future reference. I reached the closer of
the two and turned down it, breaking into a run the instant I
was out of the Ihmisit's sight. The alley was short enough that
a determined quarry might be able to disappear out the other
end before an equally determined pursuer could reach the corner
and regain eye contact. The question was how much effort the
Ihmisit was willing to put into this, and what kind of physical
shape he was in.

I was nearly to the end of the alley when my straining ears
heard the soft *clump-clump* of a walking Ihmisit switch to the
pitter-patter-pitter of a running one. But at least he didn't seem
to be armed.

"Stop, human," a voice demanded hoarsely from behind me.
"Stop, or I will shoot."

I grimaced. So much for him being unarmed. Unless he was
bluffing.

In general it wasn't a good idea to call a bluff like that.
Especially when you didn't have any cover; even more especially
when you'd choreographed the confrontation in the first place. I
trotted to a halt and turned around, holding my package in front
of me like a small and brightly wrapped shield. The Ihmisit had
slowed to a fast jog, his left hand gripping a partially concealed
handgun tucked behind his waist sash. "What do you want?" I
called.

"I mean you no harm," he said, coming to a more conversational distance of three meters before stopping. "You are Gregory Roarke?"

"Who?" I countered, frowning. As my father used to say, *Unless the guy asking who you are is holding a wad of cash, you might as well lead with a denial.*

"Gregory Roarke," he repeated, drawing his gun fully into view and pointing it at me. It was a Pickering 202, I saw, a nice little 2mm job that was a favorite among people who wanted to look fearsome but weren't willing to spring for something pricier or more effective.

"Never heard of him," I said. Still, getting shot would definitely hurt, and even with a Pickering if the slug found the right spot it could be fatal. So I kept my hands in sight, one of them flat beneath my package, the other one holding onto the box's side, and waited for him to figure out his next move.

The move really should have been obvious, and I was vaguely surprised that it took him another few seconds of consideration to come up with it. "Your package," he said. "Set it on the ground."

"But it'll get dirty," I protested, nodding at the nice gift wrapping. "It's a gift for my mother."

"Set it on the ground," he repeated, gesturing with the Pickering. "There."

With a theatrical sigh, I squatted down and started to set down the box, shifting my left hand to the side of the box nearest me as if the weight balance had changed. Then, abruptly, I gave the box a hard shove upward and forward, sending it flying in a tight arc straight at the Ihmisit's face.

Leaving my formerly concealed plasmic resting neatly on my right palm.

The Ihmisit reacted instantly to the object hurling unexpectedly toward him. Unfortunately for him, his species' hardwired response was to fling both arms up in front of him, crossed at the forearms, to protect his eyes.

Which, even more unfortunately, put his Pickering completely out of firing position.

"Just freeze right there," I told him, closing my hand around the plasmic's grip and flicking off the safety. "No need for anyone to get hurt."

He froze, all right, his arms still crossed—the box had landed harmlessly on the ground in front of him, but no one ever said reflexes were always on the mark—the insectoid antennae jutting out from just above his eyes gone rigid. "You," he said, his tone making the word an accusation.

"Yes, me," I agreed, rising back to my feet. "As for you, you've just cost me a—well, actually, I have no idea what that gizmo was, but it cost me fifty commarks. But never mind that. What do you want with me?"

"You are Gregory Roarke?" he asked.

"Yes, he is," a woman's voice came from behind me. "Holster it, would you, Roarke?"

Keeping my plasmic pointed at the Ihmisit, I turned my head. Standing at the end of the alley, her Siskrin plasmic held casually in front of her and not quite pointed in my direction...

"*Mindi?*" I said, frowning.

"I'm flattered you remember me," she said with just a hint of sarcasm. "Really, Roarke, just holster it."

I looked back at the Ihmisit. "Him first."

"Dukor, put it away," Mindi said soothingly. "It's all right— we're all friends here. Aren't we, Roarke?"

"Not sure I'd put it *that* strongly," I cautioned as the Ihmisit reluctantly tucked his Pickering back behind his sash.

"Well, we're not enemies, anyway," Mindi amended, walking toward me. "Unless this has pushed it over the line?"

"Depends on what you want with me," I said, slipping my plasmic back into its holster. Mindi was a bounty hunter I'd run into on a couple of jobs, and while I didn't know her well enough to either like or dislike her, she'd always struck me as professional enough. Whatever was going on, at least it wasn't personal. Probably. "You got here fast. Where were you hiding?"

"I wasn't," she said. "I was just doing my famous follow-him-from-in-front routine."

"Ah," I said, nodding. So she'd been a block or so ahead of me, where I wasn't paying any particular attention, while Dukor shepherded me in her direction and kept her apprised of my position and any change of direction via phone. "I don't remember you working with partners before."

"Not working with them now," Mindi said, holstering her plasmic as she walked past me. "Partners are way more trouble than they're worth."

The Ihmisit rumbled something rude-sounding. "You know what I mean," Mindi chided him as she pulled out a hundred-commark bill. "Pleasure doing business with you, Dukor. Remember to keep an eye out for any place a weapon could be hidden. Roarke doesn't shoot the second he gets an opening. The next guy might."

Dukor took the bill, gave her another rumble, gave me a dark look, then turned and stomped back down the alley. "Here," I called, retrieving the gizmo and tossing it to him. "Souvenir."

He didn't even bother to turn around, but just let it rattle to the ground in front of him. "Or not," I added.

"Local talent," Mindi explained as we watched him go. "Unfortunately, the follow-in-front thing requires two people."

"I seem to remember you also being pretty good at following from behind."

"Not with someone of your caliber and reputation," she said. "And yes, that's a compliment. So what are you doing on Vesperin?"

"Still waiting to hear what you want with me," I reminded her.

"Actually, not a thing," she said, eyeing me curiously. "A notice went out that you can pick up some fast cash reporting on the presence and social life of one Gregory Roarke, bounty hunter."

"*Former* bounty hunter," I corrected her automatically, feeling my eyes narrow. "What do you mean, social life? Like which parties I'm being invited to?"

"More like where you're going and who you're seeing," Mindi said. "You still with, ah, what's-her-name—the Kadolian?"

"Selene," I supplied. "Yes, and we're crocketts now."

"Maybe *you* think so," Mindi said. "Not according to the notice. It specifically labeled you as a hunter. So who've you made mad?"

"You mean lately?" I shrugged. "No one, as far as I know. Were there any addenda to this notice? Like *detain* or *shoot*?"

"If there were, you'd already be in restraints," Mindi said, eyeing me curiously. "Interesting. So who did you meet in that half-built building?"

"Who says I met anyone?" I countered. "Actually, I was just looking for a good view of the enclave."

"*Sure* you were," Mindi said. "You really are a rotten liar, you know."

"So I've been told," I conceded. "Sorry; client privilege."

"I thought you were a crockett now."

"Not according to your notice," I pointed out. "If I'm going to be tagged as a hunter, then hunter rules should apply. Tell you what—I'll trade you. A name for a name. Who's handing out cash for Gregory Roarke gossip?"

"Uh-*huh*," Mindi said, her face taking on a knowing look. "*A* name, huh? Let me guess. You don't really know her name, do you?"

I waved a hand. There were times I wasn't much of a bluffer, either. "I can give you the name I was given. Probably an alias, but it might have cropped up before."

"Hardly worth the effort, then, is it?" Mindi pointed out. "But I can't deliver on my side, either, so I suppose it comes out even. The only name on the mail drop is *Hades*."

"As in, *go to*?"

"More likely as in *king of the Old Greek mythological hell*."

I scowled. "So we've got ourselves a literary type."

"Or someone who likes to pretend he or she is," Mindi said. "There are plenty of those out there. So where are you heading after this?"

"Back to the ship to put my feet up and have a drink," I told her. "After that, I don't know. Probably get back to crocketting."

"Yeah, I'm sure," Mindi said, pulling out her phone. She peered at it, and I could see her eyes moving back and forth as they read a brief message. "Interesting work, crocketting, out there at the edge of nowhere."

"Not so much the edge as the middle," I corrected. "No one's interested in real estate that's *too* far off the beaten path."

"I'll take your word for it," she said. "Well, I've got to go. Work, work, work. Been nice talking to you."

"Likewise," I said. "We'll have to have a drink together someday."

"Sounds good," she said. "Oh, and I'll take that name now. Even a bogus one is worth that extra two hundred commarks."

I frowned. "Two hundred on top of...?"

"On top of the five I'll already get for reporting your presence on Vesperin."

I gave a low whistle. "Five plus two is a lot of money."

"Especially for this much vague." She shrugged. "But as long as it's coming in my direction instead of going the other way I'm good with it."

"Understandable," I said. "Though as my father used to say, *Deep pockets are great when you're digging into them; not so great when you're being dug out of them.*"

"Don't worry, this is a one-off deal," Mindi assured me. "If I was going to chase someone around, I'd pick someone a *lot* better looking."

"I'll remember that when I finally get around to having my face changed," I said. "She introduced herself as Piper."

"As in Pied Piper?"

"No idea," I said. "I'm not as literary as some people. Do I get a cut of that seven hundred, by the way?"

She raised her eyebrows. "Only if you think I hold promise for future colonization. You're a crockett, remember?"

"Right," I said. "It's hard to keep track of me sometimes."

"I'll bet," she said. "See you around, Roarke."

With a friendly nod she turned and headed down the alley in the direction her hireling had taken. I watched until she disappeared around the corner, then continued on toward the end I'd been heading for when all those guns started pointing at me. I reached the end of the alley, joined the pedestrian flow on that street, and turned back in the direction of the *Ruth*.

And as I looked casually around me for indications that Mindi might have hired more than one local to keep track of me, I pulled out my phone.

Selene answered on the first vibe. "Are you all right?" she asked anxiously.

"I'm fine," I assured her, frowning. There were faint voices in the background. "Where are you?"

"The StarrComm center in Mikilias," she said. "I thought I should call in an update."

I sighed silently. Three guesses as to how the admiral had taken the news that we were now traveling with a professional assassin.

"What did he say?"

"Nothing yet," she said. "I'm still waiting for a booth. The line's pretty long, too, so I might be a while. Where did she go?"

"Tell you later," I said, looking around for one of the floating signs that marked the enclave's runaround stands. Nothing. "Let me find a runaround and I'll join you."

"That really isn't necessary," she said. "I'm armed, and the city seems safe enough."

"It's not the city I'm worried about," I told her. "Sit tight—I'll be there as soon as I can."

I keyed off and called up a map of the enclave on my info pad. Ihmisits, unfortunately, tended to be homebodies, and in an area the limited size of this particular enclave they tended to do most of their traveling on foot. There was only one official runaround stand, and it was a solid kilometer away.

I craned my neck, hoping to spot one that the renter had finished with and was now parked along the street. But there was nothing in sight. My best and fastest alternative, I concluded reluctantly, would be to continue on to the spaceport.

For a moment I was tempted to just call it quits, call Selene back and tell her I was going back to the *Ruth* instead, and let her handle the call. The admiral probably wouldn't be as hard on her as he typically was on me.

With a sigh, I turned back toward the spaceport. Partners might be trouble, as Mindi said, but Selene, at least, was worth that trouble.

It took me half an hour to get back to the spaceport's runaround stand, and another half hour to drive across Mikilias to the StarrComm center. I'd reached the big white building and was looking for a place to park when I heard the gunfire.

By the time I was able to push my way to the front of the crowd gathered outside the StarrComm center, a group of k'Tra badgemen and medics were already on the scene. Four bodies were lying on stretchers, three of them completely covered in the universal sign of respect for the deceased, while three medics had finished their stabilization work on the fourth victim and were rolling the stretcher toward the ambulance. One of the medics leaned over the figure, apparently listening, then half turned to face the crowd. "Is there a Gregory Roarke here?" he called.

I felt my heart freeze. I'd tried calling Selene a dozen times since I heard the shots, but she'd never picked up. "Here!" I shouted, raising my hand as I pushed my way through the last two lines of gawkers between me and the line of badgemen keeping the crowd back. "I'm Roarke."

"She's calling for you," the medic said. "Hurry, please—we need to get her to surgery."

One of the badgemen started to step in front of me, probably intending to ask for ID. He took one look at my face and thought better of it. I covered the twenty-meter gap at a dead run—

And found myself gazing down into Mindi's pale face.

My first reaction was sagging relief that it wasn't Selene. My second was a flash of anger toward whoever the hell had done this to her.

She was barely conscious, her eyelids drooping, the agony starting to fade from her face as the painkillers kicked in. But she was still aware enough to recognize me and give me a wan smile. "Pied Piper, eh?" she murmured, the words muffled by her oxygen mask.

"Who did this, Mindi?" I asked. "Did Piper do it?"

There was no response. Her eyes closed and a huff of breath went out of her parted lips as she lost consciousness.

"That's all for now," the medic said, shouldering past me as he and the others went back to rolling the stretcher. "Hospital, Fourth and Dwint. You can talk to her later."

"Meanwhile, you can talk to *us*," the badgeman put in.

"Sure," I said, watching numbly as they loaded her into the ambulance. I'd seen worse than that—lots worse, including some absolute slaughters. But seldom had I seen someone I'd been talking to barely an hour earlier suddenly fighting for her life with no idea what had happened.

Worse, it sent memories of Selene's own near fatal shooting surging up through my stomach, throat, and brain and threatening to overwhelm me.

And then, as if teleported there by the sheer force of my anguish and fear, Selene was suddenly at my side. "Gregory?" she whispered.

"Roarke?" the badgeman prompted. "We need your statement. Don't wander off."

"I'll be right back" I said. I took Selene's arm, as much for my own reassurance as for guidance, and started us back toward the line of k'Tra badgemen. "It was Mindi," I said. "Do you remember her?"

"Yes, I think so," Selene said, her eyes following the ambulance as it pulled away. "I'm sorry—I didn't want my phone on in there and never turned it back on."

"It's okay," I said. "Are you all right?"

She nodded. "I was still inside when the shooting started."

"So you didn't see any of it?"

"No." She touched her fingertips to my hand, still closed around her other arm. "Gregory, Nikki was here."

"Yeah, I got that impression," I said grimly, looking at the bodies now being loaded into the other ambulances. No hurry on those, obviously. "Any idea of the weapons involved?"

She inhaled slowly, her nostrils and eyelashes fluttering. "There was a plasmic and at least one mid-caliber firearm," she said. "I think the three dead men were shot with the plasmic. Mindi was shot with the firearm."

"Dead *men*?" I asked. "All three were human?"

"Yes." She paused, apparently just noticing the oddity of that. "Three humans killed together in a k'Tra city. That seems... unusual."

"It does, doesn't it?" I agreed. "Hold on a second."

We reached the badgeman line and I started working us back through the dissipating crowd. Now that the show was over and the bodies were out of sight, the onlookers were returning to their regularly scheduled lives. "Okay," I said when I judged we were clear enough of everyone not to be overheard. "Fact one: Mindi carries a Siskrin plasmic, so she *could* have been the main shooter. Fact two: she got a message just as we were wrapping up our conversation in the Ihmis enclave."

"Was it a hunter notice?"

"In hindsight, I'd say that's likely," I agreed. "And if she was here hunting, maybe our three less fortunate souls were, too. Did you see any other humans waiting in the StarrComm center?"

"There were a few," she said slowly. "But that's probably not unusual, given that it's the closest center to the human enclave."

"Which unfortunately just confuses the issue," I said. "Okay, try this. Did you see an older man there: medium height, slender but working on a paunch, white medium-length hair, no beard, facial wrinkles, overall salesman air?"

"No," she said. "But the waiting room was large, and there were people in the booths I wouldn't have seen. Who is he?"

"Horace Markelly, the man Nikki came to see. *Just* to see," I added as Selene's pupils went suddenly tense. "She looked at him, declared him off-limits, and left."

"What do you mean, off-limits? Off-limits how?"

"I'll tell you later," I said. "The point is that she told me she'd been offered a contract on him and was going to turn it down. I'm thinking her prospective client may have hedged his bets by putting extra backup in the area."

Selene pondered that another couple of steps. "If one of the bodies was Markelly, who were the other two? Bodyguards?"

"Well, he *did* have four heavies hanging around," I said, frowning. "But they were all Yavanni. Maybe they were Markelly's business associates, people he met up with after Nikki and I left. Or else they're random citizens who got caught in the crossfire."

"If that's the case, whoever shot them was a terrible hunter," Selene said, contempt in her pupils.

"No argument here," I agreed heavily. Licensed bounty hunters were required by law and ethical guidelines, not to mention sheer personal pride, to keep collateral damage to the absolute minimum. A two-to-one innocent-to-target ratio was both incredibly amateurish and completely unacceptable. "Anyway, there's nothing more we can do here. Let's see if the runaround I rented is still where I parked it and get back to the ship."

"All right." Again, Selene hesitated. "Gregory, how sure are you that Nikki turned down that contract?"

"Not sure at all," I said. "All I have is her word on the subject."

"So she may have been lying," Selene said. "She may have said that to calm you, then come to the StarrComm center and killed him anyway."

"*If* one of the deceased is Markelly," I cautioned. "We won't know that for sure until the badgemen release their names."

Still, Mindi *had* dropped Nikki's name there at the end. Why should she do that if Nikki wasn't the one who'd shot her?

"Yes," Selene said, coming to a sudden stop. "Wait a moment. We're going back to the *ship*? Right now? What about our report?"

"The admiral will keep."

"What about the badgemen?"

I looked back over my shoulder. The badgeman I'd talked to had been pulled elsewhere. "I'll send them a statement," I said. "Right now, I want to get back to the *Ruth* before Nikki does."

"She can't open the entryway."

"Yes, that's the theory," I agreed. "You want to give it a field test?"

"Not really," Selene murmured. "I think I see a runaround over there. Let's take it."

CHAPTER SEVEN

For once, my fears proved groundless. We made it back to the *Ruth* to find the entryway still sealed and Nikki nowhere in sight.

We went aboard and I started the preflight while Selene called the tower to get us a lift slot. "Well?" I asked when she signed off.

"Forty minutes," she reported. "We can extend that if Nikki doesn't get here before then." Her pupils went a little darker. "*If* we still want her aboard."

"*You* want to tell her we're abandoning her on Vesperin?" I countered. "More to the point, do you want to tell Floyd and Cherno?"

"And we just pretend the StarrComm shooting didn't happen?"

"We didn't see it," I reminded her, painfully aware of just how thin that particular sheet of ice was. Especially given Mindi's name drop. "All we know for sure is that Nikki was at the Starr-Comm center sometime before or during the shooting. Possibly calling her client to tell him the deal was off, like she'd told me she was going to."

"Yes, you said you'd explain about that later," Selene said. "This would seem to be a good time."

"Okay," I said. "Just bear in mind that it sounds weird to me, too."

I went through the whole off-limit former client explanation

71

that Nikki had laid out for me. It sounded better this time through, though I could see several ways an enterprising person could game that kind of system. "So if she's telling the truth Markelly would be untouchable," Selene said thoughtfully when I'd finished. "But the man who tried to hire her to kill him wouldn't?"

"Because he tried to hire her but she turned him down?" I shrugged. "That's how it reads to me."

"So if the other client was here to watch Nikki work, and Nikki talked to Markelly about it, Markelly might have hired her to kill him instead?"

"I suppose that's possible," I said slowly. That possibility hadn't even occurred to me. "Though showing up to watch your hired killer work sounds pretty stupid. You'd do better to be halfway across the Spiral meeting with top government officials when it went down."

"Unless he thought that was what everyone would expect him to do," Selene pointed out. "And where you are doesn't really matter when you've hired out the job. What the badgemen follow then is the money trail."

"I suppose," I said. "And given that the trail was half a million commarks long, he might very well want to see for himself that everything went as planned."

"I don't suppose she was careless enough to mention her client's name."

"You don't get to her level by being careless," I said. "No name, no hints, not even a planet. But if one of today's victims turns out to be one of Markelly's rivals, we'll know who to start pointing fingers at."

"Starting with us," Selene said in a low voice. "Do you suppose that's why Gaheen hired us for this job?"

I frowned. "Not following."

"Let's say he puts out a contract on Markelly," Selene said. "Part of the deal with Nikki is to arrange her transport to and from Vesperin."

"We're crocketts, so our schedule is all over the map," I said slowly, starting to see where she was going with this. "We show up someplace and then disappear for days or weeks at a time."

"And Floyd will have told him we have several false ship IDs."

I made a face. One of which we were using right now, in fact. With a professional killer aboard, I'd decided early on that

I didn't want the *Ruth* to be one of the dots the badgemen might soon be connecting. "He also knows we have shadowy friends in high places. If we happen to attract official attention, they would probably try to get us clear."

"Which would then muddy our connection with Gaheen himself."

"Right," I said. "And like Cherno said, we were the only ones Gaheen knew would make this kind of deal in exchange for a portal."

"Other than the Patth."

I snorted. "Somehow, I can't see Nask agreeing to cart an assassin around the Spiral."

"He carries Expediters all the time."

"There's that," I conceded. "Though they're really more all-around troubleshooters than just killers." I shook my head slowly. "No, Gaheen's target wouldn't be Markelly. This might have been a test run, a shakedown cruise to see how well we and Nikki work together. If so, his real target would be down the line somewhere."

"Another four and a half weeks away, if what Cherno said about a six-week time limit was accurate."

"Or that number could have been a diversion," I pointed out. "Or Markelly was a side job that Nikki decided to pick up given she already had free transport for the next few weeks."

Selene gave a sudden shiver. "We keep calling her Nikki," she said softly. "I keep thinking of her as Piper. We need to remember that we have no idea who this person actually is."

"Well, we know she's the same flavor of assassin as the real Piper," I said. "But you're right, we still don't know why the two of them switched on us. Can you pull up Floyd's list of planets?"

"Certainly." A moment later, the thirty names came up on one of the helm displays. "Are we going to one of those next?"

"That *is* what we're supposed to be doing," I said. "I presume that after this Nikki's going to at least want a breather before she wants us to take her somewhere else. We might as well throw a dart at this list and see which one seems the most likely place for a Gemini portal to be lurking."

"She's here," Selene said.

I looked at the entryway display. Sure enough, Nikki had appeared and was walking up our ramp.

At least I assumed it was her. The veil was the same, but the rest of her outfit had changed from black and dark green to a patterned maroon with blue highlights. "Nice reversible outfit," I commented, getting out of my seat. "I'll go let her in. You stay here and keep an eye on our lift slot."

Nikki was waiting patiently when I opened the entryway. "Nice outfit," I commented, stepping aside to let her pass. "Even the cut and hang look different from the other side."

"Thank you," she said, pulling off her veil. "I'm always amazed at how easily such an obvious gambit fools people's eyes. I trust you have a lift slot set up?"

"Thirty minutes," I said, a knot forming in my stomach as I sealed the entryway behind her. Fresh from a kill, calm as a solar minimum, and ready to make herself scarce. "You always in this much of a hurry afterward?"

She gave me a measuring look. "I take it you heard about the StarrComm center?"

"I was *at* the StarrComm center," I retorted, my underlying fear of this woman suddenly vanishing into the memory of Mindi's drawn face. "And you'd better hope to hell you're not the one who shot Mindi."

"That the girl bounty hunter?"

"Yes," I bit out.

"No, I didn't shoot her," she said. "She caught a round from one of the other three hunters."

I frowned. *Three* hunters? Subtracting whoever the target had been, that left only two additional bodies "What do you mean, three? Did the last one get away?"

"Not unless the morgue has takeout," Nikki said, frowning.

"Then who was the target?"

Her face cleared. "Ah," she said. "No, you've got it backward, Roarke. The target wasn't any of the deceased.

"The target was me."

"I think now that what I thought was distraction was just that he was juggling two different StarrComm calls at the same time," Nikki said.

"Yours and one of his other people in the same center," Selene murmured.

I looked at her, noting the mix of reluctance and antipathy in her pupils. I'd offered to take Nikki's statement in the dayroom, where Selene could watch and listen via intercom without having to be in the same room with her. But Selene had insisted on being physically present, and since we were too close to lift for both of us to be out of the cockpit she and I were seated at our usual helm and plotting table stations while Nikki stood in the open hatchway.

It was, I had to admit, the ideal setup if Selene was going to perform her magic in regards to the olfactory changes that might indicate a lie. Less ideal was the fact that my partner was now stuck three meters away from our assassin.

"I doubt his stooge was at the Mikilias center itself," Nikki said. "Too much risk of me spotting him. Better to put him on the other side of the planet and just have him phone out the hunter notice." Her lip twisted. "There would certainly be no problem figuring out where *I* was."

"How did they know it was you?" Selene asked. "They couldn't see your face."

"The outfit *is* pretty distinctive," I pointed out.

"Yes, that's probably what they zeroed in on," Nikki said ruefully. "In retrospect, I should have switched before I made my call."

"That must have been the notice Mindi was looking at just before she left me," I said. "So how long exactly did it take you to turn down your prospective client? Or is he just the talkative type you can't shut up?"

"Not long, and no," Nikki said. "I assume you're wondering why I was at the center long enough for that kettle of vultures to gather."

"Basically," I confirmed. "Setting up a new job?"

She shook her head. "No, I was just making some other calls. One to each of my three mail drops..." She paused, her eyes suddenly hard on me. "And one to Cherno, trying to find out what's going on with you two."

"What do you mean?" I asked carefully.

"You two," Nikki repeated. "This ship. Your connection to him. This ridiculous six-week delay between picking me up and the job."

"I assume there's always some prep work."

"On the ground, yes," Nikki said. "But not usually six weeks' worth. Certainly not six weeks gallivanting around the Spiral."

"What did he tell you?" Selene asked.

"Nothing," Nikki said. "Oh, he talked a lot. Lots of nice-sounding purr words and bafflegab. But he didn't *tell* me anything."

She folded her arms across her chest. "Except that you're looking for something that has a bearing on the job. So. Your turn."

I shook my head. "If Cherno won't tell you any more than that, we shouldn't either."

"What if it's something I need to know?"

"It isn't," I assured her. "Or at least, it isn't at the moment. You'll know when it's time."

"Almost exactly the words he used," Nikki growled. "It just better not impact the job, or the price goes up. All right. First thing I need to do is to make some more calls."

"To whom?" I asked.

"To people," Nikki said in a tone that strongly discouraged further discussion of the point. "If my prospective client was behind this, he needs to know that he missed."

"*And* that he should now start watching his back?" I asked.

"I'll leave that part to his imagination."

"Okay," I said, keeping my voice steady. "Actually, we should check in with someone, too. Once we lift, we'll head across Vesperin to Lotearro or Blipni—"

"No," Nikki interrupted. "They know I'm here, and may have all the local StarrComm centers covered."

I looked at Selene, saw the reluctant agreement in her pupils. If the notice had indeed been a general bounty alert, every hunter on Vesperin would know about it by now.

Actually, given that Bounty Hunter Central had a permanent StarrComm repeater booth on every major planet in the Spiral—as did most interstellar governments—every hunter everywhere would know about it by now.

Nikki might have been reading my mind. "Or maybe they've blanketed the whole Spiral," she said. "Though if it *is* a general, you could tap in and see if you can figure out what's going on."

"Let's not try drawing any more attention our direction than we have to," I said, a sudden thought occurring to me. One of the names on Floyd's list . . . "How about Lucias Four?"

Nikki shook her head. "Never heard of it."

"It's a very minor colony about seven hours away." I gestured to Selene, who nodded and pulled up the planet's stats on one of her displays. "More of a glorified crop research station, actually," I continued. "It's got...let's see"—I peered past Selene's shoulder—"only about a hundred people there. But it's a Crodalian Enterprises operation, which means they've got enough backing to have their own StarrComm array."

"That's a lot of money to spend for a hundred people," Nikki said suspiciously.

"Crodalian really likes their people to stay in touch with each other," I said. "I once did a job for one of their subsidiaries, and I can tell you they have money to burn."

"And there *is* a StarrComm facility listed," Selene added, pointing to the relevant line on the planetary stat listing.

"So I'm thinking we go there, beg, borrow, or buy a few minutes on the system for our calls and be off again before anyone off-planet has any idea we're there." I held a hand up. "At the very least I think I can guarantee there won't be any hunters nearby."

"Yes," Nikki said thoughtfully. "All right, it sounds reasonable. So what exactly do *you* want with the place?"

"As I said, to make some calls."

"I mean what else." Nikki pointed to the display where I'd pulled up Floyd's list. "Lucias Four is one of the places you were already looking at. Very convenient that they just happen to have what I need, too."

"Fine; you caught me," I admitted. "Yes, we *do* also need to take a look at the place. But our target is a group of alien ruins on the other side of the planet, and we don't have to land to check them out."

"Some kind of fancy sensors?"

"In a way," I hedged. "The point is that I can pick our in-vector so that we swoop over the ruins before continuing on to the research station. It'll cost us an extra three hours at the most, probably closer to two."

"What if someone spots us incoming and sends out the word?" Nikki asked.

"To whom?" I countered. "Three hours incoming plus an hour at the research station isn't enough time for any hunters to get to Lucias before we're long gone."

"The *Ruth* also won't be using the same ID that we are here," Selene said. "That will blur any connection with Vesperin."

"*And* we'll be going in as crocketts," I added. "Nothing

remotely odd about crocketts checking out an unexplored part of a mostly virgin planet."

Nikki hesitated, then nodded. "All right, you've sold me. Make it happen."

Considering how fast those hunters had responded to the notice it was clear that whoever targeted Nikki had a lot of money or influence or both. Enough, possibly, to call in favors or pull strings and strand us on Vesperin.

But of course, that would require him to know which specific ship Nikki was flying on, and the ID that ship was currently flying under. Without those, he didn't have a chance of finding us, certainly not with the brief window he had to work with.

We lifted on schedule, without a whisper of complaint or suspicion, and were on our way to Lucias Four.

And if we were very, very lucky, the pot of gold at the end of the rainbow.

We reached the planet, coming in on a vector that would take us over the ruins Floyd's list had marked. A hundred kilometers short of the site, Selene dipped us low into the stratosphere and I launched the shiny new bioprobes the Icarus Group had bought for us.

Nikki had retired to my cabin for a nap a couple of hours previously, and I'd expected her to sleep through the whole procedure. To my mild surprise she showed up in the control room hatchway two minutes after I sent the probes on their way. "Anything wrong?" she asked.

"Not at all," I assured her. "I just launched the bioprobes. Did you feel a kick?"

"Yes, a small one," she said, her eyes flicking across the displays. "Woke me up."

"Occupational hazard," I said, nodding. "I used to sleep on hair-trigger alert when I was on a hunt, too."

"Not quite the same," Nikki said. "So those little missiles of yours just swoop down, scoop up some air samples, and then come back up?"

"Basically," I said. "The actual procedure can be complicated, but that's what it boils down to. Once they're back Selene and I will sort out the spores, seeds, and anything else they picked up, seal them into ampules, and file them away for delivery to our client."

"What happens to the samples if you don't have a client?"

"Crocketts nearly always have a client," I told her. "Running a planet on spec usually isn't cost-effective. Though sometimes if you're passing a wild-card system that isn't on your schedule you may swing in for a quick scoop. If the samples show promise but your client isn't interested, you can buy a certified storage vault at an Association facility while you try to hunt up a buyer."

"Who may never materialize?"

"Who often doesn't," I agreed. "See *on spec* above."

"Yes," Nikki said thoughtfully. "All in all, I think I prefer my job. At least there aren't any doubts about what you're getting into. How well do you know her?"

I frowned. "Who, Selene?"

"Mindi," Nikki said. "When you thought I'd shot her you looked ready to jump me, suicidal odds or not."

"Oh," I said. "No, she was just an acquaintance. It was just..."

"Just that you knew her at all?" Nikki offered.

I felt my throat tighten briefly. "Basically."

"I understand," Nikki said. "*Assassin* is a pretty nebulous concept to most people until they know someone connected to a job."

"I suppose," I said. "You're sure they were coming after you, right?"

"Oh, yes," Nikki said, a sort of mask settling over her face. For a few minutes she'd been able to talk to me almost like a real person. Now, suddenly, she was a professional killer again, with all the distance and psychological walls the job entailed. "For whatever it's worth, if there'd only been one or two I'd have just disabled them instead of killing them outright."

"If for no other reason than so you could interrogate them?"

She flashed me an approving half smile. "I can see why Cherno keeps you around," she said. "Exactly." The smile disappeared, and the mask came down again. "But with four of them moving on me, three with guns already in hand, I didn't have that luxury."

I took a deep breath. A part of me still wanted to hate this woman, and all of me still didn't like her. But having been in similar situations I couldn't really argue with either her reasoning or her response. "At least you saved Mindi for last," I muttered.

Nikki shrugged. "Of course I did. She was the one who hadn't drawn."

I nodded. More logic, more cold-blooded calculation, and

again I couldn't really fault her. "So which one of them shot her? Do you know his name?"

"Don't know any of their names," Nikki said. "One of the questions I plan to ask on that StarrComm call."

The intercom pinged. "Gregory, we're getting a signal from the surface," Selene said. "They say this is a private and restricted area, and that we need to recall our probes immediately and leave."

I frowned. "Since when is this part of Lucias private?"

"I don't know," Selene said. "There wasn't anything about that in the listing."

"Maybe someone bought the planet since it was updated," Nikki suggested.

I scowled. Crodalian Enterprises *was* known for quick and sometimes heavy-handed business dealings, and they certainly had speculation money to drop on a virgin planet if they thought it might turn a profit someday. "Tell them we understand, and that we'll be out of here as soon as we can," I told Selene as I cancelled the probes' programming and keyed for retrieval. "Should be about ten minutes."

"Understood." The intercom clicked off.

"So much for your little side trip," Nikki commented.

"It was a long shot anyway," I said. "And it may not be a total loss. The probes got deep enough to have grabbed at least a few samples. Feathers in particular are really good at grabbing altitude."

"Interesting," Nikki said. "Let's hope you get lucky."

"Let's hope," I echoed. "But as my father used to say, *Lady Luck usually sticks with the people she's already friends with.*"

"That's not you?"

"She barely even knows me."

Five minutes later, I used the *Ruth*'s twin tight-core grav beams to pull the bioprobes back to the ship and into their aft starboard and port bays. Selene got us out of the area, and as we let the autopilot sweep us in a gentle arc toward the other side of the planet she and I went to the clean room to run the samples. Not for spores or feathers, but for the telltale scent of portal metal.

Of course, as my father also used to say, *Lady Luck's bad-news sister, on the other hand, will hang out with pretty much anyone.*

There was no portal scent that Selene could detect. But there was another molecular trace that I'd neither expected nor wanted.

"You've got to be kidding," I said, staring at her across the examination table. "There are *Patth* down there?"

"I wish I was," Selene said, her pupils looking pained. "But they're definitely there." Her nostrils twitched twice. "It would seem they're working off the same list we are."

"More likely they worked up their own," I growled. Stupidly obvious now, of course. Nask had the same baseline data on the Erymant Temple and grounds that we'd given Cherno, and they were just as eager to find the other end of the Gemini as he was.

Actually, probably more so. Whatever the details of Cherno's acquisition of the Patth's new toy, I doubted it had been an amiable transaction.

Unfortunately, the fact that the Patth were digging into the Lucias Four ruins also guaranteed their presence at or near the research station. And, more to the immediate point, at or near the station's StarrComm facility.

Selene would have been following the emotional aspect of my analysis via the subtle changes in my scent, and she knew me well enough to have tracked me to my current conclusion. "What do you think?" I asked anyway.

"I think we have to keep going," she said, her pupils showing resigned reluctance. "If we take off now, they'll think we spotted something."

"And even if they're not set up to chase us, the word will go out instantly to every Patth and Expediter in the Spiral," I said heavily. "Sort of wishing now that we'd used one of the other IDs."

"We couldn't," Selene said. "Not if we wanted to come in as crocketts. The *Ruth* is the only ID that matches that job."

"Unfortunately, it's also the ID that matches *us*," I said. "Well. Nikki needs to make some calls, and so do we. We'll just have to hope that whoever the Patth have at the StarrComm building doesn't have any instructions concerning us."

"Yes," Selene murmured, looking in the direction of the dayroom where Nikki had gone for a snack while we worked. "And not just for our sake."

"No," I said, wincing "For his."

CHAPTER EIGHT

The research station consisted of a set of five interconnected buildings and a single landing pad along a narrow dirt road about a kilometer to the north. A patchwork quilt of test crop fields of various sizes surrounded the pad and buildings, extending from a group of hills to the northwest to a narrow river running along the eastern edge of the grounds and nearly to the horizon in all other directions.

The pad was a standard hinterlands design: a single flat repulsor-equipped pad big enough to handle a medium transport or small freighter and flanked by a pair of no-frills but sturdy-looking grav beam towers. The area around the pad had been deserted as we put down, but by the time I'd powered the engines to standby and we headed down our ramp's zigzag configuration a man and an open-topped car were waiting for us.

"Any particular objectives here you have in mind?" Nikki asked softly from behind me as we made our way down the zigzag.

"Making our calls and getting out in one piece," I said. "That's about it."

"And no one dying," Selene added from behind Nikki.

Nikki grunted. "No guarantees on that last one. But I'll try."

"Greetings," the man called as we reached the ground. "I'm Dr. Elfred Landon. Your visit is something of a surprise, to say the least. I assume you're the Gregory Roarke who called in to us?"

"I am," I said, nodding politely. "These are my partners, Selene and Nikki."

"Welcome," Landon said. "What can we of Landon Station do for you?"

"First of all, thank you for allowing us to land," I said. *Landon Station.* So he'd named the place after himself? "I know you and your colleagues are doing important work out here, and we have no desire to interrupt or otherwise cause any disruption."

"I would hope not," Landon said. "At the same time, you were rather evasive when you spoke earlier with Dr. Stuart."

"Yes, and I'm sorry about that," I said. "But we needed to be circumspect. We're crocketts, as I told Dr. Stuart. We were doing a survey a few light-years away from Lucias Four, found something completely unexpected that we believe our client would be interested in, and came here hoping you'd permit us to buy some time on your StarrComm array to report in and ask for further instructions." I offered my most disarming smile. "In these things, as I'm sure you know, time is of the absolute essence, and your base and StarrComm facility are hours closer than anywhere else."

"I understand," Landon said. "But our array is normally only for our own researchers' use." He pursed his lips. "On the other hand, as a scientist I'm certainly well acquainted with surprise discoveries."

"And the need to follow up on those discoveries as quickly as possible."

"Indeed." His eyes flicked across all of us, lingering a moment on Selene. Probably wondering what species she was. "And of course, the only reason we're here in the first place is because the company's own crockett report hinted at potentially useful soil and native flora," he continued. "So I have a soft spot for people like you. Let me speak with the StarrComm technician and see what can be worked out."

"Thank you," I said. "That would be very much appreciated."

"Happy to help." Landon's wrinkled face creased in a smile. "And in case you were wondering, the station is named for my aunt, not me. I'm as egotistical as any other scientist, but I'm not *that* egotistical."

"The thought never even crossed my mind," I assured him.

"I'm sure it didn't," he said, still looking amused. "Please; follow me."

The car Landon had brought was every bit as uncomfortable as one would expect from a purely utilitarian vehicle. But it was roomy enough, and it beat the hell out of walking. As my father used to say, *Riding is always to be preferred, unless it's going to attract unwanted attention.* In this case, I was pretty sure there would be unwanted attention around every corner, but there was nothing we could do about that.

And the car was still faster than walking.

The dirt path Landon drove us along was bordered on both sides by the test plots I'd seen on our way in, squares that ranged anywhere from garden-sized arrays three meters across to farmer-sized fields that were a good ten by ten. Landon identified each crop as we passed it, just a name as we drove by the smaller plots, a name and a brief description or history during the additional time we had alongside the larger ones. I listened with half an ear, noting with annoyance that the brisk wind was rolling over us from the direction of the *Ruth*, which would severely limit Selene's ability to pick up any scent clues from the base itself until we were practically on top of it.

If Selene was worried about that, it didn't show in her pupils. To the contrary, she seemed fully immersed in Landon's running commentary. That, or she was far better at faking interest than I was.

The StarrComm facility was inside the northernmost of the five linked buildings, the first structure we reached after passing through the test fields. It was tucked away like an afterthought at the eastern end of a large cafeteria. The array grid itself was nowhere to be seen, of course—its land and power requirements would have taken up the research station's entire complement of cropland and overwhelmed their modest reactor. It would be kilometers away, probably planted in the woodlands I'd seen beyond the hills to the northwest.

Landon was leading us across the cafeteria toward the unla-beled door he'd identified as the StarrComm control room and privacy booth when Selene gave out a small and nearly silent gasp. I turned to her, my stomach tightening as I spotted the sudden tension in her eyes.

I took her arm reassuringly with my left hand, casually dropping my right hand to my hip and plasmic concealed beneath my loose jacket. On Selene's other side, I saw that Nikki had picked up on Selene's reaction and hooked one thumb casually on the edge of her belt sash. The StarrComm door swung open.

Standing there facing us, his mahogany-red face set in stone, was a Patth.

"Ah—Uvif," Landon greeted him casually as we continued forward. "This is Mr. Roarke. He's a passing crockett who needs to use your facility to contact his client. Is there any way he can buy a few minutes of time?"

For a moment Uvif stood in silence. I felt Selene twitch, and looked casually over my shoulder to see that an Iykam had slipped into the cafeteria and was standing stiffly just inside the door.

"There will be no trouble with his request, Dr. Landon," Uvif said. "There will also be no charge for his time."

I turned back to the office. The Patth had stepped out of the doorway and was gesturing inside. "I greet you, Mr. Roarke. Please; the facility is yours."

I felt my throat tighten. Over the past couple of decades the Patth had wormed their way into practically every major industry in the Spiral, and StarrComm was no exception. I knew they could tap into the system and search out supposedly private conversations at will, with only the huge amount of StarrComm traffic and the finite number of Patth eavesdroppers putting a limit on their goal of galactic omniscience.

But with a Patth sitting right here knowing where the call originated, it would be laughably trivial for them to not only trace my call but probably record it as it happened.

As my father used to say, *It doesn't take much of a change in circumstances to make even the most lively plan roll over and die.* There was no chance now that I could update the admiral and the rest of the Icarus Group on what had been happening with us and Nikki. Bad enough that the Patth might be able to sift out a private conversation a few days or weeks from now, when it hopefully would be of only limited use to them. I had no intention of letting them record and distribute what I had to say in real time.

"Thank you," I said, inclining my head to Uvif. "But as we

humans say, *ladies first.* My associate Nikki also has a call she needs to make. With your permission, I'll wait to make mine until she's finished."

Out of the corner of my eye I saw Nikki's forehead crease a bit. A person in her line of work would be very sensitive to atmosphere, and she clearly recognized there was something going on between Uvif and me.

But most of my attention was on the Patth. I was hardly an expert on their facial expressions, but the disappointment that flickered across his face was obvious. Clearly, he'd hoped I would assume he hadn't recognized my name and would make my call, giving him the chance to score the double triumph of getting not only my conversation but also the Icarus Group's contact number.

Still, as my father used to say, *Get used to disappointment. It's the only thing besides lima beans where the supply has always exceeded the demand.*

"I see," Uvif said, sounding a bit deflated as he looked back and forth between Landon and me. Maybe he was trying to think of some reason why I could make calls but Nikki couldn't.

If he was, he missed his opportunity. "Thank you," Nikki said brightly, already moving toward him. "I appreciate it."

For a second Uvif looked like he still might try to object. But if so, he was again too slow on the uptake. Nikki strode past him, giving him a genial smile as she closed the door behind her.

"Excellent," I said briskly, mostly to distract Landon from any confusion he might be having about what had just happened. Uvif's Plan A was over and done with. The big question now was whether Plan B involved letting us walk out of here, or whether it would include a shade more violence.

Which meant that my Plan B now was to see what kind of resources the Patth had available to work with beside the single Iykam standing behind us. "While we wait for her to finish, Dr. Landon, perhaps you'd be kind enough to give us a quick tour of your facility."

"I don't know," Landon said, looking uncertainly back and forth between Uvif and me. "Surely your associate won't be long."

"Our client is unfortunately quite wordy," I said. "Though of course she'll cut the call short if one of your people needs to use the facility." I gave him my best ingratiating smile. "The truth is that I'm fascinated by what you're doing here. As a crockett I've scooped up a lot of alien flora, but I've never seen what happens once I hand it off to my clients."

Landon's face cleared, and he waved at the door behind the Iykam. "All right, but it will have to be quick," he said. "We have a great deal of work yet to complete before we retire for the night. This way, please."

As my father used to say, *Give a man a fish and he'll eat for a day. Ask him about his passion and he'll talk until the fish rots.*

I'd wondered if the Iykam would insist on tagging along, which I didn't want. Fortunately, Uvif was apparently wary enough of Nikki that he didn't want to be left alone with her. I caught his subtle hand signal to his guard, and when Landon led us out of the cafeteria the Iykam stayed put.

The tour was indeed quick, bringing to mind the whirlwind metaphor for such things I remembered hearing when I was younger. But Landon was up to the task, rattling off names, numbers, facts, histories, hopes, suppositions, and personal anecdotes with a speed that rivaled even that of Bolfin quick-talkers. Once again, I listened just closely enough to be able to put in an occasional interested-sounding comment while I spent the bulk of my attention on doors, windows, blind corners, potential cover, and items that might be utilized for attack or defense.

Selene, for her part, didn't bother with any comments, but spent the entire time sniffing and fluttering her eyelashes.

We were halfway through the fourth building when Landon got the call I'd been expecting.

"Uvif says your friend is finished," he announced as he put away his phone. "Time for us to head back."

"Can we finish the tour first?" I asked. "This whole operation is fascinating."

"Sadly, no," Landon said. "We'll need to send our daily report in about an hour, and you still have your own call to make."

"Understood," I said. "Still, with any luck we'll be back this way again in the future. Maybe we can finish the tour then."

"Maybe we can," Landon said as he turned and began retracing his steps. "It's been a treat to share some of our trials and successes with genuinely interested parties."

He opened the connecting door and started down the passageway leading back to the third building. As he did so, I dropped back to Selene. "Well?" I murmured.

"One more Iykam," she murmured back. "Fifteen humans. No additional Patth."

So of the hundred or so residents listed in the planetary stats, eighty-five of them were out in the fields or working in the building that we hadn't gotten to. Under the circumstances, much better odds than I'd hoped for. "Call Nikki and have her meet us at the car," I told her. "Tell her to make it look and sound casual, like she's going out for fresh air or something."

Selene nodded and pulled out her phone. I left her and hurried forward, reaching the passageway door just as Landon reappeared. "Is there a problem?" he asked.

"No," I said. "No problem. Why?"

"I thought I'd lost you," he said, looking over my shoulder. "What's she doing with her phone?"

I looked back. Selene had closed her eyes and was holding her phone pressed to her forehead. "She gets headaches sometimes when she hears and sees too much this quickly," I told Landon. "Her species' version of a migraine combined with sensory overload. Her phone has a setting for a low-frequency vibration that helps lower her blood pressure and ease the pain."

"Oh," Landon said, sounding both confused and interested. "I'm sorry—I didn't realize the tour would affect her like that."

"No apology needed," Selene assured him, opening her eyes briefly and then closing them again.

But not before I spotted the amusement in her pupils. One of the side benefits of partnering with a rare species like Selene's was that I could make up pretty much any physical or psychological quirk for her that I needed to fit a given situation, and no one could call bull on me. It was an endless reservoir of excuses for me, and a correspondingly endless source of entertainment for her.

Which wasn't to say I should push it. "Another minute and she'll be fine," I assured Landon. "She'll catch up as soon as she's able to travel."

"I think she should come with us now," he said, his eyes going suddenly hard. "In fact, now that our security chief has finally returned from the fields, I think it's time we all had a conversation together."

"What are you talking about?" I asked, putting on my bewildered face as I silently berated myself for taking Landon at face value. Of course the head of a multi-billion-commark research facility wouldn't let strangers wander around without wondering if they were corporate spies here to steal his work. All the smiles and tours had been his way of stalling until the people charged with protecting his little fiefdom made it back from their other duties.

"I'm talking about a former crockett—yes, *former* crockett—named Gregory Roarke and his team of troublemakers," Landon said darkly. "According to Uvif, the Patth have a deep file on your activities throughout the Spiral over the past year or so."

"I think Uvif has me confused with someone else," I said stiffly. "Do I look like a troublemaker? Does *she* look like one?" I pointed sharply at Selene with my left hand, jabbing my finger toward her like I was trying to stab her.

An experienced bounty hunter or even a moderately aware civilian would never have fallen for such a simple trick. But Landon was neither. Even as he pulled out his phone, his eyes reflexively followed my finger toward Selene.

And by the time his gaze returned to me I had my plasmic out and pointed at him.

"Easy," I cautioned as his eyes and mouth went wide. "And no, we're not here to steal any secrets. We really did only want to make some StarrComm calls."

"You won't get away with this," Landon said, the words coming out mechanically. Apparently, his expectations about upper-level gentlemanly espionage didn't include weapons.

"Probably not," I agreed. "Selene?"

She stepped to Landon's side and plucked the phone from his frozen fingers. "There were storage closets lining the passageway," she reminded me.

"Yes, there were," I agreed, motioning with my plasmic. "Just ease back into the passageway, Dr. Landon. No screaming or other noise, of course."

If I'd said *shouting* instead of *screaming* he might have considered risking it. But *screaming* came packaged with images of pathetic and laughable losers, and I could see in his face that the thought of looking like that had driven off any such temptation. Taking a deep breath, he turned and stalked back to the passageway door.

As my father used to say, *Offering someone the smart option is good. Offering him the dignified one is often better.*

Ninety seconds later, Landon was secured in the nearest closet. "Did you get through to Nikki?" I asked Selene as I took Landon's phone from her and tossed it into one of the other closets.

"Yes," she said. "She'll meet us at the car."

"Good." I pointed to a nearby exit door. "Time to go cross-country. This way."

Nikki was waiting at the car when we reached it, her eyes methodically sweeping both the nearest doors and the landscape around us. "What's wrong?" she asked as we arrived.

"Nothing," I said, motioning her and Selene to get in as I climbed into the driver's seat. Like most company vehicles I'd seen in secure or isolated facilities, it didn't require a key. "Well, the Patth in there probably wants to kill me," I amended as I started the engine. "Aside from that we're good. You get what you needed?"

"No," Nikki said as she got in the car behind me. She had two guns in hand now, I saw: a Fafnir plasmic like mine and a Jaundance 4mm. "But not from lack of trying. Business or personal?"

"Mostly business," I said as I pulled onto the narrow road leading back to the *Ruth*. The top of the ship was visible over the patches of waving grain and low shrubs, but the underside was still out of sight.

Still, with the wind that had been at our backs earlier now blowing in our faces... "Maybe some personal thrown in," I added. "Selene? What've we got?"

"Two armed humans." She paused, and I risked a glance at her to see her eyelashes fluttering as she tried to isolate something very faint. "Firearms, I think. I can smell lubricating oil."

"As expected," I said, nodding.

"Why as expected?" Nikki asked.

"Firearms are better than plasmics in frontier situations," I told her, frowning. Did she really not know that?

No, of course she didn't. An assassin who charged half a million commarks per hit would be going after the high and mighty, who were mainly to be found in cities or private fortresses. Country life would be way outside her professional experience. "Better range and stopping power for varmints and predators, easier to maintain, and if you've got propellent and a supply of slugs you can easily reload the cartridges. Any idea where that other Iykam could be?"

Selene shook her head. "Somewhere behind us, probably."

So two armed humans in front of us, a Patth and two armed Iykams behind us. Terrific. "Guess we'll have to play this by ear. Any of these plots seem of particular interest to Landon?"

"Yes, two of them," she said. "One was about four back from the *Ruth*. It had green and yellow spotted leaves, with a sort of…" She waved a hand helplessly. "They're hard to describe."

"No need," I assured her. "Just point me to the plot when we get there. You said there were two?"

"The other one's coming up now," she said, pointing. "Four plots ahead."

"Here they come," Nikki warned.

I half turned to look over my shoulder. Three more cars were visible back there, roaring toward us in clouds of dust, the narrowness of the road forcing them to go in single file. "Selene, get ready to take the wheel," I said, looking forward again. "I'm getting off at this first plot. Nikki, Selene will drive you to one of the other plots and stop. Wait there, watch the guards at the ship, but don't make any moves unless I do. Got it?"

"What's the plan?" Nikki asked.

"No time," I said. "Just play off my cues. I'll have my phone on so you can listen in on what's happening here."

"There," Selene said, pointing to a group of purple-flowered bushes with clusters of low-hanging nuts or fruits.

I slammed on the brakes, threw the car into park, and hopped out. Selene slid into my seat, shifted back into drive, and roared off again. I keyed on my phone and put it in my pocket, then drew my plasmic. Keeping my arms at my sides with the weapon pointed at the ground, I turned to face the approaching vehicles. Landon was at the wheel of the lead car, I could see now, with Uvif beside him and the two Iykams in the back seat behind them. With all the dust they were churning up I couldn't see into the trailing cars, but I would have bet good money that they were full of researchers and every single gun in the station.

Under other circumstances, I could imagine Landon hitting the accelerator and doing his best to run me down. But with me standing motionless, armed but not directly threatening anyone, there really wasn't any way for him to justify that. Still, he let the car come uncomfortably close before braking hard and slewing to a halt five meters away.

The Patth was out of the car practically before it stopped, the two Iykams right behind him, moving to flanking positions on either side of him. Landon was only slightly behind them, while the two cars behind him similarly stopped and began disgorging their passengers.

And from the number of rifles I could see flailing around as the researchers sorted themselves into a confrontation line I was pretty sure I'd called that one right, too.

"Dr. Landon," I called over the burble of auditory chaos accompanying the general scrambling. "I strongly suggest you keep your people back if you don't want a disaster on your hands."

"You suggest that, do you?" Landon snarled back, his voice rich with rage and mortification. He'd thought he was being clever, inviting potential spies into his web, only to have them completely turn the tables on him. "You think you can take all of us? Is that what you think?"

"We came to make a StarrComm call, not to steal your secrets," I called. "We've made our call, and now we just want to leave."

"You may find that difficult," Uvif put in. The Iykams, I noted with interest, were standing stiffly with their hands inside their loose robes but hadn't yet drawn any weapons. However Uvif had arranged to be in charge of the StarrComm facility, there was a fair chance he'd pitched the Iykams as assistants instead of bodyguards.

All of which, in retrospect, made a lot of sense. If the portal-hunting group on the other side of the planet managed to dig something out of the ruins they would want all other communications with the outside universe locked down until they could get the equipment here to cart it off.

"We didn't steal any secrets," I repeated, looking directly at Uvif now. "Nikki's call had nothing to do with your operation. You know that."

Landon half turned to look at the Patth, his eyes narrowing slightly. StarrComm communications were supposed to be strictly private, only my comment implied that wasn't the case. At least, not here on Lucias Four.

And since Landon had no inkling of what the other Patth

on the planet were up to, his natural conclusion would be that Uvif had wormed his way into Landon Station for the purpose of spying on his precious crop research.

"The point is that we just want to leave," I continued. "And with the minimum of damage."

Landon's head snapped back around to face me. "What do you mean?" he demanded.

"I mean this." Raising my arm from my side, I pointed my plasmic directly at the crop plot beside me.

And suddenly, the whole group went very still.

As my father used to say, *If you do it right, threatening to punch someone in the face is as effective as actually punching him, and it takes a lot less effort.*

Landon took a step toward me, close enough now that I could see the veins in his neck throbbing. "Roarke, if you so much as..." He broke off.

Though as my father also used to say, *Of course, if you do it wrong, you're the one who'll probably end up with a faceful of fist.*

"We just want to leave," I said again, resisting the impulse to take a step backward in response. "No harm, no foul, and you'll never see us again."

For another eight heartbeats we all just stood there, the air crackling with tension, all the guns in the world—possibly literally, for a change—pointed at me. I kept my plasmic pointed at the plants, wondering distantly whether I'd have time to set them on fire if Landon called my bluff, or even if I would consider it justified to do so.

Then, to my relief, Landon sagged a little. "Go," he muttered, giving me a short, rather tired nod. "Just go."

I nodded back. "Thank you," I said. "If you'll be kind enough to call your men back from my ship—"

"No," Uvif snarled. He made a twitching motion with his hand.

And suddenly both Iykams were pointing corona guns at me.

"Uvif?" Landon demanded, his mouth dropping open as he again turned to stare at the Patth. "What in hell's name—?"

"Silence," Uvif cut him off. "This human is a threat to the Patthaaunuth. He cannot and will not be allowed to leave."

"Uvif—"

"I said *silence!*" Uvif snarled. "Step aside or burn where you stand."

Landon drew himself up. "How dare you threaten a senior researcher of Crodalian Enterprises—"

"Fool!" Uvif cut him off. "Who do you think owns Crodalian Enterprises and your pitiful little research station? *We* do."

Landon shot a startled look at me, then turned back to Uvif. "I had no idea—"

"Or so he says," I spoke up quickly. As my father used to say, *Always have a bigger bluff ready in case they call your first one.* "You have any actual proof of that, Uvif? I'll bet you don't."

"*You* be silent," the Patth retorted. "You may speak once you are in Patthaaunuth custody."

"I don't think so," I said calmly. "You see, I know how the Patth do things. You want to take over Crodalian Enterprises, all right, and the fact that you're playing StarrComm tech here tells me that Dr. Landon's project is the key."

Uvif gave a sort of rumbling snarl. "I am finished trading words." He gestured the Iykams forward. "Take him."

"No," Landon said, his voice suddenly calm. "Take *them*."

And abruptly the guns that had been pointed at me were pointed at Uvif and the Iykams.

Uvif actually sputtered. "You foolish humans. The Patthaaunuth will tear you down to your bones."

"Put your weapons down," Landon said. His voice was shaking a little, but his face and stance were firm enough. "Pillay, put them in the fertilizer storage room."

"If I were you, I'd call your head office as soon as they're secure," I offered as two of the men strode up behind the Iykams and relieved them of their weapons. "Tell them what happened and that you need backup as fast as they can get it to you. I don't know what kind of force the group on the other side of the planet can muster, but they're bound to at least have a few more like these two. Still, once your story is out they should be leery about doing anything that will make it worse."

"And you?" Landon asked, turning his eyes back on me.

"Like I said, we came to make a call," I told him. "But just like you have a soft spot for crocketts, I have a soft spot for people getting screwed over by the Patth." I gave him a nod, turned, and headed at a fast jog for the *Ruth*.

I half expected to get shot in the back, or at least ordered to stop and come back. But Landon apparently had had all the intrigue and potential weapons fire on his plate that he could handle for one day. Besides which, even if his people were able to take me down there would still be Nikki and Selene to deal with.

Halfway to the *Ruth* I passed the two men who'd been guarding the ship, hurrying the other direction. We eyed each other as we passed, but none of us said anything.

Nikki was waiting beside the car when I reached it. "Are you insane?" she demanded.

"Probably," I conceded. "Selene gone inside?"

"Yes." Nikki slipped her plasmic back into concealment, keeping her Jaundance and most of her attention on the distant group behind us as she followed me to the ship. "What if Landon changes his mind and decides not to boost us?"

"He will," I assured her. "The main reason spaceports use pad repulsors and perimeter grav beams is that thrusters fired at ground level make a mess of everything in their path. If Landon was worried about me scorching his favorite test plot, he sure as hell won't want us burning everything aft of the ship on our way out."

Still, I felt a flicker of relief when whoever was in charge of Landon Station's lift system did indeed kick in the repulsors and grav beams with only slightly less efficiency than I'd seen elsewhere in this kind of rural setup. I returned the favor by keeping the thrusters on lower power than usual until we were well clear of the station and the crops.

Half an hour later, without any Patth ships having peeked over the horizon from the other side of the planet, the *Ruth*'s cutter array sliced us into hyperspace and we were gone.

CHAPTER NINE

"You're either the biggest idiot I've ever met," Nikki accused as she paced restlessly across the dayroom's limited floor space, "or three degrees short of suicidal."

"I don't see the problem," I said mildly from my fold-down seat as I took a sip of my drink. I understood the need to bleed off excess energy and adrenaline after a particularly trying encounter like the one we'd just had, but even just sitting here watching her walking back and forth was making me tired. "I got us in, you made your call, and I got us out again."

"You *don't*?" Nikki countered. She spun around in mid-pace and shot a look at Selene, seated to my left on one of the other fold-downs. "Please tell me *you* see the mess your boss has dropped us into."

"I don't know what else he could have done," Selene replied stiffly. "He couldn't let us be captured."

"So instead he makes enemies of the whole damn Patth species?"

"The Patth didn't like us long before Uvif's Iykams pulled their guns on us back there," I said. "And Selene's right. If you were listening, you certainly saw that Uvif was all but salivating over the chance to bring us in."

"I *was* listening, and that raises a whole raft of other questions,"

Nikki said acidly. "But that's your problem, and you're welcome to it. *My* problem is that for the next few weeks I'm joined at the hip to you two and your feuds. I get shot at enough without drawing extra fire just because of where I'm standing."

"I know, and for what it's worth I'm sorry," I said. I didn't particularly relish my current spot next to a working assassin, either. "I was pretty sure there would be a Patth keeping an eye on the research station in case the dig crew needed to send any messages. But I thought he'd be more embedded into the staff and would be out monitoring the crops or something. I didn't expect he'd be in direct charge of the StarrComm facility."

"Like I said: an idiot," Nikki said. "You should always have a plan ready for the worst-case scenario."

"I usually do," I said. "And again, I *did* get us out of there."

For a moment Nikki glared at me. Then, she seemed to shake away the emotion. "At least you recognize the problem. The question now is how you're going to solve it."

"We solve it by finishing the job Cherno set for us," I said. "Then we and you go our separate ways."

"All of us still riding together until then?"

"That's how Cherno set it up," I reminded her.

"Cherno didn't know you were going to paint a luminous target on our backs," Nikki countered. "All right. Let's start with what exactly you're looking for."

"We can't really—"

"Stop," Nikki said, her voice suddenly deathly quiet. "Enough of the stalling. What you're doing and where you're going to do it are now life-or-death decisions. I need to know what's going on, and I need to know before we touch ground again."

I looked at Selene, caught the reluctant agreement in her pupils. And it wasn't like Nikki wasn't eventually going to find out about the portals. A few weeks early couldn't hurt. "All right," I said, waving at the foldout couch. "You're going to want to sit down for this."

"I'm fine," Nikki said.

"Whatever," I said. "Bottom line: Cherno has an alien device stashed away at his mansion. It's a portal of the type we call a Gemini that can instantly send a person to another portal multiple light-years away. He's got one end; we're looking for the other."

For a moment Nikki stared at me, her face unreadable. She

looked at Selene, then back at me. Then, her eyes still boring into my face, she backed over to the couch and lowered herself onto it. "Really."

I nodded. "Really."

"You've seen it work?"

"I've ridden it myself," I assured her. "Not Cherno's Gemini, but others like it. Trust me: as insane as it sounds, the damn things do indeed exist."

"And there's another one just sitting around?"

"More likely buried or half buried in or near alien ruins," I said. "Hence, the list Floyd gave us on Xathru."

"And there's probably not just one," Selene added. "There may be dozens of them scattered across the Spiral."

"Dozens, or hundreds," I said. "There's really no way to know."

For a moment Selene was silent, gazing off into the distance as she digested all that. Then, her eyes came back to focus. "I'll assume for a moment that all that is true," she said. "So if I had one of these things—"

"*Two* of these things."

"*Two* of these things," Nikki continued, "you could send me into someone's bedroom or private office or something?"

"No, you can only go back and forth between the portals," I said. "You leave one end and go to the other."

"Yes, I got that," Nikki said. "But if you were able to get one of the portals into someone's office you could do that?"

"It would have to be one hell of an office," I said. "Gemini portals are spheres about twenty meters across."

"Oh," Nikki said, momentarily taken aback. "You could have mentioned that."

"Sorry," I said. "The big sphere's twenty meters across, with a conjoined smaller sphere about fifteen."

"Got it," Nikki said, and I could see her shuffling this new data into her mental swirl of ideas and possibilities. "So he just tripped over this thing one day?"

"I don't think so," I said. "It's in a quick-build structure on his property, and it's still sitting on the cargo straps they used to haul it there."

"So it *is* portable," she said thoughtfully. "If it's too big for someone's house you could still move it onto their land and inside their outer security ring."

"Theoretically, sure," I said. "Be a bit hard to hide a twenty-meter sphere in a Zen garden."

"There are always possibilities," Nikki assured me. "You just have to train yourself to think that way. How long has Cherno had the portal?"

I thought back. It had been four months since Nask and the Patth sneaked the portal off Fidelio, but I didn't know when along its journey Cherno had managed to hijack it.

But there *was* someone who might know. I hadn't thought about Trent for a while, but if he'd been involved in the theft he would know those details.

I felt my throat tighten. I'd wondered once if his invitation to join his crew meant he was planning to steal the other end of Cherno's Gemini, but those speculations had taken a back seat to everything else that had happened since then.

But if he had even a hint of where that portal was, maybe he and I should renew acquaintances.

Meanwhile, Nikki was waiting for an answer. "No more than four months," I told her. "Probably somewhat less."

"So he's been thinking about this for a while," she concluded. "And the fact that he's linked me up with you tells me he's figured out a way to get his portal inside his target's security."

"I suppose that's possible," I said, my thoughts still on Trent and the possibility of tracking down the other Gemini through him. "Still be a hell of a stunt to park one on someone's lawn without them noticing it."

"Trust me," Nikki said dryly. "There are plenty of the rich and powerful who could drop something that size onto their estates and never know it was there. So where does this little treasure hunt of yours start?"

"Hopefully, on one of these planets," I said, standing up and pulling out my info pad. I could see in Selene's pupils that she'd sensed I'd had a sudden thought, but she knew better than to ask in front of Nikki. There would be plenty of time to talk about Trent when we had more privacy. "Cherno's people made up a list of possible spots," I continued, pulling up Floyd's planetary list and handing the pad to Nikki. "I'd probably start with one of the higher spots, but at this point it's mostly a dart toss."

"I see Lucias Four is there," she commented, flashing a baleful look at me before returning her attention to the pad. "You could have told me that was what you were looking for from the start."

"The point about it having a private StarrComm facility was equally valid," I said with a shrug. "No reason we can't do two things at the same time."

"Funny you should say that," Nikki said. "I see Niskea is two down from the top. Interesting."

I frowned. There were a lot of adjectives I'd heard applied to Niskea over the years, but *interesting* had never been one of them. "Something there catch your eye?" I asked.

"Not my eye, no," she said. "There's a part of Rosselgang City informally called the Badlands. Ever hear of it?"

I winced. Every hunter in the Spiral had heard of the Badlands. For way too many targets it was their final attempt to hide from justice.

Unfortunately for them, in this case hiding from justice also meant hiding from civilization. The Badlands was a two-kilometer-square enclave of criminal rule surrounded by a city and planet that didn't want them there but hadn't figured out a way short of tactical nukes to get rid of them.

Though as was the case with most other defiant strongholds in the Spiral, there were rumors that the Rosselgang government left the Badlands alone because there were quiet fortunes to be made through bribes, smuggling, and protection agreements. "The place is hardly a secret," I said. "I've heard hunters talk about targets disappearing in there. Most of them never found out whether the fugitives are still there or were able to slip out."

"Most likely they settled down there," Nikki said. "The more valid question was whether they settled aboveground or below it."

Selene shifted silently in her seat. Her pupils showed revulsion, but I couldn't tell whether it was directed toward Nikki or the Badlands. "So; important safety tip," I said. "There's supposed to be a small spaceport near one edge of the enclave that's barrier-ringed and relatively safe."

"It's actually very safe," Nikki said. "No one wants to have to go into badgeman territory if they need to get cargo in or themselves out, so everything inside the port fence is a steel-skinned neutral zone." She raised her eyebrows slightly. "*Outside* the fence it's a different story."

"I take it you have business in there?" Selene asked.

"You sound like you're hoping I won't make it out," Nikki said, a little too calmly. "No, no business, just a purchase I need to make." She paused. "Actually, it'll be a custom order, so it may take a while."

"Okay, that works," I said, trying not to think of what sort of nastiness an assassin's custom order would include. "We can just head over—"

"How long a while?" Selene asked.

"I'm not sure," Nikki said, eyeing her thoughtfully. "Could be as little as a day. Could be two or three."

"Even more perfect," I said. "As I was starting to say, we'll drop you off, then head over to the ruins—"

"No," Nikki interrupted. "We can go look for Cherno's portal after I'm finished."

"You mean in a day or three?" I asked pointedly. "Or maybe more? You *do* remember we're running on a timer here, right?"

"I've seen what happens when you get on the ground," Nikki said. "I don't want you wandering off somewhere, getting into trouble, and leaving me stranded."

"Won't happen," I promised. "We'll be good little boys and girls, take a quick look around, and head straight back."

"Besides, I would think the Badlands would be the perfect place for you to retire to," Selene put in.

Nikki's eyes narrowed. She opened her mouth—

"Let's stick to the point, shall we?" I spoke up quickly, motioning Selene to drop it. Most of the time she was able to sit on her feelings toward Nikki, but her bubbling animosity could come out at the most awkward moments. "Nikki, we can't just sit around doing nothing. We have to find the other end of Cherno's portal, and our timeframe is looking very thin."

"Don't worry about it," Nikki said, her gaze lingering on Selene another moment before shifting to me. "In my experience, when a client says there's only one shot at something, it's nothing but eagerness and hyperbole. There's always a second opportunity somewhere down the line, and usually a third and a fourth. Maybe they're not as neat and simple as the first opening, but they're always there."

"Cherno may be forgiving toward *you*," I told her. "There's no guarantee that same restraint holds for Selene and me."

"Why wouldn't it? Aren't you the only ones who know how to find this portal?"

"We're the only ones he knows personally," I said. "But there are others out there he might be able to get to. And as my father used to say, *It doesn't matter if you can't be replaced if the other guy thinks you can.*"

"Don't worry, Cherno's not that stupid," Nikki soothed, setting my info pad on the couch beside her. "Anyway, the conversation's over. We land at the Badlands, you wait there while I handle my business, and then we can get back to your hunt." She stood up and waved a hand toward the bridge. "And the sooner you set course for Niskea, the sooner that all happens."

With that, she gave each of us a polite nod and headed out into the corridor and aft toward her cabin.

For a moment Selene and I just looked at each other. Then she stirred. "I'm sorry, Gregory," she said in a small voice. "I didn't mean to...are you angry?"

"Yes," I confirmed. "But not at you." I glowered out into the corridor. "And if she thinks we're just going to sit on our hands while she goes shopping for snow globes or whatever, she's sadly mistaken."

"You think we can lift from the Badlands without her knowing about it?"

"Oh, I'm sure she'll have that covered," I said. "But just because the *Ruth* stays on the pad doesn't mean we have to be aboard. Let's go lay in a course and find ourselves some options."

Usually I left the bridge hatch open when I was in there, both for the ventilation and for the mostly false sense of roominess it created. This time, even with Nikki presumably locked in her cabin, I made sure to close and lock it.

Looking up Niskea's coordinates and setting our course took about ten minutes. I ran the engines to plus-twenty, the highest setting I was willing to risk, which would burn fuel like crazy but would also shave twenty percent of the time off our trip. Even with that, though, we were in for a solid four days in hyperspace, days we were effectively useless. More than once I'd reflected that Cherno's six-week timetable was ridiculously optimistic for the size job he'd handed us.

But then, at the time he'd set his plans he'd thought we would be able to turn on his damn portal for him. So much for the best-laid plans.

I felt my throat tighten. No. Not *his* portal. Sub-Director Nask's.

I gazed at the nav reading, wondering yet again how in hell's name Cherno had gotten the portal away from the Patth. Wondering, too, whether Nask had made it out the other end alive.

And it belatedly occurred to me that if Trent had been part of it, there might even now be Patth Expediters closing in on him. Eager though I was to find out what he knew, he might not be a healthy person to stand next to at the moment.

As my father used to say, *Don't spit at someone who's armed and angry, and don't stand next to the guy doing the spitting.*

"Gregory, look at this," Selene spoke up from the plotting table behind me.

"What've you got?" I asked, turning around.

"The spaceport Nikki wants us to land in is only about six blocks from the edge of the Badlands," she said, handing me her info pad. "If we can pick up a runaround inside the port fence, it should only take a couple of minutes to get clear of the area."

"That assumes no one tries to stop us," I pointed out, looking at the street map she'd pulled up. Scrimshaw Avenue, the major thoroughfare that marked the northern boundary of the Badlands, was indeed six blocks away from the spaceport.

Only that six blocks translated to nearly half a kilometer. Plenty of time for the locals to peek through a runaround's windows and see that there were strangers among them.

On the other hand, newcomers to a place like the Badlands ought to be relatively common. Furthermore, if I gave the gawkers my best scowl they might be persuaded to exercise the better part of valor and leave us alone. "And then we grab an aircar and head over to the ruins?" I asked doubtfully.

"Or we start by calling the admiral," Selene said, reaching over and tapping a spot on the pad. "The nearest StarrComm center is only ten kilometers away."

I nodded, mentally sifting through the possibilities. The ruins on Cherno's list were a good eight thousand kilometers out from the Badlands. A quick trip there and back would be possible if Nikki's errand took the full three days she'd mentioned; not so much if it only took one. But a conversation with the admiral should only cost us a couple of hours.

"Sounds like a plan," I agreed, handing back the pad. "Okay.

We'll wave good-bye to Nikki, then see what transport we can get. We probably do owe the admiral an update."

I looked over at the Niskea course display. "And he owes *us* a list of planets to look at. We should probably remember to remind him of that."

The Badlands spaceport was a textbook example of the economical use of space, its eight landing pads cramped together in an area where more respectable spaceports would only have four. But the *Ruth* was compact, and I was a reasonably good pilot, and we made it to our assigned pad without any trouble. Nikki made a couple of phone calls as we powered down, and by the time I'd arranged for refueling she was ready to head out on her buying spree.

"Final instructions," she said as the three of us met by the entryway. She was dressed in the same black-and-dark green wrap, hat, and veil she'd been wearing when we met, the same one she'd worn during her Vesperin reconnoiter. Apparently, it was her walkabout outfit of choice even when it made her identifiable to hostile hunters.

Though maybe being identifiable here was an asset, especially when your name was Piper.

"We'll start with the obvious: stay put," Nikki continued. "I've reserved the pad for six days, and spaceport operations are monitored, so don't try to sneak it out of here."

"I thought you said it would only take three days," I reminded her.

"It will," she said. "An artist like Franck never needs more than three days for a custom job. But it's only money, and it doesn't hurt to make people think you'll be staying somewhere longer than you actually will. People making plans usually scale their timetables based on how long they have to carry them out."

I nodded. "Like Cherno and his six-week countdown."

"If that's supposed to remind me to hurry, consider it noted," she said. "Item two: don't let anyone else aboard the ship. The fuelers and port authorities are bonded, so they should be safe enough, but anyone can just stroll in through the gates and no one will stop them."

"Usually we only allow friends aboard," Selene murmured.

"Good," Nikki said, ignoring the implied swipe. "If you get

hungry, the local area has plenty of places you can call for delivery. Just leave payment at the top of the zigzag, have them do the same with the food, and you're good."

"Or we could just go out and get it ourselves," I said. "Sampling the local color can be fun."

"In this case, it probably won't," Nikki said. "On our way in I took the liberty of sending Planetary Control your bounty hunter ID. An hour or two, and everyone in the Badlands will know you're here and will probably assume you're chasing a target."

I stared at her, a tight feeling in my chest. I'd deliberately come in under my crockett ID and license to avoid that exact misunderstanding. "What the hell did you do *that* for?"

"To make sure you stay put," she said calmly. "I don't want to come back to the *Ruth* to find you two off playing tourist. That timetable you just mentioned, remember?"

I looked at Selene, saw my same anger and frustration reflected in her pupils. But what was done was done, and there wasn't anything we could do about it. "Or you could just make sure to call when you know how long this is going to take."

"I'll try," she promised. "I'll definitely call when I'm heading back. Believe it or not, I don't want to spend any longer here than I have to, either. Any questions?"

"No, I think you've thoroughly boxed us in," I bit out.

"Good," Nikki said. "And it's not so much a box as it is a fortress. Be good, and enjoy the local food."

She gestured to the entryway. I opened it and she headed out, exuding casual confidence as she walked down the zigzag. I leaned my head out as she descended, studying the perimeter fence, the nearest gate, and the small operations and entry building beside the opening. The street beyond the fence, the one that offered the quickest route out of the Badlands, looked narrower than I would have liked, but it was broad enough to avoid getting instantly flanked by people emerging from buildings, alleyways, or side streets. There wasn't much vehicular traffic, but there were enough pedestrians moving back and forth that at least a traveler wouldn't feel completely conspicuous.

The perimeter fence itself, I noted, was little more than a token chain-link style that anyone with even a modicum of determination could easily climb or breach. Apparently, Nikki had been right about agreements among the locals being the true guarantee of the port's security.

She'd also been right about how easy it would be for someone to wander in.

I waited until she'd reached ground level and was crossing toward the gate and office before closing the entryway and turning to Selene. "Okay, she's on her way. What have we got?"

"Nothing," she said, her pupils showing frustration as she worked her info pad. "There aren't any runaround stands in or near the port, and none of the cab companies will send a driver into the Badlands."

"Terrific," I growled. "What about outside the Badlands? Any runaround stands there?"

"There's one two blocks north of Scrimshaw Avenue," she said. "Once we get out we might be able to pick up one and drive ourselves back here."

"It's getting there in the first place that's the problem," I said heavily. "Like I said, nice little box."

"Yes, it is," Selene said. "Are we going to stay in it?"

I thought about Nikki's warnings about the Badlands, and her underhanded trick of broadcasting my hunter ID to all the lowlifes around us. Cheap manipulation, and I'd never liked being manipulated. "As my father used to say, *Do a little more each day than is expected of you, and more will be expected. So don't do more. Do different.*"

Selene's pupils were showing wariness. "Meaning?"

"Meaning that if we can't get a ride, we'll just have to walk," I said.

"Do you think it's safe?"

"If Nikki can do it, so can we," I said firmly, hoping I wouldn't end up eating those words. "Grab your jacket, phone, and plasmic, and let's go."

CHAPTER TEN

We had to pass by the operations office on our way to the gate. The female Ulkomaal at the desk didn't say anything, but I had the impression she was watching us closely as we passed her window. Briefly, I wondered if she recognized us, and whether the Ulko people might still remember my part in helping Ixil free the two slaves back on Pinnkus.

Probably not, and at any rate that incident wouldn't do us any good here. Whether or not the Ulkomaals held any residual gratitude, this particular one was living and working in a criminal enclave. Even if she did recognize us, she wasn't likely to be inclined to stretch her neck out for outsiders.

Six blocks. Half a kilometer. Anywhere else in the Spiral, I reflected as we set off down the walkway, that would have been a nice ten-minute stroll or a brisk five-minute walk.

But here, with the lingering looks of pedestrians and idlers on us as we passed, and the brooding buildings with all those overlooking windows hemming in close around us, I felt like a fish in a bowl surrounded by a houseful of hungry cats.

Nikki had said that it would be another hour or two before everyone in the Badlands knew who I was. Two blocks into our walk, I decided she'd seriously underestimated the speed of gossip.

But at this point there was really nothing we could do but

keep going. It was nearly as far back to the *Ruth* as to the relative safety of the city beyond Scrimshaw Avenue, and I knew from experience that projecting even a hint of fear or unease would only encourage those who were already inclined to be trouble. So I kept us moving, alternating a straight-ahead stare like that of a man on a mission with quick measuring scans of my surroundings like a man who was nevertheless not stupid or unaware of those around him.

Checking to see how Selene was doing could be interpreted as uneasiness, so I didn't. But she was keeping up with me, and her stride was as firm as mine, and I had no doubt she was exuding the same air of confidence that I was.

Three blocks to go. Halfway through the gauntlet, and so far no one had done anything but stare, glare, or glower. As my father used to say, *If someone wants to think he's tough because he's good with looks and insults, by all means let him have his delusions. There'll be a lot less paperwork for you to fill out afterward.*

Unfortunately, even if none of this bunch wanted to take me on, they all had friends. I spotted at least four young men and two women furtively pull out their phones as Selene and I approached, and I was pretty sure they hadn't suddenly decided to call for takeout.

Still, three blocks didn't give anyone very much response time. With luck and a little intimidation this should work.

We were midway down the fourth block when I heard a sudden intake of air from beside me. "What is it?" I asked quietly.

"It's Trent," Selene said, sounding more puzzled than worried. "He's here."

I sent a quick look around us. If he was anywhere nearby, he was keeping to the shadows. "Where?"

"I don't know," she said. "Too many scents, and the airflow is restless. But he *is* here."

"I believe you," I assured her. "But that doesn't make any sense. Why would he be on Niskea, let alone in the Badlands?"

"He must be hunting one of the targets here," she said. "You said there were dozens of them."

"More likely hundreds," I said, appreciating the irony of it all. Nikki had tried to lock us into the *Ruth* by broadly hinting to the locals that I was in the Badlands to snatch one of their neighbors, and now here Trent was apparently doing that exact same thing.

Earlier, I'd thought about trying to contact him to pump him for information about his proposed hijacking. With him right here, it would be trivial to set up a meeting.

Assuming, of course, that we survived the next few minutes. "Whoever he's here for, it has nothing to do with us," I told Selene. "Though if we're lucky, and worse comes to worst, he may show up in time to be a distraction."

We were a block and a half from the wide avenue ahead when worse indeed came to worst.

Their move was casual enough to look at first like just a group of young men crossing the street, but quick enough to effectively cut off any options I could try. Five young thugs lined up across the street ten meters in front of us, and as I glanced over my shoulder I saw that five more had similarly cut off our retreat.

"Hello, there," I called, offering them a friendly wave and my best oblivious smile. As my father used to say, *If you appear to be a naïve grinning idiot, most people will look down on you, which puts you in perfect position for a quick uppercut.* "I think we're lost. Can you tell me where Joji's Cajun is?"

"They're closed today," the one in the middle called back.

"That's a shame," I said, letting my smile slip a little. The place had certainly looked open when I'd spotted it down one of the side streets we passed a couple of minutes ago. "Someone told me they had great food. Can you suggest an alternative?"

"How about you chew on one of these, Mr. Big Man Bounty Hunter?" the thug countered. Reaching inside his jacket, he produced a long, nasty-looking knife. "Goes down real smooth," he added, holding it up to show me.

I huffed out a silent sigh as his four companions picked up on the cue, one of them producing a knife of his own, the other three pulling out pairs of fighting sticks. They were great weapons if you were expecting close-in work: cheap, effective, and didn't leave behind any ballistics or spectral profiles to tag you for the killing.

But the absolute first rule of knife fighting was to always point your weapon at your opponent's eyes so that he couldn't tell how long it was. By that standard, this guy was a rank amateur.

Still, he probably had a lot more experience attacking with a knife than I had defending against one. And it was a really *long* knife.

"Hey, there's no need for hostility," I protested, letting my waving arm drop back to my side. My plasmic was still hidden away, but I could get it out faster than any of them could move into stabbing distance.

But that would instantly escalate the situation, and I needed to try all the other options first. "I'm not here to bother you or anyone else," I assured him. "I just want to go to the Starr-Comm center across town and send a message. Nothing to do with anyone here."

"Sure," the thug grated out. He took a step forward, his four companions following suit. "A hunter suddenly shows up here, and we're supposed to believe he's just sightseeing? Sure."

"This doesn't have to go any further," I said, trying one last time.

"Neither do you," he shot back.

"Yeah. Funny," I said, looking around. The passersby and shoppers had all come to a halt and were gathered around us like spectators in an open-air arena waiting for the main bout to begin. The probability that with its current configuration the fight was likely to be over very quickly didn't seem to be affecting the anticipation level.

And it occurred to me that not producing a weapon might actually have worked against me. The toughs had now tagged me as an easy target, and if their ambition matched their swagger and amateurism they would be happy with any kind of victory, even an easy one. In fact, with that type, the easier the better.

"But you're forgetting one thing," I said, pointing to the shop directly to my left. It was a rolled-meat store, I saw, with a metal frame supporting a colorful cloth awning that stretched over the walkway almost to the street itself. "See that place over there?"

And as the thugs' eyes reflexively followed along that line, I slid my plasmic out of concealment.

"You're forgetting that the people over there don't want to spend the rest of the day smelling burned flesh," I continued, hefting the plasmic a little for emphasis. "Well, human flesh, anyway. I'm sure their rolled meat is delicious. So let's do this. We all agree that you're courageous defenders of your turf, that we're cowards who aren't worth the trouble of fighting, and that you chased us out of the Badlands fair and square. Okay? Then we can all just get on with our lives. Sound good?"

An experienced fighter with a grasp of combat odds and cost/benefit ratios would already have concluded that the vague and unconfirmed suggestion that I *might* be hunting someone wasn't worth losing at least three to five members of his team, especially since he himself would probably be the one I'd shoot first. But as I'd already noted, these toughs were anything but experienced. "Oh, yeah, big hunter man," the thug sneered, taking another step toward Selene and me. Again, his flankers followed his lead, but it seemed to me that this time they hesitated just a bit before moving closer. "You going to shoot us down, huh? You think you can get all of us—*all* of us"—he waved his hand in a wide arc that encompassed the watching crowd—"before we tear you to little pieces?"

"I don't think there'd be much tearing," I replied. "Most of these people are smart enough to realize this isn't their fight. Actually, it's not *your* fight either—like I said, we're not here to take anyone." I held up a finger. "And just as a grammatical point, you shouldn't say before *we* tear you apart, but before *they* tear you apart. Because you won't be one of them."

For a second he seemed puzzled. Then the confusion cleared from his face and he gave me a vicious smile. "You don't think I've got the stomach to do it, huh?"

I sighed. As my father used to say, *Sometimes subtlety just isn't worth the effort. In those cases, and with those people, make sure you have a brick handy.* "Actually, I was referring back to my earlier comment about burnt flesh," I told him. "Which would be yours."

His face hardened. "You want a piece of me, hunter?" he demanded. "Go ahead. Shoot."

"Thanks for the offer," I said. "But I think I'll go with a more imposing opponent."

Without waiting for his response, I shifted my aim and sent a plasma shot into the rolled-meat shop's awning.

There was a chorus of mixed screams and screeches from the onlookers gathered beneath the cloth as it burst into smoky flame. "There you go," I said to the thug, sparing a quick glance at the burning cloth to confirm that no one was in any immediate danger. I'd picked that particular awning because of its isolation from any other flammable objects and for the metal frame that looked sturdy enough to keep it safely suspended in the air while the fire burned itself out.

The fact that it was also sending up a thick column of black smoke as it burned that could already be seen for a couple of kilometers was just a nice bonus.

"I saw a firefighter substation a block past Scrimshaw Avenue on our way in," I said, raising my voice to be audible over the screeching of the onlookers and the crackling of the flames. "I figure it'll take them about three minutes to get here. And fire-fighters are usually accompanied by badgemen."

"You figure that, huh?" the thug called. If he was worried about the authorities charging in on his private battlefield, he was hiding it well. "Got news for you, hunter: Badgemen don't come into the Badlands. Neither do firefighters. We're on our own." He lifted his knife. "Which means *you're* on your own. How does that go? *If you run...?*"

"*...you'll only die tired,*" I finished the sentence as a sinking feeling settled into my stomach. And with that, I was out of choices. If Selene and I were going to get out of this alive, I was going to have to shoot. To wound if possible, but to kill if necessary.

Worse, with us at the short end of ten-to-two odds, I was going to have to attack first. Even with the argument of self-defense on my side, in the eyes of Commonwealth law shooting first would make me the aggressor. "I don't suppose you'd be interested in handling this like real men," I offered. "No weapons, hand to hand."

"Why, you think that'll hurt less?" one of the other thugs jeered.

"Maybe not, but it'll certainly take longer," I told him. "Nice street fight, lots of spectators. I'm thinking you'd have time to set up some wagers on the outcome, maybe make yourself a little extra cash."

The thug's eyes flicked over my shoulder, possibly double-checking that there was no official response on the way to deal with my casual arson. "You think stalling is going to do you any—?"

"I'll take a piece of that," a voice came from my right.

I sent a frown that direction. A short, wiry-looking man with a messenger bag over his shoulder had pushed his way to the front of the crowd. "Fact, I can run the action for you," he continued as he walked briskly toward the line of thugs. "Got seed money right here—just give me a minute to set up a wager grid."

I refocused my attention on the thugs as the newcomer slid the bag off his shoulder and popped the sealing strap. The leader seemed completely dumfounded by the unexpected intrusion into his moment of glory, especially the man's assumption that we were indeed going to exchange our armed standoff for a full-on showground brawl. Beside me, I heard Selene's breath catch in her throat...

And then, in a single smooth motion, the thin man threw his bag at the second knife-wielding kid's face and threw himself at the chief thug. A snap-grip on the thug's right wrist with his left hand—a half pivot as he snaked his right arm up under the thug's armpit—the very audible *crack* as he broke the thug's right elbow—letting go of the thug's wrist to deliver a short but devastating palm-heel blow to the side of the kid's neck—

A scream of surprise and pain came from behind me. I spun around toward the line of thugs behind us, bringing my plasmic to bear—

To find a taller and more strongly built newcomer with a similar messenger bag across his back had already introduced two of that group to the pavement and was in the process of taking down a third.

I turned back, a single glance at Selene showing she was as astonished by the sudden flurry of violence as I was. The thug spokesman was sprawled unconscious on the ground now, his knife lying a meter away on the pavement, and the thin man was in the process of taking down the other kid who'd been carrying a knife, the one he'd thrown his bag at. The other three—

The other three, fighting sticks still in hand, were in full-fledged retreat, running like maniacs through gaps that had miraculously opened up for them through the surrounding crowd. Some members of the crowd had likewise suddenly discovered they had business elsewhere and were moving away nearly as fast.

I looked behind me again. The large man was standing calmly among the crumpled figures of the three thugs he'd taken out, the other two having vanished like their comrades into the landscape.

"Are you all right, Mr. Roarke?" the thin man called.

I turned back to face him. He had retrieved his messenger bag and looped it back over his shoulder and was walking toward Selene and me. "I am now," I said. "To whom do we owe thanks for the timely assist?"

"Call me Huginn," the thin man said. "This is my partner, Muninn. I'm glad we caught you before you left the Badlands."

"Oh?" I asked carefully as Muninn came up to join us. "That sounds like you were looking for us."

"Yes, we were," Huginn confirmed. "Our boss would like a brief word with you to discuss your current situation and activities."

I felt my throat tighten. Cherno hadn't said anything about requiring periodic reports, and given that all we had right now was a nicely balanced stack of nothing, I hadn't thought that calling him was worth the StarrComm fees. Apparently, he thought differently. "Certainly," I said. "Selene and I were heading to the StarrComm center anyway. Do you have a vehicle handy, or shall we find a runaround?"

"Actually, we're not going to the StarrComm center." Huginn looked around. "But we should probably continue this conversation elsewhere." He gestured ahead toward the busy thoroughfare of Scrimshaw Avenue. "After you."

"Thank you," I said, frowning as the four of us started off. Did no StarrComm mean Cherno was already here on Niskea? I thought about asking as we walked, decided there were still too many ears around who didn't need to know our business.

Three minutes and a wide pedestrian crossing later, we were finally and officially out of the Badlands. "Okay, here's the deal," I said as we paused. "As I said, we need to go to StarrComm and make a call. After that, we'll be happy to accompany you wherever we need to go."

"Sorry," Muninn said harshly. "The boss wants to see you now." His eyes shifted to Selene. "And *only* you."

"I'm sorry, too," I said. "Selene and I are a package deal. And we really need to make that call."

Muninn shook his head again. "I just said—"

"Not a problem," Huginn cut in calmly. "You and Muninn go see the boss. I'll take Selene to the StarrComm center, wait while she makes her calls, then escort her back to the *Ruth*. Will that be acceptable?"

My first instinct was to ask him to choose between *no* and *hell no*. The absolute last thing I was willing to do was leave Selene with a total stranger, especially a stranger who'd demonstrated an ability to dispense the kind of near-lethal violence I'd seen from him. "And if I say no?"

Huginn gave me a microscopic smile. "Please don't make me insist."

I braced myself—

"It's all right, Gregory," Selene spoke up. "I'll go with him."

I stared at her, feeling my jaw drop a little. "Selene, what in—?"

"It's all right," she repeated. "Mr. Huginn won't hurt me." She looked at him. "Will you?"

"As long as you're with me, you'll be absolutely safe," Huginn said. The words were calm and polite, but there was an undertone of steel in his tone that promised *very* bad things to anyone who tried to interfere with that promise.

Or maybe that was just wishful hearing on my part. With the two of them standing right there, and my plasmic back in concealment, there wasn't a chance in hell I could prevent them from doing anything they wanted.

And frankly, if Cherno was going to be mad at me, it would probably be just as well if Selene wasn't there.

As my father used to say, *You can accept the inevitable with grace, or you can scream like a spoiled two-year-old. Screaming doesn't gain you points with anyone.*

"Fine," I said, fixing Huginn with a hard look. "But if anything happens to her..."

"Nice to meet you, Mr. Roarke," Huginn said. "I'm sure we'll see each other again soon."

We found the runaround stand, grabbed ourselves a pair of vehicles, and headed off in our respective directions.

I'd expected Muninn to take me to some fancy restaurant for our meeting, or maybe for a longer drive out of the city to a secluded estate. To my surprise and mild concern, he drove instead to another spaceport inside the city limits, this one twice as big as the one in the Badlands but far more upscale. He parked us beside a ground-to-orbit shuttle, and we were barely aboard and strapped into our seats when the perimeter grav beams winked on, pulling us up off the pad, and the pilot took us up toward space.

I stared out the window as the planet receded beneath us, my nagging feeling of discomfort keying up a couple of levels. A shuttle parked in a premium field that was almost certainly reserved for high-end starfaring ships, and a launch slot that could apparently be moved instantly to the head of the line. Either of those would be a solid flag of money or power; the two of them together doubled that conclusion.

Trouble was, Cherno was a criminal lieutenant, and people in that position typically tried to keep a lower profile than that. Part of the goal was to avoid attention from the badgemen, but most of it was because they didn't want to look like they had ambitions against their own bosses.

Had I been wrong about who Huginn and Muninn were working for, then? Could Gaheen himself be here? The one time I'd met the newly crowned big boss of the organization, we'd had a short but civil enough conversation. But if he'd traveled all the way from Huihuang to check on my progress, today's meeting might not be nearly as friendly.

Especially since he knew now that I'd come to his mansion as part of an effort to assassinate him. An unwilling part, true, and I'd also been instrumental in keeping that murder from happening. But I'd dealt with enough crime bosses to know that sometimes important details like that got lost in the shuffle.

And then, even as I was mentally rehearsing what I was going to say, I caught sight of the vessel our shuttle was headed for and my whole scenario went straight off the cliff.

It was a Patth ship.

And not just any Patth ship. It was the *Odinn*, the private transport of Sub-Director Nask. The Patth who'd once kidnapped and threatened me, and whom I'd threatened in return.

He was also the Patth I'd last seen hurrying a Gemini portal off Fidelio, to the consternation of Jordan McKell and the rest of the Icarus Group. The portal that was now sitting in a private warehouse on Cherno's estate.

And whether Nask was still alive or the *Odinn* was now the property of his successor, this meeting could very easily go badly. Very, very badly.

CHAPTER ELEVEN

The shuttle docked, and Muninn led the way onto the *Odinn*.

I was expecting an escort, and for once today I was right. Six Iykams were waiting, their expressions the dark neutral of soldiers who'd been ordered to be polite but really, really didn't want to. They formed a traveling box around me, and with Muninn again leading the way we headed forward. Two corridors later, he opened a hatch and motioned me inside.

And once again I came face-to-face with Sub-Director Nask.

As my father used to say, *When the time comes when your worst enemy is down and out and near death, try not to gloat.* I didn't particularly like Nask, though he was hardly my worst enemy. But even if he had been, there was nothing about the setting facing me that even remotely encouraged gloating.

Nask was lying in a contour couch, a wraparound console with half a dozen glowing displays behind and above his head. Three monitor lines and two tubes led from the wraparound and disappeared beneath the temperature-regulating blanket that covered him from the neck on down. His mahogany-red face was drawn and a little pale, but his eyes were bright and alert. "Mr. Roarke," he said. His voice was raspy, but the words were clear enough. "Thank you for accepting my invitation."

"You're welcome," I said as Muninn stepped to Nask's side

and turned to face me, his expression a sort of stoic glower. Someone else who really didn't want to be polite. "Though if you'd just asked me, your people wouldn't have had to do any leaning. Don't take this the wrong way, but you look terrible."

Nask managed a decent impression of a Patth smile. "I also feel terrible," he said. He looked sideways up at Muninn, who nodded acknowledgment and made a gesture to our escort. "But the pain and weakness are comforting reminders that I'm still alive."

"I'm glad," I said as the Iykams disappeared out into the corridor and the hatch closed behind them. "You may not believe that, but I genuinely am."

"Perhaps," Nask said. "I have a question."

I nodded, wondering uneasily where exactly this was going. The Iykams might be out of position, but if my answer was the wrong one Muninn could certainly take me apart without any of their help. "Which is . . . ?"

"Recall first that you once asked me a similar question," he said, "stating that I was the only Patthaaunuth you knew personally who wasn't stupid. I preface mine with the similar qualifier that you are the only human I know who isn't a wanton and bloodthirsty murderer. So answer me this: Did you or anyone else in the Icarus Group steal my portal and attempt to kill everyone aboard the freighter?"

I took a careful breath. That was indeed the question I'd expected. "No," I said as calmly and firmly as I could. "I wasn't involved, and neither was anyone with Icarus."

"How do you know?" Muninn demanded suspiciously.

"A reasonable question," Nask agreed. "You do not appear to me to be at the head of their rankings. Could they have done this act without you?"

"I'm sure they do a lot of things without me," I said. "But this one I'm sure of." I braced myself. "Because I know who has it."

People talk about an atmosphere turning electric, but I'd rarely seen one actually do so. This was one of those times. Muninn straightened up to an even more intimidating height than he'd already been born with, and Nask actually sat up a little. "Who?" the Patth asked.

"His name is Cherno," I said. "He's a criminal, one of Gaheen's top regional lieutenants. Sorry, but I don't know either of their first names."

"Muninn?" Nask invited.

Muninn's eyes bored into me another moment as he pulled out an info pad and got to work. "Robertine," he said. "Robertine Cherno." He worked at the pad some more. "Mustam Gaheen."

"And how do you know Cherno has our Janus portal?" Nask asked.

Again, I braced myself. "Because I've seen it."

"Where?"

"I don't know," I said. "We were taken there aboard one of Cherno's yachts, then moved to an opaqued aircar and van. I know it's within a nine-day flight of Xathru, but it could be anywhere in that sphere."

Nask looked up at Muninn. "You will seek out this Robertine Cherno," he said in a graveyard voice. "When you find him, you will have him killed."

"Whoa," I said, holding up a hand. "Let's see if we can find another way first, shall we?"

"Why?" Nask countered.

"For starters, because he has some heavy-hitters of his own on the payroll," I said. "Not to mention at least one high-priced assassin. You try a frontal assault, and a lot of people will get killed, including a lot of your Iykams."

"The Iykams' job is to serve the Patth, wherever and however the Patth choose," Muninn said stiffly.

"Very commendable," I said. "Also very wasteful if there are better ways. Did I also mention that it's a big Spiral and that we have no idea where Cherno and the portal are?"

"You said *we*," Nask reminded me. "Was Selene also aboard?"

"Okay, maybe we have *some* idea," I conceded. "The area around the hangar on Cherno's planet included a mix of fir trees and Vyssiluyan pampas grass, with water and algae nearby, which we assume was a pond or lake and not a river. Nearby species included humans, Doolies, and Mastanni, plus other odors too faint to identify. Cherno's mansion had scents of hyacinth and masala chai, and his garage had Craean lubricating oil for his cars."

I'd been keeping an eye on Muninn while I rattled off the information, and was mildly amused to see the growing disbelief in his expression. Apparently Nask hadn't gotten around to telling his minions about Selene's remarkable abilities.

No, I realized suddenly. Not a minion. Given his position

beside Nask, the dismissal of the Iykam guard, his competence at unarmed combat...

"By the way, I see you've picked up a new pair of Expediters," I added, looking back at Nask. "I hope neither of them wants to kill me this time."

"That depends," Nask said coolly. "If you're telling the truth about your involvement in the Janus theft, then no, you have nothing to fear. If you're lying..."

He stopped, leaving the rest of the threat unspoken. But it wasn't like I couldn't connect that particular pair of dots. "I'm not lying," I assured him. "And while I won't presume to tell you that I'm as upset as you are about the theft, I *am* on your side as far as getting it back is concerned."

"Really," Nask said, his tone saying he didn't believe that for a minute. "*Now* you drift into untruth territory."

"Actually, I don't," I said. "Back when I was a bounty hunter I watched a lot of targets being poached from one hunter by another. I lost a couple that way myself once or twice. It seldom seemed right, and it never seemed fair."

Muninn gave a snort. "Even children over five know life isn't fair."

"Actually, children as young as two know it," I said. "As my father used to say, *A child's first word is usually not* Mama *or* Dada, *but* Mine. *Don't expect that priority to ever change.*"

"Yet it changed for you," Nask said.

I shrugged. "Having your arm shot off can do things to your view of life."

"In my experience, it usually just makes you more bitter," Muninn rumbled.

"You want something less naïvely altruistic?" I asked, feeling a stirring of annoyance. I'd never yet met an Expediter who I really got along with, and Muninn and his buddy were falling right into that pattern. "Fine. Sub-Director Nask had the perfect opportunity to sabotage the Icarus Group's portal on Fidelio and he didn't. As far as I'm concerned, that earned him the right to the one he took."

"Aside from the fact there was little you could do to stop us?" Nask asked with a faint smile.

"We have the chance now," I said bluntly. "Cherno's already offered us the portal."

For a moment both of them were silent. "Yet you tell me where it is," Nask said at last.

"The description I gave you is hardly definitive," I said. "Oh, and I also have a sketch of the mountains visible through his office window, which I can give you before I leave. But that's not going to help you much, either."

"Yes," Nask murmured. His brief surge of energy had passed, and he again sagged in his bed. "Let us leave that aside for the moment. Why are you traveling with a hired assassin?"

"That was Cherno's price for giving us the portal," I said. "Piper came aboard on Xathru—"

"Who?" Muninn cut in.

"Right," I said, scowling to myself. "I keep forgetting. A woman named Piper was brought to the *Ruth*, but before we lifted she was quietly swapped out for a woman calling herself Nikki."

"Interesting," Nask said. "Muninn, I take it you know Roarke's current passenger?"

"I've never met her, but I know her reputation," he said. "Her name is Nicole Schlichting, and she's—"

"*Nicole Schlichting?*" I echoed, a sudden knot forming in the pit of my stomach. "We have *Nicole Schlichting* aboard our ship?"

"I take it you know her, too?" Nask asked.

I swallowed hard. Nicole Schlichting was half legend and half watchword among both criminals and bounty hunters. Virtually nothing was known of her: not her face, her voice, her origins, her associates, or where she currently made her home. She was a ghost, able to find and get to her target through even the tightest security. She'd killed dozens or hundreds or thousands, depending on which rumors you believed. She was smart, dependable, ruthless, and she never, ever—

"And she never misses," I murmured. "She told me that herself. *Damn* it all. And I never put it together." I focused again on Muninn. "You're absolutely sure it's her? I thought no one knew what she looks like."

"*We* do," Muninn said, "Rather, the Patthaaunuth do. And yes, you were seen with her after her near-miss on Vesperin," He was eyeing me curiously, I noted, as if wondering at my reaction to her name.

Maybe he didn't put as much stock in the rumors as the rest

of us. Or maybe the Path had come to an agreement with her, and as one of their agents Muninn had that same immunity.

Immunity . . .

"Your part of the bargain was to bring her to Niskea?" Nask asked.

With an effort I dragged my mind away from Nicole Schlichting and her unerring eye. "Our part was to take her wherever she or Cherno wanted," I said. "So far our travels all seem pretty random, or at least unfocused."

"Not to the Yellowdune ruins in Niskea's northern continent?" he pressed.

"Actually—" I broke off as a minor mystery suddenly came clear. "*That's* why you're here, isn't it?" I said. "You're overseeing the Path search of Yellowdune for the other end of your portal."

"It seemed to me that finding that end of our Janus would be the quickest way to retrieve our stolen property," Nask said.

"Definitely worth trying," I agreed. "That explains all the tension at Lucias Four, too. You're hitting as many planets on your list as you have resources for."

"Indeed." Nask offered a faint smile. "I should perhaps mention that your recent visit there has damaged Arbitor Uvif's standing considerably."

"That was not my intent," I assured him. "All I wanted was the StarrComm facility. If I'd known you had such a tight lock on the planet I'd have chosen somewhere else."

"No apologies needed," he said. "Uvif has always had a higher opinion of himself than he merits. But you speak of our list. I assume the Icarus Group has a similar list of their own?"

"I'm sure they do," I said. "So far they haven't shared it with us. Our current list came from some fast research by Gaheen's people after we told Cherno the same thing. *Mostly* the same thing, anyway."

"Mostly?"

"He wanted us to activate the portal. I told him it could only be activated from the other half of the dyad."

Nask looked up at Muninn. "Our understanding of the physics was that the portals in a Janus dyad were identical."

"As far as I know, they are," I agreed. "But Selene pitched him an impressive song and dance about master/slave tech, and Cherno didn't really have a choice but to accept it."

"Why would she do that?" Nask said.

I looked him straight in the eye. "Because she smelled your scent inside," I said. "We've known Cherno stole it from you since the beginning of this job. That's why we've been stalling him off."

"Because you care so much about the Patthaaunuth and Patthaaunuth possessions?" Muninn sneered.

"In truth, he does," Nask said thoughtfully. "Within his personal parameters of fairness and justice. Where then does that leave us?"

I focused on the medical wraparound. Horribly injured during Cherno's bloody hijacking, possibly having skated very close to death, Nask was nevertheless here overseeing his people's efforts to find the other end of their stolen portal. Or, if that didn't work, to maybe find a new and unrelated one they could call their own.

Maybe even a portal like the original Icarus.

"Tell me how Jordan McKell found the original portal," I said. "I assume you know."

"Of course I know," Nask said. "Don't you?"

"As you pointed out earlier, I'm hardly at the top of the group's pecking order," I said. "Let's start with where they found it."

Nask hesitated, then gave a small shrug. "It can hardly be considered a secret anymore. An archeological group found it in a set of ruins on Meima."

"The Trandosh dig, I assume," I said, nodding. That particular set of ruins were midway down Cherno's list.

"Yes," Nask confirmed. "I'm told they originally thought it to be a stardrive that would outstrip even the Talariac's capabilities. Only later did they realize its true nature."

"And were probably as flummoxed by it as you were."

"The Patthaaunuth already had some inklings," he said evasively. "Why do you ask?"

"Curiosity," I said. "I hate working on a puzzle when I know someone's got some of the pieces in his pocket."

"As you seem to also have," Nask said. "Would you care to share them with me?"

"As my father used to say, *Speculation is like a pleasant aroma you can't quite pin down and that nine times out of ten will lead you in the wrong direction.*"

"Very true," Nask said. "Just the same, I would like to hear it."

"Oh, come on—let's be sporting about this," I chided. "You've got the same data I do, and a hell of a lot more resources."

"You have the Icarus Group."

"*When* they're willing to talk to me," I said. "Which is usually only when they need something."

Muninn took a step toward me. "Roarke—"

"That's all right, Muninn," Nask said. "Mr. Roarke is right to be discreet. I also genuinely believe he would prefer the Patthaaunuth have the portal than the criminals Gaheen and Cherno."

"I would," I confirmed, a swirl of thoughts and plans joining all the speculation already whizzing around my brain. "In fact, I'll go further. If you'll grant me a favor, I'll do everything in my power to get Cherno's portal back to you."

"You said he'd offered it to the Icarus Group," Nask said.

"So he did," I said. "Like I said, let's be sporting."

Again, the room filled with silence as the Patth sub-director and his Expediter studied me. "Very well," Nask said at last. "I accept. What is this favor?"

I took a careful breath. "I need a million commarks."

I hadn't yet had a chance to see Muninn truly surprised. The facial expression alone was worth the price of admission. "A million—? Are you out of your *mind*?"

"Agreed," Nask said calmly.

Muninn looked down at him, treating me to a nice reprise of the facial show. "Sub-Director—"

"Mr. Roarke isn't betraying his people for money," Nask said, his eyes on me. "Whatever this need, it will be connected to his promise."

"And if all that high-minded talk of fairness was just smoke rings?" Muninn persisted. "And there are protocols that need to be followed for transferring a sum that large."

"As for the first, remind me to someday tell you about Brandywine," Nask said. "As for the second, there will be no questions. You'll draw the necessary bank checks from my personal account before Mr. Roarke leaves the *Odinn*. Do understand, Mr. Roarke, that I don't particularly like humans in general or you in particular."

"I feel the same way toward you and the Patth," I said evenly. "But I think there are some areas where we can find common ground. Brandywine was one. This is another."

"We shall soon find out," Nask said.

"We shall," I agreed. "One last thing. Do you have a mail drop or other number in case I need to contact you?"

"If there's need for communication, Sub-Director Nask will contact *you*," Muninn put in.

"And if Sub-Director Nask doesn't realize we need to talk?" I asked.

"Roarke—"

"Calmness, Muninn," Nask interrupted mildly. "Mr. Roarke is right. You can call this number, and the message will get to me." He rattled off the standard eighteen digits of a StarrComm number. "I trust you won't need to write that down?"

"No, sir, I've got it," I assured him. Years of memorizing StarrComm contact information for people who also didn't want such things written down had honed my memory skills considerably. "Thank you."

"I'll expect to hear from you in due time," Nask said. "Until then, best of fortune in your hunt. Muninn, please escort him back to the Badlands and his ship."

"Thank you in turn, Sub-Director," I said, giving him a small bow. "I wish you a speedy recovery."

"Thank you," Nask said. "And may we exact an equally speedy vengeance upon those who murdered my people."

I swallowed. "Yes. Indeed."

My biggest fear on the way down was that Nask would call ahead and order Huginn to do something vague but nasty with Selene, if only to safeguard the million commarks now tucked away in my wallet. To my relief, I arrived at the *Ruth* to find Selene already aboard and Huginn long gone.

"How is Sub-Director Nask?" she asked after we'd both expressed our relief that the other was unharmed and retreated to the dayroom.

"Banged up pretty badly," I said, wincing at the memory. "He was apparently aboard the transport when Cherno's men hit it, and only survived because they thought he was already dead. I'll have to remember to get that whole story next time we meet." I cocked an eyebrow at her. "You knew it was Nask, didn't you? You smelled him on Huginn and Muninn."

She nodded. "I didn't want them to know I could do that." Her pupils went rueful. "And I knew that if Nask was asking for you, and if they were Expediters, there was probably no way to get out of it."

"True on all counts," I agreed. "Though I spent several bad

minutes after recognizing the *Odinn* wondering if Nask was dead
and his successor was looking for a scapegoat. I trust you got
through to the admiral?"

"I did," she said. "And Huginn kept his word about letting
me make the call in privacy."

"Given the Patth ability to tap into StarrComm's system,
not sure how much of a sacrifice that was on his part," I said.
"Okay. Go."

"The admiral is not at all happy with how this is going,"
Selene said. "He furthermore pointed out that once Cherno gets
the portal working he has no reason to keep us alive."

"Known that one for a while," I agreed. "Just means we need
to keep him needing us until we're ready to bail."

"That was what I told him," Selene said. "I also told him
about Cherno's six-week timeline and suggested he try to find a
likely target for Nikki and figure out where that target would be
at that time. That might narrow down the possibilities."

"Sounds reasonable," I said. "Especially since her half-million
commark fee puts her skills out of reach of most locals. Someone
big or famous or powerful, then."

"That was the admiral's conclusion, too," Selene said. "He
also warned that even if her fee eliminates local politicians or
troublemakers the potential target list will likely be longer than
the roster of possibilities for Cherno's mystery planet. But he
promised to try."

"Good," I said. "Speaking of mysteries, Muninn also told me
that our friend Piper is in fact Nicole Schlichting."

Selene's pupils went wide with surprise and dread. "*The* Nicole
Schlichting?"

"That's what he says," I said. "Now that I think about it, I
really ought to have picked up on it earlier. The half-million
commark fee, the never-miss boast—they should have clued me
in that we weren't talking about a run-of-the-road assassin."

"And the part about not targeting people who've hired her?"

I shrugged. "That was a new one on me, but why not? It's also
not the sort of thing you talk about in public. I'm pretty sure
her clients and prospective clients are fully aware of it, though."

"Very likely," Selene said, some of the anxiety in her pupils
giving way to thoughtfulness. "But then why tell you?"

"Why let us see her face in the first place?" I countered.

"Why offer me details about her that might help me figure out who she is? I don't have answers to any of those."

"And why is an Expediter able to identify her when InterSpiral Law Enforcement can't?"

"All good questions," I agreed. "Hopefully, we'll be able to get some answers down the road."

"Yes," Selene murmured. "Though you know, that half-million commark protection guarantee might not be a bad idea. Announcing that such a payment will keep a person safe from her would probably bring in billions from people with rich enemies and bad consciences."

"True," I said. "On the other hand, that half million isn't just a retainer. You have to also hire her to kill someone."

"People with bad consciences usually have someone they want dead."

"I suppose," I conceded. "Maybe she's saving a public announcement and cash-grab for her retirement party. Anything else from the admiral?"

"He gave me the Icarus Group's list of ruins that might match those of the Erymant Temple." Pulling out her info pad, she handed it over. "Tell me what you see."

I ran my eye down the list. Niskea, Kiva, Jondervais, Lucias Four . . .

I frowned, running it again. Niskea, Kiva, Jondervais, Lucias Four . . .

I looked up at Selene. "Meima," I said. "It's on Cherno's list, but not the admiral's."

"I noticed that, too," Selene said. "An accidental oversight, do you think?"

I snorted. "With detail-obsessive Admiral Sir Graym-Barker? Not likely." I handed the info pad back. "Even more interestingly, Nask told me that the Icarus—McKell's original portal—was discovered in a dig on Meima. Coincidence?"

"With alien portals? Not likely," Selene said, a touch of humor in her pupils. "Maybe that's the reason the admiral left Meima off the list. Because they already found a portal there."

"Maybe," I said. "On the other hand, there were two Geminis on Fidelio, and right next to each other, too. Who says there can't be two on Meima?"

"True," Selene said, watching me closely as the humor faded

from her pupils. "But Geminis are single-route portals. The Icarus is full-range. If the—what do we call them, Gregory, the ones who built the portals? We have to call them *something*."

"I suppose we could go with *the Builders*," I said. "Or we could try for something catchier, like maybe the *Portalines*?"

"Or the *Icari*?"

I mentally tasted the word. Not only was it catchy and classical sounding, but McKell would probably hate it. "Sounds good," I said. "Icari it is."

"All right," Selene said. "So if the Icari had a full-range portal already there, why would they also need a Gemini?"

"Good question," I agreed. "Maybe *because* the Geminis are single-routes?"

Some puzzlement rose into her pupils. "I don't follow."

"Not sure I do, either," I conceded. "But here's how I see it."

I paused, frowning, as my phone vibed. Who on Niskea even had my number? I keyed it on. "Roarke."

"This is Nikki," Nikki's familiar voice came.

I scowled. No, not just *Nikki. Nicole Schlichting.*

But that was a conversation for another day. "Hi," I said as casually as I could. "How's the shopping trip going?"

"It's going fine," she said. "I just called to tell you I'm going to be longer than I originally expected."

"How much longer?"

"Possibly as long as five days."

I hissed silently. Her three-day side trip had already threatened to gouge a big divot out of our already tight schedule. Throwing in two more days would shred it completely.

Unless I was right about Meima, which would make the delay mostly irrelevant. But again, a conversation for another day. "You sure you can't get what you need somewhere else?"

"Like I told you earlier, an artist like Bonno can take up to five days for a custom job," she said. "Maybe even six, but probably only five. I just called to say this would be a good time for you to go do your touristing bit."

"I thought you wanted us to stay here."

"That was before Bonno decided it would be five days," she said with exaggerated patience. "Like I said, an artist. Just be back before the reservation runs out on the pad or you'll lose it."

"Understood," I said. "Any good restaurants to recommend?"

"Do I look like a food critic?" she shot back. "Just be back in five or you'll buy yourselves a little slice of barbequed hell."

"Got it," I said. "We'll see you soon."

"Count on it," she said. The phone made a double click and went dead.

I lowered the phone and looked at Selene. "You heard?"

She nodded. "She said that Bonno could take up to five days for the job."

"Right."

"But before she left, she told us *Franck* never needs more than *three* days."

"Right again," I said. "So: new names and new numbers. Thoughts?"

"I think it's obvious," Selene said quietly. "She's trying to send us a message."

I nodded. "Which means she's in trouble."

"Yes," Selene said. "And needs us to come rescue her."

CHAPTER TWELVE

The first step in any target hunt was to put the clues together. This was no different, I decided, except that in this case the person in question *wanted* to be found.

"Let's start with the names," I told Selene as we pulled out our info pads. "We've got *Franck* and *Bonno*. See if you can find anyone in the Rosselgang City population listings who could conceivably be given those nicknames."

"You mean like *Franckbonno*?" she asked, working at the pad.

"Exactly," I said. "Remembering that whoever might have been listening in on her side of the conversation doesn't know we know the *Franck* part."

"So then maybe *Bonno Franck*?"

"Yes, but probably not that obvious," I said, keying in my own search to focus on the other hints Nikki had fed us.

I wasn't expecting much from the three day/five day inconsistency. There'd been no reason for Nikki to give us an incorrect or clue-heavy number before she left the *Ruth*, and whoever was with her right now would presumably have heard the latter number, so she probably couldn't do anything with that. The *maybe even six* comment, though, had possibilities.

First check was a city calendar to see if anything special was happening in six days. I got the info pad sorting the list from

most publicized to least, then started a check of every restaurant, café, or street stand that featured human-style barbeque.
I'd delivered that cue straight onto her plate, and someone with
Nikki's intelligence would hardly have failed to pick it up and
run with it.

"I think I may have it," Selene spoke up. "What do you think
of *Francksibon Picker*?"

"I think that parents who gave a child a name like that ought
to be prosecuted," I said, running through the possibilities. Both
Franck and *Bonno* would work as a nickname for a name like
that. "It's also exactly the sort of jawbreaker that no one in his
right mind would use in daily conversation if there was something easier available. Quick question: Can you check and see
how many Badlands given names end in -*bon*?"

"Looks like quite a few of them," she said, tapping her pad.
"There are also several families whose names begin with *Bon*."

"So calling him Bonno wouldn't have been distinctive enough
to raise any eyebrows among her captors," I concluded. "I think
we may have a winner."

"Maybe," Selene cautioned. "The problem is that there are
five Francksibons listed."

"You're kidding. *Five* of them?"

"Could be a family name," Selene offered.

"Or they're all named after some famous criminal we've never
heard of," I said. "Still wouldn't burden a dog with a name like
that. Any of the five identified as gunsmiths?"

"Did she say her contact was a gunsmith?" Selene asked, her
pupils frowning. "I never heard that."

"She didn't, but I doubt she came here for a packet of candy
curls," I pointed out. "What else could he be except a gunsmith?"

"A security expert?" Selene suggested. "A break/enter tool-
maker? An explosives maker?"

"Okay, fine—there are other options," I conceded. "Let's start
with gunsmith anyway."

"None of them are listed with that specialty," Selene said.
"One is listed as a pawnshop owner, one buys real estate, one
runs a restaurant, and the other two aren't connected to any
particular business."

"What kind of restaurant?"

"A Najiki pondo."

I scowled. About as far from human-style food as you could get.

And, of course, even criminals secure inside a criminal enclave weren't stupid enough to openly advertise their skill at blowing things up. "New tack. Any of their addresses have a six in them?"

She worked at the pad. "No," she said. "But two of the addresses have threes."

I shook my head. "No good. There was no reason for Nikki to have folded a clue into the number of days she originally gave us."

"Unless she was already anticipating trouble."

"Well...yeah, I suppose," I said, scowling at my own pad. "Which then begs the question of why she would want to come here in the first place. Okay, let's try this. Here's a map of all the barbeque places in the Badlands. See if any of the Francksibons are within six blocks of any of them."

"All right," she said, peering at the map I'd sent and getting to work. "But I think it begs more than one question."

"Such as?"

"Who in the Badlands has suddenly decided to bother her?" Selene asked. "Before she left the *Ruth* she seemed comfortable with the idea of going outside. Furthermore, her use of a nickname for Picker suggests she knows him reasonably well."

"I assume you're adding her scent during that last conversation into that calculation?"

"Yes, of course," she said, as if it was obvious. Which it probably was. "She was very calm. And if someone *is* threatening her, why is she still able to call us without interference?"

"And without a very specific script in front of her," I said, nodding. "Because the phrasing, tone, and cadence matched the way she's been talking the whole trip."

"Plus there's the barbeque reference."

"Plus that," I agreed. "Anything?"

"I don't know," she said, her pupils looking puzzled as she gazed at her pad. "The Picker pawnshop is close to one of the street carts. But the carts move every day, so I'm not sure that does anything for us."

"Okay," I said slowly. "But most of the street carts I've seen don't move all that much. In fact, a lot of them are required by local regs to stick to the same corner or at least stay on the same street."

"Yes, they are," Selene said, with a sudden cautious enthusiasm as she tackled her pad again. "And if this cart stays on the same street..."

She looked up at me, her pupils clear and determined. "That would put it between five and six blocks from the Francksibon Picker pawnshop."

"Really," I said, pulling up a local map. "Mark it for me, will you?"

The two marks appeared on my pad, currently five blocks apart but with the potential to be six. "Looks like we have a winner. So next question is, what do we do about it?"

"What do you mean?" Selene asked, her pupils frowning. "We rescue her, don't we?"

"That's certainly what Gaheen and Cherno would want us to do," I agreed. "My question was, why us?"

"Why *not* us?" Selene countered.

"Lots of reasons," I said. "Start with the fact that Nikki's an assassin. On a lot of Commonwealth worlds, as you yourself pointed out once, just the fact that we're carting her around would tag us as accomplices."

I waved a hand to take in the area around us. "Now, there are probably a lot of people in the Badlands who wouldn't care about that, especially since they're more or less immune from trouble from the badgemen in here. So why didn't she call one of them for help?"

"Maybe she did," Selene said. "Maybe they all turned her down."

"Given the size of the money stack she can offer?" I shook my head. "Unlikely."

"Then it's because she doesn't trust any of them."

"Yeah, that's where I landed, too," I said grimly. "Which leads to the unpleasant possibility that someone's ready to offer more for her skin than she can outbid."

"That would have to be a *lot* of money," Selene pointed out. "At half a million per job, even if she only does one a year—"

"Like I said: a money stack," I agreed. "So who could offer more than her nest egg is worth?"

"And why does she think we would turn it down?" Selene added. "Does she think we're too honorable to betray her?"

"More likely she thinks we won't know about the offer because we won't get the memo," I said, pulling out my phone and keying for bounty hunter notices.

Unfortunately, all the stories about the Badlands and its magnet effect for the scum of the Spiral were right. There were at least fifty pending notices that named Niskea and Rosselgang City. I glanced down the list, but didn't spot Nikki's name. "Do me a favor and sift through this after you lift," I said, standing up and keying the list over to her. "See if you can find something that connects to our wayward passenger."

"Wait a minute," she said. "I'm leaving? I thought I was going with you."

"I wish you were," I said. "It would make finding Nikki a whole lot easier. But if that call was being listened in on, they might get suspicious if we don't take her up on her suggestion to go touristing. So you're going to head up and out, do circles around Niskea for a couple-three hours, then come back. If we're lucky, that'll be long enough for me to find her and spring her from whatever vultures are perched over her."

"And if it isn't?"

"Let's just hope it is," I said. "As my father used to say, *Always look on the bright side of life except when it ruins your night vision.* Give me five minutes to get off the ship, then call control and take the first lift slot they've got. I'll wait inside the south gate until you're off, then head out."

"How are you going to get off without them seeing you?"

"If they've got eyes all around the *Ruth*, I can't," I said. "I'm hoping that when Nikki said they were monitoring spaceport operations she meant someone was just watching the electronics from a distance. Regardless, I'll just have to risk it."

"And if there are people waiting outside the fence for you?" she persisted, her pupils showing nervousness. "You won't have any Expediters around this time to protect you."

"Unless Nask decided to have one of them keep me on a short leash," I pointed out. "It would be a very Patth thing to do."

"But you won't know if you have backup until you need it."

"There's that," I admitted. "But I don't see what else we can do. Anyway, I know how to disappear into a crowd. And it's easier alone than if you were with me."

"I know," she murmured, reaching up to touch her white hair. "All right, if you think it's best."

"I don't think it's *best*, but I think it's the hand we've got to play," I said. "I'll be okay."

"I know," she said again, her pupils about as unenthusiastic as I'd ever seen them. "Please be careful."

"I will," I said, heading for the dayroom hatch. "And watch the approach when you come back. The crosswinds make landing kind of tricky."

Sixteen minutes later, I stood just inside the spaceport's south gate and watched as the *Ruth* roared its way into the sky.

I waited until it had disappeared beyond the sprinkle of high clouds. Then, trying to convince myself this was of course going to go smoothly, I passed the operations office—this one had a stone-faced human at the desk instead of an Ulkomaal—and once again headed into the Badlands.

After the reception Selene and I had gotten on our last jaunt outside the perimeter fence, I was expecting that trouble would start gathering around me within the first block. To my mild surprise, no one at this end of town seemed to be paying any particular attention to me whatsoever. Certainly there were no lingering looks, surreptitious phone calls, or people fingering weapons. Either the denizens in this part of the Badlands were less curious or lethal toward strangers, or else word of what happened to the last batch of toughs had made it this far and no one wanted to volunteer for the encore performance.

The barbeque street cart Selene had tagged was about three blocks south of me and two blocks east, with the pawnshop that was my ultimate goal two more blocks south and one west. Assuming that Nikki had gone straight to meet Picker there was no reason for her to have made a point of noticing a barbeque cart two blocks off her direct path. That suggested that the cart owner might be another acquaintance, possibly someone who could give me more information.

Detours through potentially hostile territory could be dangerous. But then, so could diving into trouble with a shortage of hard intel. I flipped a mental coin as I hit the third block, weighed the risks, and turned east.

The street was long and wide, clearly one of the Badlands' major thoroughfares, with at least eight street carts spaced out along the relevant two-block section. I started along the walkway, keeping my neutral, minding-my-own-business expression in place and watching for the sign that would mark my goal. I passed a stir-fry cart, then a gelato vendor, spotted the barbeque cart's sign up ahead—

"*Roarke?*" a surprised voice came from behind me.

I turned. Standing there, looking as astonished as he sounded, was Trent.

In retrospect, it shouldn't have been a surprise. Selene had already told me she'd picked up his scent.

But that was before we'd been attacked, watched a pair of Expediters take out our attackers, had an awkward conversation with Nask, and been tasked with rescuing our murderous passenger. Frankly, I'd forgotten about Trent.

"I thought it was you, but I didn't believe it," he continued. "What in Salmon Hill are you doing here?"

"Being a tourist, of course," I said. "I read somewhere that the Badlands were one of the great attractions of the Spiral."

"If you mean they attract scum, you're right," he said, his surprise giving way to a knowing smile. "You sly and clever dog. You're hunting again, aren't you? Who's your target?"

"No, really," I assured him. "Well, okay, I'm here to do some recon. But I don't have a target."

"In that case, you are the luckiest jackdaw I've ever met," he said, his knowing look turning into cheerful anticipation. "I've got a target—a *huge* one—and I could really use your help. You in?"

"Really, I can't—"

"You, me, and two other hunters," he cut me off. "One target, known location, practically nonexistent security."

"Except the security of being in a place that doesn't like hunters."

"One reason I could really use a fourth on this one," Trent said. "Bounty is two million, which works out to half a mil for you. What do you say?"

"I say it's very tempting," I agreed, thinking fast. Whatever trouble Nikki was in, having three other hunters with me could make the extraction a whole lot easier. Assuming, of course, I could keep Trent and his buddies from figuring out who they were helping me spring.

As my father used to say, *There are two ways of keeping people in the dark: pointing the light somewhere else or blasting it straight into their eyes.* "But I need to finish my own sweep first," I continued. "Who's your target, and when are you planning to move on him?"

"On *her*," Trent corrected. "And brace yourself. The target is Nicole Schlichting."

I'd been prepared to act surprised with whatever name Trent dropped. In this case, I didn't have to act at all. "You're kidding," I said. "You talking about *the* Nicole Schlichting? The assassin?"

"The one and only," he assured me. "You're next going to ask who in hell puts out bounty notices on assassins. Answer: I don't know, and I don't care. He pays well; end of story."

"He certainly does," I said, grinding my teeth. So much for getting Trent to help me rescue her.

Unless we could spring her from her current trouble, and then she and I could manage a double-reverse and get her away from Trent?

I gave a silent sigh. Against Trent alone, maybe. Against Trent plus two other hunters, not a chance. Nothing I could do now except short-circuit this whole thing, and the faster the better.

Fortunately, I knew exactly how to do that.

"Well, under the circumstances, I think my recon can wait," I said. "You said you know where she is?"

"Mostly," he said. "We've got it narrowed to a single block a couple of streets south of here." He pointed behind me and across the street at a seedy-looking taverno. "I was just talking with Beeks and Jingo about how to narrow that down when I spotted you through the window. Come on, let's see if their search has come up with anything."

We crossed the street and made our way back and into the taverno. The main seating area was only sparsely occupied, but apparently even that level of privacy wasn't good enough for Trent. Instead, he led me upstairs to a small private room with a single door, two small round tables with four chairs each, and a sidebar with several bottles of beer and a couple of unused glasses. The wall had a single wide window looking out onto the street, presumably the one Trent had spotted me through.

There were two large men seated at one of the tables as we entered, a glass of beer in front of each of them. Their eyes followed me as I made my way to the empty chair Trent gestured me to. "This is Roarke," Trent told them as he sat down at the remaining chair, where another half-full beer glass awaited him. "This is Beeks; that's Jingo. Beeks, get him a beer, would you?"

"Sure," Beeks said, giving me a speculative look as he stood up and crossed to the sidebar. He picked up one of the bottles and one of the glasses and started pouring.

And with one-third of my opposition now standing with his back to me, it was time to make my move. I looked idly out the window and let myself stiffen. "What the—?"

"What?" Trent demanded, half standing up to look past Jingo's shoulder. Jingo, with his back to the window, had to turn all the way around in order to see.

"That woman across the street," I said, pointing with my left hand. "That's Schlichting,"

And in that moment of misfocused attention, I neatly flipped the three knockout pills I'd surreptitiously pulled from their hiding place into the three glasses of beer sitting momentarily unattended on the table.

"You're kidding," Beeks said, my beer glass still gripped in his hand. "*That's* Schlichting?"

"How would you even know?" Jingo asked suspiciously. "No one's ever seen her face."

"Trust me," I said. "Maybe *we* haven't seen her face. But the Patth have."

"Who says?" Jingo demanded.

"Like I said: the Patth," I said. "I was aboard one of their ships not two hours ago. They showed me her picture and some video clips."

"*Who* showed you her picture?" Trent asked. "Which Patth?"

"No, wait a minute," I said, letting myself wilt. "False alarm— it's not her. Her gait is wrong."

"Her *gait*?" Beeks echoed. "What is she, a racehorse?"

"And what are you, her trainer?" Jingo added, clearly impressed by his own wit.

"Which Patth?" Trent repeated, more insistently this time.

"I told you, they showed me videos—"

"*Which Patth?*"

Unfortunately, there was no way out of it. "His name is Sub-Director Nask," I said. "Master of the ship *Odinn*. Why, is that important?"

He eyed me a moment, then gave a small shrug. "It isn't," he said. "I was just curious. Ah," he added as Beeks set my glass in front of me and resumed his seat. "So. All the more reason to be glad I spotted you. We had a vague idea what she looked like, but it wasn't nearly definitive enough. We were going to have to let her make the first move, and hope we survived it. Now that you know what she looks like, we've got both the numbers *and* the initiative."

He lifted his glass. "A toast, gentlemen. To Lady Luck for setting up our target and for sending Roarke our way. May she continue to smile on us."

We all raised our glasses. "To Lady Luck," we said in unison, and drank.

I had set my glass down and was preparing to launch into a long-winded scheme for getting to Nikki when the world suddenly went dark.

CHAPTER THIRTEEN

I awoke in stages, the first being the vague awareness that I was conscious, the second being that the side of my head was pressed against a hard surface, the third being that that same part of my head hurt.

The fourth stage was gaining enough awareness to wonder what the hell had just happened.

Carefully, I opened my eyes. I was still in the same private taverno room I'd started in, with the same round table and the same smell of beer.

And with the same companions.

It was like a scene from some community service video warning against the hazards of excessive alcohol and drugs. Trent, Beeks, and Jingo were passed out in their chairs, their heads resting sideways on the table just as mine had been. My first fear was that they were dead, but then I spotted the slow torso rhythms that showed they were still breathing. I gazed at them for a minute, and only then did it occur to me to look at my watch.

I'd been asleep for nearly twenty minutes.

I looked at Trent again, taking a few deep breaths to clear the cobwebs out of my lungs and hopefully my brain. Clearly, just as I'd drugged them, they'd also drugged me.

The only thing that had saved me was that my knockout pills lasted longer than theirs.

I frowned, rubbing the side of my head as I looked at the three sleeping beauties. Okay, so I'd been drugged. Beeks had done the deed, but I couldn't imagine he would do such a thing on his own initiative.

So why would Trent want to drug me?

Because he didn't want to split the bounty on Nikki? Ridiculous. He was the one who'd called me in on this. Furthermore, if he knew even vaguely where Nikki was he would surely have realized I was going the wrong direction. All he needed to do was let me stride off into the sunset, and he'd have been rid of me.

Maybe it would make sense after the rest of my drug-induced stupor went away. Somehow, I doubted it.

But whether it did or not, I didn't have the time right now to pick at it. Nikki was in trouble, and I'd just lost half an hour out of whatever window there was to get her out of it.

Speaking of windows...

Carefully, trying to expose myself as little as I could, I sidled over to the window and took a long look outside. If Trent had watchers waiting down there for the signal to come haul my carcass away, I didn't see them.

But whether they were there or not, it was time to go. Checking to make sure my plasmic was still in its concealed holster—it was, and the power pack was still in place—I headed out the door and down the stairs. The main taverno room had a few more patrons than had been there earlier, and I had a couple of tense moments as I crossed to the exit. But no one did anything more than give me wary looks, and a moment later I was back on the street.

My earlier plan had been to check out the barbeque street cart before approaching Picker's pawnshop. But with that lost half hour, and a lot of customers now lined up at the cart, I decided it would have to be the direct approach instead. I headed south again, trying to watch everywhere at once, and finally came in sight of my destination.

I'd looked for watchers outside Trent's taverno and hadn't seen any. The reason for that now seemed obvious: Every single one of them had apparently taken up posts here on Picker's street.

I studied their stakeout pattern as I walked casually down the street toward the pawnshop, and quickly realized that my first assumption had been wrong. These weren't more of Trent's men and women, who would have set up an interlocking web around their target. These were simply a collection of bounty hunters, each working independently, which meant each was in conflict with the others as they jockeyed for the best spots or sat off in the rear in hopes of snatching Nikki from whoever got to her first.

There were a lot of problems with a setup like that. But the biggest and most useful, at least to me, was that there was no effort at mutual support. If I looked hard enough, I should be able to find someone who was completely out of view of all the others.

I was halfway down the first block when I spotted him.

He was a big man, with blond hair and beard and what looked to be a permanent scowl, the latter likely being the reason for his current solitude. He'd planted himself beneath an alley-side window of the building next door to Picker's, clearly expecting Nikki to find a way across and then sneak down the side of that building while everyone else was focused on the pawnshop.

Not a bad strategy, actually. I'd also noticed the pipe bridge that linked the two rooftops as I came down the street, a pathway that could theoretically be used to travel between them. It would be tricky to keep any of the hunters below from spotting such a move, but I had no doubt Nikki could pull it off.

I continued down the street, noting the overall sense of tension increasing with every step I took toward the pawnshop door. I reached it and passed without pause or even a glance, feeling the tension take a corresponding dive. Despite the larger, block-wide cordon, it was clear that some of them, at least, had narrowed it down to the pawnshop.

Which was fine with me. The more the hunters concentrated on the pawnshop, the less they'd be looking in all the other directions.

I made my way to the end of the street and turned the corner. More hunters loitered on this side of the block, probably focused on the building that backed up behind the pawnshop. I continued past without looking at them, and again turned at the next street. There were a couple of hunters here, but since this side featured an entirely different group of buildings, there wasn't a lot of point in guarding it, though there might be a way for Nikki to get through to the building that backed up to Picker's. Still, I suspected these particular hunters would probably have preferred to take up station in the alley if Scowly hadn't planted himself there first.

With luck, that spot might yet become available.

I continued to the alley and turned into it, walking straight into what was probably Scowly's best glare. "Butt out," he growled as soon as I was close enough for him to deliver a warning without raising his voice enough to attract attention. "Butt out, or be sorry."

"You think I *want* to be here?" I growled back, starting to pull out my info pad. "I was told to give you the latest from the boss."

"What boss?" he retorted. "I work alone." He lifted the edge of his jacket to show his holstered Libra Gold 4mm. "And take your hand off that thing."

"It's just an info pad," I said, coming to an awkward halt and letting my pad slide back into its pouch. "You're not—? Sorry, I thought you were with us. My mistake."

I turned and started to retrace my steps back toward the alley mouth, stroking my left thumbnail to activate the mirror there and holding it where I could see behind me. Scowly might be proudly independent, but no hunter with any brains let fresh intel just walk away from him.

He didn't. He came up behind me with a speed and silence that were particularly impressive given his size. "What's your hurry?" he muttered practically in my ear as his hand closed around my arm. "I'll just take that—"

His threat broke off into an agonized squeak as I jabbed my elbow into his solar plexus. The impact loosened his grip on my arm; spinning on my heel, I turned to face him and slammed my fist into his throat. He staggered a couple of steps backward...

And to my surprise and dismay, he shook his head as if clearing it, rubbed briefly where my elbow and fist had tried to dent him, and started forward again.

My first and probably smartest instinct was to turn and run. He couldn't shoot me without the risk of the noise alerting his quarry and the other hunters, and if he chased me too far he would lose this prime spot.

But then I thought about Selene, and what she would say if I left Nikki twisting slowly in the wind.

Which was a puzzle all in itself. Selene didn't like Nikki—that much was painfully obvious. At the same time, it was equally clear that she didn't like the thought of abandoning even an assassin to the dregs of the hunter community.

Again, a conversation for another day. In the meantime, Scowly was striding purposefully toward me, and unless I did something fast there might not be any other days for all these conversations that kept stacking up. "Hold it," I snapped, snatching out my plasmic and holding it uncertainly in front of me.

Despite his obvious pain, Scowly managed a smile. Like all experienced hunters, he was good at reading people, and he could tell that I wasn't prepared to shoot him down in cold blood. I started to back away; he compensated by picking up speed. He stretched out his hand as he reached me, intent on grabbing the plasmic. I countered by smoothly drawing it back and to my right, wondering if he would recognize that I was deliberately drawing him out of position.

He didn't, or if he did it didn't penetrate his angry resolve fast enough. His grasping fingers were nearly to the weapon—

And as they closed over the muzzle I let go, spun to my left on my right heel, and stuck my left leg out behind me directly in his path.

If he'd been going slower he might have been able to dodge the leg sweep. But with his speed and his single-minded fixation on disarming me before I fired he didn't have a chance. His shin hit the back of my leg, and he had just enough time to let out a strangled gasp before he fell face-first onto the pavement. He put out both hands, trying to stop his fall, and mostly succeeded, even managing to keep hold of his stolen plasmic. He twisted around onto his back as I regained my own balance and threw myself at him, wasting his last precious second trying to get the plasmic turned around in his big hands and aimed at me.

I was sailing through the air toward him in full belly-flop formation when he finally got the weapon in position and squeezed the trigger. He had just enough time to register that nothing had happened when I slammed down on top of him.

My elbow in his stomach hadn't knocked the wind out of him the way I'd hoped. My full body weight landing squarely on top of his torso did. He puffed out an agonized explosion of air, and into his wide-open mouth I popped one of my knockout pills.

He was still struggling to recover from my body slam when

the drug sent his eyes rolling upward, loosened his muscles, and sent him to dreamland.

Breathing hard, I climbed off him, untangled my plasmic from his limp fingers, and retrieved the power pack I'd ejected from the weapon just as he was grabbing it. A quick check of both ends of the alley to make sure I hadn't attracted unwelcome attention, and I tucked the weapon back out of sight.

My phone vibed in my pocket. Sifting through Scowly's pockets with one hand, I fished out my phone with the other and keyed it on. "That you?" I asked.

"Yes," Nikki's voice came back. "What the hell are you doing out there?"

"Clearing away some of the riffraff," I told her, frowning. There shouldn't be any way she could see me from Picker's building. Had she gotten free and somehow made her way across to the building beside me?

"And making enough noise doing it to wake up every badge-man in Rosselgang City," she retorted. "You've got a plasmic—next time just shoot him. It'll be a lot quieter."

"You're welcome," I growled. There was a folded paper in Scowly's inner pocket, and I pulled it out. "What are you doing wandering around? I thought you were a prisoner."

"Who told you *that*?"

"So the deeply coded phone message was just you having some fun?" I asked sarcastically as I unfolded the paper. "I assumed it meant you were in trouble and couldn't talk freely. My mistake."

"Oh, I'm in trouble, all right," she said. "But it's not as simple as that. Are you finished there?"

"Unless you want to complain about my rescue technique some more."

"Maybe later," she said. "Head back out the alley, turn right at the end, and take the first door. Beloi Apartments. I'll meet you inside."

I frowned. From Picker's shop, to the building overlooking the alley, to the apartment building on the next street over. Was the whole block honeycombed with secret tunnels? "Fine. I'll be right there."

"And make it snappy," she added. "Sooner or later, they're going to storm this place, and I'd just as soon not be here when that happens."

"Right," I said, grimacing as I unfolded the paper and saw what was on it. "I think I can second that."

The apartment building was unlocked. Resisting the urge to draw my plasmic before entering, I pulled open the door and went inside.

The entryway lights, which had probably never been any great shakes to begin with, were dim or out completely. It made for plenty of shadows, and I spotted Nikki lurking in one of them. She waited until I'd closed the door behind me, then moved in and locked it. "This way," she muttered, and led the way down a short corridor to a janitor's closet. Unlocking it, she went inside and rolled up the spill mat on the floor to reveal a trapdoor with a short flight of steps leading downward. We headed down into a basement area, a big one, with walls that were beyond the reach of our small flashlights.

"So this is how you got out of Picker's place?" I asked quietly as we headed across the floor. "Nice. Covers the whole block, I assume?"

"Yes," she said. "Been sealed since the original owners sold off the buildings about eighty years ago. Franck and his former partners started buying up the buildings twenty years ago and opening them up to the basement again."

"Handy."

"Secrets usually are."

We reached another stairway, she got the trapdoor above us open, and we headed up. Three minutes later, we were in a spacious workroom above Picker's pawnshop.

An older and rather corpulent man was waiting for us, an artistically designed but nonetheless very nasty-looking plasmic rifle pointed at me as I followed Nikki through the hidden doorway. "Mr. Picker, I presume," I said, inclining my head and holding out my hands to show they were empty. "Given the lack of reaction from my associate here I assume you're not the current threat?"

Picker grunted, his eyes flicking to Nikki. "He always this wordy?" he rumbled.

"He tends that way," Nikki agreed. "But right now, he's my best path out of here."

"If you say so," he said, lowering his plasmic a little but keeping it ready.

"I say so," Nikki said. "Nice of you to join us, Roarke."

"The pleasure's all yours," I said. "So I gather Mr. Picker is more of an ally than a jailer?"

"Who said anything about him being a jailer?"

"That's usually what's implied when someone wraps their call for help inside a lot of obscure language and vague clues," I growled. "You could have saved us a lot of time and effort if you'd just said everything in plain language."

"I couldn't," Nikki said. "Someone might have been listening in."

"Like Selene?"

"Like someone you might have been having a drink with," she said. "A hunter, or worse."

"What would be worse?"

"Never mind," she said. "That being said, it took you long enough to figure out the clues. You usually need luminous trail markers when you're on a hunt?"

"Oh, I don't know," I said. "If you subtract the half hour I spent sleeping off a Mickey Finn, I think I did pretty well."

I had the modest satisfaction of seeing her actually look surprised. "You were *drugged*? How? Where?"

"We can talk about that later," I said. "Right now, let's focus on the task at hand. Tell me about the immediate threat, and why exactly you dragged me here." I gestured to Picker and his rifle. "It's not like you needed the extra firepower."

"Of course I need it," Nikki said. "You expect Franck to open fire on his neighbors?"

"Ah," I said, nodding as it started to come clear. "Let me guess. My part was to charge to the rescue, all square-jawed and steely-eyed, so as to draw all that brooding attention out there. Then, while they were all focused on killing me, you'd slip out the back door?"

"Mostly," she said without any embarrassment I could detect. "Except that I assumed you were good enough to just lead them away and not die in the process."

"I'm flattered you think so highly of me," I growled. "But I can't help noticing that you were prepared in case I wasn't as good as you thought."

Her lips compressed briefly. "I had to consider all the possibilities. You understand."

"I suppose," I said. "I'll just point out that I can do an exceptionally fine diversion when I know that's what I'm being asked to do. Trying to play me doesn't gain you anything, and even costs you a little."

She inclined her head. "Point taken. I'll remember that in the future."

"Yes. About that future." Keeping my movements slow and nonthreatening, I pulled out the paper I'd taken from Scowly. "The hunters out there have a pretty good sketch of your face." I flipped it open and held it up in front of her. "They also have your name...Nicole."

For a moment the room was silent. I kept my eyes on Nikki, but also kept Picker at the edge of my vision. So far he seemed to be following Nikki's lead, but depending on how dark he thought she wanted to keep her secret it was possible he would take action on his own.

Apparently, Nikki thought so, too. Taking a deep breath, she made a calming twitch of her fingertips toward her friend. "Like I told you, it's *Nikki*," she corrected, her voice studiously neutral. "My parents are the only ones who ever called me Nicole. You really think this is a good sketch?"

"I think it captures you pretty well."

She shook her head and handed it back. "Not even close."

"Next time I'll call in an art appraiser." I said, clamping down on a sudden flash of anger. Her complete nonchalance at the deception she'd pulled was unbelievable. "You know, it would have been awfully handy to know from the beginning who exactly we were dealing with. But again, that's for later. Right now we need to figure out how to get us clear of the mousetrap out there. Any thoughts?"

"You already know we can get to any building on this block," she said. "That includes the café on the corner, the Beloi Apartments, a dress shop, a hardware store, and Franck's pawnshop downstairs."

"What was your plan assuming I was able to draw them off?"

"Get a wig and new clothing from the dress shop and slip out." She nodded toward the paper I was still holding. "That sketch may not be good, but it's unfortunately good enough."

"Agreed," I said, a slightly crazy plan starting to form in the back of my brain. If she couldn't *walk* out of here..."Any idea how many hunters we're facing? I counted nine on my way in, but those were the obvious ones."

"I'd say at least fifteen," she said. "Some more competent than others, of course."

"As is the way of things," I said. At least with Trent and his buddies snoozing away the afternoon we were three down from where that number might have been. "Can we get to the roof?"

"I don't know," Nikki said. "Franck?"

"There's an access hatch on the top of the Beloi," Picker said, frowning at me. "But it's four stories straight down, and the street's too wide for you to jump it."

"Not planning to jump," I assured him. "Okay. Let's take a look at that dress shop and see what we've got to work with."

"You have an idea," Nikki said, looking closely at me.

"I do." I gave her a tight smile. "As the fashion industry is fond of saying, we're going to create a new you."

The dress shop was across the alley from the apartment building Nikki had brought me in through. She led me back down to the common basement, up another hidden stairway into the shop's back room, and up the regular staff stairs to the second-floor stockroom. There, we found the treasure trove she'd mentioned: clothing, wigs, makeup kits—everything for the discerning woman navigating the criminal paradise that was the Badlands.

More important, at least to me, were a couple of damaged mannikins awaiting refurbishing. We collected what we needed, cleared off a sewing desk, and got to work.

"This doesn't have a chance in hell of working," Nikki warned as she struggled to untangle a bleached blond wig I'd found in a corner behind some bolts of cloth. "You know that, don't you?"

"As I already told you, I'm open to suggestions," I reminded her. "But I think you're selling the power of suggestion short. As my father used to say, *Assumptions are like body odor. Most people don't know when they're making them.*"

"Your father had a bizarre sense of humor."

"I prefer to think of it as delightfully unique."

"It's still bizarre."

"Probably," I said. "Tell me about the man who hired you to kill Horace Markelly."

"I can't talk about my clients."

"He isn't a client," I reminded her. "You turned him down, remember?"

She pursed her lips, forehead wrinkled in thought. "There are still limits. What do you want to know?"

"Mostly why the hell he's so hot on taking you out," I said. "The attack in Mikilias was bad enough, with four hunters competing for the dubious honor of trading shots with you. But whipping the Badlands into a frenzy is a whole new level of crazy. You said you talked to him from the Lucias Four research station?"

"Yes," Nikki said, still looking thoughtful. "He swore he hadn't put out a notice on me. That whatever happened in Mikilias wasn't him."

"You believe him?"

She shrugged. "I did at the time," she said. "Not as sure now. I *did* tell him that if it was him, and if he ever tried something like that again, I'd burn him to the ground." She gave me a bitter edged smile. "I'm pretty sure *he* believed *me*."

"That seems reasonable," I said, feeling my stomach tighten. "So if it wasn't him, who else could it be? Who have you seriously annoyed lately?"

She looked down at the wig in her hands. "This is way past annoyance, Roarke. Whoever it is has my face. *Nobody* out there is supposed to have my face."

"You meet all your prospective clients wearing the veil you had on when you came aboard the *Ruth*?"

"Always," she said. "Sometimes I arrange the meet at a masque where everyone's already disguised."

"Handy," I said, frowning at her. Considering her occupation, I wasn't at all surprised that she was fixated on keeping her anonymity.

Yet she'd had no problem letting Selene and me see her face aboard the *Ruth*.

But then, we hadn't known who she really was. Did that make a difference? "New question," I said. "Why—?"

"Can we save the questions for later?" she interrupted. "We have work to do here."

"Which will go just as quickly with conversation as it will with silence."

She snorted. "Let me guess. Your father used to say something about that, too?"

"I remember a line about idle hands, but it doesn't really apply here," I said. "My question was, what was that whole Piper charade about?"

"What Piper charade?"

I eyed her. She was still working on the wig, a perfect blend of interest and puzzlement on her face. "The Piper charade," I repeated. "Wherein you have Floyd bring a woman wearing your travel gear and veil to the *Ruth* and tell us she's our passenger, and then go off, switch clothes with her, and come aboard pretending to be her."

"I have no idea where you got such a ridiculous—"

"I don't know if she voluntarily changed clothes with you or you killed her and stole them," I cut her off. "Don't really care, either. I just want to know *why*."

Nikki gave me a long, measuring look. Then, she shrugged. "I don't know," she said. "Best guess is that Cherno decided to trade up."

"What do you mean?"

"I mean he decided at the last minute to hire me instead of Piper."

I frowned. I'd assumed Piper was just a stand-in that Nikki had hired for the occasion. "You're saying Piper's another assassin?"

"Of course," Nikki said. "Cherno wouldn't have hired her if he didn't know she could handle it. She specializes in the surreptitious, subtle jobs. She's good enough, I suppose, but she's not me."

"Because she sometimes misses?"

Nikki eyed me coolly. "Yes."

For a moment I was tempted to push back at that claim. But it seemed pointless, and anyway she was about to get a chance to prove it. "So Cherno just fired her?"

"More or less," Nikki said. Her voice had changed subtly, but I couldn't tell what that meant. "She got paid—she told me that. He told us to have her meet you instead of me and then I would switch out with her. He didn't explain, and I didn't ask."

"Seems overly complicated," I said. "Especially with the veil making you pretty anonymous to begin with."

She shrugged. "For half a million commarks I'm willing to make reasonable accommodations. When is Selene due back?"

I checked my watch. "Any time now," I said, pulling out my phone. "Let me try to call her."

She answered on the fourth vibe, with the news that she had indeed returned safely and the *Ruth* was back on our assigned pad. I gave her a quick update of the situation, omitting the Trent part for a later time, and told her about the plan.

She wasn't any more enthusiastic about it than Nikki had been. But unlike Nikki, she at least accepted the basic psychology involved. I gave her our location, we set a time, and I keyed off.

"And that's that," I said, putting the phone away. "Let's get this wrapped up."

"And give them a show?" Nikki asked.

"Trust me," I said. "They'll be talking about this one for years to come."

CHAPTER FOURTEEN

———— ❖ ————

The Beloi building wasn't the tallest one in the Badlands, but it was the tallest in this particular nine-block neighborhood square. The height was useful, but even more so were the five shack-like structures that dotted the flat gray slate, ostensibly containing a pair of water tanks, elevator machinery and access to stairs, antenna clusters for the residents' use, and even a compact solar power collector. Since most buildings I'd seen across the Spiral managed to do without all of those except the elevator housing, my guess was that the others were mostly there to provide cover for activities that might be shady or nefarious by even Badlands' standards.

Nikki and I lugged our gear up the stairs and laid it out in the visual shadow of the elevator housing. "Okay," I said, running my eyes over everything. "You and Franck's gun at peace with each other?"

"If you mean am I ready, yes," she said, peering down the barrel of the custom-made plasmic rifle Picker had been pointing at me earlier. She'd burned through an entire power pack fine-tuning its aim on Picker's indoor range, but when she was finished she confirmed that she could indeed do what I needed done. "Franck really was right about your wordiness."

"Nervous habit," I said, giving a quick look around at the

various Badlands rooftops that were higher than ours, the closest one a good five blocks away. No one was visible skulking around on any of them.

But then, I hadn't expected to have any such company. A good sniper could make a kill shot from there, but settling down in a location like that would never even occur to a bounty hunter. Not only was it useless as a surveillance point for street-level activity at our distance, but when a hunter's payment was dependent on hauling in the target—or, if the client wasn't fussy, the target's body—it would take far too long to get to the scene after a kill or incapacitation.

And of course, if there were other hunters present, which there usually were, some unprincipled type was bound to move in and poach the target for himself.

"Looks clear," I announced, returning to Nikki. She had our creation, whom I'd dubbed Lady Smirks, ready in her harness, dressed in the clothing, hat, and veil that Nikki had been wearing when she left the *Ruth* a few hours ago.

Only not quite the same. The mannikin we'd borrowed for the job was only about three-quarters human size, so we'd needed to do a quick tailoring job to make the clothing fit it.

Nikki had never been enthusiastic about this plan. Now, as she propped Lady Smirks up against the elevator housing wall, she looked even less so. "I don't know, Roarke," she said. "They're bound to see this thing's too small to be a person."

"I don't think so," I said. "At this distance human eyes can't measure scale with any accuracy, especially with no reference points around. It's also too light to be human, but they won't know that, either. And on top of that, we have you and the vaunted Schlichting marksmanship to sell it."

"Assuming they don't see the shots."

"Plasmic shots in broad daylight are notoriously hard to see," I pointed out. "No, this will work. The only unknown at this point is how many stragglers we'll have to go through on our way out."

"That won't be a problem," she said softly. "All right. Call Selene and let's do this."

I nodded and keyed my phone. Selene answered—"Go," I said.

I got her acknowledgment and put the phone away. I took a moment to check Lady Smirks's wide-mesh macramé harness, making sure not to disturb the thin elastic bands on the tops of the mannikin's wrists or the more rigid ones holding them at her sides. Thirty more seconds, I estimated...

And there it was, rising into view across the rooftops between us and the spaceport.

One of the *Ruth*'s bioprobes.

"Get ready," I told Nikki, getting a grip on the mesh. I'd told Selene to run the probe as slowly as she could, but they weren't exactly designed for a lazy afternoon saunter, and it was burning its way toward us like an anti-armor missile. I saw it shift direction just a bit as Selene fine-tuned its altitude and heading...

I stepped away from the elevator housing to face the incoming probe, Lady Smirks balanced against my back and the top of the weighted harness ready in my hands. The probe flew over the building across the street—passed over the street itself—crossed the edge of our apartment building—

And as it roared toward me I hurled the mesh as high up into the air as I could. The probe's nose hit it, catching one of the large mesh holes and yanking Lady Smirks up off the roof. The probe continued on over the next street and the hunters undoubtedly looking upward to see what was going on. A couple of shots rang out from below, and I heard one ricochet off the probe's belly.

Sitting with her back braced against the elevator housing, sighting along the plasmic's barrel, Nikki fired twice. The first shot hit the thin cord anchoring Lady Smirks's left wrist to her side, releasing the arm to snap upward on its elastic strap to the mesh anchoring the mannikin to the probe. The second shot hit the similar cord tying down Lady Smirks's right wrist.

Only instead of snapping up all the way to the mesh, this arm raised just to the mannikin's forehead, treating the watchers below to a sarcastic salute.

The masquerade alone would probably have convinced the hunters that their quarry was flying the coop. But the movement of the mannikin's hands, the first to a steadying grip on her harness, the second in a mocking gesture, would have put even the most skeptical observer's doubts to rest. That was indeed Nicole Schlichting riding the missile now blasting its way out of the city, and their siege had just been breached.

It was only as I finished running through the satisfaction of a plan well executed that the full significance of what had just happened caught up with me.

I looked down at Nikki in her new blond wig as she worked at disassembling the plasmic rifle. Two thin cords on a rapidly moving target... and she'd nailed them both with a single shot each.

A shiver ran up my back. *I never miss,* she'd told me once. My brain might have accepted that, but my more practical and cynical gut had continued to cling to the comforting thought that no one was *that* good.

Only she was. She really, truly was.

She finished packing up the rifle and stood up. "So," she said in a conversational tone, as if she did this sort of impossible thing every day. "Back to the ship?"

"Unless there's somewhere else you'd rather be," I said, trying for the same casual tone.

"Not really," she said. "Let me give Franck back his gun and pick up my package and I'll be ready."

I suppressed a wince. Somehow, in and among all the other things that had happened since Nikki left the ship, I'd almost forgotten she'd come here to get something. Something handcrafted, most likely expensive, and almost certainly lethal. "Sure," I said. "I'll walk you back and make sure you and Selene are safe, then I've got one more errand to run before we leave. Don't worry, it won't take long."

"I wasn't worried," she said, regarding me thoughtfully. "Need any help?"

As my father used to say, *Unless you really, truly have it nailed down, grab any help that's offered to you. Especially if it's a hammer.*

Yes, I wanted help. I wanted Jordan McKell, Ixil, and every other field operative the Icarus Group had on tap. I wanted a couple of platoons of EarthGuard Marines and a flight of Siroc pursuit fighters, with maybe a side order of Royal Kalixiri commandos tossed in.

But none of them were available. And if there was one thing I'd figured out for sure, it was that I didn't want a hammer like Nikki wandering around outside the *Ruth* any more than she absolutely had to.

"Thanks," I told her. "But I've got this."

Trent came back to consciousness via roughly the same stages I'd gone through earlier. "Welcome back," I said. "Don't try to rub your eyes, because you can't."

For a moment he continued to sit there with his head resting on the taverno's private room table, blinking his eyes as he
worked his way to full consciousness. I saw his shoulders move
as he tried to bring his arms out from behind his back, realized they were restrained at the wrists, and gave up the effort.
"Roarke," he said, his voice a little croaky. He worked moisture
into it as he sat upright. "What the hell did you do to me?" he
demanded, sounding better this time.

"Nice," I complimented him. "Confusion, outrage, and righteous
indignation, and you're not even completely up to speed yet. If
I didn't know better, I'd say you'd had Shakespearian training."

His eyes narrowed, just noticeably. "What do you mean?"

"I mean that was a great performance," I said. "But we'll
skip the curtain calls for now. I want to know who put out the
bounty notice on Nicole Schlichting."

"Yeah, I'll bet you do," he said, his eyes flicking around the
room. "Is she here?"

"No," I said. "Well, maybe no, anyway. Hard to tell with a
master ghost-walker like her. So?"

"So what?" he countered, giving the room another sweep,
pausing on the chairs where his cohorts had been sitting earlier.
"What did you do with Beeks and Jingo?"

"Me? Nothing," I said. "No, the badgemen did all the heavy
lifting. Did you know they both had bounties on them?"

His throat worked. "No, I didn't."

"Too bad," I said. "You could have made a little extra money
today on top of the—well, on top of the nothing, actually. Who's
gunning for Schlichting?"

"You're a funny man, Roarke," he said softly. "You might
want to think about how easy it is to make a laughing man
stop laughing."

"I already don't laugh nearly as much as I used to," I said.
"Come on, Trent. Simple question, simple answer. Let's match
them up and we can both call it a day."

For a long moment he stared at me. "I don't know who put
out the notice," he said at last. "I already told you that."

I shook my head. "Oh, Trent," I said with a sort of weary
regret. "Trent, Trent, Trent. Are we *really* going to have to do it
that way?" I made a show of pulling out the knife I'd pilfered
from his pocket while he was still asleep. "Fine. If you insist."

"I don't know what you—"

And right in the middle of his sentence he snapped his arms out from behind his back and lunged at me, one hand aiming for my knife hand and the other clawing for my face. Reflexively, I twitched back in my chair.

And watched him fall flat on his face half a meter short of his twin goals as the restraints I'd used to anchor his ankles to his chair went taut. He mostly got his hands under him in time to break his fall, but I heard the painful *oof* of forcibly expelled air.

"So I take it you're not going to cooperate?" I suggested, standing up and moving around behind him.

"Go to hell, Roarke," he managed. "You and your tame buddy Nask can both go to hell."

"Yes, I seem to be making that trip a lot lately," I said as I returned his knife to my pocket and drew my plasmic. "As for Nask, I'm pretty sure he's already there. Last chance, Trent. If you don't have a specific name, I'll settle for a list of possibles."

I paused, waiting. He didn't reply. "Suit yourself," I said, backing toward the door. "If you change your mind, just leave the name in a message in my mail drop. There'll be money in it, too. Good money."

He snorted, turning his head to glare up at me as he peeled himself up off the floor. "You really think you can buy me?" he demanded.

"If you're not in the hunter business for the money, what the hell *are* you in it for?" I countered. "Speaking of which, the paperwork on Beeks and Jingo should be ready for me at the badgeman office. See you around."

I backed out of the room, closing the door behind me. The restraints tying him to the chair were pretty tough, and I had his knife, so it would be awhile before he could get free. Plenty of time for me to get to the badgemen and collect my money.

Or at least that was what I hoped Trent would think. In fact, I had no intention of going anywhere except straight back to the spaceport. If Trent still had resources in the Badlands, better for him to mount a Light Brigade charge at a bunch of badgemen than at the *Ruth*.

Still, it would have been nice if he'd loosened up and given me at least a starting point for nailing down Nikki's obsessive stalker. Unless we could clear that up, we were going to be looking over our shoulders until we finished whatever job Cherno had signed her up for and could finally say good-bye.

But as my father used to say, *It's amazing how many people who see you breaking eggs will automatically assume you're making an omelet.* If Trent wouldn't give me the name, maybe there was another way to get it.

Nikki was waiting inside the entryway when I arrived at the *Ruth*, displaying some residual annoyance that I hadn't let her come with me to confront Trent. "About time," she said.

"Took him longer to wake up than I expected," I explained as I sealed the entryway hatch behind me. The long, hardside travel case she'd brought back from Picker's place, I noted, was resting against the corridor wall behind her. Whatever was in there, she apparently didn't want to let it out of her sight. "Selene on the bridge?"

"Yes, getting us a lift slot," Nikki said. "Did he talk?"

"Oh, he certainly talked," I told her as I headed forward. "Trent's a really good talker. Doesn't mean he actually *said* anything."

"So you got nothing."

"I wouldn't say that," I said. "There was a time or two that he hesitated when he should have been spitting curses at me, and once when he said something he probably shouldn't have."

"What was that?"

"Still need to cogitate on it," I told her. "Don't worry, I'll be happy to share when the time comes."

I'd be sharing with Selene, anyway. Not sure how much of anything would be going Nikki's direction.

But there was no point saying that out loud. Especially since she'd probably already figured it out.

"Sure," she said. Collecting her travel case, she took a few long strides and caught up with me.

Selene was in the pilot's chair when we arrived. "Any trouble?" she asked. Her voice was calm, but her pupils showed her relief that I was back safely. They went a little more stiff as she spotted Nikki in the corridor behind me.

"No, Trent pretty much lived up to my expectations," I said. "Did you get the note I sent?"

"Yes." She flicked another look at Nikki, who'd stopped in the bridge hatchway, then swiveled around to point at the plotting table and the Yellowdune map she'd pulled up. "Poloran Spaceport is the closest to the ruins themselves. Klax River Field, on the western edge of the city of Klaxorr, is closest to the StarrComm center, about thirty kilometers away. I'm assuming you want the latter?"

"Yes, if you can get us in," I said, tapping a spot on the map only three kilometers from the StarrComm center. "What about this one?"

She craned her neck to look. "Private field."

"Of course it is," I growled. "Commarks to commas who owns it."

"The Patth?"

"Congratulations, you've won a comma," I said. "Do we have a lift slot?"

"Fifteen minutes, and I've got tentative confirmation on Klax River. We should have full approval before we lift."

"You're not going to the ruins themselves?" Nikki asked. "I thought that was why you wanted to come to Niskea in the first place."

"Changed my mind," I said. "Selene, did you get a chance to look through the Rosselgang hunter notices?"

"Yes," she said, handing me her info pad. "The target name is different, but if you pull up the picture it looks like the one you described."

One glance was all I needed to see that it was indeed the sketch of Nikki's face that Scowly had been carrying. "That's it," I confirmed, keying for the full notice. Contact information... there it was. A standard mail drop, with the name *Hades* associated with it. The same name Mindi had mentioned on Vesperin. "Okay, we've got a plan," I said, wondering distantly if Mindi had pulled through. "Nikki, better head back to the dayroom and strap in."

"Where are we going after Klaxorr?" she asked, not budging.

"We can talk about that later," I said.

"We've still got fifteen—thirteen—minutes," she said. "We can talk about it now."

Sternly, I told my temper to go have a time-out. "Fine," I growled. "After Klaxorr we're going to head to the Trandosh dig on Meima."

"I thought Meima was low on your list."

"*Unlikely* doesn't necessarily mean *wrong*," I pointed out. "As my father used to say, *The battle is not always to the strong, nor the race to the swift, and if you have inside information to the contrary a small bet can pay off big.*"

"And if you're wrong?" she pressed. "Meima's a long ways away, and Cherno won't be happy if you run down his clock."

I grimaced. That thought had been hovering at the back of my mind for quite a while now. "You were the one who said there's always a second opportunity somewhere down the line," I reminded her.

"Yes, and there always is," she agreed. "The question is whether he'll be patient enough to wait for it. If not, he may cut all three of us loose."

And if he did that, the severance package he offered would probably not be pleasant. "Unfortunately, we don't have many other options," I said. "If you look at the other places on his list, there's really only enough time to look at one of them. I've got a feeling about Meima."

"A *feeling*?"

"At this point in the chase, gut feelings are as much use as actual data," I said with a shrug. "Doesn't mean we won't try to hedge our bets as best we can. Meima's fifteen days away, but we can trim that to eleven if we run at plus-thirty."

"That will require extra fueling stops."

"I've factored those into the timeline."

"What about the extra fuel cost?" she persisted. "Do you have enough to cover it?"

I thought about Nask's million commarks tucked away in my wallet. "We should, yes," I said. "Like I said, I think it's our best option."

"I suppose we'll find out," she said. "So why are we going to Klaxorr?"

I looked at Selene, noting the wariness in her pupils. "Hopefully, to get you out from under this bounty notice."

"How do you propose to do that?" Nikki asked.

"I don't know," I said evasively. "But I'll think of something."

Unlike the port in the Badlands and the one Muninn had used to get us to the *Odinn*, Klax River had been built in a fairly open area with plenty of room to grow. The landing cradles were large, relatively new, and nicely spaced out. I put us down in our assigned spot without trouble, and while Selene arranged to have our fuel tanks topped off I headed to the nearest runaround stand, grabbed a vehicle, and headed for the StarrComm center.

It was still late morning on this side of the planet. Traffic was fairly light as I left the port, but got steadily denser as I approached and then passed the edge of Klaxorr city proper. More than once, as the rest of the vehicles around me unexpectedly slowed or even stopped, I wondered if I should have called up to the *Odinn* and asked Nask to let us put down at their private field instead of Klax River.

But then, that would have tainted one of the two prongs of this experiment right from the start. So I kept going, stopped when the traffic stopped, went when it went, and fantasized about Nikki sitting on the runaround's roof shooting the more annoying drivers for me.

As my father used to say, *There may come a day when the nasty things we merely think about will become actual crimes. Do not hope for that day.*

I reached the StarrComm center to find it would only be about twenty minutes before I could get a booth. I found a seat in the waiting area, working out my message and keeping an eye on the other patrons. None of them seemed especially interested in me, but of course that was exactly how a properly trained observer would look.

But at least no one glared or approached or took a shot at me. All things considered, that was already better than most of the rest of my day had been.

Finally, it was my turn. I closed myself into my assigned booth, fed money into the slot, and punched in the number on the bounty notice Selene had tagged for me. The mail drop came up, the *Ready* notice came on, and I took a deep breath.

"Hello, Hades," I said into the microphone. "My name is Gregory Roarke. I have your target in hand and will be bringing her to Barcarolle on Meima, where I'll be happy to turn her over to you. Let me know when you've arrived and we can arrange a meeting. Make sure you have the payment money in hand. Here's my mail drop info for when you're ready to make it happen."

I gave my number and signed off. Prong One of the experiment was underway. Time to return to the *Ruth* and see if Prong

Two would pan out. I collected my change, walked past the desk and through the waiting area, and headed out into the midday sunshine.

To find Nask's man Huginn waiting for me.

He was sitting on one of the benches along the approach walkway, as if waiting for someone or pausing in a lunchtime stroll to sit and watch the clouds drift past overhead. But he stirred as I stepped into view through the doors, and as I headed toward the parking area he got casually to his feet. "Morning, Roarke," he called as he sauntered toward an intercept. "Nice day, isn't it?"

"Getting a bit warm for my taste," I said, waiting until we were in better conversation distance before stopping. "If you're looking to make a call, this would be a good time. Not too many people in there right now."

"Yes, the pre-noonday lull," he said, nodding. "So what brings you to Yellowdune?"

"Yellowdune?" I echoed, looking around. "I thought this was Klaxorr. Those runaround nav systems are just useless, aren't they?"

He smiled, but it was a mechanical thing without any genuine humor behind it. "You know what I mean."

"No, I don't think I do," I said. "Perhaps you can explain it to me?"

For a moment he just looked at me, probably trying to decide how sarcastic I was being and whether I'd crossed the line to where he would be permitted to do something about it. "You and Schlichting made a lot of noise in the Badlands today," he said. "Stirred up the whole city, for that matter."

"Yes, but we all got out alive," I said. "That makes it a draw in my book. By the way, I hadn't had a chance yet to thank you for getting Selene to and from the StarrComm center safely. I owe you. *And* Sub-Director Nask."

"I'm sure Sub-Director Nask appreciates it." He gestured toward the walkway bordering the StarrComm center grounds, a winding promenade lined with trees and contoured flower beds. "Walk with me."

"I really should get back to the *Ruth*," I said, not moving. "We need to get going, and I think we've probably worn out our welcome on Niskea."

"Not sure how much welcome here you had to begin with," he said. "Where are you going?"

"To our next destination," I said. "Not entirely sure where that is yet."

"Ah," he said, gesturing again. "Walk with me."

As my father used to say, *One invitation is a request, two is an order, three is a threat. Try very hard not to let it get past two.* "I'd be delighted," I murmured.

We headed out—westward, I noted, though I suspected it was the relative lack of other people in that direction that was important rather than the direction itself. "As I was saying," Huginn continued, "you and Schlichting made quite an impression on the Badlands today."

"I hope you're not blaming me for that," I said. "She was the one who set the whole mess in motion."

"So the available evidence would indicate," he said, a bit reluctantly. "There is, however, a school of thought that says trouble clusters around certain specific individuals." He gave me a sideways look. "Sub-Director Nask considers you to be in that category."

"Not sure I'm flattered," I said cautiously. The relative lack of witnesses out here might make private conversation easier, but it also lent itself to equally private violence. "If it makes you feel any better, I really *don't* go looking for trouble."

"Perhaps," he said. "If it makes *you* feel better, the sub-director also has you in the category of efficient people who achieve their chosen goal with very little wasted motion."

"I'll take that as a compliment," I said. At least it sounded more like one than the troublemaker thing. "Your point?"

"My point is that, as far as I can see, nothing you've done on Niskea has been wasted motion," he said. "Including your trip here to Yellowdune."

"Except that I'm not *at* Yellowdune," I said as patiently as I could. "Even if I was, I wouldn't be looking to cut in. Sub-Director Nask wouldn't be supervising personally unless you were here in force, which as far as I'm concerned means this particular set of ruins are all yours."

"I suspect the Icarus Group would disagree."

"Probably," I had to admit. "But the Icarus Group isn't here. It's just you and me."

"Is it?" he countered, turning finally to look squarely at me. "Because this is what *I* think, Roarke. *I* think the whole Badlands thing was just a very loud diversion, something to get everyone looking and thinking in the wrong direction while you and Selene sneaked off to Yellowdune and located the portal."

"Really?" I said, giving him a patient look. "Just like that? You've been searching for who knows how long, and we just waltz in and undercut you? Who do you think we are, the Wizards of Camelot?"

"There was only one wizard," he corrected absently. "Merlin. And don't bother denying that you have some kind of special talent for these searches. I can't see any other reason the Icarus Group would keep you around."

"Well, there *are* our sunny dispositions," I said. "As my father used to say, *Never underestimate the value of an honest, friendly smile for persuading people not to shoot you.* But fine, let's assume Selene and I are crackerjack at such things. Do you see her anywhere around? Or any other Icarus operatives, for that matter?"

"Just because I haven't seen them doesn't mean they aren't here," he said. "Tell me why you left a perfectly good StarrComm center in Rosselgang and flew all the way out here just to use the Klaxorr one. Especially since you've already said that you're in a hurry."

"One: The Rosselgang StarrComm center is hardly even moderately good, let alone perfectly good," I said. "It requires me to travel through a particularly nasty part of the Badlands, and one trip like that per day is my limit. Two: I hoped that if I dropped in this close to your Yellowdune operation that you or Muninn would show up for a closer look."

"And I have. So?"

"So I was hoping to ask you for a favor."

His cheek muscles twitched. Clearly, that wasn't the answer he was expecting. "A *favor*?"

"Yes," I said. "Selene, Nikki, and I need to go to Meima. I thought maybe Sub-Director Nask would be willing to fly us there."

"*What?*"

"I'm supposed to meet someone in Barcarolle on Meima," I explained. "I don't know where he's coming from, but it would be handy if I could get there ahead of him, or at least sooner than he expects. A ride aboard a Talariac-equipped ship would cut the travel time to a quarter of what the *Ruth* would take."

He was staring at me now as if I'd suddenly gone senile. "Are you serious?" he demanded. "Do you think anyone here would let you—?" He broke off, actually sputtering.

"Okay, so it was a long shot," I conceded. "But it was worth a try."

He snorted. "No. It wasn't."

"Or it wasn't," I said. "Well. Nice chat, but I have places I need to be."

"Places like Yellowdune?"

"I already said no," I said. "If you'd like, you're welcome to come to Klax River with me and watch the *Ruth* take off."

"As if that would prove anything." He stared at me a moment longer, then the corner of his mouth twitched. "I'm beginning to see why Sub-Director Nask once offered you an Expediter position. You have the full range of arrogant confidence that the Patthaaunuth look for in applicants."

"I'll take that as a compliment, too," I said. "Well. Good-bye, Huginn."

"*Au revoir,*" he corrected. "Means *until we meet again.*" He raised his eyebrows slightly. "Because we *will* meet again."

A shiver ran up my back. Between him, Muninn, and half the Spiral's bounty hunters, if I'd deliberately set out to make myself a new roster of enemies, I doubted I could have done a better job of it. "I'll look forward to it," I said. "One last question: Do you have any idea who this *Hades* is, the one behind the bounty notice on Schlichting?"

"None at all," he said. "Nor do I care. *Au revoir,* Roarke."

"Right," I murmured. "*Au revoir.*"

CHAPTER FIFTEEN

Traveling for eleven days at plus-30 wasn't nearly as easy as it sounded. At that power output the engines had an enhanced tendency to go off-synch, and I spent a lot of time on the bridge tweaking them back on track again. I also discovered that running them that hot added an additional harmonic to their usual rumble, an odd sound that cost me a few hours of sleep over the first couple of days until my brain learned to recognize it and edit it out.

As I'd told Nikki, I'd factored the additional time that would be required for fuel stops into my eleven-day estimate. Finding planets that were on our least-time vector as well as offering a fast fueling turnaround was something of a challenge, but our spaceport data files were up to date and Selene was mostly able to find exactly what we needed. Six days into the trip we unexpectedly ended up spending an extra four hours at one of the ports when a routine mid-fueling status check turned up three engine components that our mad dash across the Spiral had stressed to the point of unreliability. Fortunately, the port had the parts we needed and piling an additional three hundred commarks on top of the regular bill bought us the expedited service we needed.

Nikki kept mostly to herself during the trip, locked in her cabin for hours on end with whatever was inside her fancy new case. Occasionally she would emerge and ask for something from the *Ruth*'s stock of tools and analysis instruments. I would get whatever she needed, accept her perfunctory thanks, and watch her disappear back into her cabin. Occasionally she would have meals with us, but her earlier talkative phase seemed to have passed and most of the time she simply chose what she wanted from the dayroom's pantry, heated it if necessary, then once again disappeared into her cabin.

She also seemed to be going out of her way to avoid interacting with Selene, though that might have been my imagination. Whether or not the snubbing was deliberate, it was clear that Selene was more than happy to keep their mutual distance.

We were fifteen hours from Meima when I decided it was time Nikki and I had a private talk.

It took nearly a minute and three separate sets of knocks before she finally unlocked the cabin hatch. "Yes?" she asked, her face and voice making it clear that she wasn't in the mood for interruptions.

"I wanted to tell you we'll be on Meima tomorrow," I said.

"Thank you." She reached for the hatch control—

"I also wanted to talk to you about a job," I added.

Her hand paused, hovering over the control. "What sort of job?"

"The kind you get paid for."

She snorted. "Right," she said. "Like you have the means—"

She stopped in mid-sentence, her gaze shifting from my face to the fan of ten hundred-thousand-commark certified bank checks I held up in front of me.

For a moment we stood that way, silent and still. Then slowly, reluctantly, she returned her eyes to my face. "Come in," she said, her tone subtly changed as she stepped aside out of the hatchway.

"Thank you." I walked over to the fold-down desk and chair across from the bed, laid the checks on the desk, and sat down. Nikki closed and sealed the hatch and, after a moment's hesitation, went over to the bed and seated herself on the edge.

"I'm listening," she said.

"You said earlier that your fee was half a million," I said. "I have twice that here."

"So I see," she said. "Let me guess. This Trent bounty hunter?"

"No, I can handle Trent," I said. "I have something more interesting in mind. First of all, let me make sure I'm clear on how exactly this works. I hire you for half a million and give you a name, and assuming he or she isn't on your untouchables list I'm permanently immune from anything anyone might want you to do to me?"

"A name and all the rest of the necessary data," she corrected, her face taking on a knowing expression. "You can't just say *John Wong* and put yourself on the list while I try to figure out which of the millions of John Wongs you're talking about."

"Sure, obviously," I said. "But I hand you money and specify a target, and that does it?"

"Yes," she said, the knowing look deepening. "Though as you said, that target can't be on my list. So who do you anticipate is going to hire me to take you out?"

"Me? No one," I said. "I mean, really. Can you see anyone in my circle of acquaintances having a spare half mil lying around?"

"*You* have a full mil," she said, gesturing to the checks on the desk. "Where did you get it, anyway?"

"An anonymous benefactor," I said. "I can't say anything more."

"Not a problem," she said. "Just bear in mind that it's only the person who hands me the money who goes on my list. Just because *you're* on it doesn't mean your anonymous benefactor will be. Who's the target?"

"In a minute," I said. "First, I'm curious. Why did you let Selene and me see your face when you've worked so hard over the years to stay anonymous?"

"Not really any of your business."

"Actually, I think I can make a case that it is," I said. "Now that your secret is out, at least among some of the bounty hunter community, Selene and I have the same bull's-eye painted on our backs that you do."

Nikki gave a little snort. "Hardly. What would anyone gain by taking you out?"

"What would anyone gain by taking *you* out?" I countered. "As far as I've been able to ascertain, there are only six planetary warrants on you, and you have to be physically on those worlds before a hunter can make a move. Just hauling you in from somewhere else won't work." I raised my eyebrows. "Especially given the likelihood that such a brazen hunter would get himself killed en route."

"Could be revenge, then," she said, ignoring my little addendum. Probably figured it was obvious. "There are people out there who blame me for killing their friends or business associates." She considered. "Considerably more people than are, in fact, justified in that belief. If that matters to you."

"It does," I said, though offhand I wasn't sure how much. Whether she'd murdered ten or a thousand, she was still a murderer. It was something I needed to remember. "A name like yours probably attracts copycats."

"Along with people who are too cowardly to take responsibility for their own actions," she said, her lip twisting with contempt. "You had something of a name yourself back in the day. You must have dealt with some of that."

"Not really," I said. "When you're swapping out warm bodies for cold cash you have to physically show up at a badgeman office. We have more of a problem with other hunters slipping in to poach a target."

"Especially for you, I'd guess," she said, eyeing me curiously. "I understand you were more of a throw rug for that sort of thing than most other hunters."

"You mean because I wouldn't shoot a poacher on sight or suspicion?" I countered, feeling my stomach tighten. "Yeah, I probably lost more than my share of targets to the opportunists. But as my father used to say, *Just because you let someone live doesn't necessarily mean he's happy with that life.* A lot of the poachers I ran into had bigger problems than just me, and I doubt most of them ever worked them out."

"In other words, they eventually got themselves killed, only not by your hand?"

"I'm sure some of them did." With a couple of them, I certainly hoped that was the case. "But that reputation had a few side benefits that I doubt any of the poachers ever understood. I got at least two dead-or-alive targets to surrender instead of shooting it out because they knew I wouldn't kill them in cold blood as soon as they showed themselves."

"Probably figured they could find a way to get the drop on you along the way to the payment."

"I'm sure some of them thought that," I agreed. "Didn't do them any good, as it turned out. But as my father used to say, *Sometimes one of the rewards of being a nice guy is that the other guy's not-so-nice hopes get dashed that much harder.*"

"That's cute," Nikki said. "Enough stalling. Who's my target?"

I braced myself. Here was where it was going to get tricky. "The name's in here," I said, pulling out a sealed envelope and setting it on top of the bank checks. "My one condition is that you not open it until I tell you to."

Her eyes narrowed. "Excuse me?" she said, her tone gone suddenly ominous.

"You'll have the million and the envelope," I said, fighting to keep my own voice casual against that look and voice. "When I say the word—"

"No," she cut me off. "No, let me be clearer. *Hell* no. Who do you think I am, some stock-manipulating futures broker?"

"I'm offering double your usual fee," I reminded her.

"I don't care," she said. I'd expected her to start getting angry at this point, but she was still projecting that ominous calm.

Which, in its own way, was more terrifying than black disdain or even loud fury would have been. "Will you at least think about it?" I asked.

"This conversation is over," she said. "Take your money and your envelope and go."

There was clearly no point in continuing. Silently, I picked up the envelope and the bank checks and put them back in my pocket. "Thank you for your time," I said, and left the cabin.

Selene was on the bridge when I arrived. "Everything all right?" she asked, her pupils wary as her nostrils flared a bit in my direction.

"Just had a talk with Nikki," I said, keeping my voice casual. So far I hadn't shared any of this plan with Selene, nor had I told her about the million commarks I'd talked out of Nask. If I was lucky, she'd never have to know about either. "Told her we were about to hit Meima."

"Yes," Selene murmured, her eyelashes going into their flutter. She could tell something was off with my current emotions, and was trying to figure out what it was. "Did she happen to mention why she'd been spending so much time in her cabin?"

"I assumed she was playing with her new toy," I said, frowning. "Was there more to it than that?"

"I don't know," she said, her pupils frowning in turn. "It's just...that cleaner/enhancer you use sometimes on your arm?"

Reflexively, I flexed the fingers of my artificial left arm. The prosthetic was mostly self-maintaining, but the manufacturer recommended that its electronic and mechanical systems be looked at and maybe cleaned or tweaked once or twice a year. "The Tixi 455, or the CorroStop?"

"The one for the sensors and the sensor leads."

"The Tixi 455," I said. "What about it?"

"I smelled something similar a few hours ago when I happened to bump into her in the dayroom," she said. "It wasn't the same thing you use, but it was similar."

"I suppose that makes sense," I said, running the possibilities through my mind. "She's way too good a shot to get it all from long practice and clean living. A prosthetic arm, maybe with an exotic targeting sensor setup in the knuckles of her gun hand, would go a long way to explaining it." I cocked an eyebrow. "*Does she have a prosthetic arm?*"

"I don't know," Selene said. "The scent from yours is a permanent part of the *Ruth*'s air filtration, which makes it nearly impossible to sort out whether any of it is coming from her. The only way to be sure would be to run a close-scent examination."

"As in sniffing up each of her arms?"

"Yes," she said, apparently missing the utter ridiculousness of the picture her comment had created in my mind. "If you can come up with an excuse that will persuade her, I'm willing to try."

"I'll see what I can do," I said. "But as my father used to say, *It's easy to persuade someone to do what he already wants to do. The tricky part is convincing him he wants what you want.* But we'll keep a prosthetic arm as our working assumption. You find us a landing field yet?"

"There are three possibilities," she said, pulling up a map of Barcarolle and the Trandosh archeological dig, a vast area a few kilometers southwest of the city that included about five square kilometers of hills, woodlands, and a small creek. "Perhaps more like two and a half."

"*Half* a spaceport?"

"A moment," she said, touching a spot in the northwest part of Barcarolle proper. "This is the city's main spaceport. It's a fair distance from the dig, but it will be easier for the *Ruth* to sit there without drawing unwelcome attention."

"Especially if we use one of our fake IDs," I said, nodding. "Next?"

"The dig also has its own landing field," she said, pointing to a much smaller spot at the southern end of the dig's boundary. "It's generally only for people from the three universities who've been working the area for the past fifteen years, but we might be able to come up with a story that will get us in."

"That might be tricky," I said. "Even if we could, the *Ruth* would stick out pretty badly among those boxy midsize freighters universities usually pick up on surplus. What's the half port?"

"Here," she said, pointing to a wide, deep pit just west of the dig area's center. "It's not listed as functional, but you can see the mountings for a pair of perimeter grav beam towers."

I frowned at the image, an unpleasant chill running up my back. "Just one pair?"

"Yes." She looked at me, and I could see in her pupils that she had tracked to the same conclusion I had. "Do you think... the *Icarus*?"

"Why else would there be a couple of grav towers out in the middle of nowhere?" I asked. "That must be how they got the thing off the ground. I assume the towers themselves are gone?"

"I don't see them on the satellite views," Selene said. "But they could have just been folded down and buried under a loose layer of dirt and plants."

"Or disassembled but still nearby," I said, studying the image some more. "Either way, they might be quickly available if someone finds something else that needs to be lifted. I presume the main focus of the dig has moved somewhere else on the site?"

"Yes, it seems to be over here," she said, moving her finger to a raggedly forested area half a kilometer west of the grav tower mountings. "The terrain there seems to be mostly small hills."

"And small depressions," I said absently, a fresh plan beginning to form in the back of my mind. My original thought had been to get us downwind of the dig and then move in from there, hoping Selene picked up a trace of portal metal. But if those hills were what I was starting to suspect they were... and if my current theory on Nask's missing Gemini portal was correct...

"Gregory?"

I snapped my attention back to Selene. She had the nostril-and-eyelash thing going again. "It's okay," I assured her. "I've been working on a theory, that's all. And I think I just figured out where to start testing it."

"In the Trandosh dig?"

"That's the place," I confirmed. "Go ahead and ask for a slot in the main Barcarolle spaceport. We're going to have to travel no matter where we put down, and we might as well go for as much anonymity as we can get."

"And Nikki?"

I rubbed my cheek. I didn't really want her along with us on this one.

On the other hand, I didn't really want her alone on the *Ruth*, either. "We'll let her decide what she wants to do," I said. "Maybe we'll get lucky and she'll want to go off and sample the Barcarolle nightlife."

"Yes," Selene murmured. "Because Nikki wandering around a city by herself never leads to trouble."

I huffed out a sigh. "Yeah. Good point."

The landing in Barcarolle went smoothly and, as far as I could tell, without anyone paying any untoward attention to us. We put down in our assigned pad—it was flat rather than a cradle, which meant having to deal with the zigzag instead of the much easier ramp—set up a schedule for the fuelers and the maintenance people, and got ready to head out.

Nikki wasn't really interested in staying with the ship. Nor was she particularly excited at the prospect of coming with Selene and me. She absolutely wasn't interested in investigating whatever passed for entertainment on Meima. In the end, she somewhat reluctantly opted to tag along with us.

As we walked down the zigzag, I tried to figure out whether or not I was happy with her decision. By the time we reached the runaround stand, I gave it up as not worth the effort.

With the wind currently consisting of light and variable breezes from the northwest, I took us in a looping path around the southeast side of the dig. Finding a low but promising ridge in the middle of the airflow, I ushered Selene up the grassy slope to the top.

Given the sheer size of the grounds, I didn't really expect her to get anything at that distance. Still, I'd held some private hopes, and couldn't help feeling a bit of a letdown when her efforts came up dry.

"I'm sure the view here is lovely for people who like this sort of thing," Nikki said in a muffled voice. She'd passed up her usual city-strolling wraparound for a pair of rugged jeans and a fleece-collar jacket more suitable for tramping around the countryside, plus heavy boots and gloves, and she'd swapped out her fashionable veil for an allergy mask. The mask was a better overall match for her ensemble, but the thickness of the material made her a lot harder to understand. "Whatever you're hoping to accomplish out here, I don't think it's working."

"Don't worry, this was just Act One," I assured her as we retraced our steps down the hill toward our runaround. "Act Two should be much more interesting."

"It had better be," she warned. "Otherwise, I'm taking the runaround back to the ship and you two can find your own way home."

"Trust me," I said. "You remember me telling you about the portals? Let's go see the spot where the very first one was found."

I hadn't expected there to be a plaque, or a collection of personal and historical items, or scribbled notes from the archeologists and techs who'd found the portal and built the *Icarus* around it. Even so, the site was something of a letdown.

"So where was the portal?" Nikki asked as we gazed into the tiered hole from our chosen spot at the crater's southern rim. The ground on this part of the rim was a good six meters higher than the surrounding terrain, higher even than the ridge we'd just climbed to the southeast. Apparently, this was where the original digging party had piled all the dirt they'd dug out.

"It was somewhere down there," I said, looking once into the pit and then turning my attention to the surrounding terrain. Selene had said the archeologists were currently working to the west, among the hills and dips we'd noted earlier. Unlike the area immediately around the pit, the ground in that direction boasted a sparse covering of maybe a dozen varieties of trees and bushes. From our current vantage point I could also see there was more bumpy ground to the southwest, though the hills there seemed fewer and farther between. But they were definitely there.

I shifted my attention northward, then east. Fewer trees in both directions, plus flatter ground—pretty much the same as the landscape we'd just driven through south of the Icarus pit.

A lot of small hills to the west, occasional ones to the north and southwest, nothing at all anywhere else. Exactly what my current theory predicted.

Which didn't necessarily mean I was right, of course. I'd charged off in the wrong direction many times before.

But if I *was* right, the end of the rainbow ought to be due west, just beyond the hilly section.

"Interesting," Nikki murmured.

"What is?" I asked, turning back to her. She was gazing west, her eyes tracking down the edge of the crater ridge we were currently standing on. As far as I could tell, there was nothing down there but dirt, some scraggly bushes, a couple of broken retaining walls, and a whole bunch of random chunks of concrete.

"That bush down there, the set of three about a hundred twenty meters away," she said, nodding toward the cluster. "There's an animal lurking beneath the middle one."

I frowned. The bushes' branches had decent overall coverage, spreading out a good half meter to all sides. But even though they were slender and their associated leaf complement was somewhat sparse, I couldn't see anything in there except the ground itself. "What kind of animal?" I asked. "We talking something dangerous, like whatever the local equivalent of a wolverine or rattlesnake is?"

"Depends on what you consider dangerous," Nikki said. "I think it's a Kalixiri outrider."

I felt my mouth go suddenly dry. A Kalixiri outrider? As in maybe one of *Ixil's* outriders?

Silently, I cursed my own stupidity. Of course it was one of Ixil's. The fact that Meima hadn't been on the admiral's list of possible portal locations was, in retrospect, an obvious indicator that the Icarus Group was doing something here and didn't want Selene and me crashing their party. Especially not with someone like Nikki in tow. And depending on the seriousness of the project, it might reasonably include one of the group's chief troubleshooters, Ixil or Jordan McKell or both.

And of course, the fact that we'd come in under one of the Icarus Group's fake IDs would have been an instant flag for whichever member of their team was monitoring the local traffic. We might as well have brought a bullhorn and maybe shot off a few flares.

Still, as my father used to say, *When you get that dazzling flash of insight, make sure the other guy doesn't know you've gone temporarily blind.* "A Kalixiri *what*?" I asked.

Nikki gave me an incredulous look. "You seriously don't know what Kalixiri are?"

"Of course I do," I said with the proper edge of offended professionalism. "Scaly, lizard-faces, smarter than they look. Are you talking about the furry ferrets some of them carry around as pets or something?"

"They're hardly *pets*," Nikki said, her bemusement edging into scorn. "They're called *outriders,* and they act as the Kalix's scouts."

"Really?" I asked, looking back down at the bush. This time I spotted a small movement from beneath the leaves.

"What could someone possibly be scouting here?" Selene asked. "We're not doing anything illegal." She looked pointedly at me. "We're certainly not doing anything very interesting."

"Just because there's nothing here doesn't mean we won't find something somewhere else," I said stiffly, silently giving thanks for a partner who was smart enough and quick enough to play a deflection when the situation called for it. If that was Pix or Pax down there, he probably wasn't so much scouting as he was keeping track of us. "As for the thing down there, whatever the Kalixiri think it's good for, it's still just an animal. Probably out hunting grubs or plants or whatever."

"It's stupid assumptions like that that usually get a person killed," Nikki said tartly. "Let's follow it and figure out what it's doing."

"Yes, but—fine," I conceded with an air of irritated resignation. "Whatever. Go on, we're right behind you."

We headed down the ridge, Nikki taking the lead, Selene following, me bringing up the rear. If that was Pix or Pax, and if he'd been ordered to find us, he ought to be on his way back to Ixil by now to report.

But he was still crouched unmoving beneath the bush. Was he not, in fact, watching us, but on some other mission entirely? Or had Ixil's instructions to him missed the possibility that we would spot him?

Abruptly, Selene's stride faltered. "Northwest," she said urgently, pointing toward another set of bushes fifty meters away. "Brown and gray with white spots."

Reflexively, I dropped my hand to my plasmic's grip. There was something brown and gray over there, all right. Something three times the size of a Kalixiri outrider, and with the jaws, teeth, and claws of a predator.

And it was moving slowly and stealthily in the outrider's direction.

I muttered a curse. Whatever orders Ixil had given the outrider, self-preservation probably superseded them. Worse, I couldn't let the animal be killed or even injured, which meant coming to his defense. Nikki would certainly wonder at my sudden change in attitude, and a suspicious assassin wasn't exactly an ideal traveling companion.

I was still trying to come up with a plan when Nikki produced her Fafnir from inside her coat and casually fired off a plasma shot toward the stalking predator. It jerked back as the shot splattered on the ground in front of its snout, then turned and bounded away through the dirt and undergrowth until it was lost to sight behind one of the hills.

I took a deep breath. "Well," I said lamely. "That worked."

"Couldn't have it distracting our outrider," she said, slipping the Fafnir back into concealment. "Now we can watch and see where it goes."

"Yes," I said. "Good plan. I thought you never missed."

"I didn't miss," she said, throwing a puzzled look at me. "I wasn't trying to kill it. Why would I? I just needed to nudge it back. A plasmic shot a few centimeters in front of an animal's snout usually does the trick."

"Yes, I suppose that's reasonable," I said. Fifty meters away, a precise shot, and as far as I'd been able to tell she hadn't even taken time to aim. Definitely some kind of sensor-link to her gun hand.

Except that she was still wearing her gloves, which meant my theory that the sensors were in an artificial hand's knuckles was now out the window.

In or around her eyes, then? But putting sensors in either of those places was notoriously difficult to do without leaving marks, and there was nothing anywhere on her face that I could see.

"There it goes," Selene said.

I looked back at the three bushes. The outrider was on the move, all right, scampering in a zigzag path away from us toward one of the sections of broken retaining wall.

"Come on," Nikki said, starting down the slope after him. "Don't get too close—we don't want to spook it."

Privately, I thought it unlikely that getting too close was going to be a problem. The outrider was faster than we were and clearly knew where he was going, while we had to pick our way carefully over the rocks and debris lest one of us twist a knee or ankle.

He reached the retaining wall and disappeared behind it. Nikki muttered something under her breath and picked up her pace. I did the same, catching up with Selene and risking my footing by taking a quick look into her eyes. Her pupils showed a fresh revelation, something no doubt gleaned from a new scent in the air—

"There!" Nikki snapped, pointing. "Hell."

I grimaced as I spotted the reason for her annoyance. The outrider we'd been following had emerged from the retaining wall right where it had gone in and was now proceeding southwest at a good clip.

The problem was that another outrider had also appeared, this one from beside a bush at the other end of the wall, and was making his way northeast toward the other side of the Icarus pit.

"Which one is ours?" I asked, slowing.

"Good question," Nikki agreed. "Any idea?"

"That one," Selene said quickly, pointing at the outrider heading northeast.

A little too quickly, maybe. "How do you know?" Nikki asked suspiciously.

"I just do," Selene said, her voice again a bit rushed.

"Good enough for me," I put in. "Selene and I will follow that one—you track the other."

"Or vice versa," Nikki said, her eyes narrowed as she looked back and forth between us. "I'll take that one." She gestured toward the outrider Selene had tagged, still making his way around the pit. "You two can have the other. What are you waiting for? *Go*."

"Yeah. Fine." With a show of reluctance, I unglued my feet from the ground and headed off after our designated outrider. "Come on, Selene."

As my father used to say, *Your first goal is usually to prove yourself trustworthy. But sometimes it can be even more useful to prove the exact opposite.*

We found Ixil lying in one of the pits a few meters back from the retaining wall where Pix and Pax had set off on their diversionary runs. "We thought the two of you would show up sooner or later," he said without preamble, sounding rather unhappy with us.

Possibly his unhappiness was just with the current situation. But probably it was with us.

"We thought it might be a good place to find the other end of Cherno's portal," I said, looking over my shoulder. From halfway down Ixil's pit I could see the top of Nikki's head as she followed the other outrider. "I'd ask why Trandosh wasn't on the list the admiral gave us, but we don't have the time. Who else is here?"

"Jordan and a small dig crew," he said. "Is that the assassin the admiral told us about?"

"Yes," I said. "And she's touchy about her anonymity and can shoot a commark cent off your head, so warn everyone to keep their distance. What exactly are you doing here?"

"Investigating," he said, the vague word and leave-it-alone tone telling me it was none of my business. "You?"

"Like I said, looking for the missing end of Cherno's Gemini portal."

Ixil cocked his iguana-like head. "You're not joking, are you? Do you seriously expect to find a second portal here?"

"Why not?" I countered. "Fidelio had two Gemini portals sitting practically back-to-back."

"Yes, but those were Geminis," he said. "Icarus is a full-range portal. Why would the creators bother putting a Gemini this close to it?"

"The Icari," I corrected him. "Selene and I are calling them the *Icari* now. Classier name. I have a theory."

I looked back around. Nikki had paused and seemed to be searching for something. Had the outrider given her the slip? "Unfortunately, there's no time for that, either. But if I'm right, the portal will be west of here, probably near where the series of hills and dips ends."

Ixil looked at Selene. "And you think that why?"

"I'll tell you tomorrow," I said. "Get some ground turned over out there, focusing on area rather than depth. With luck, Selene and I should be able to leave Nikki on the *Ruth* and come give you a hand locating it. If enough of the scent gets through—"

"A moment," Ixil cut me off. "You told the admiral your passenger's name was *Piper*. You're on a first-name basis now?"

"Sort of," I said, taking a step back. Nikki had definitely stopped. "Lot of smoke and mirrors on this one. We have to go."

We met Nikki about midway from where we'd all started. "Any luck?" I asked.

"No, it disappeared behind some rocks and more of this broken concrete," she said. "Maybe you're right. Maybe it was just hunting for food." She eyed me thoughtfully. "Though that raises the whole question of what a Kalix is doing out here in the first place."

"Maybe he's with one of the archeology groups," I offered. "Or maybe he's a tourist looking for souvenirs. People collect the strangest things."

"Maybe," Nikki said. "We might want to look around a little more."

"Well, if you want to do it today, you're doing it on your own," I warned. "I need to head over to the Barcarolle Starr-Comm center and check for messages."

"From?"

From the guy who put out the bounty notice on you. The guy I promised to deliver you to. "No one in particular," I said aloud. "You just never know when something interesting might pop up."

The message I'd hoped for was indeed waiting in my mail drop. *Arrived in Barcarolle on Meima. Will be waiting at Bosling Red taverno every day at nine p.m., local time, until you arrive. Have package ready for pickup.*

I scowled at the note. I'd hoped to announce my own arrival and maneuver him into sending a follow-up note suggesting a time and place for our meeting. With only one StarrComm center in Barcarolle, I might then be able to spot him as he went into or out of the center when sending that message.

Of course, that assumed he'd use the Barcarolle facility instead of taking the trouble to fly off to one of the planet's other half dozen locales. He might be cagey enough to do that. But now even that vague hope was gone. With his proposed meeting schedule already in place, there was no need for him to do anything more than show up and wait for me to make contact. I could either follow up on his terms, or give up and chuck the whole thing.

I thought about Nikki, and what she would say if she found

out what I was doing. But this had to end, and tonight was as good a time as any.

I pulled out my phone and punched for Selene. "Everything all right at the ship?" I asked when she answered.

"Yes," she said. "Is there a problem?"

"Probably," I said. "We got an answer, and it looks like the game is on. I need you to meet me at the Bosling Red taverno in"—I checked my watch—"half an hour."

"Do you want me to bring Nikki?"

"No," I said. "But be sure to pack your plasmic. There's a good chance we're going to need all the firepower we can get."

CHAPTER SIXTEEN

———— ❖ ————

The Bosling Red turned out to be a reasonably upscale place, with soft lights, softer background music, tasteful décor, and an impressive wine list. I got there forty-five minutes before the designated meeting time, with Selene arriving about two minutes behind me. I'd picked out a small, round, two-person table that offered a fairly decent view of the main door and, more importantly, a perfectly positioned airflow toward Selene from the extra chair I'd borrowed from one of the other tables. If our guest was planning any shenanigans, the subtle changes in his scent should give us at least a few seconds' warning.

We watched as customers filed in, a fair mix of humans and aliens, watching for a familiar face or at least someone who looked like they were here for a business meeting. We got two false starts, lone patrons who paused by the door and searched the room before spotting and joining their respective groups.

Then, at precisely five minutes to nine, a man strode in.

Not just any man. If some lunatic genetic engineer had deliberately set out to load the most sheer intimidation he could into a single package, this would probably be the result. He was massive, a good half head taller than me, with a broad chest, muscled shoulders and arms, no neck to speak of, and a face that would probably curdle milk when he was smiling and terrify babies when he wasn't. His beady eyes swept the room.

And came to rest on me.

"Selene?" I murmured as he started toward us.

"Clothing is local style, and no one seems to be paying particular attention to him," she murmured back. "Probably a well-known resident."

I nodded. I'd noted those same two points and reached the same conclusion. "Hired muscle, then. Let's see how he smells when he gets closer."

The man maneuvered the rest of his way through the tables and came to a stop behind our empty chair. Up close, he looked even bigger than he had from across the room. "Roarke?" he rumbled in a voice that matched the rest of his intimidation level.

"Yes," I confirmed. "You?"

"Call me Basher," he said. He frowned briefly at Selene as if wondering what species she was, then seemed to give up the effort. His eyes flicked to our hands, making that long count up to four to confirm they were all visible on the table. "Where's the package?" he asked, pulling out the chair and dropping into it.

"Nearby," I said. "Where's the money?"

He eyed me a moment, then pulled a thick envelope from his jacket pocket and pushed it across the table toward me. "You want to count it?"

"Absolutely," I said, making no move to pick it up. "Selene?"

She took the envelope and sniffed at it, then opened it and did the same to the stack of certified bank checks inside. "Yes," she said.

"And . . . ?" I asked, nodding toward Basher.

She nodded. "Yes."

"Thank you," I said. So the scent I'd been expecting was on both the bank checks and Basher himself. My suspicions about Hades' identity had indeed been correct. All as expected, but it was nice to have confirmation. As my father used to say, *Accusing someone without proof can destroy a relationship, bring embarrassment, or get you shot. So can accusing someone* with *proof.* "And thank you for the delivery, Basher. But we need to speak to your boss now. You want to give Hades a call and invite him to join the party?"

For a fraction of a second Basher's eyes widened before he could narrow them back down. "I don't know any Hades," he rumbled. "You have the money. I want the package." He leaned a little ways over the table and flexed his fingers. "Unless maybe you want me to do a grip workout on your neck."

I gave a theatrical sigh. "Basher, have you ever heard of a rooster-spur boot?"

He blinked. "A what?"

"A rooster-spur boot," I repeated. "It's a fighting shoe with a double-hook knife that comes out of the toe."

His gaze dropped briefly to the table, as if he could see my feet through the opaque surface. "So what, you're going to *kick* me?"

"You weren't listening," I said patiently. "I *could* just kick you, sure. A knife to the shin or kneecap would hurt like hell and pretty much end your day. But I could also scoop it up behind your ankle and hook your Achilles tendon. That would end your entire week and take a lot of medical work to repair."

I let my expression harden. "Or I could slice across the back of your knee and cut the popliteal artery. That would end everything, since you'd bleed out in about half a minute."

He was staring at me, his mouth slightly open, looking rather like a beached fish. Furtively—or at least as furtively as someone that size could manage—he tried to ease back from the table and hopefully out of the reach of the terrifying footwear I'd just described.

A useless effort, as I'd already hooked my instep around the front leg of his chair. It would be trivial for him to break that tenuous grip, of course, but he'd probably seen enough knife fights to know how fast a stab wound could be delivered and wasn't anxious to test my speed with such things.

I let the tense standoff go on another two heartbeats. Then I lifted a hand, palm upward in invitation. "Hades?" I prompted.

"I'm here," a voice came from behind and to my left.

I half turned in my chair to look. Trent was walking up behind me, a longer-hair wig, muttonchop sideburns, and a short Fu Manchu mustache wrapped around his face. Against the wall behind him and downwind of us I spotted an empty two-person table, probably where he'd been sitting while he watched our drama play out. He was just putting away his phone, clearly how he'd been monitoring our conversation. "There you are, Hades," I said, beckoning to him. "Grab a chair."

"No need," he said. "Basher was just leaving." He stopped a couple of meters short of our table and sent a leisurely look around the taverno. "So where is she?"

"She's close enough," I told him. "First, we need to talk."

Trent pursed his lips, still studying my face. Then, with a microscopic shrug he started walking again, circling the table and stopping beside Basher. "That'll be all, Basher," he said, motioning the big man to get out of the chair.

"But—" Basher gestured helplessly at me.

"There's no such thing as this ridiculous chicken shoe he was blathering about," Trent said impatiently.

"A *rooster-spur boot*," I corrected him. "And actually, it *does* exist. I saw a couple of guys fight with them once."

"Sure you did," Trent said. "Good-bye, Basher."

Basher lurched to his feet and took a hasty step back from the table. Trent pointed him toward the exit and sat down in the vacated chair. Basher turned toward the door.

And paused, frowning at something across the room. "Mr. Trent?"

"Good-*bye*, Basher," Trent repeated, more firmly this time.

Basher's lip twitched. He nodded silently and headed for the door.

"Local talent?" I asked, watching Basher wend his way through the room. Halfway across he slowed, his eyes once again lingering on something near the bar before he resumed his pace.

"You don't really think I'd partner up with an oaf like that, do you?" Trent countered scornfully. "How did you know?"

"That you're Hades?" I shrugged. "It was pretty obvious after you drugged me in the Badlands instead of enlisting me to help capture her. So when did *you* know she was traveling with us?"

He gave a small shrug. "After she shot her way through those hunters on Vesperin," he said. "I checked the records, saw the *Ruth* was there the same time she was, and came to the logical conclusion."

"More of a lucky guess than a conclusion," I said. "Considering how many people and ships must have been on Vesperin at that time."

"You were also seen together on Balmoral."

"Extrapolating from two data points is still building on wet sand," I warned. "How did that point you to Niskea?"

"There are two or three master gunsmiths she's worked with over the years," he said. "I figured she might want something special on hand, flipped a coin, and ended up with Niskea." He favored me with a small smile. "And yes, we also had the other places covered."

"Very efficient of you," I said. "Who's *we?*"

"Myself, my client, and my client's other front men."

"Not really helpful," I pointed out. "How about a name?"

"How about not?" he countered. "Come on, Roarke. You know how the confidentiality thing works."

"Okay, fine," I said. "So here's the deal. I have a job to do, Nikki has a job to do, and until those jobs are finished I can't let you have her."

His face hardened. "*You* can't let us have her? And how exactly do you intend to stop us?"

"Oh, you'd be surprised how good crocketts are at disappearing," I said. "All those lovely inhabitable but uninhabited worlds you can sit on with all the air and water you could possibly want."

"I thought you said you had a job to do."

"I'm told it's open-ended."

A muscle in Trent's cheek twitched as he clenched and then unclenched his jaw. "I presume you have a counteroffer?"

"You and your client take a step back and let us finish our respective jobs without interference," I said. "Once Nikki's off the *Ruth*, whatever any of you want to do is none of my business."

"And if I refuse?"

I shrugged, trying to look casual. I'd beaten Trent once, which I was pretty sure he was also thinking about. But that had been as much by luck as by skill, and I had no desire to try for a rematch. "Then we'll just have to disappear until your client loses interest or kicks you off the job."

"And you're very good at the disappearing, or so you say," he said. "Let's try another approach." He leaned back in his seat, stretching his arms straight to either side as if easing tired or cramped muscles and joints. He brought them back in again—

And suddenly there was a Libra 2mm cricket gun gripped in his right hand.

"Here's the new deal," he said in a tone that managed to be conversational and threatening at the same time. "We're going to go outside—you first, Selene next, me last. I only have six shots, as I'm sure you already know, but if you make trouble all six will be going into her back. I genuinely hope you believe me."

"I do," I said, trying to work some moisture into a suddenly dry mouth. "Believe me in turn when I say that if you hurt Selene, you'll die tonight."

"Good," he said with another small smile. "We understand each other, then. Ready?"

"One question first," I said. "Well, one question and one comment. Do you really think even six shots from a cricket gun will be enough to take down someone like Nicole Schlichting? Even if she doesn't, you know, get in the first shot?"

"Don't worry, this is just an opening conversation piece," he said, tapping his left elbow gently against his side for emphasis. "I have more in reserve. Everyone up, please. Nice and easy—we don't want to draw unwelcome attention."

"I still have a comment," I reminded him, making no move to stand up. "The most useful thing about hiring local talent like Basher is that they *are* local. They're familiar with the streets and shops, can fit in with the citizenry, and know all the workers and patrons of places like this."

Trent's eyes narrowed slightly. "Your point?"

"My point is that when someone like Basher spots something off-kilter," I said calmly, "you really ought to pause and let him tell you about it." I nodded over his shoulder.

He smiled. "You don't really think—?"

He broke off, his smile vanishing, his face and body going rigid as the muzzle of a plasmic pressed briefly against the back of his neck. A plasmic concealed from casual view by the serving tray of the bogus waiter Basher had spotted and puzzled over earlier.

The bogus waiter Jordan McKell.

"Nicely done, Selene," I complimented her.

"You said you wanted extra firepower," she reminded me. "This seemed the best option."

"Absolutely," I agreed. "Hello, McKell. We were just talking about you."

"So I heard," McKell said. "Who's this?"

"A man who's going to wish he'd taken me up on my offer." I reached across the table and took hold of the Libra's muzzle. For a second Trent resisted; then, reluctantly accepting the inevitable, he released his grip on the weapon. "Selene?" I prompted as I turned the Libra around to point at its previous owner.

She stepped around the table, probed delicately beneath the

left side of Trent's jacket, and came up with a nasty-looking Ryukind plasmic. She pocketed the weapon and resumed her seat.

"Thank you," I said. "So: let's recap. The new arrangement is for you and your client to back off until Nikki is off our ship for good. Right?"

Trent looked like he'd just bitten down on an especially sour lemon, but nodded. "Fine," he said.

"And you're going to rescind the bounty notice."

"Fine," he said.

"And make sure that your client doesn't reinstate it."

The imaginary lemon seemed to get a little sourer. "He won't be happy."

"You'll just have to find a way to make sure he is," I said. "But however you need to do it, the notice is rescinded."

"No, not rescinded," Selene put in. "Mark it as fulfilled."

"Excellent idea," I agreed. "That way no one will stay on the hunt hoping the notice will come back at a future date."

Trent sent Selene a look that could frost liquid steel. "Fine," he said again. "As soon as I'm back on my ship I'll square it."

"Excellent," I said. "And just to make sure"—I picked up the envelope of bank checks Basher had left there, held it up for Trent's inspection, and slid it into my jacket pocket—"I'll be hanging onto this for the moment. You'll get it back after Nikki's off the *Ruth* and I alert you that she's fair game again."

Trent stiffened. "That wasn't part of the deal."

"Not the original deal, no," I agreed. "But that was when I was going to be a gentleman and trust you to keep your end. As my father used to say, *Trust is like a mirror. Break it, and you'll have seven years of bad deals.*"

"Yeah," Trent growled. "Cute. My client isn't going to be happy to hear I've lost his money."

"Why tell him?" I asked. "Like I said, you'll get it back. Then you can go after Nikki and earn it."

"What if someone gets to her first?"

I cocked an eyebrow. "Gets to *Nikki*?"

"Point," he conceded reluctantly. "Can I go now?"

"I think we'll all go together," McKell put in. "I'd hate for you to catch your death sitting out there in the cold waiting to ambush us."

"Anyway, Basher might be waiting to inquire about hazard

pay," I added as we all stood up. "We'll see you to a runaround stand before we leave."

We didn't escort him all the way to a stand, of course—we also couldn't have him grabbing a vehicle and following us. But we did leave him in sight of one before the three of us piled into McKell's runaround and took off into the night.

"Very much appreciate the assist," I said to McKell as he headed toward the spaceport. "You can just drop us anywhere near the south entrance."

"I've got a better idea," he said. "Let's go to the *Stormy Banks*. I can fix us a drink." He threw me a sideways look. "And you can enlighten me as to what the hell game you're playing this time."

CHAPTER SEVENTEEN

———— ❖ ————

"Nicole Schlichting," McKell said, shaking his head with a mix of awe and disbelief. "The legend herself. I'd make you a small wager that she's still considered a myth among a sizeable percentage of the badgemen out there."

"A couple of weeks ago I'd have been right there with them," I agreed, taking a sip of my cola.

"And you're sure it's her?" McKell pressed. "*Really* sure, I mean? It's not just her calling herself Nikki?"

"Very sure," I said. "I have direct confirmation from people who should know."

McKell's eyes narrowed slightly. "Which people? ISLE badgemen?"

"Let's just say they're people who know things and leave it at that."

For a second I thought McKell was not, in fact, going to leave it at that. But then there was a small vibration from the phone he'd set on the *Stormy Banks*'s dayroom table beside his drink. "Report from Ixil," he announced, picking up the phone and peering at the display. "Your passenger seems to be doing some work on her new toy."

"Is she, now," I said. On the drive to the spaceport McKell had told us Ixil was planning to let himself into the *Ruth* through our secret entrance and send Pix and Pax through the ship's air ducts to check on Nikki. Apparently, he'd succeeded. "Details?"

"He says it looks like an Ausmacher missile-slug sniper rifle," McKell said. "Pax couldn't get a clear enough look for Ixil to identify the model."

"Well, whichever one it started life as, it'll have been modified," I warned. "She picked it up from a gunsmith on Niskea."

"Or the gun might be standard issue and her friend just provided her with specialized ammo," McKell pointed out as he keyed in a return message. "I've seen that happen on occasion. But I'll tell Ixil to get whatever else he can on the gun." He finished his message and set the phone down again. "Let's talk about Trandosh. Why do you think there's a portal at the end of the hilly section?"

"Why do *you* think there's one here?" I countered.

McKell frowned. "Who said we do?"

"If you're not portal-hunting, why are you and Ixil here?" I asked. "I can't believe you haven't got more pressing duties than taking a fond-memories tour."

McKell paused, and I could see him working through just how much he could or should tell us. "Icarus was unique," he said at last. "You remember that with Firefall the Patth had to wait until a destination code was punched in before they could get their own portal's address?"

I nodded. Considering everything else that had been clustered around that puzzle I wasn't likely to ever forget. "Sure. So?"

"So that wasn't the case with Icarus," he said. "It was already on and set for Alpha. That's why when I accidentally triggered it that's where I ended up."

I looked at Selene, saw her pupils starting to register the full implications of what McKell was saying. "So you want to know who set it up?"

"Who, and why," McKell said. "We've looked around Alpha as best we can using small orbital drones, but so far we haven't found any clues as to why the Icarus portal might have been preset for it."

"Any idea how much time has passed since the portal was activated?" I asked. "I mean originally, not since you went through?"

"Good question," McKell said. "One estimate puts the portal ages at between ten and fifteen thousand years."

"So it was sitting there, primed and on standby, for at least ten thousand years?"

"As you may have noticed, the portal creators—"

"The Icari," I corrected.

"The *Icari* made these things to last," McKell said, giving me a look of strained patience. Apparently, he wasn't any more impressed by our name for the portal's creators than Ixil had been. "Or it could be worse. If we take the state of the Trandosh ruins into account, that number could go up to forty or fifty thousand years."

"No," Selene murmured. "It's closer to ten."

We both looked at her. "How do you know?" McKell asked.

For a second I caught a glimpse of some deep emotion in her pupils. Then they cleared, and she was back to her usual calm self. "The Trandosh ruins aren't a good indicator," she said. "Remember how well-preserved the Erymant Temple complex is. The buildings there haven't survived forty thousand years of natural erosion and weathering."

"*If* both sites were built by the Icari," McKell cautioned. "They may not have been."

"They were," I said. "Selene's right. The reason Trandosh is so badly ruined is because it was attacked."

"Really," McKell said calmly. I'd expected my statement to have thrown him at least a little. "By whom?"

I paused, trying to organize my thoughts. I needed to convince him if we were going to find the other end of Cherno's portal before our clock ran out. But at the same time I needed to avoid the facts that would run the conversation off the road, or violate the admiral's order to keep Nask and the Patth out of it. "Let me go back to the beginning," I said. "Remember my theory about Popanilla?"

"That Shiroyama Island was a prisoner-of-war camp set up by the Icari?" McKell shrugged. "It was an intriguing idea, anyway."

"*I* thought so," I said, filtering the annoyance out of my voice. I'd pitched that suggestion to McKell and the admiral, neither of whom had greeted it with any discernable enthusiasm. They still preferred their original theory that the place was the scene of some great ancient battle that the Icari had used a Gemini portal to get to. "Now assume there was another prison somewhere, this one for political prisoners instead of military ones. Assume further that those prisoners were able to get access to their end of their Gemini, that it led here to Meima, and that they and however many friends had already gathered here attacked the government center where the Icarus portal was located."

"To what end?"

"What do you think?" I countered. "Control a full-range portal like Icarus and you can go anywhere. You can escape, launch further attacks—the sky is literally the limit."

Selene muttered something in her own language, her pupils suddenly stricken. "The hills and dips," she said. "You're saying the dips are bomb craters from the battle?"

"More likely the result of mortars or antipersonnel rockets," I said, a ghostly image rising in front of my eyes of men and women charging furiously across a killing field. "Smaller charges, more precise, safer for use near your own people and facilities."

"So they were running from their portal to the Icarus," Selene said slowly. "That's why you think it's at the far end of the hill section."

"Right," I said. "All the attackers were in that zone. No point wasting ammunition elsewhere."

"Interesting theory," McKell said. "One problem: What makes you think this portal, if it exists, is the other end of Cherno's Gemini?"

"There was just something about Cherno's place," I said, putting all the quiet earnestness into my voice as I could. As my father used to say, *When you want someone to swallow a plate of malarkey, make sure it's the best-tasting malarkey you've ever baked.* "I can't really put it into words, but I'm convinced the other end is here."

McKell shook his head. "Sorry, Roarke. I can't just—"

"I could smell it," Selene said suddenly.

McKell broke off in mid-sentence. "What?"

"The aromas that I smelled near where the Icarus was found," she said. "I could smell them in Cherno's portal." She looked at me, her pupils rippling with the tension that came from a basically honest person lying her butt off.

"Wait a minute," McKell said, frowning. Fortunately, he wasn't nearly as good at reading her as I was. "You're saying that some of the cross-transfer air from ten thousand *years* ago is still in that portal?"

"You know how well those complex molecules can cling to

surfaces," I improvised. "It's the whole basis for Kadolian scent tracking. If Selene says she smelled Trandosh in Cherno's portal, you can believe it."

McKell grunted. "You could have said that in the first place," he growled. "Instead of that *just something about Cherno's place* nonsense."

"I probably should have," I said, making sure I sounded properly chastened. "I guess sometimes you just want to be trusted for yourself."

"Yes, well, that's not the way to go about it," McKell said, his eyes shifting back and forth between us. He still wasn't buying it, not fully.

But he also couldn't refute it, not in any objective way. Selene's abilities were far enough off the edge of the map that he could accept her conclusions or reject them but couldn't really challenge them.

"Fine," he said at last. "Anyway, any portal we find is a win for us, even if it isn't the other end of Cherno's. Let's assume you're right. How do we proceed?"

"As I told Ixil, we start by turning over some of the soil out past the hills," I said. "You don't need to dig too deep, just enough to bring some portal metal molecules to the surface. Selene and I will give you a few hours' head start, then come by and see if she can spot anything. If she can, great. If she can't, we repeat the process."

"What about Schlichting?"

"We'll check the bounty notices when we get back to the *Ruth* and see if Trent has closed down the one on her," I said. "If he has, she should be able to go anywhere she wants without drawing any trouble."

McKell's lip twisted. "If her reputation is even close to the reality, I doubt you have to worry about her."

"I was more worried about the person or persons who instigated the trouble."

"Good point," he said. "All right. As soon as you're safely on board, I'll have Ixil retrieve Pix and Pax and sneak back out. We'll get started at the dig at first light."

"Thanks," I said, draining my glass. "While you're at it, ask him to get every bit of data he can about that Ausmacher gun and ammo. I want to know exactly what we're up against."

"I don't think you need to be concerned about it," McKell said. "She's not going to open fire with a sniper rifle inside the *Ruth*."

"I'm not thinking about us," I said. "I'm thinking about her target."

McKell shook his head. "There's really nothing you can do about that," he said heavily. "If someone like Schlichting misses her target the first time, she's just going to try again later."

"So she told me," I said. "But I won't have any control over her actions then."

"I don't think we have any control over her *now*," Selene murmured.

"Then maybe we should try to get some."

McKell looked at Selene, then back at me. "You're not thinking this through, Roarke," he said. "The only thing getting in Schlichting's way will accomplish is getting you and Selene in her crosshairs, too."

"Maybe." I took a deep breath. Clearly, neither of them was getting it. "Look. Nikki is aboard our ship. *Our* ship. We may not be legally responsible for her actions, but those actions still reflect on us. I don't want to be associated with a murder, plain and simple. If she wants to kill someone after she leaves, you're right, I can't stop her. But as long as she's aboard my ship, I have to at least try."

Again, McKell looked at Selene. "For what it's worth, I *do* understand what you're saying," he said. "I'll just point out that while you're not responsible for Schlichting, you *are* responsible for Selene. Don't put her in danger just to satisfy some vague sense of justice."

"I won't," I assured him.

"Good. See that you don't." McKell stood up and gestured to the dayroom hatch. "Time to go. Come on, I'll drive you back to the *Ruth*."

Nikki was still in her cabin when we arrived. I knocked, and when she answered I told her we were back, that I was locking down the *Ruth* for the night, and asked if she needed anything.

She didn't. She also didn't ask where we'd been, and I didn't offer to tell her.

I returned to the entryway and double-locked it, then went to the bridge to make sure the pilot board was similarly locked down. After that it was finally to the dayroom, where Selene had in the interim set the table and prepped a late dinner for the two of us. I sealed the dayroom hatch, and for the first time in several hours we finally had some privacy.

"Interesting evening," Selene said, her pupils studiously neutral as I poured us some wine. Having been threatened with a strangulation and a shooting, and having had to navigate the minefield that was McKell's innate grid of suspicions, I decided I could bend my earlier vow and have a little alcohol. "I assume you have some thoughts?" she added.

"One or two," I said, sitting down across from her and picking up my fork. "Number one is to thank you for backing me up with McKell about Cherno's better half being on Meima. I don't think he'd have been nearly as willing to cooperate without your vote of confidence."

"You're welcome," she said, her pupils shifting to a thoughtful look. "I wish the admiral hadn't ordered us not to tell him where Cherno's portal came from."

"I'm not thrilled by that, either," I conceded. "He's not going to be happy when he finds out, and just because it's not our fault doesn't mean he won't blame us for it."

"I suppose." Selene speared herself a chunk of broccoli. "When are you going to tell me what kind of deal you made with Nask?" She put the vegetable delicately in her mouth. "Or weren't you planning to?"

Briefly, I thought about denying that I'd even met with Nask personally, let alone come to any agreements. The less she knew about any of that, the cleaner she'd come out when the inevitable fallout came roaring down on me.

But of course she'd smelled Nask's scent on me when I came back from my visit to the *Odinn* and knew who I'd been keeping recent company with. "No, I can tell you," I said reluctantly. "I should probably mention first that he's in pretty bad shape. When Cherno's team hijacked the Fidelio portal, they apparently killed every other Patth aboard."

"Thirty of them, if Trent was telling the truth."

I winced. I'd forgotten that number. "Probably," I said. "Nask's own survival was a combination of luck and the raiders' inattention."

"I'm sorry for him," Selene said, her pupils showing no genuine regret that I could see.

"If you're not, you should be," I said bluntly. "He's still our best window into what the Patth are thinking and doing, and on top of that he owes us a favor that we'll be collecting on when the time is right. His death would put us back to Square One."

"Whereas we're now all the way to Square Three?"

"Probably more like Square One-and-a-Half," I conceded. "The Patth are hardly known for their eagerness to make friends. The point is that we don't want some other go-getter taking the portal mandate away from him."

Selene looked down at her plate, picking out a piece of chicken. But when she raised her head again I could see some reluctant agreement in her pupils. "All right," she said. "I'm glad he's alive, and wish him a speedy recovery. What deal did you make?"

"You're not going to like it," I warned. "I promised I would do everything in my power to get his portal back to him."

Her pupils turned a sort of stunned flatness. "The portal you promised the admiral?"

"The portal *Cherno* promised the admiral," I countered, hearing the defensiveness in my voice. "I never made any promises one way or another."

Selene remained silent, but it wasn't hard to guess what she was thinking. I might not have explicitly told anyone I'd hand the portal over to the Icarus Group, but that had certainly been everyone's expectations. Including my own. "How do you intend to go about doing that?" she asked.

"Still working on it," I said. "Look, I know you don't agree, but this is—"

"Who said I didn't agree?"

"Uh . . ." I broke off, staring at her. With anyone else I'd assume it was sarcasm or a setup to some withering retort. But Selene didn't work that way. Besides, I could see the calmness right there in her pupils. "You *don't* disagree?"

She turned her attention back to her plate. I sat quietly, waiting as she pondered her way through three more bites. "Back on Fidelio you pointed out that Nask could have sabotaged our Gemini portals, but didn't," she said at last. "At the time, you used that as your argument for why we shouldn't begrudge the Patth obtaining theirs."

"And that would still be my argument," I agreed. "Plus the fact that a lot of Patth were killed during the hijacking, which will have made everyone from the Director General on down *very* unhappy. Returning the portal to them would go a long ways toward convincing them that the Icarus Group had nothing to do with it."

"I don't know how convinced they'll be regardless," Selene warned. "But you're right, it's certainly the best first step." She studied me. "What did Nask give you to bring aboard the *Ruth*? A communicator of some kind?"

For a second I just stared at her. How had she—?

Of course. She'd smelled Nask's scent on me when I returned from the *Odinn*, but after several showers and clothes launderings the scent was still there. Ergo, Nask had given me something that hadn't gone through any of those cleaning processes.

That something being the million commarks currently tucked away in my wallet.

As my father used to say, *Sometimes the full truth makes things more complicated than you can afford. In that case, just tell the half that keeps things simple.* "He gave me some spending money to cover unanticipated expenses," I said. Which was completely true, though certainly not how Selene would take it. "Anyway, right now Nask and Cherno are the future. The Trandosh ruins are the present, and we need to get some sleep if we're going to dig us up a portal tomorrow."

"Yes," Selene said. "Speaking of ruins, have you really changed your mind about Shiroyama Island?"

I had to play back my memories of the evening's conversations before I could pick up on her reference. "You mean that it was for Icari political prisoners? Yes. For one thing, the place is just too *nice.* There's those mountains, shoreline, forests, plus plenty of flat ground where you can house a bunch of people in relative comfort. It's way too nice a spot to park a bunch of your enemies."

"Not to mention the comfortable climate."

"Exactly," I said. "It's the kind of place mid-level functionaries put people they might be answering to again someday. And second, there are those armbands like the one you found. You don't need to pamper enemy prisoners by letting them keep their rank insignia. In fact, taking those away would be an easy way to add some extra humiliation to their exile."

"But again, you'd want to treat political prisoners with more respect," Selene said. "Yes. So how do you think it worked?"

"The escape?" I felt my throat tighten as I again visualized the Meima killing field. "I'm guessing the Popanilla crowd had help from someone on Fidelio in taking over their portal. They came through, hurried across the Erymant grounds to the other Gemini—"

"Not bothering to do any damage to the structures along their way."

"Probably doing their best *not* to damage anything, in fact," I said. "That kind of noise would draw attention, which was the last thing they wanted. The minute the Fidelio authorities were alerted, they would have moved to lock down the Gemini portal to Meima."

"And the rebels couldn't stay on Fidelio because there was no full-range portal there?"

"That's my guess," I said. "I'm thinking Fidelio was a minor administration complex. A way station for the rebels on their way to the *real* prize."

"Meima and Icarus."

"Right," I said. "The full-range portal and the people who ran it were their ultimate goal. Also note how the rebels were able to completely circumvent the whole purpose of having two different Gemini portals close together in the first place. That transfer gap was supposed to keep any prisoner escapes confined to Fidelio and not let them get to Meima."

A hint of contempt drifted into Selene's pupils. "Someone wasn't doing their job."

"Or someone had been suborned or was already dead," I said, wincing again. "We don't know how big or widespread the uprising was."

"But we *do* know the Meima administration center was completely destroyed."

"Eventually," I said, frowning. "Not necessarily all of it at that time."

But if it *was* mostly destroyed in that first attack, then we might also have the answer to McKell's puzzle.

We finished the rest of our meal in silence. "What do we do if the portal's not there?" Selene asked as we collected the plates and flatware.

"Then Nask and Cherno stop being the future and become the present," I said grimly. "A very, very unhappy present."

CHAPTER EIGHTEEN

Nikki was gone when I woke the next morning, but she'd left a note at the entryway that she was heading to the StarrComm center to check her mail drop. I got some deep-maintenance tests going on the *Ruth*'s engines and sensor systems, and when Selene woke we had a leisurely breakfast and discussed the day's strategy. At about ten-thirty I got a call from McKell saying they were ready for us, and we snagged a runaround and headed for the western end of the Trandosh ruins.

McKell and Ixil were waiting alone when we arrived. "I sent the other diggers for an early lunch," McKell explained as we walked over to them. "I didn't think they needed to see our secret weapon in action."

"They certainly earned a break," I commented, looking around. The whole area looked like it had been attacked by a garden party of compulsively neat moles, with an ordered array of thirty-centimeter-deep holes spaced a couple of meters apart, each hole with its own pile of excavated dirt beside it. "I guess it's Selene's turn now."

"Yes." Selene took a step toward the grid, took a few tentative sniffs, then waved the three of us downwind toward one of the mounds at the eastern end of the field. "It'll be easier if you're out of smelling range."

"Right," I said, beckoning to the others. "Signal if you get anything."

A minute later McKell, Ixil, and I were seated along the base of one of the hills. "Last night I ran an analysis of the ground-piercing radar images for these mounds," Ixil said as we watched Selene move methodically along the grid, pausing over each hole and dirt pile to sniff the air. "If you look at it properly the data are indeed consistent with a series of mortar blasts modified by a few thousand years of erosion. I'm surprised no one noticed that before."

"You said it yourself," I pointed out. "You have to look at the data with that possibility in mind. No one saw it because no one was looking for it."

"Yes," McKell said thoughtfully. "Makes you wonder what else is out there that no one is seeing."

"It does indeed," I agreed. "As a matter of fact, I have a couple of ideas about that."

"Would you care to share with the rest of the class?"

"Let's wait until we see what Selene turns up," I said, peering off to my right as a movement caught my eye. One of Ixil's outriders had rounded the hill we were sitting against and was hurrying toward us. "Trouble?" I added, nodding toward the animal.

"Not necessarily," Ixil said thoughtfully as he held out his arm. "I have them patrolling the area. Still, he *does* seem to be in a hurry." The outrider ran up to us—it was Pix, I saw now that I could clearly see the markings in his fur—and scampered up Ixil's arm. He settled into his usual position on the Kalix's left shoulder and dug his long claws through cloth and skin and into Ixil's nervous system. Their symbiotic linkup connected their minds and memories—

"We have a visitor," Ixil announced, still sounding thoughtful. "It's your friend Trent."

"Well, *that's* awkward," I said, scowling. "Damn. I would have sworn we weren't followed."

"Maybe you weren't," McKell said, craning his neck to peer as far as he could around the side of the hill. "Any chance he might be interested in the ruins for some other reason?"

"I can't see him being interested in anything he can't trade for quick cash." Glowering, I got to my feet. "I guess I'd better go talk to him."

"You want me to come along?" McKell asked, starting to get up.

"No, thanks," I said, waving him back down. "I'd rather the two of you keep an eye on Selene. You have a location on Trent?"

"About two hundred meters that way," Ixil said, pointing over his shoulder to his right. "He was moving slowly, so he shouldn't have wandered too far."

"Unless he's picked up speed," I said, starting around the other side of our hill. "Back in a minute."

I didn't see anyone moving as I maneuvered my way through the hills and pits toward the one that ought to give me a vantage point above Trent's last known position. I reached my target hill and started up. Midway to the top, mindful of the fact that he was probably at least as good a shot as I was and that he had a lot more motivation to make trouble, I dropped to hands and knees and continued my journey in a commando's crawl.

The centuries that had elapsed since the battle had left the hills covered in a spiny, purplish ground cover that seemed to have as many prickles as it did actual stalks and slender leaves. Fortunately, while the prickles were annoying, the barbs were thin and flexible enough that they didn't penetrate the skin of my hands. I reached the top of my hill and cautiously eased my head up for a look.

It was Trent, all right. He'd made it about half a hill closer than Ixil's estimate, heading toward the flat section of the ruins Selene and the others were working. Fortunately, he was moving slowly enough that my hill still put me on the high ground above him.

It was a perfect setup for a sniper attack, and my plasmic had more than enough range to make it a quick kill. Fortunately for Trent, I had neither the inclination nor any excuse for that kind of action.

What I *did* have was motivation to try to get him off our backs. Drawing my plasmic, I aimed carefully at one of the small bushes just behind him and fired.

With a muffled *whoosh* the bush burst into flames. Trent reacted instantly, leaping a meter forward and dropping into a crouch, a weapon magically appearing in his hand. His head whipped back and forth, his eyes darting everywhere as he tried to locate the source of the attack.

In this case, it was an exercise in futility. For all a plasmic's shortcomings in the areas of range and stopping-power when compared with a chemical or missile-slug firearm, the weapon had the advantage of being virtually silent. A warning shot that landed behind a target where he hadn't been able to see its visual track might as well have come straight down from God.

"Roarke?" he called softly, his voice barely audible over the rustling of trees and bushes. "Schlichting?"

I thought about dropping a second shot beside him, but of course this time he was likely to see it, which would make it pointless and probably a little childish. "Hello, Trent," I called instead. "Just drop the weapon, there's a good boy."

Even with the background noises, he had my location before I'd finished my order. For a moment he stared up at me, probably gauging his chances for a successful hit against the small target cross-section I was currently presenting. Then, very deliberately, he stood up and just as deliberately tucked the gun back into its waist holster beneath his jacket. "I just want to talk," he called, raising his hands to shoulder height.

"I'm listening."

He looked around again, his gaze sweeping across the various hilltops. "Your bodyguard taking the morning off?"

"There's one easy way to find out," I said, wishing now that I'd accepted McKell's offer of backup. Trent was in a lousy combat position down there, but as my father used to say, *When arrogance and pride arrive at the party, logic and reason collect their coats and leave. If the pride is also wounded, tactical sense usually leaves with them.*

"No, thanks," he said, raising his hands a little higher. "You and Selene out for a stroll, I take it?"

"Bird-watching," I told him. "I trust you didn't come all the way out here just to play Twenty Questions."

"Actually, you're not far off," Trent said. "I have a few questions I need to ask you. Simple questions, nothing that would violate confidentiality or bring trouble to anyone. A few simple answers, and I'll disappear from your life forever."

I felt my eyebrows go up. He had questions for *me*? "If any of them involve Nikki, you're out of luck," I warned. "I already told you she and I have jobs to do."

"Yes, I remember," he said. "And I have no further interest in her."

"I'm sure she'll be happy to hear that," I said. "Would these questions be the same ones you were planning to ask when I woke up after you drugged me on Niskea?"

Even at our current distance I could see his face darken. "Yes, and I'm truly sorry about that. Rest assured that I reprimanded Beeks *very* severely for his impudence."

I frowned. "Are you telling me Beeks drugged me on his own initiative?"

"Of course," Trent said. "I would never have—"

"Without any orders from you?"

"I just said that."

I shook my head sadly. "Oh, Trent, Trent," I said putting some theatrical regret into my voice. "I realize some people get so used to lying that the fibs just pop out of their own accord. But are you *really* going to stand there and tell me that an underling— who *you're* paying—would drug an invited houseguest without specific orders to do so?"

He drew himself up. "I've told you what happened. If you're not willing to accept the truth, I can't make you."

"You're absolutely right," I agreed. "What you also can't do is continue to waste my time." I lifted my plasmic a bit. "The only question is whether you walk back to your vehicle and drive away on your own, or whether you get to ride with a couple of medics while they try to assess how badly charred your leg is."

He snorted. "You're bluffing. I've read your file. You wouldn't shoot someone in cold blood."

"You'd be surprised at how often those bounty hunter files miss something," I said. "Anyway, I'm not the only one out here, remember? I'd make a small wager that my bodyguard wouldn't hesitate a bit to take you down. And not just an injury, but permanently."

Once again his eyes flicked around the area. But this time, when he turned back to face me, some of the defiance in his face and body language had faded. Tactical sense had apparently returned to the party, possibly bringing pizza. "This isn't over, Roarke," he warned. "I'm going to get the answers I want. One way or another."

"Next time try saying *please*," I said. "Oh, and before you go, just put your weapon on the ground, will you?"

Silently, he pulled out his gun and set it on the prickly grass. "Do take good care of it," he said softly. "I'll be retrieving it and the others you took away from me very soon, and you wouldn't like what I charge for damage."

"I'll keep that in mind," I said. "Good-bye, Trent."

I watched him make his way back around the hills and dips, wondering if I should follow to make sure he really left. But with this terrain there was no way I could keep him continually in sight, and I had no doubt he had a backup weapon tucked away somewhere. A couple of seconds on his own, and he would have little trouble getting the drop on me.

Still, as long as he thought there were two of us watching him, he would probably withdraw and look for a more promising time and place. And given that there really *were* two watchers who would be dogging his every step—Pix and Pax—we ought to be safe enough, at least for the moment.

So I waited until he was out of sight, gave it another couple of minutes to see if that wounded pride might still be doing his thinking for him, then went down and retrieved his weapon— this one a Golden 6mm—and returned to where I'd left McKell and Ixil.

I'd expected to find them still seated against the hill, watching Selene doing her sweep. Instead, they were about a third of the way out in the field of holes, digging industriously at the ground while Selene stood to the side watching them.

I hurried toward them, my heart suddenly pounding. Selene looked up at me as I approached and gave a silent nod. McKell also looked up, then returned to his digging. "Any idea how deep?" I asked as I came up to them.

"Not very," Selene said. "A meter, maybe two."

"That's to the top, of course," McKell added, tossing another shovelful of dirt off to the side. "Those hills the mortar rounds threw up must have been impressively high for a few thousand years of erosion to have filled in this much around the rest of the portal."

"Unless it was partially buried to begin with," I said, eyeing the deepening pit. "Time to call back your other diggers?"

"I've given them the rest of the day off," McKell said. "I think we can handle this ourselves."

"Agreed," I said, thinking fast. If this was indeed the other end of Cherno's portal . . . "I'd like to ask a favor," I said. "If and when we confirm this is the portal we're looking for, I need you to activate it, and then pull back. Cover the entrance a little or otherwise disguise it, and put everything else on hold for a few days."

McKell paused, his shovel dug partway into the dirt. "Excuse me?" he asked.

"I know you'll want to shout the good news to the admiral and get a crew in here to dig it the rest of the way out," I said. "But it's important that we keep this discovery strictly to ourselves for the moment."

"Yes, I understand what you're asking," McKell said. "Still waiting for the reason."

"I wish I could give it to you," I said. "Later, I will. For now, I'm just asking that you trust me."

"Ixil?" McKell invited, his eyes still on me.

"The admiral won't like it," Ixil pointed out. "The longer we wait, the higher the probability that the Patth will learn about this and move to take it away from us."

"There aren't any Patth ships on Meima at the moment," I said. "I checked this morning before we left the *Ruth*."

"You really *were* convinced we'd find a portal here," Ixil murmured thoughtfully.

"Yes, I was," I confirmed. "I'll also point out that without Selene and me it might have been years before you even thought to look for it."

McKell and Ixil eyed at each other. "He has a point," Ixil said. "His theory about an attack on Meima was the key."

"I suppose," McKell conceded reluctantly. "How long will you need us to sit on this?"

"A few days," I repeated. "Right now, that's as definitive as I can be."

McKell grunted and resumed his digging. Three shovelfuls later he paused again and gave a brief nod. "A few days," he said. "No more. And if whatever it is happens sooner, you let us know sooner."

"Agreed," I said. "Selene?"

"We're getting closer," she said.

"All right, then," McKell said. "Let's find this thing."

"And let's make sure Pix and Pax are on the watch," I warned. "Even if Trent doesn't come back, there may be other inquisitive eyes out there."

"Don't worry," Ixil assured me. "They've got it covered."

They kept at it for another half hour, at which point I took over Ixil's shovel so that he could concentrate on coordinating the outriders' patrols. Selene watched us work, keeping track of the scent and occasionally fine-tuning our direction to keep us directly over the portal's highest point.

Twenty minutes later, we hit portal metal. An hour after that, we'd widened the hole sufficiently for someone to get down there and access one of the hull's hatches.

That someone, inevitably, was me.

"Remember, just a quick in and out," McKell reminded me for the third time as I gazed through the hatchway. The opening was on the bottom of our pit, but at the top of the receiver module, which meant the portal's internal gravitational field would be pointed the opposite direction to Meima's.

Still, that just meant that I'd need to roll into and around the opening, the same maneuver I'd done a hundred times between various portals' receiver modules and launch modules.

Sometimes I couldn't believe I'd actually become proficient at such a bizarre skill.

"I ran the activation procedure and everything seems all right at this end," McKell continued. "All you need to do is confirm the portal works—one trip there, one trip straight back. No surveillance, no recon, no walking up to Cherno and asking when's dinner. And if the other end isn't Cherno's..." He paused, his expression clouding over.

"I'm sure it is," I said.

I truly hoped it was, anyway. Because if it *wasn't*, Selene, Nikki, and I were gazing into a pit of trouble way deeper than the one we'd just dug.

"You usually are." McKell gave a brisk nod. "Good luck."

I nodded back and stretched myself out in the dirt alongside the portal opening. A good thing I hadn't dressed for the occasion. Checking my plasmic to make sure it was secure in its holster, I rolled into the opening, around the rim, and inside the portal.

No matter how many times I did this there was always a flicker of disorientation as gravity abruptly changed direction. That moment had gotten shorter over time, but it had never completely gone away. I got to my feet and made my way through the soft directionless light to the rectangular opening that marked the

entrance to the launch module. Once again I settled down beside
the gap and rolled inside.

I stood up, taking a moment to look around. The first thing
I checked was the section of the curved deck where the control
board containing the home and destination panels would be on
a full-range portal like Icarus. There was nothing there, fully
confirming this was indeed one end of a Gemini portal.

Now came the real test. I walked to the black-and-silver
extension arm and wrapped my hand around it. The module
sensed my presence, and the local gravity shifted again, sending
me smoothly upward along the arm. I reached the luminescent
gray end; bracing myself, I closed my hand firmly around it.
There was the usual tingle as the blackness dropped over me—

And a couple of seconds later I was floating in the center of
a Gemini receiver module.

I took a careful breath as the internal gravity caught me and
floated me gently toward the surface. I was hardly in Selene's
league, smelling-wise, but my comparatively frail human body
did have a decent enough set of olfactory receptors, and the air
surrounding me did smell very much the way I remembered the
air in Cherno's warehouse enclosure.

The portal's gravity did its usual trick of suddenly increasing
in the final meter of my descent, dropping me a bit hard onto
the deck. But again, I was ready for it. Keeping my hand on my
plasmic, I headed around the curved surface to the opening, lay
down beside it, and carefully looked out.

A rush of exhilaration swept away a level of tension that
I'd carried so long I'd forgotten it was there. I was indeed in
Cherno's warehouse, and we had indeed found the other end of
his Gemini portal.

Two seconds later all that low-level tension reversed direction
and came flowing straight back again. Now that this particular
hurdle was past, we still had the fact that Cherno and Nikki
were planning to murder someone.

I gave the visible parts of the warehouse a slow, careful scan,
straining both eyes and ears. There was no indication that anyone was in here besides me. In retrospect, given how important
the portal apparently was to Cherno's plans, I would have been
surprised if he'd shared the secret with anyone he didn't absolutely have to.

Did that mean there also weren't any guards in the tunnel leading to and from his mansion?

Carefully, I eased my way out of the portal. Crouching beside the opening, I gave the warehouse another visual scan, this time looking for cameras. The same logic that said no guards also suggested no cameras, but there was a chance Cherno was the type who liked to keep an eye on his possessions. But again, there was nothing I could see.

I shifted my eyes to the trapdoor leading down into the tunnel. McKell had said no recon, and I mostly agreed with him. But at the same time it would be handy to know if Cherno had hedged his bets by at least covering the approach to his prize. Walking across the room, I knelt down beside the trapdoor and lifted it a couple of millimeters. For a full minute I stayed there, again listening hard. No creaks of a chair being moved, no shuffling of feet, no sipping of a drink, not even any heavy breathing.

As my father used to say, *Sometimes the best way to prove your innocence is to deliberately stroll into a trap.* I'd never fully bought into that one, but this might be the time to test it. Lifting the door all the way, I headed down.

The lights that had illuminated the tunnel during our last trip had been turned off, leaving the whole passageway in darkness. I fished out my flashlight and turned it on.

Once again, my gamble had paid off. The tunnel was deserted.

I focused on the elevator at the other end, briefly wondering if I might be able to make it three for three. But as my father used to say, *Stupidity is like a childhood disease. The later in life that you catch it, the worse it is.* Still, there was no harm in taking a closer look.

The elevator itself was as I remembered it: heavy metal doors, an even heavier metal frame, and a single call button. What I hadn't noticed my last time here was the pair of fifteen-centimeter-square ventilation grilles—one set half a meter above and to the left of the elevator door, the other set a few of centimeters above the floor directly beneath the first—that were circulating air through the tunnel and, via the gaps around the trapdoor, into the portal's warehouse.

And air systems, as I'd learned a long time ago, could be very handy.

The lower grille was fastened to its housing with four screws, one in each corner. I unscrewed them, took off the grille, and shined my light inside. The duct ran horizontally for about ten centimeters, then made a right-angle turn and continued straight up. The inner walls had probably started out smooth, but years of sitting untended in the underground damp had left patches of corrosion and pockmarks where some of the metal had flaked off.

I'd be surprised if any of Cherno's people had even considered the possibilities the ducts offered to someone like me. But then, I'd be surprised if any of them had ever seen a Kalix and his outriders in action.

Fortunately for me, I had.

As was usual for systems that didn't have to support any weight except its own, the ducts were made of soft and fairly thin metal. A few minutes with my multitool's auger, and I'd reamed out the screw receptacles enough that the fasteners simply rested inside without the threads engaging anything. I replaced the grille, slipped in the decorative but now useless fasteners, and headed back down the tunnel to the warehouse and the portal.

Two minutes later, I was once again on Meima.

I arrived in the receiver module to find McKell striding along beneath me heading for the launch module. "It's all right," I called down to him. "I'm here."

He looked up, his determined expression momentarily softening, then roaring back full strength with a side order of anger. "Where the *hell* have you been?" he demanded.

"Looking around a little," I said, wishing I could speed up my downward drift. Floating helplessly in the air, I was in perfect position for McKell to unload whatever choice invective he'd picked up during his long-past days in the EarthGuard auxiliary.

"I thought I said no recon."

"This wasn't a recon," I protested. "I was just looking around a little."

"What's the difference?"

"Recon requires you to fill out paperwork."

I could tell he wanted to roll his eyes at that one. But he didn't, probably figuring it would be beneath him as my supposed superior to show that kind of reaction. Besides, I'd come back in one piece and not bleeding, and that surely counted for something. "So?"

"It's the other end of Cherno's Gemini, all right," I confirmed.

"There were no guards, either by the portal or in the tunnel leading into the mansion."

"I'd make a small wager that there are eyes on the other end of the elevator."

"Not a wager I would take," I agreed. "But there's an air duct by the elevator that one of Ixil's outriders—"

"Hold on," McKell interrupted. "If we're going to talk strategy, let's take it outside. No point having to go through it twice."

Five minutes later we'd rejoined the others on the surface, Selene had expressed relief that I was back, Ixil had added his own vote of disapproval of my actions, and they were finally ready to hear my plan.

"As I was telling McKell, there's an opening to a ventilation grille at the bottom of the elevator shaft that Pix or Pax should be able to get into," I said. "It'll be a straight-up climb, but the duct metal is soft and a bit corroded, so I'm hoping navigation won't be too much of a problem."

"How big is the duct cross-section?" Ixil asked.

"About like this," I said, making a frame with my hands.

"That should work," Ixil confirmed. "I assume you want him to be a scout?"

"Not a scout," I corrected. "A courier."

I laid out my plan for them. Midway through the explanation, Selene pulled out her info pad and started silently working it. "I know the gadget I need exists," I concluded. "I've seen them once or twice. The question is whether we can find one in Barcarolle, or even just somewhere on Meima."

"*And* find one that's small enough to be carried through the ducts," McKell added.

"There's that," I conceded. "Ixil?"

"The dimensions are really the only question," he said, holding out his arm as Pax came trotting up with the latest scouting report. "Pix and Pax can carry considerable weight, even with the kind of climb you describe."

"I'm not finding anything readily available for sale in the area," Selene reported. "But do you really need something that specialized?"

"She may be right," Ixil said as Pax climbed up his arm and sunk his claws into the Kalix's shoulder. There was a moment of silence while Ixil retrieved the creature's visual memories, then a second moment while he issued the animal his new patrol instructions, and Pax was off again across the landscape. "It sounds like the analysis software is the trickiest part," he continued. "We should be able to put something together that will function well enough for what we need."

"I have no idea how to do that," I admitted. "But I'm sure you two are way better at gadgetry improv than I am. The question is whether you can throw something together in the next day or so."

"I think we can," Ixil said. "Is that when you're going back?"

"That was my thought," I said. "Cherno's probably getting pretty nervous, and having us show up a few days ahead of his deadline should help calm him down."

"There's one other thing to consider," McKell said, his voice going a shade darker. "Once he knows the Gemini is active, does he really need you and Selene anymore?"

I felt my stomach tighten. "Good question," I said. "Not sure I've got an answer for it yet."

"Well, let's be sure we do before you go charging off," McKell said. "We don't have any cavalry available to send to the rescue."

"Understood," I said. "First things first. We need you to make me my new toy." I nodded toward the hole. "And we need to disguise this thing somehow."

"Already covered," McKell said. "Here's what we have in mind..."

CHAPTER NINETEEN

———— ❖ ————

McKell called his technique *hiding the tree in the forest*. I called it *work the new guy until he drops*.

As my father used to say, *The new guy always gets the pointed end of the stick. Try not to be the new guy.*

The concept was straightforward enough. We had a big, brand-new hole that might as well include a banner inviting the Patth and everyone else to take a closer look. McKell's solution was to seal up the portal, ladle enough dirt on top to hide the metal and make it look like we'd given up, then dig three more holes roughly the same size and depth elsewhere in the field.

It was a reasonable enough plan, I had to admit, especially as sundown approached and Ixil suggested McKell and I just start a fifth hole as if planning to come back the next morning. With four and a quarter major pits, the promise of more to come, and a whole field full of the pilot holes McKell's team had dug earlier, the Patth could spend days trying to find whatever it was we were looking for.

The downside was sweat, fatigue, and the promise that a lot of previously underutilized muscles were going to ache the next day.

"I assume you want us to come back tomorrow and do more digging?" I asked as we loaded the shovels back into McKell's runaround.

"No, I'll put our other people on it," McKell said. "They might as well earn their keep. You and Selene should focus on how you're going to play things once your new gadget is ready."

"With special emphasis on how to stay alive once Cherno knows his Gemini is functional," Ixil added.

"It's at the top of our list," I promised. "Let us know when the gizmo is ready."

My arm and back muscles were already stiffening up as we returned our runaround to the stand and walked back to the *Ruth*. My rumbling stomach reminded me that we hadn't eaten since breakfast, and for a moment I enjoyed a private fantasy of Nikki, freshly back from the StarrComm center, surprising us with a hot meal laid out on the dayroom table.

Sadly, there was no meal awaiting us.

Neither was there a Nikki.

"She *was* here, though, wasn't she?" I called back to Selene as I looked into the dayroom. There was no sign that she'd cooked or eaten anything in there since our departure, or for that matter had even dropped in.

"Yes," Selene called back from her own inspection of the engine room. "Her scent is fresh."

"So, a few hours?"

"Less," Selene said. "Probably less than an hour."

"And no notes?" I asked, opening the hatch to her cabin for a quick peek inside. She hadn't answered a knock when Selene and I had first arrived, but I needed to make sure she hadn't been taken ill or was otherwise incapacitated. No one inside. I started to close the hatch—

And stopped. Lying on her bed was her phone.

"Selene?" I called, stepping into the cabin. As far as I could remember, Nikki had never left the ship without her phone riding securely in its holder on her left hip. Why would she break that pattern now?

Selene appeared in the hatchway. "What is it?"

"This," I said, pointing to the phone. "Did she have it when she left this morning for the StarrComm center?"

"Let me see."

She stepped over to the bed and knelt down beside it. Leaning over the phone, she sniffed, nostrils and eyelashes working as she sampled its scent. "Is there a Zulian restaurant near the center?"

I pulled up the memory of my last visit there. Across the street from the center was a short row of restaurants... "Yes," I said. "There's a Zulian, a Bulgrenist, and a Yavanni."

"Yes, I can smell all three," Selene confirmed. "The Zulian spices are more pungent, and adhere better to a phone's casing."

"So she made it to the center and back again," I said slowly, trying to think it through. "And then left again, but didn't take her phone. Why would she do that?"

"Are you sure she had her phone all the other times she left the ship?" Selene asked.

I thought back, pulling up mental image after mental image. Nikki on Balmoral...on Vesperin...on Lucias Four...on Niskea... "Yes," I said. "Every single time." I waved at the phone. "Until now."

There was a short pause. "You and I have traveled places without our phones, too, on occasion," Selene reminded me. "Usually when we were concerned that someone might track us."

"Right, but that's *us*," I said. "Nikki surely has the best track-and-hack-proofing in the Spiral."

"Unless she's concerned she could be facing something new."

"From where?" I countered. "If no one on Vesperin or in the Niskea Badlands has the kind of fancy gear that can punch through her guardware, there sure as hell isn't anyone on Meima who can."

Abruptly, Selene stiffened. "Yes, there is," she said. "Jordan McKell."

I stared at her. "Are you saying that the Icarus Group...?"

"You said Nikki has the best available guardware for her phone," Selene said. "But surely the admiral has high-level resources of his own."

"*I* would if I were sitting on an Icarus-size keg of dynamite," I agreed. "But how would Nikki know—oh."

"Yes," Selene said "Ixil's outriders. Nikki saw them."

"Well, she saw *Kalixiri* outriders," I said. "But there's no reason for her to think they belonged to Ixil, or to any Kalix in particular."

"Unless she knows more about Icarus than she's let on."

"Or was recently *told* more about Icarus than she's let on," I said.

And with that, the rest of the pieces I'd spent the past few weeks poking at suddenly fell together. "Oh, *hell.* Come on." I grabbed Selene's arm and hurried us down the corridor toward the entryway. "If he hasn't got her now, he will soon."

"Who?" Selene asked, catching up with me.

"Who else?" I retorted. "Trent."

McKell answered on the second vibe. "Trouble?" he asked without preamble.

"Triple helping," I said. "Nikki left the ship without her phone, and I think Trent's got her."

"I thought we'd convinced him that his plan was a nonstarter."

"*We* were convinced," I said, keying the entryway and ushering Selene onto the zigzag. "Him, apparently not so much. What kind of tracking resources do you have available?"

"I'm not sure you're allowed to know about—"

"Stop it!" I snapped. "This is no time to play protocol. Nikki's in danger, which means Selene and I are in danger. What kind of tracking can you do?"

There was the soft hiss of a sigh. "There are a couple of things we can do with phones," McKell said reluctantly. "But if she left hers behind they're worthless."

"How about tracking runaround rentals? Can you do that?"

"Yes, but not in real time. There would be a ten- or fifteen-minute delay to get that data."

"Good enough," I said. "As long as you *can* do it—and as long as Nikki knows you can do it—that's all I need."

"Wait a minute," he objected. "How would Nikki know that?"

"From Trent," I said as we reached the bottom of the ramp. "We're heading out now. Call you later."

I keyed off. "Where are we going?" Selene asked.

"We'll start with the runaround stand," I said, settling into a brisk walk. No point switching to a sprint until we had some idea how long a race we were looking at. "Can you smell her?"

"Yes, she came this way," Selene said. "No more than half an hour ago, either. I'm sorry, I should have said something on our way in. I assumed I was getting her scent from when she returned to the *Ruth.*"

"Not your fault," I said. "I'd have assumed the same thing. The crucial question is whether she grabbed a runaround this time. I'm guessing she didn't, but we won't know until we get there." A sudden thought struck me, and I pulled out my phone and punched again for McKell. "Question," I said when he answered. "Do you still have that bounty hunter persona you used on Brandywine?"

"Yes, but it would take way too long to get into the makeup and prosthetics."

"Don't need you to," I said. "What I need is for you to put out a bounty notice on Nikki offering five million commarks."

For about five of our hurried steps he didn't reply. I listened to the silence, lining up my reasoning, arguments, and pleas for when he turned me down.

I frowned, listening closer. Was that traffic I was hearing in the background? Or was I just combining his silence with the sounds coming into my other ear? "McKell?" I prompted. "I really need—"

"Done," he said. "Five million commarks for delivery alive, reply and confirm to the attached mail drop. I assume you wanted me to use the same sketch you brought from Niskea?"

"Yes," I said, mentally tossing my prepared speech out the airlock. Even now, McKell could sometimes surprise me. "Don't worry, you won't have to pay up."

"The admiral will be glad of that," McKell said dryly. "Anything else?"

"Not that I can think of," I said. "We strained Trent's budget when we confiscated his blood money. Hopefully, the news that Nikki's life is worth five million to him will buy us some time. Thanks."

I keyed off as we trotted up to the runaround stand. "Okay, Selene. Work your magic."

There were half a dozen vehicles parked in the stand. Selene walked past them, sniffing at each but not bothering to stop, until she reached the end of the group. She took four steps past it, paused—

"She went by," she said, picking up speed. "This way."

"Good," I said, smiling tightly. So, warned that someone might be able to track runaround rentals, she'd opted to walk. "Hopefully, we'll still be in time to save her."

"I don't understand," Selene said as we picked up our pace. "Nikki knew someone was trying to kill her. Why would she let Trent lure her out of the *Ruth*?"

"By offering her something she needed," I said. "Or maybe

something he just convinced her she needed. Remember the Tixi 455 you smelled in her cabin earlier? That was her fiddling with her enhanced targeting prosthetics."

"You think so?" Selene asked doubtfully. She paused, crouched down to sniff at the pavement, then straightened up and continued walking. "Those enhancements require an optical component, and facial inserts are usually quite visible."

"The key word being *usually*," I said. "Nikki was smarter than the average assassin, or maybe just had more money or influence. For her inserts she went to the best in the business: the people who've been doing facial grafts for nearly thirty years."

Selene spun around, and even in the dim light I could see the shock in her pupils. "Are you saying...the *Patth*?"

"Who else?" I said, hearing an edge of bitterness in my voice. I really, *really* should have seen it sooner. "How else could Trent know about Icarus and its capabilities? How else did he know enough about Nikki's inserts to be able to lure her out with a promise that a tech was available in Barcarolle to work on them? For that matter, how did Nask's associate Muninn even know what she looked like when she's been so careful to keep her face hidden?"

I looked past Selene at the darkening city beyond the spaceport. "Trent's not a bounty hunter, Selene. He's a Patth Expediter."

I'd been worried that we might have to traipse halfway across Barcarolle on our unexpected errand of mercy. Fortunately, Nikki's trail looked to be ending much sooner, at a medical building only a couple of kilometers from the spaceport.

A *big* medical building, naturally, with three floors and covering half a block's worth of real estate. But that was okay, because there was only one likely destination in there for her.

"Here," I said, pointing to the listing on Selene's info pad as we walked toward the building's main entrance. "This optometrist suite on the second floor at the south end of the building. Trent will have told her he had a place with full optical and eye-treatment equipment. She'd have been suspicious of anywhere else he tried to send her."

"All right," Selene said, taking a lingering look at the building's layout and then putting the pad away. "How do we get in?"

"Hopefully, the same way she did." I nodded toward the main entrance, a pair of glass doors beneath a large but tasteful sign proclaiming the place to be the WHISPER PARK HEALTH CENTER. "We'll start with the front door."

Sure enough, Nikki's scent trail led straight to the doors. "Is this where she went in?" I asked, trying the handles. Both doors were locked down solid.

"No," Selene said, sniffing at the doors. "She knocked on this one—right here. But then..." She took a few steps to her left, then backtracked and headed a few steps to her right, checking the scents in both directions.

I looked up at the sign over the doors. It was mounted a couple of centimeters away from the outer wall on slender but sturdy-looking spacers. If the sign and spacers were strong enough to hold Selene's weight, and if I could get her up there, she should be able to get to the nearest set of second-floor windows. If the tenants of those offices had been a bit careless with their external security, that might be our way in.

Of course, that further assumed that none of the pedestrians or motorists traveling the nearby streets noticed or cared that their local med center was being broken into. Would Trent risk Nikki's entry being observed by those same potential witnesses? Or would he use another entrance?

Sure enough. "She went this way," Selene said, heading off to our right toward the south end of the building.

"Got it," I said, catching up with her. "So Trent was probably waiting inside, and when she knocked he waved her to a side door where the whole thing would be less visible."

"Yes, that makes sense," Selene agreed.

Abruptly, she stopped. "Gregory, there's a dead person some-where over there."

I clenched my teeth and drew my plasmic. Or maybe stealth hadn't been Trent's only reason for getting Nikki out of the public eye. "Show me."

Selene led the way to the end of the building and around the corner. Midway down the side, slumped against the wall in a pool of darkness and blood, was a dead man.

I felt a flicker of relief that the victim wasn't Nikki. Unfor-tunately, it didn't look like it was Trent, either. Trying to watch every direction at once, I knelt down beside him and played my flashlight's lowest setting across his blood-soaked shirt. "Knife wound, looks like," I told Selene.

"Instantaneous?"

"Pretty much." I straightened up and again looked around. He couldn't have made it very far with a wound like that, and there'd been no blood trail along the ground as we came around the building. Unless his death and Nikki's presence at this same time and place were pure coincidence, I was guessing that either she or Trent had done this.

As my father used to say, *Nothing in this universe is completely pure, be it motives, coincidence, or luck.*

"She went in here."

I looked up. Selene had continued on another five meters past the body to a discreet side door and was sniffing the handle. "You sure?" I asked.

"I'm sure." She tried the handle. "This one's locked, too."

I frowned down at the body, trying to work through the logic. If Trent had killed the man before Nikki arrived, he would hardly have directed her to a door where she had to step over a corpse to get there. Ergo, it was likely that this was Nikki's handiwork. Moreover, her choice of a knife instead of her Fafnir or Jaundance suggested a reluctance to draw attention with either the plasmic's flash or the firearm's bang.

"He must have been right up in front of her," Selene murmured thoughtfully. "Why would she kill instead of just disabling him?"

"Because she felt threatened," I said, nodding as the scheme came together. "Because Trent *told* her she was being threatened. Odds are this is another of his local-talent thugs, only this one masquerading as an Icarus troubleshooter."

"Trent shouts a warning as he opens the door for her," Selene said, her pupils showing understanding and revulsion. "Tells her to run, that he's Icarus and that he's going to attack her."

"Only instead of running, she counterattacks," I said, opening the bloody jacket and starting to check the pockets. "Clever, really. Telling her there are enemies outside focuses her attention out here instead of on him."

"I thought you took all of Trent's thug-hiring money," Selene said.

"I expect Expediters have access to a pretty generous credit line," I said. Nothing in the jacket. I shifted to his trouser pockets. "Let's just hope he wants to get some of it back."

"Is that why you asked McKell to put out a bounty notice?"

"Exactly," I said, smiling as my fingers found what they'd been looking for. "And once again, Trent doesn't understand what happens when you hire local talent. Local talent wants to be versatile, so that you'll remember them fondly afterward and maybe hire them again. So when you tell someone you want them to act threatening, they don't just bring a gun and attitude to the table. They want to be ready for anything else you might decide you want from them."

I held up the dead man's compact burglar kit. "Such as a little break-and-enter. Let's see how good a lock the medics put on their private entrance."

Not a very good one, as it turned out. Thirty seconds with my new lockpicks and I had the door open. We slipped inside, found the stairs, and headed up.

There was a soft glow coming from the frosted glass on the optometrist suite door as we emerged from the stairwell. We eased over to it, and Selene got down on the floor to sniff the air coming through the narrow crack beneath the door. She lay there a few seconds, then stood back up and pressed her lips to my ear. "Trent, Nikki, and two other men," she whispered. "In the room just off the entry foyer, I think the one to the right."

I nodded, noting that the door's hinges were also on the right-hand side. Setting up in the room on that side meant Trent would see the door opening well before an attacker could either see what was going on in there or get a weapon into firing position.

But that didn't mean there weren't other, less intrusive options available for intel, especially since our late benefactor's burglar kit included a snoop-ear auditory enhancer. I pulled it out, put the earphone into my ear, and pressed the business end against the door.

"—see why you even want this slug's money, anyway," an unfamiliar and rather surly voice came into my earpiece. "You wanted her, you got her, so what's the deal? Off her, pay up, and we can all get out of here."

"Leave whenever you want," Trent's voice came back, calm but with an air of distraction about it. "You can go too, Basher, if you want. Your money's right there. Go."

I nodded to myself. So our old taverno friend Basher was back on the job.

And if he and his thug friend took Trent up on his offer, that would reduce the opposition from three to one.

Once again, luck wasn't angling my direction. "Thanks, but I think we'll stick around," the thug said, his voice going heavily suspicious. "Anyway, that stack looks a little light."

"Ten thousand each," Trent said. "That was the deal."

"That was the deal before she offed Frog," Basher's voice put in. "I figure his share should go to Cron and me."

"You'll both get the same share she gave Frog in about a minute," Trent bit out. "Now both of you shut up. I'm trying to negotiate."

There was the brief, high-pitched squeak of chair legs shifting on a tiled floor. "Sure," Cron said. "Whatever you say, boss."

I pulled the snoop-ear away from the door. "Trent, Basher, a man named Cron, and none of them seem in a hurry to leave," I told Selene. "Good news is that Trent seems to be buying McKell's bounty pitch and is apparently trying to talk up the price."

Selene nodded. "What's our plan?"

I drummed my fingers silently on the grip of my holstered plasmic as I looked at the door. It would be easy enough to unlock and open, but I would need a diversion if I wanted to get into the room without getting shot.

Maybe even a double diversion. "Go to the roof," I said, looking around the hallway. A half-meter-long cylindrical fire extinguisher in a wall recess caught my eye. "Take that extinguisher and find some rope or cable."

"We're doing a whiplash?"

"Yes," I confirmed. "And the timing will be critical."

"I understand. Buzz coordination?"

"Yes," I said again. "One-two-three. Signal when you're ready."

She stepped over to the extinguisher, pulled it from its nook, and disappeared back into the stairwell. I took a deep breath and returned to the door. It would take a few minutes for Selene to get into position, and I might as well see if Trent was making any progress bargaining McKell up from his five-million-commark offer.

But whatever was going on in there, it was happening without any real conversation. I could hear vague muttering, either from Trent on his phone or from Basher and Cron talking quietly together, and I heard one more of the noisy chair shiftings. I also thought I heard a low moan or two, but that could have been my imagination. I unlocked the door, still listening, then put the burglar kit against the wall where it would be out of the way.

Almost time. I pulled out my phone, confirmed it was on vibe, and slipped it into my top shirt pocket where its quiver would be clearly felt against my chest. Drawing my plasmic, I prepared myself mentally for action.

I'd been crouched there another minute and a half, trying to guess from the suite's floorplan and the voices I'd heard earlier where Trent and the others might be, when my phone buzzed a single vibration.

This was it. Still listening to the snooper-ear, I rested my gun hand thumb against my phone's *Send* key and with the other hand carefully turned the doorknob and eased the door open a crack.

No reaction. I opened it a couple of centimeters more.

There it was: the subtle but unmistakable sound of sharply inhaled breath. Trent or one of the thugs had spotted the opening door.

I tapped the phone key twice. The phone did a quick three-buzz vibe—

And from inside the suite came the crash of breaking glass.

I gave Trent and the thugs a quarter second to react to the sudden noise from behind them, then threw the door all the way open and launched myself into a flat dive through the opening into a spacious reception foyer. I hit the floor and rolled up into a crouch, plasmic ready.

To discover that I'd miscalculated.

The three men—Trent, Basher, and an unfamiliar face I assumed was Cron—were exactly where I'd hoped and assumed they would be. They were on their feet in the middle of a comfortably large examination room beyond a wide archway, the chairs they'd been sitting on shoved back out of their way, all three turned halfway toward the smashed window behind them where the fire extinguisher Selene had pendulumed through the glass was still swinging on the extension cord anchoring it to the rooftop. It was a perfectly executed whiplash, with the extinguisher the second punch of the one-two-three punch of me opening the door, Selene smashing the glass to simulate a commando attacking a criminal's hideout, and me entering the room while everyone's weapons were pointed in the wrong direction. Even better, my opponents were nicely grouped together, an easy three-shot that could take out all of them if I so chose.

Except that they were standing on the far side of a lounge-style examination chair that was directly in my line of fire. A chair on which a half-conscious Nikki was currently lying.

And as the eyes and guns started to swing back toward me, I realized my hoped-for high-ground position was suddenly squarely at the bottom of the hill.

But as my father used to say, *Sometimes you'll be dealt the worst hand you can imagine. All you can do is play what you've got, and try to have a spare card or two tucked up your sleeve.*

I had a couple of such cards. Time to see if I could get to one of them.

My first shot slammed into Basher's upper shoulder, the lowest spot on him I dared target with Nikki in the way. He jerked violently with the impact, one leg buckling beneath him in reaction and sending him into a twisting tumble out of sight to the floor. My second shot, intended for Trent's shoulder, missed as he reflexively twitched out of the way. His gun still wasn't lined up on me, but he was starting to duck down behind the exam chair in response to my sudden appearance. My third shot went into the ceiling above him, shattering the acoustic tiles and raining dust and shards down on him.

My fourth went into the ceiling halfway between Nikki and me, sending a second cascade of dust swirling across the battlefield.

The impromptu smoke screen wouldn't last long, I knew, and Trent certainly wouldn't expect me to politely remain where I was until he could see clearly enough to shoot. The archway between the foyer and the exam room was the best cover I had available, with the left side the easiest for a right-handed person like me to fire around. Trent would know that, and might figure I'd go for the less obvious right side of the arch instead.

Time to pull out the first of my sleeve cards. Ignoring both sides of the archway, I instead leaped and rolled straight ahead to the foot of Nikki's chair. Turning onto my side, I curled myself around the base and peered upward along the chair's other side.

Trent was crouched a meter back from the chair, trying to wave away the dust cloud with his left hand while tracking back and forth across the archway with his gun. Two meters farther back, Cron was wiping furiously at his eyes, his own weapon flailing. I lifted my plasmic, trying to get a bead on Trent's gun hand.

But my movement had caught his attention. His gaze dropped, his eyes locking onto mine as his face hardened into a snarl.

He leaped to the side, getting around behind my head where I couldn't get a clear shot, his muzzle lowering to point down at me. I twisted back the way I'd come, trying to get around the other side of the chair's base. But he was on his feet, and I was on my side, and I had zero chance of getting to cover ahead of him. I braced myself, wincing helplessly as his gun steadied on my chest.

"Trent!" a shout came from the broken window.

My eyes flicked past Trent's side. Selene was hanging outside the building from another extension cord, her head and torso framed in the window, her plasmic pointed into the room in a two-handed marksman's grip. Trent took another quick step to the side, putting Nikki between him and Selene and taking himself entirely out of my limited range. He swung his gun around toward this new target—

Lifting my plasmic, I once again fired into the ceiling above him.

Through the fresh cloud of debris came the soft *crack* and muzzle flash of a 3mm gun from where I'd last seen Cron. An instant later the shot was answered by the brighter streak of a plasma blast. Cron gave a sort of gurgle, and fell to the floor. I blinked at the dust swirling around my eyes and shifted my attention back to Trent.

To find that he had disappeared.

I rolled back around the chair and came up onto my feet, squinting through the dust still raining down in the foyer. The suite's outer door was still open, and there was no sign of Trent.

"Gregory?" Selene called hesitantly.

"Yeah, hold on," I called back. Keeping an eye on the door and foyer, I backed to the window, brushed away the bits of broken glass with the muzzle of my plasmic, and helped her inside. "Your timing was perfect," I said. "Thanks for being my second sleeve card."

"Pardon?"

"Tell you later," I said. "Get outside—the smell in here can't be very pleasant for you. I'll finish up."

She nodded, her pupils showing the queasiness of being in the same room as plasmic-burned flesh, and headed for the door. "And watch out for Trent," I called after her. "He might still be nearby."

She waved a hand behind her in acknowledgment, and was gone.

Basher was lying on the floor, gripping his shoulder where I'd shot him and swearing feelingly. He looked to be out of the fight, but I kicked his gun away from him just to make sure. Reaching into his jacket pocket, I pulled out his phone, punched the emergency call button to summon the medics, and dropped it beside him.

Cron, with Selene's shot having burned out the center of his chest, was out of not only this fight but all future ones as well. Bracing myself, I turned to Nikki.

My worst fears, that she'd been given a lethal dose of something and had simply refused to indulge Trent with a quick death, turned out to be overly pessimistic. She was still largely out of it, but from her slack face and dilated pupils it was clear she'd simply been given something to keep her quiet for a while. I had no idea what Trent had used, but the usual treatment for such drugs was to let the victim sleep it off. Getting an arm under her shoulders, I lifted her off the chair, shifted her into a fireman's carry, and headed out.

Selene was waiting just outside the door we'd come in through, plasmic in hand. "There's no sign of Trent," she reported as we headed back toward the main street running along the front of the clinic. "There's a runaround stand a block to our left."

"Good," I said. The thought of carrying Nikki all the way back to the *Ruth* hadn't been a cheery one. "Let's try to be gone before the badgemen get here."

"I'll go ahead and get one," she volunteered, shifting to a faster pace. "And on the way back," she added over her shoulder, "you can explain that reference to sleeve cards."

CHAPTER TWENTY

Nikki didn't talk during the ride back to the ship. But she was clearly starting to recover from her ordeal, and by the time we arrived she was able to work her way out of the runaround with only little help from me. Nevertheless, she accepted my arm around her waist as we negotiated the zigzag. At the entryway I turned her over to Selene, told Selene to lock the hatch behind me, and went back to return the runaround to its stand.

Selene had Nikki settled down on her cabin bed when I returned. "Any trouble?" I asked, watching as Nikki tried to get her boots off. With her fingers still not entirely up to speed, the task was apparently presenting some difficulty.

"No," Selene said. "Any sign of Trent?"

I shook my head, watching Nikki fight with her boots. The whole scene was awkward and clearly annoying to her, but from my vantage point I had to admit that it was also rather entertaining. "If you didn't smell him out there, he must have decided to call it a night. You want any help with those, Nikki?"

She didn't answer, but simply focused harder on the task. Two tries later, she managed to pop the fasteners and get them off. "No, thank you," she said. She dropped the boots on the floor beside the bed and somewhat reluctantly looked over at me. "I suppose I owe you some thanks. I walked into that like a novice."

"You're welcome," I said. "But how about we skip the thanks and instead tell us the story of tonight's adventures?"

"Sorry," she said. "Most of the details are confidential."

"Of course," I said. "I assume we're talking about details like how you got your targeting implants from the Patth? And how someone left a message in your mail drop telling you they needed adjusting, and how lucky you were there happened to be a qualified tech right here in Barcarolle? And how he warned you that some nasty people were out to get you, so you needed to leave your phone on the *Ruth*? And how you were barely to the spot when one of those nasties jumped out of the shadows—"

"Enough." Nikki's voice was quiet, but there was something in her tone that instantly cut off my blather.

"Right," I said. "Sorry. On second thought, I guess we don't really need to discuss it. Unless there was something you wanted to add?"

For a long moment Nikki just stared at me. I held her gaze, wondering distantly how accurately she could shoot while hung over from Trent's drugs. "To you," she said at last. Her eyes shifted to Selene. "Just you."

Out of the corner of my eye I saw Selene stir. But she remained silent. "Sure," I said. "Selene, would you mind fixing us something to eat? I think we could all use a good meal."

"And some wine," Nikki added. "Or something stronger if you have it."

"I'll see what I can find," Selene said evenly. I wanted to turn to her, to look into her pupils and find out how she was taking Nikki's abrupt dismissal. But there was something about Nikki's expression that warned me not to look away.

Selene went out, I closed the hatch behind her, and Nikki and I were alone. "Okay," I said. "I'm listening. Did I get anything wrong?"

"Nothing important," she said evenly. "Tell me about your part of the evening."

I shrugged. "We figured out what was going on and followed you," I said. "Then—"

"Tell me *everything*."

I clenched my teeth. It had been a long evening, following an even longer day. My muscles were stiff and aching, I was hungry, and there was still someone out there gunning for me. "We rescued you," I said. "What more do you need?"

Her throat tightened. "The reason."

I frowned. "Reason for what?"

"You don't like me, and you hate what I do," she said. "So why did you save me?"

I sighed. "Because you needed saving," I said. "You mind if I sit down?"

She nodded toward the fold-down seat. "Go ahead."

"Thank you." I walked over and dropped into the seat. Even at rest my muscles hurt. "Okay, look. No, I don't like your job. I don't necessarily dislike you, but that's because you mostly keep to yourself and don't give us a chance to form an opinion of you as a person."

I paused, but she remained silent. "You're aboard my ship," I continued. "Anything that happens while you're here reflects on Selene and me. I don't want you killing under these circumstances, but I also don't want you getting killed. Does that make sense?"

"Not really," she said, studying my face. "So the three bounty hunters I killed on Vesperin don't count? Or the thug Selene shot an hour ago?"

So she'd been aware enough to at least follow some of the clinic fight. Good—that meant I wouldn't have to repeat any of it for her. "I've killed my share over the years, too. Killing in self-defense is different from killing in cold blood."

"Is it?"

I shrugged. "It's different enough not to trigger the same gag reflex in my conscience. Maybe I'm not being consistent, but the law mostly agrees with me." I shifted in my seat, wincing as new aches reverberated through my body.

Nikki was silent another moment, her eyes still on me. "Did you find the portal?" she asked. "Trent said that once you found it you wouldn't need me. What did he mean by that?"

"No idea," I said. "Besides, what either of us wants or needs is irrelevant. It's Cherno who's calling the shots." I winced. "So to speak."

Nikki gave a small snort. "You *do* like to push the limits, don't you?"

"It just slipped out," I assured her. "Did Trent say anything else?"

She shook her head. "It's all still pretty fuzzy. Maybe I'll get some of those memories back when this stuff wears off."

"Let's hope so," I said. "When I thought he was a hunter targeting you, I at least had a handle on him. Now that I know he's an Expediter, I have no clue what he's going for."

"He's an *Expediter*?"

"Yes," I said, frowning at her. "You hadn't figured that out?"

"No," she said grimly. "But now all that soap he pitched about my implants and Patth techs makes sense. I should have realized there was no way he could have set me up without inside information."

"That was what I figured, anyway," I said. "The only part I don't have yet is what he wants with you. You sure he didn't say anything about that?"

"Only that you wouldn't need me," she said.

I stared at her, a sudden horrible realization flashing across my mind. Some of the things Trent had said...had done...had *not* done...

"Anyway, I should probably let you get some rest," I said, standing up as casually as my aching body would permit. "Selene should be here soon with some food and drink for you. Best thing for you is to eat up and then get some sleep."

"I agree." She closed her eyes. "Roarke?"

"Yes?"

This time she was silent long enough for me to wonder if she'd fallen asleep. "That envelope you showed me," she said, her eyes opening again. "You still have it?"

It took me a moment to remember what she was referring to. "The one with the name inside?"

"Yes," she said. "Get it. *And* the money."

"Sure," I said, backing to the hatch. "Be right back."

Selene wasn't in the dayroom when I arrived, but the three meals she'd prepared were waiting on the table, one of them arranged on a tray. I grabbed the envelope and money from my locker, then picked up the tray and returned to Nikki's cabin. "Here's your meal, too," I said, setting the tray down on the nightstand. "Hope it's okay—looks to be one of our prepacked stews."

"It'll be fine," she said. "The envelope?"

I handed it to her, followed by the ten hundred-thousand-commark bank checks Nask had given me. "Understand that I'm not promising anything," she warned, running a quick count of the notes and then slipping both them and the envelope under her mattress. "I still don't trust you enough to take any of this at face value."

"No problem," I said. "When the time comes...well, let's just leave it at that."

"For now." With an effort, Nikki pulled herself up into more of a sitting position and transferred the tray to her lap. "Good night, Roarke."

"Good night," I replied. "Pleasant dreams."

Her throat worked briefly. "Always," she murmured.

Selene was waiting for me on the bridge, seated in the pilot's seat and gazing thoughtfully at the monitor boards. "You heard?" I asked as I eased down into the plotting table seat.

"Yes," she said. "I gather she didn't notice the intercom was on?"

"If she did, she didn't say anything," I said. "I assume you turned it on when you were helping her into bed?"

"Yes," she said. "When did you take out the indicator light?"

"On the way to Meima," I told her. "One of the times she was showering. Since she'd never yet used the intercom to call either of us, I figured it was safe. Oh, and I turned it off again when I set down her tray. Any thoughts on our conversation?"

"Only that I'm still confused about what Trent is doing here." She half turned, and I could see sudden awareness in her pupils. "But you aren't confused anymore, are you?"

"I don't think so," I said. Once again, reading my mood from my scent. "Though it wasn't until just now, when Nikki mentioned Trent saying I wouldn't need her, that it finally jelled."

"And?"

"And for once our highly trained Expediter got it exactly backward," I said ruefully. "Remember he said he'd seen us pick up Nikki on Balmoral? That was right after we came back from our meeting with Cherno, which I'm guessing Trent also knew about."

"How could he have known that?"

"Floyd and Cherno would have been messaging back and forth while Floyd tried to get us pinned in a corner while he gave us Cherno's sales pitch," I said. "Given the kind of backdoors the Patch have into StarrComm and every other high-tech system in the Spiral, it would have been easy for Trent to pick up on that."

"Out of trillions of communications every day?" Selene objected. "No, not even with computerized searches. Not unless—" She broke off.

"Not unless he was specifically looking for us or references to us," I finished the sentence for her. "I submit that Trent's been stalking us right from the beginning."

"The thing with Oberon," Selene said slowly. "He maneuvered us into helping capture him, didn't he? With the scent of portal metal on his clothing as bait."

"Which meant he'd been in contact with a portal, which makes sense now that we know who he is," I said. "We also know now that his description of Nask's freighter's hijacking was probably also accurate."

"So why did he offer you a hijacking job?" Selene asked. "Was he trying to see if you'd be willing to do something like that?"

"If I'd be willing, and if I *had* been willing," I said. "I think he suspected me—and by extension the Icarus Group—of hitting Nask's freighter. I think he was hoping I'd let something slip that would prove it."

She shivered. "Just as well you didn't accept the job."

"And you have no idea how close I came to doing so," I said, wincing at the memory. "I thought seriously about leading him on, giving him some rope in hopes of squeezing some information about Nask's portal out of him." I gestured aft toward Nikki's cabin. "Either way, I think he'd put enough pieces together to suspect Cherno was involved. Nailing the Icarus Group would just be a bonus."

"Which was what he thought he'd discovered when he saw us with Nikki?"

"Maybe," I said. "At least he would have seen it as a lead to follow up on." I shook my head. "And that was the point where he took his set of dots and connected them in exactly the wrong way. In a nutshell, he thinks Cherno hired Nikki to be my bodyguard."

Selene turned to face me, her pupils brimming with disbelief. "*What?*"

"You heard right," I assured her. "Though again, it wasn't until today that I had all the pieces myself. When Trent and I were talking out in the Trandosh ruins—I think I told you this—he said there were questions he wanted to ask me. He also asked if my bodyguard was taking the morning off."

"I assumed he was talking about McKell."

"So did I," I said. "Only afterward did it occur to me that he was taking a close look at all the hilltops around us. *All* of them, not just the close ones. Now, an Expediter will presumably know a lot about Icarus personnel. McKell's good, but I doubt he's an expert sniper."

"If he is, no one's ever mentioned it."

"True, though that's not the sort of topic that gets brought up at parties," I said. "But we know—and Trent knows—that Nikki *is* a sniper."

"So she's the bodyguard he was talking about?"

"It's the only way I can make it make sense," I said. "What's especially ironic is that when we were waiting for you to send the probe to lure the hunters away from our rooftop in the Badlands, I remember thinking that we were completely exposed up there, and that if a sniper just wanted to take out Nikki he could do it from any of the surrounding rooftops. But I also knew that someone shooting from that distance couldn't get to the scene before someone else grabbed the body and trotted off to claim the bounty. So I put it out of my mind."

"But if Trent wanted to get you alone for questioning, that would have been the perfect setup for him," Selene said.

"Exactly," I said. "The irony of the situation being that he was busy sleeping off my knockout pill and completely missed his chance."

"Actually, it's worse," Selene said quietly. "He had you, Gregory. Right there and drugged, with me in the *Ruth* and Nikki halfway across the Badlands. If you hadn't also drugged him and the others . . ." She shivered.

"Yeah," I said, feeling a little chilled myself. I'd come *that* close, and never even known it. "I wish I knew what these questions of his are."

"*I* wish I knew who he was working for," Selene countered.

"Whoever it is, he's not a friend of Nask," I said ruefully. "Back on Niskea he threw a snarl at me about my 'tame buddy Nask.' I thought at the time the phrase seemed both highly conversant and deeply disrespectful. But things happened, and my focus moved on, and I never got back to thinking about the possible implications. He's probably working for another sub-director who wants Nask's position."

"Maybe we can ask him when we catch up with him again," Selene suggested.

"Somehow, I don't think we're going to be the ones doing the catching," I said darkly. "Trent hasn't completed his job yet, and he strikes me as the persistent type."

"I'm afraid I have to agree," Selene said. "Do we have a plan?"

"Right now, we're mostly treading water," I said. "As of this afternoon, we couldn't move until McKell and Ixil got the equipment I need. As of this evening, we also can't move until Nikki flushes Trent's drugs out of her system."

"Yes," Selene said. "One more thing. While we were out rescuing Nikki, McKell was aboard the *Ruth*."

"Was he, now," I said, nodding as I finally understood the background noises I'd heard on my second call to him. He'd been in a runaround, coming over to take advantage of the fact that the *Ruth* was temporarily unoccupied. "Any idea what he was doing?"

"Nothing specific," Selene said. "But I do know he spent time in Nikki's cabin."

"Checking out her gear, probably," I said. "Certainly taking a good look at her new Ausmacher."

"You think he might have sabotaged it?"

"I hope not," I said. "She's bound to check everything before we get back to Cherno, and if she spots any problems we're the ones she'll blame."

"I'm sure McKell considered that."

"Well, if he didn't there's nothing we can do about it now," I said.

"No." Selene paused. "This envelope you got for Nikki. May I ask what was in it?"

"Just a name," I said with forced casualness, even knowing that the change in my scent would instantly clue her in that it was more important than I was making it sound.

"And the money?"

"It's something I can't talk about right now," I said. "You just have to trust me that it's important."

"All right," she said calmly, her eyelashes fluttering a second and then coming to a halt. "Are you ready to eat?"

"Very ready." Bracing myself, I levered myself out of the chair. It hurt just as much as the last time I'd done this. "And then I'm going to get some sleep."

"You look like you need it," Selene said, standing up. Her version looked a lot more graceful and less painful than mine. "Can you make it to the dayroom?"

"Of course," I said with what dignity I could muster. "But I may let you handle all the cleanup this time."

I slept for nearly ten hours, and when I pried my eyelids open I felt a solid fifty percent better than I had when I'd collapsed on the foldout couch the previous evening.

Which wasn't to say the aches and stiffness were gone. My body was clearly going to be reminding me of the afternoon's exertions for another couple of days at least.

Selene was on the bridge, working on a meal bar and breakfast cola she'd managed to sneak out of the dayroom without waking me. "Good morning," she greeted me as I walked in. "How do you feel?"

"Better than I should, worse than I could," I said, lowering myself gingerly into the plotting table seat. "Anything from Nikki?"

"She was up earlier, but then went back to her cabin," Selene said. "I offered her a meal bar, but she said she wasn't hungry."

"How's the internal cleansing going?"

"She still smells a little odd," Selene said. "But not nearly the way she did last night. I think her body's well on its way to flushing out Trent's drug."

"So she shouldn't need you to stay here and babysit?"

"I shouldn't think so," Selene said, her pupils shifting to wariness. "Is there something you need me to do outside the ship?"

"As a matter of fact, there is," I said, mentally preparing myself. This was not going to go over well, on a number of different levels. "Remember the alien armband you found on Popanilla?"

"The one that was stolen from me, and which I never did get back?" Selene asked pointedly.

"Yes, and I'm sorry about that," I apologized. "I'll talk to McKell, see if he can retrieve it. My question is whether it had a distinctive smell."

The wariness in her pupils went a little deeper. "Yes," she said. "There was a certain... It wasn't portal metal, but it had some of the same flavor. Is that why you thought the people who'd been on the island were Icari political prisoners?"

"Actually, I didn't even think about asking you about the

various scents until a little while ago," I said. "But the fact that there's a connection in their scents does tend to support that conclusion." Once again, I braced myself. "There were bones there, too, the bones of the previous inhabitants. I don't know if we ever saw any unburied ones, but—"

"We did," Selene said, a quiet revulsion flicking briefly across her pupils. "I did, anyway. They were..." She trailed off.

"They were long dead, and there was nothing you could have done for them," I put in firmly. "Did they also have a distinctive smell?"

Selene closed her eyes, her nostrils doing the sort of half-speed twitching I'd sometimes seen when she was searching for a particularly elusive olfactory memory. "Yes," she said. "But it was faint." She opened her eyes again, and this time her pupils showed resignation. "You want me to search for bodies out there, don't you?"

"Actually, I just want you to search for *one* body," I said. "One specific body, and it won't be in the killing lane between the Gemini and the Icarus."

Her reluctance eased a little. "Limiting the search area will help," she said. "But it's still a large area for a single Kadolian."

"I think we can narrow it down a little more," I said, pulling out my info pad. A quick search of the Spiral's archives—"Here," I said, handing it to her. "This is the Erymant Temple area. Let's assume the Trandosh ruins followed a similar design pattern, though the complex here was probably bigger and more extensive."

"All right," she said, scrolling through the pages of images and schematics.

"Let's further assume the Icarus portal was about the same place as the Fidelio one we dug out," I went on. "What you're looking for is a secure building or section of a building, with no windows, thick walls, and limited access. Your search will be inside that room or building, and between there and the place where they found the Icarus."

"They were waiting for someone," Selene murmured, still staring at the Erymant images. "That's why the Icarus was still active and preset for Alpha. Someone went through, then waited for someone else. Someone who never arrived."

I felt my stomach tighten. Even as I had visualized the long-past Trandosh killing field, I could now see a distant glimpse of the doomed straggler, falling in a blaze of enemy fire or suffering the more horrible death of being crushed by collapsed walls or ceilings. "That's what I think, yes," I said. "He had to be someone important for them to risk their enemies using the open portal to come through behind them."

I reached over and touched her arm. "The search won't be pleasant. If you're not sure you can handle it, just say so."

She was silent another moment. "I can handle it."

"Thank you," I said. "You'll have your plasmic, and I know there are at least two other archeological teams in the area, so it's about as public as any open ground can be. You should be safe enough."

"And Trent is looking for you, not me," Selene said with a touch of dry humor. "Don't worry, I'll be fine. And if he comes anywhere near the area I'll know it."

"Good," I said. "I'll alert McKell, too. Maybe he or Ixil can keep an eye on you."

"I'm not worried," she said. "One question. If I find an armband or bones in the right place, how will I know it's the person I'm looking for?"

"Trust me," I said grimly. "If I'm right about this, you'll definitely know."

I'd expected it to be another two or three days before McKell and Ixil were ready with the equipment I'd requested. To my mild surprise, it was late afternoon that same day when Ixil showed up at the *Ruth* with the gadget in hand.

Nikki was asleep, and Selene was still out at the Trandosh ruins. I left a note for the former, gave the latter a quick call, then threw together a go bag with toiletries and a change of clothing. Half an hour later, Ixil and I were in his runaround heading back to our end of the Gemini portal.

Time to renew acquaintances with Robertine Cherno.

CHAPTER TWENTY-ONE

Cherno's end of the Gemini was still deserted when Ixil and I arrived. I double-checked the warehouse, just to make sure there weren't any guards hidden off to the side, then did the same for the underground tunnel. Once again, Cherno's desire for secrecy outweighed his need for security.

Ixil and I didn't talk as we made our final preparations. There was no need. We'd worked out the plan while we were digging our giant gopher holes in the Trandosh field, and we both knew our roles in this little drama. Ixil got Pax into a custom-made harness, gave him his final instructions via their neural link, and then the outrider and I headed out. Pax rode atop my go bag as I negotiated the trapdoor and headed down the tunnel. At the elevator I pulled open the ventilation grille, ushered Pax inside, then put the grille back in place.

Then, taking a deep breath, I punched the elevator call button.

I assumed there would be an armed escort waiting for me when the door opened, but the car was empty. I went inside, punched the up button—the car had only the two buttons—and headed up.

The welcoming committee I'd expected was waiting at the top, looking alert, intimidating, and surprised by my sudden appearance from a supposedly empty elevator. More proof, if I'd needed it, that Cherno was playing his cards close to his chest.

Still, confused or not, they were good at their jobs. They frisked me, taking my plasmic, phone, info pad, and multitool, then rummaged briefly through my go bag and confiscated that, too. Once I was deemed harmless enough to meet their boss, they led me to Cherno's office.

There'd been no way to calculate what time of day it would be when I arrived, but for the plan to work it needed to be late afternoon or early evening at the earliest. For once things turned out even better than I'd hoped, the view out the office window showing the starry blackness of full night. Even better, the forest and distant mountains showed a small directional glint, the sign of at least one planetary moon. My guards sat me down in the chair I'd used the last time I was here, told me to wait, and filed out.

I was being watched, of course. That was a given. Fortunately, there was nothing in here I needed to see. Flexing my still-sore muscles a couple of times, I settled in to wait.

Three minutes later, the door again opened, and Cherno strode into the office.

"So you found the other end," he said briskly as he circled around behind the desk and sat down. His hair was a little disheveled, and his eyes a bit on the bleary side, and he was dressed in a sort of evening robe of red silk with gold highlights. The black sky outside hadn't told me what part of night it was, but judging from Cherno's appearance it looked like I'd arrived after his bedtime.

Perfect.

"Yes, we did," I confirmed. "Sorry it took so long, but we *did* make it within your deadline."

"Yes, you did," he said, nodding. "And for that, I imagine there'll be some bonus money in it."

"I thought our payment was to get the portal."

"That's your *group's* payment," he said. "As you said before, you and Selene don't get anything. I'm planning to rectify that omission." His eyes flicked over my shoulder, as if he was suddenly noticing that I was alone. "Piper didn't come with you?"

I was on the edge of correcting him when I remembered that he didn't know we knew who Nikki really was. "She's still a bit under the weather," I told him. "But she should be ready to travel tomorrow, or the next day at the latest."

"She came down sick?"

"She came down drugged," I said bluntly, watching his expression closely. "Someone tried to take her out."

I'd already been ninety-nine percent sure that Cherno hadn't had a hand in Trent's actions. The sudden rigid look on his face filled in that last one percent. "Is she all right?" he asked.

"She's fine," I said, shifting again in my seat. "He wasn't trying to kill her, just put her out of action for a while."

"Looks like he tried to do the same to you," Cherno said, eyeing me.

"It's nothing," I assured him. So he'd spotted the slight hesitancy in my movements. The man could definitely be observant when he wanted to be. Something I needed to keep in mind. "He tried, he failed, and it's over. So when do I get to hear about the main event?"

His eyebrows rose slightly. "What main event is that?"

"Piper's main event," I said. "Don't we at least get to know why she's here?"

"She's an assassin," he countered coolly. "Why do you *think* she's here?"

"I was hoping for something a bit more specific."

"You want specific?" Cherno asked. The veneer of civilization was still there, but it was showing some strain. "I'll be specific. It's none of your business."

"Yes," I murmured. "See, the thing is that it's at least a *little* our business. We've been seen with Piper, the *Ruth* has been seen carting Piper around the Spiral, and there are way too many badgemen who'll remember all of that when Piper's job goes down. If her target is a major political or social leader, we need to be ready to disappear for a while."

For a long moment I had the sense that he was thinking about ordering his thugs to take me out into the forest and make me disappear permanently. Then, his lip twitched in a sort of wry smile. "I suppose that's reasonable. Fine. The target's a local politician—a Senator Gilles—who's trying to put the planet's entire drug industry under direct government control. As you may know, Mr. Gaheen is trying to shift our organization's illegal drug operations into more acceptable channels."

"I'd heard that, yes," I said. In fact, I'd seen some direct evidence of that tentative shift a few months back. Whether Gaheen was genuinely trying to go legit or whether this was just a new approach to money-laundering remained an open question. "I assume moving the industry to the government would mean taking all control away from the various entrepreneurs and private companies here?"

"Officially, yes," Cherno said. "Less officially, Gilles has made it clear that he's willing to discuss granting government licenses to favored companies and individuals."

"The level of favoredness scaling to the amount of money changing hands?"

"You understand how this works," Cherno said with an edge of contempt. "And of course, it's not just how much money flows in, but how often. You see why Mr. Gaheen has decided this scheme needs to be cut off at its root."

"Yes, absolutely," I agreed. "I assume Senator Spoilsport has other political plans and views that have rubbed his colleagues and constituents the wrong way? Plus a few strictly personal enemies?"

"You're asking if there are other people out there who want him dead?"

"Exactly," I said. "As my father used to say, *The best place to hide a tree is in a forest, and the best place to hide after a job is among a bunch of people who are mad that someone else got there first.*"

"Interesting way to put it," Cherno said. "In this case, your father is right. Combine that with the very local nature of the man and his crusade, and I think a week or two on a beach somewhere should be all you need until the storm blows over."

"Yes, it does sound that way," I agreed. I gave a big yawn. "Sorry. It's been a busy few days."

"So it would seem," Cherno said. "I'm told you brought an overnight bag."

"Yes, sir, I did," I said. "I don't mean to impose on your hospitality. If it's not convenient for me to stay here, if one of your people could take me to the nearest town I can get a hotel."

His lip twitched, just enough to show his first thought was that I was trying to get someplace where I could figure out where in the Spiral I was. "Why not simply go back?" he asked.

"I'd rather not chance it," I said. "With the portal freshly opened, I was warned to give it about twelve hours between the first two or three transits. There's no sign of trouble with it," I hastened to add. "I'd just rather err on the side of caution."

"I suppose that makes sense," he said. There was still some suspicion lurking in his eyes, but my argument sounded reasonable, and at any rate there wasn't any way he could really argue the point. "Under the circumstances, I think it best for you to stay here for the rest of the night."

He tapped a key on his desk. The door behind me swung open, and one of the men who'd met me at the elevator stepped into the office. "Yes, sir?" he rumbled.

"Has Floyd returned yet?" Cherno asked.

"No, sir," the guard said. "But he sent a message saying he'd be back early tomorrow morning. I mean *this* morning," he corrected himself.

"Good," Cherno said, shifting his attention back to me. "Mr. Roarke, this is Yimm. He'll be taking care of you tonight."

"Hello, Yimm," I said politely. The thug didn't bother to respond, but just eyed me like he might look at a bug that was reputed to be venomous.

"Yimm will show you to the guest suite and get you anything else you need," Cherno continued. "You said twelve hours?"

"Yes, sir."

"Good." Cherno glanced at his desk clock. "Tomorrow at noon Yimm will bring you back here. Your watch on local time yet?"

I peered at my watch. It had indeed recalibrated, showing the time to be one-thirty in the morning of a twenty-eight-hour day. "Yes, sir," I said. "So noon is at fourteen o'clock?"

"Yes," he said. "That'll make it about thirteen hours since you got here. That work for you?"

"It should be fine, yes," I confirmed.

"Good," Cherno said. "Yimm will bring you here at noon. I'll turn you over to Floyd, and the two of you will go bring Piper to me. Got it?"

"Got it, sir, yes."

Cherno's eyes shifted to Yimm. "Escort Mr. Roarke to the guest suite, give him his overnight bag, and get him anything else he wants."

"Yes, sir," Yimm said, gesturing me toward the door. "Mr. Roarke?"

"Thank you, Mr. Cherno," I said, getting carefully out of the chair, making sure it looked harder and more painful than it actually was. As my father used to say, *People usually underestimate those who are sick or in pain. More importantly, they also tend to inflict less additional pain of their own.* "Any chance I can also have my info pad? I could do a little reading before settling down."

"You'll get it back later," Cherno said. "If you get bored, go out on your balcony and look at the stars. It's very relaxing."

"Understood, sir," I said. "Thank you again. And may I say, I'll be glad to see this job through to its conclusion."

"As will I, Mr. Roarke," Cherno said. "Get some rest. Yimm will be outside your room if you need anything."

"I'll remember that," I said, nodding. I'd also remember the darker message lurking beneath that offer: Don't try to leave.

But that was okay. Everything I needed to do tonight I could do right from Cherno's guest suite. "I'll be ready to go at noon. Sleep well, Mr. Cherno."

The guest suite was the same one Selene and I had spent a few hours in during our last visit nearly six weeks ago. Then, we'd stayed mostly in the conversation room, but this time I made a point of giving myself the complete tour. The suite was bigger than most of the apartments I'd lived in, and more luxurious than any of them. The beds were emperor size, and looked extremely comfortable.

But testing them would have to wait. Right now, I had work to do.

The last time we were here I'd assumed the place would be loaded with hidden cameras and microphones, but hadn't dared go on a search for them. This time, knowing that I held the key to Cherno's assassination scheme and that he therefore couldn't simply have me shot, I wasn't nearly so worried about the consequences of that kind of chutzpah. Tossing my jacket onto one of the beds, I started my search.

To my surprise, the surveillance equipment I'd expected to find wasn't there.

On one level, it was a relief that my next task would now be infinitely easier. On another level, it raised a host of discomfiting questions. Were the people Cherno usually hosted in this suite the sort who would take a dim and possibly lethal view of being spied on in the more intimate moments of their lives? Had someone higher up the food chain than Cherno—maybe even the big boss Gaheen himself—found the cameras and ordered them removed under pain of death? Had some enterprising badgeman found a way to hack into the system, and tearing them out was purely an act of self-preservation on Cherno's part?

As my father used to say, *There's always a bigger shark and a faster gun.* Cherno might be the distrustful type, but he could hardly have achieved his exalted status in Gaheen's organization without learning when and where to be discreet.

Or, there was another possibility, one that on reflection made even more sense in the current scenario. But that thought and its implications could be put aside until later.

Each of the suite's rooms had its own set of ventilation grilles. I chose the ground-floor vent nearest the tunnel elevator and got to work.

Yimm and his fellow thugs would have scanned the contents of my go bag for anything unusual or contraband, but I'd have bet good money they would miss the set of tiny plastic screwdrivers Ixil had sewn into the bag's edge piping. In this case I would have won that bet. I worked the proper driver out of its hiding place and unscrewed the grille. They'd left me my flashlight; turning it to its lowest setting, I set it inside the air duct to give Pax something to aim for. Setting the bag aside, I went to the kitchen nook and picked out a nut bar, then opened the balcony doors and stepped outside.

Cherno had been right. The view was indeed magnificent. The starscape was as glorious as any I'd seen in my travels, the reflected glow from the two tiny moons too dim to interfere with the starlight except in the areas directly around them. The forests and mountains, as I'd already noted, had taken on an ethereal appearance in the light. It was the sort of spectacle artists would attempt to capture in paint, and poets would try to describe in words.

Me, I was just pleased that my balcony had a view of the northern sky.

Pax was waiting when I returned, his little nose twitching with what I privately called his what-did-you-bring-me look. I unwrapped the nut bar, and while he enthusiastically tackled it I unstrapped McKell's gadget from his harness and went back out onto the balcony.

The first part was easy. I turned on the air sensor, a simpler version of the samplers in the *Ruth*'s bioprobes that would pull in pollen, spores, and other biomolecules, as well as calculating the atmospheric percentages of oxygen, nitrogen, carbon dioxide, and a couple of other gasses. While the sampler was doing that, the internal compass checked the strength of the local magnetic field—planets without such fields generally were slathered in too much cosmic radiation to be habitable—and fixed the direction of magnetic north. With that direction now defined, I took several wide-angle pictures of the sky. There were a lot of stars up there, but the Icarus Group's computers were quite good, and comparing the pictures with known star charts should narrow my location down to a few dozen light-years.

Now came the tricky part. Balancing the gadget on the balcony railing with the camera pointed toward magnetic north, I set the time-lapse for fifteen minutes. The star trails it recorded would create arcs centered on the celestial north pole, allowing the Icarus analysts to calculate the declination between magnetic and true norths.

The fifteen minutes seemed to take the equivalent number of hours, but at last it was over. I shut down everything, closed all the covers and lens caps, and returned to the suite.

Pax had finished half his nut bar and was looking ready to find a good spot for a nap. But he brightened up as I stuffed the gadget in his harness and ushered him back into the duct. I waited until he'd scampered off the way he'd come, then retrieved my flashlight and screwed the grille back into place. My last task was to return the screwdriver to its hidden compartment, and make a quick dinner for myself from the suite's food stock.

I also made sure to munch down the rest of the nut bar, lest some sharp-eyed thug notice half a bar in the morning and wonder why I hadn't finished it.

I ate quickly, my ears primed for noise or quiet commotion outside my door. The plan was for Ixil to wait inside the portal until Pax returned, but if Cherno sent anyone down there to check things out he would retreat back to Meima and come back for the outrider later when the coast was hopefully clear.

If it wasn't clear, there would be trouble. But Ixil had assured me he had that under control. He hadn't offered any details, but I gathered that anyone who blundered into him or Pax would be quietly incapacitated and taken on a one-way trip to Meima, there to be dropped into a deep and very unofficial hole until this was all over.

That would of course lead to consternation and searches at this end of the Gemini, followed by a rude awakening for Cherno's resident house guest. At that point all I could do would be to act bewildered and proclaim my innocence, and hope Cherno bought it. It wouldn't hurt to make sure he remembered he still needed me to bring Nikki to him.

As my father used to say, *Sometimes it's useful to pretend you know more than you do. Usually, it's the other way around.*

The bed was as comfortable as it looked. I set my watch's alarm for eleven o'clock and turned off the light.

I was gazing out the window at the starscape when I fell asleep.

CHAPTER TWENTY-TWO

I slept through until my alarm, with no loud voices or bright lights to indicate that Ixil or Pax had been spotted or that any of the local thugs had quietly disappeared into the night. Certainly no large men with guns intruded on my slumber. I showered and dressed, then built myself a nice breakfast from the nook's supplies. At three minutes to noon Yimm came to collect me, and with my go bag dangling from the big man's fist we walked to Cherno's office.

Cherno and Floyd were waiting when Yimm ushered me inside. "Mr. Roarke," Cherno greeted me. "I trust you slept well."

"I did, sir, very much so," I said, nodding to him and then doing likewise to Floyd. "Hello, Floyd. You're looking good. What have you been doing with yourself these past few weeks?"

"Working," he said. The word and tone conveyed absolutely zero information, as they were undoubtedly meant to. "You ready to go get Piper?"

"Yes, I'm ready to go," I said. "No, we're not getting Piper, at least not right away."

"That twelve-hour waiting period?" Cherno asked.

"Actually, after this second transit we'll probably be able to drop the cooling period to three hours, maybe even less," I said. "I'll give the techs a call when we get there and confirm that."

"Just make sure you don't push too hard and disable it," Cherno warned. "I don't want your people claiming I sold them damaged goods."

"That won't be a problem," I assured him, eyeing Floyd's expression and the slight puzzlement there. Clearly, there was still a part of this job that he hadn't been read into. "Anyway, if anything happens to it, I'm sure the techs can put it right again. As long as we have possession of the portals, that's all that matters."

"Glad to hear it," Cherno said. "Yimm, see them to the elevator. I'll expect to see the two of you again soon."

"And Piper," I said.

Cherno's lip twitched in a smile. "And Piper."

Yimm took us to the elevator, handed me back my go bag, and pushed the call button. The door opened without delay, indicating the car was already waiting.

Which didn't necessarily mean there weren't thugs lurking in the tunnel or by the portal. If Cherno had any lingering doubts about me or my slightly contrived overnight stay he'd have made sure the car was waiting when I was ready to use it, if only to leave me with the impression that I was totally in the clear.

Still, there was nothing in Floyd's body language to indicate I was under any special scrutiny. If I was being offered hanging rope, my traveling companion probably wasn't in on it.

If Selene had been here I could have been a hundred percent certain of that. In her absence, I'd just have to do the best I could.

The elevator reached the bottom and we headed off down the tunnel. I noted in passing that the grille Pax had used earlier was in its proper position, hopefully indicating Ixil had been able to meet him here and take him back to the portal. Unless, again, Cherno was playing things cute.

The tunnel and warehouse building were empty when Floyd and I arrived. "So how does this work?" he asked as we rolled our individual ways into the receiver module.

"We go into the launch module, we ride the extension arm, we touch the weird luminous gray part, and we end up in the receiver module at the other end," I said. "Nothing to it."

He grunted as we walked around the inside of the big sphere. "I still don't see why we needed this damn thing. We could have brought Piper in without anyone knowing anything about it."

"I've been wondering the same thing," I said. "When we were just talking about using the *Ruth*, I assumed Mr. Gaheen wanted us to bring Piper because we don't have any connection with him for the badgemen to pounce on."

"Except that you used to work for Mr. Varsi."

"Oh," I said lamely. "Right." It had been so long since I'd done anything for the organization that I'd tucked those memories into the back corners of my mind. "So...why?"

"I don't know," Floyd said as we stopped at the opening into the launch module. "Maybe you can ask Mr. Gaheen about it later. After you."

"More likely *you* can ask him." I lay down and rolled into the other sphere. I waited until Floyd had done the same, and together we walked around the sphere to the extension arm. "Mr. Gaheen and I don't really travel in the same social circles. Definitely not circles that include greedy and conniving senators."

"For the next couple of days you do," Floyd said as we stepped up to the extension arm. "We just grab here?"

"Right here," I said, closing my hand lightly around the arm. "Gravity will reverse—yep, there it goes," I added as we started floating up along the arm. "Just relax and let the module do all the work."

"So how do you know about the senator?" Floyd asked. "Better question: *What* do you know about him?"

"Just that he's trying to close down independent drug operations in the area except those who are willing to bribe him," I said. "But since we're on the subject, how many people know about this thing?"

"Which thing?" Floyd asked. "The senator's plan, or Mr. Gaheen's?"

"The latter," I said. "Seems to me that if someone loudly proclaims he's against something, and the originator of that something suddenly pops up dead, the loud someone will be pretty high on the badgemen's unpleasant-questions list."

"Come on, Roarke, give us a break," Floyd said scornfully. "We may not be all fancy-pants like you and your friends—"

We reached the luminescent gray section. I felt the usual tingle and was enveloped in the usual black shroud, and a couple of seconds later we were through.

"Whoa!" Floyd huffed. "What the *hell*?"

"Welcome to Meima," I said. "You were saying something about fancy-pants?"

It took him a couple of seconds of jerkily looking around as we started to drift toward the inside hull before he found his voice again. "Yeah," he said. "*Damn.* Yeah. I said we might not be all fancy, but we're not stupid. Only a few people know what the job is." He frowned suddenly at me. "Wait a second. Mr. Cherno told *you*?"

"Yes, which was why I asked who knows about it," I said. "I'd have thought I was pretty far down Mr. Gaheen's need-to-know list."

"You shouldn't be on it at all," Floyd said tersely. "Mr. Cherno just *told* you?"

"It wasn't *quite* that random," I assured him. "I told him I needed to know the details so that I could calculate how long Selene and I would need to go to ground. He apparently thought that was a reasonable request."

"Yeah," Floyd said, still frowning. "I guess. Mr. Cherno usually plays things closer to the chest than that. Mr. Gaheen definitely does. This thing have the same landing speed-up I saw when you came in through the one on Fidelio?"

"Yes, but it's not as violent as it looks," I said. "Just relax and keep your knees bent to absorb the impact."

For his first portal landing, he did pretty well. I had the feeling that in his younger days as one of Varsi's street-level enforcers he'd done his fair share of jumping off things. To my mild surprise the receiver module hatch was open, with nothing but dirt showing. "We underground?" Floyd asked as we walked over to it.

"Yes, but the dirt sitting there is new," I said, frowning. Surely McKell and Ixil hadn't had to fill in the hole, had they? If so, getting out of here was going to be a problem.

They hadn't, and it wasn't. Five seconds' experimentation showed that the dirt was merely a two-centimeter layer, held floating in place in the opening by the competing gravity fields of the portal and Meima itself. "I did something like this once myself," I said as I scooped up a handful of dirt and let it fall again. "See, the dirt tries to fall through into the module, but once it's here it tries to fall back through to the other side, and so ends up kind of spread out in the middle."

"Yeah," Floyd said, looking dubiously at the dirt. "You say you did this before?"

"Just the once," I said. "Though my barrier was made of burning alcohol instead of dirt. Pretty impressive, if I do say so myself. So I guess we just roll through the dirt."

There wasn't anyone visible nearby as we climbed out of the hole. But about fifty meters away was something that hadn't been there the previous day: a large marquee tent of the sort I'd seen field teams use as portable command centers and weather shelters. "I'm guessing that's our next stop," I told Floyd. "Odds are good we'll find Piper in there."

The tent was roomy, big enough to accommodate at least twenty people in reasonable comfort, which made the four folding chairs, large drinks cooler, and single occupant look rather lost amidst all that empty space.

And the odds I'd confidently professed to Floyd went snake-eye on me.

"*There* you are," McKell said from one of the chairs, raising a can of cola in greeting. "I was starting to wonder where you were. Hello, Floyd. Nice to see you again."

"Likewise," Floyd said, in a tone that was friendly enough but made it clear that he knew both of them were being more polite than strictly honest. "Where's Piper?"

"I just talked to her," McKell said. "She called earlier to say she had an errand to run, but now says she's on her way and will be here in about an hour."

"That give the portal enough time to rest up?" Floyd asked.

"It should," McKell said. "The techs will take a look while we wait for Piper, but they're pretty confident that the shakedown transit was ten by ten."

"Good," Floyd said. "Mr. Cherno won't want to sit on his hands for hours every time waiting for this thing to come up to speed."

"Considering that he's getting a whole bunch of light-years in a single gulp, I would think a short delay wouldn't be an unreasonable price," McKell said, a little stiffly.

"You want Roarke to tell him that?" Floyd countered, just as stiffly.

"The point is that the portal is working," I interrupted. I knew McKell had a less than pleasant history with criminal organizations, but there was no point in dumping any of that latent animosity on Floyd. "As soon as Piper arrives and we've run the cooling period we can head straight back."

"The sooner the better," Floyd muttered.

. McKell made like he was going to answer, seemed to think better of it, and instead turned to me. "Selene left a message for you to call her when you arrived."

"Great," I said. "I was going to ask if you'd heard from her. Any idea where she is?"

"Somewhere northeast of here, last I knew," McKell said, frowning. "She said to call, not visit."

"I'd love to," I said, heading toward the tent's door. "Unfortunately, Mr. Cherno still has my phone. Don't worry, I'll be back before Piper gets here."

Privately, I wondered if I was going to end up fudging on that promise. It was only about half a kilometer to the area where I'd told Selene to start her search, but with all the low hills and dips obstructing the view I would need to be practically on top of her before I saw her.

Maybe Selene had anticipated that, or else McKell had gotten a two-for-one deal on tents. From the top of the very first hill I climbed I spotted a small patch of white in the right direction. I went back down, circled the handful of other intervening hills, and came to a smaller version of the tent I'd just left. I looked around the area as I walked up to it, but there was no one in sight. "Selene?" I called softly.

"In here," her voice came from inside.

I pulled the flap aside. Selene was kneeling on a padded mat, a chisel and small brush in her hands, other tools laid out to either side. Directly in front of her was a two-meter-long shallow trench that she'd dug in the ground.

Inside the trench was an alien skeleton.

Not a whole skeleton, I saw as I stepped forward. It was only a partial set, possibly a torso, the bones lying in loose formation. One arm was visible, composed of either a lot of small bones or bones that had originally been longer before being broken in half a dozen places. There were no fingers; whatever had shattered the arm had apparently torn them away or pounded them into dust.

Above the torso, on top of the spot where the head had

presumably been, was a large, squarish block of stone half buried in the ground.

"I think there are three or four more of them nearby," Selene said quietly. "It looks like the ceiling collapsed on them. At least it would have been quick."

I looked at her, and at the mix of regret, sadness, and revulsion swirling through her pupils. "Thousands of years ago," I reminded her.

"I know." She touched the chisel to the ground at the edge of the trench. "It's here, Gregory."

I felt my stomach tighten. "You're sure?"

"I can smell a different type of Icari metal buried under here," she said. "Not portal or armband, but something in between."

Not as indestructible as a portal, but stronger than decorative status or rank symbols. Yes, that could indeed be what I was hoping for. "Keep at it," I told her. "I'd stay to help, but I need to get back to—any idea where I'm going back to yet?"

"Yes," Selene said. "The admiral's people figured it out last night. Ixil says it's Kanaloa. The pollen samples put Cherno's mansion in the northern hemisphere, probably the Conflor Forest region."

I pulled up a mental image of that part of the Spiral. Kanaloa was a middle-of-the-road colony planet, neither luxurious nor poverty-stricken. Its location made it a convenient gathering spot for that sector's conferences and professional get-togethers.

And if I was remembering right, it was indeed a nine-day journey from Xathru.

"Great," I said. "There's something I need you to do for me. I need you to go to the StarrComm center—right now—and call this number." I rattled off the contact number Nask had given me. "Do I need to write that down?"

"No," she said, her pupils taking on that wary look again. "Nask?"

"Nask," I confirmed. "Tell him his portal's somewhere in the Conflor Forest on Kanaloa. Also tell him the current owner is planning to use it—somehow—in a political assassination in three or four days. Not sure where or when. If he wants to get hold of it before that, he'll need to hunt it down on his own. Oh, and tell him not to bother looking for lists of Cherno's properties. The mansion he's using is borrowed."

"Really? How do you know?"

"No security cameras in the guest suite," I said. "It finally occurred to me that Cherno might not want his name associated with what's about to happen, so he found some idle-rich type who was spending a few months galivanting around the Spiral and just moved into his vacant property."

Selene's pupils twitched. "Or else killed him."

"Actually, I don't think so," I said. She'd had to focus on enough death for one day. She didn't need more ghostly images in her imagination. "If he wasn't planning to leave at some point and hand the place back to his oblivious host, there'd be no reason not to put a whole surveillance system in there."

"I understand," Selene said, uncertainly in her pupils. "Gregory, are you sure you want to do this?"

"We've been through this," I said. "Giving the Gemini back to the Patth is the only way to convince them that Icarus had nothing to do with the theft."

"I know, and I don't disagree," she said. "But you're here, and McKell and Ixil are here. Couldn't you go through to Kanaloa and capture the portal yourselves? Then you could stop the assassination and give it to Nask directly."

I shook my head. "Wouldn't work. First of all, I have no idea how many men and how much firepower Cherno has on tap."

"I only smelled four of them when we were there."

"Which was almost six weeks ago," I reminded her. "However many were there then, you can probably triple or quadruple it now that the job is almost on us. There's also Nikki, and with a half-million contract to fulfill I doubt she'd be on our side."

"No, I suppose not," Selene conceded.

"More to the point," I said, "if McKell and Ixil had the Kanaloa portal, do you honestly think they'd agree to hand it over to the Patth?"

"But it's the only way."

"*I* agree," I said. "But the admiral probably wouldn't. I think he'd say damn the torpedoes and invite Nask to take his best shot. How do you think *that* would end?"

"Very badly," Selene said, her pupils cringing. "You know what he's going to say to us when he learns what we've done, don't you?"

"I can guess," I said soberly. I'd thought about that a lot over the past few weeks. "I'm guessing we'll get his full repertoire of past and current naval vulgarities. We'll just have to hope we're too valuable to drop in a hole somewhere. Anyway, the die is cast, as they say."

"Yes," she said. "There's one other thing you need to know. When we brought Nikki back to the *Ruth* after Trent captured her, there was a new smell in the ship, something I've never smelled before. I'm not entirely certain, but I believe it came from Nikki's cabin."

"Interesting," I said, visualizing the cabin and the objects in it. Something to do with Nikki's clothing? Her toiletries? Her implants?

Her weapons?

"You think McKell might have been able to work some magic on her new Ausmacher?"

"That was my thought, too," Selene said. "But I don't know what it was, or whether Nikki found and corrected it."

I scowled. There was an easy way to check on the latter question, I knew. All I had to do was take Selene back to McKell's tent and wait until Nikki showed up. If the smell was still there, Nikki probably hadn't removed McKell's sabotage.

But if I did that, Floyd would probably insist on bringing her back to Kanaloa with us. Right now, I needed her here on Meima. "I'll see if I can find out anything," I told her. "Meanwhile, I need to get back to Kanaloa, and you need to get that message to Nask."

"Yes," she said. "Be careful, Gregory."

"Always," I assured her. "You, too."

I returned to McKell's tent well within the hour I'd promised. But Nikki was also ahead of schedule, and was already waiting inside with McKell and Floyd when I arrived, a small go bag and her long carry case on the ground beside her.

"Sorry—took me a bit to find her," I apologized as I looked over the group. Nikki was dressed in another of her black-and-green outfits with the hat and veil in place, the kind Floyd had seen when he first brought her to the ship.

Only he hadn't brought *Nikki* there. He'd brought *Piper*, and the reason for that bizarre switch was still a mystery.

"No problem," McKell assured me. "Ms. Piper was also running early."

"My errand took less time than anticipated," Nikki said.

I felt my eyes narrow as I took a closer look. Her outfit was indeed like her first one...except for the long tear in the wrap's side just under her left arm. The kind of tear made by a very sharp knife. "Glad to hear it," I said, keeping my voice casual. "Any trouble?"

"None to speak of." She reached inside the robe and pulled out a small, flat object. "Here," she said, tossing it to me. "Souvenir."

I caught it, and found myself holding a plain bifold wallet. I looked up at Nikki, saw with a sudden sense of unease that she was watching me closely. Bracing myself, I opened it.

It was Trent's.

I gazed at the ID in the left-hand window, the card every Commonwealth citizen was required to carry, the one that included Trent's name, face, and official information. In the other display window, the one facing it from the wallet's other side, was his bounty hunter license.

Hidden away behind the license was the card that identified him as a Patth Expediter.

I looked back at Nikki. "He tried to kill me," she said simply.

"Yes," I murmured. "I'll bet he's sorry now."

"I'm sure he is," she agreed.

I looked at McKell. "Are we ready?"

"*I* am," he said. I could see the questions hovering behind his eyes, along with the patience to leave them for another time. "Just waiting on the three of you."

"Then I believe the waiting is over," I said. "Can I carry your bag, Ms. Piper?"

"Thank you," Nikki said. Picking up both pieces of luggage, she handed me the go bag. "I'm looking forward to seeing how this portal of yours operates."

CHAPTER TWENTY-THREE

Nikki's only comment about the transit was to express her gratitude that it didn't spark any nausea or dizziness. Probably adding
those upsides to the list of practical possibilities she'd started
making when I first told her about the portals.

I'd expected to find a full honor guard waiting for us when
we arrived. But it was only Yimm, clearly armed, clearly bewildered by our sudden appearance. Even when Cherno had to bend
his various paranoias and secrets, he still kept that bending to
a minimum. Yimm greeted Nikki and Floyd, rather pointedly
ignored me, then escorted us through the tunnel and up the
elevator and to Cherno's office.

Cherno went through the whole welcoming thing again. Then,
as if it was just an afterthought, he turned to me. "I assumed
your partner would be with you," he said.

"Unfortunately, she had to stay behind to work on our ship,"
I told him.

"Too bad," he said, his eyes narrowing. "I wanted to thank
her personally for helping you bring Ms. Piper here."

"Hopefully, she'll be able to come by later," I said. "But as per
our talk yesterday, we need to be ready to disappear in—what
is it?—three days."

"Five," Cherno corrected me.

"Really," I said. Either Cherno's original timeline of six weeks had only been an estimate, or else the senator's schedule had changed. "In that case, maybe I should go back and give her a hand."

"Or you could stay here and keep Ms. Piper company," Cherno said. "We wouldn't want her to get bored, now, would we?"

I looked at Nikki. With her veil still in place, all I could see of her face were her eyes, and they weren't telling me anything. "Certainly not," I agreed heavily. "I'm afraid I didn't bring my go bag this time."

"Yimm can get you whatever you need." Cherno snorted. "Oh, don't look so glum," he chided in the awkwardly humorous way of a person who hasn't had to cajole or persuade anyone in years. "You'll have a few days of rest and relaxation, and then you'll be free to rejoin your partner and disappear for as long as you think necessary."

"Thank you, sir," I said.

And if what he really meant was that Selene and I would join each other in death? But there wasn't any point in worrying about that now.

Worrying about it, no. *Planning* for it, yes. "So," I said more cheerfully. "Back to the guest suite?"

To my complete lack of surprise, Nikki was given the guest suite. What I got was something that probably housed one of Cherno's guards when he had more of them on duty here. It wasn't much more than a sleeping room: no conversation area, no balcony, no spa in the bathroom, and only a limited-menu refreshment dispensary.

But the bed was reasonably comfortable.

The next four days settled into a mix of waiting and quiet. Cherno had granted me access to most of the mansion's public areas, and I took advantage of that freedom to keep track as best I could of what he and Nikki were up to.

They were clearly up to a lot. Unfortunately, most of it seemed to be happening somewhere else. They were always gone before I awoke, and usually didn't get back until early evening.

So much for me keeping her from being bored.

Late at night on the second day, I managed to sneak into the mansion's garage. The first time Selene and I had come here the place had been empty, but now it was home to a van and five aircars. I checked each of the vehicles in turn, hoping a peek at their fuel gauges would tell me which one Cherno and Nikki had used that day and maybe give me an estimate of how far they'd traveled.

Unfortunately, the garage was also home to its own fuel synthesizer, and Cherno's mechanics had evidently topped off Cherno's vehicle when it arrived home.

Only once, on the third day, did Floyd accompany the two of them on their day trip. The rest of the time he, like me, was a clearly reluctant houseguest. He spent most of his time in his room, out on one of the mansion's four balconies, or playing cards or otherwise hanging out with Yimm and the rest of Cherno's thugs.

Though after the second such game marathon I wondered why any of them bothered. Floyd, for his part, didn't seem impressed by the others' attitude or general air of competence, while Yimm and his crew clearly thought Floyd didn't give Cherno the degree of respect they seemed to think he deserved.

Considering that all of them worked for a pair of men who were ramping up to kill someone, I didn't think either side had much claim on the moral high ground.

As my father used to say, *Birds of a feather may flock together, but when they start pooping on your car they're daring you to get out the shotgun.*

It was on the fifth day that everything changed.

The place had been running at its usual degree of low-speed activity when I awoke that morning. I had breakfast, spent a couple of hours on one of the balconies trying to memorize every crag and cliff of the distant mountains in case I got a chance to look at a map or pictures of the region, then came in for lunch. I spotted Nikki once as she passed the dining room, her green-and-black outfit now reversed to its maroon-and-blue version. Cherno himself was nowhere to be seen, but I heard his voice a couple of times as he called to one or another of his thugs. After lunch I went back outside, this time focusing on the forested hills and paying particular attention to gaps that might indicate fire scars or old logging areas.

When I came back in, the mansion had gone quiet.

I went down to the garage. The last time I'd checked there had been five aircars. Now, four of them were gone, including all three of the six-passenger models. I went back upstairs and started a methodical search, looking for signs of life or, if it came to that, signs of death.

The mansion was big, and there were a lot of rooms I'd never been allowed in. There were also lots of places where a body could lie undisturbed unless someone was specifically looking for it.

I found nothing. No one alive, no one dead.

As my father used to say, *If you appear to be the last one standing, you're either the killer or the next victim.* I'd never liked that particular aphorism, and I liked it even less now.

Finally, to my relief, I found them. Or at least, what was left of them.

"*There* you are," Yimm called from the round table set up in the middle of one of the gabled top-floor rooms, swiveling his chair around to look at me over his shoulder. Floyd was sitting opposite to him, eyeing me closely, with the seat to Yimm's right occupied by a thug named Buckley. The fourth chair, the left-hand one, sat empty. "Floyd tried to invite you to the game, but he couldn't find you."

"Strange," I murmured, looking them over. Yimm and Buckley seemed to be nursing a quiet anticipation, while Floyd seemed even less happy than usual. "I wasn't exactly hiding. Maybe he didn't look very hard?"

"I looked just fine," Floyd growled. "You playing, or not?"

"I'm playing," I said, walking over to the empty chair. I rolled it out and sat down, then rolled myself back up to the table. With things clearly coming to a boil, relaxing with a good card game was the last thing on my mind.

But there were no answers anywhere else in the mansion. Maybe I could find a few in here. "What's the game?"

"Five-card stud," Yimm said, collecting the cards and starting to shuffle them. "You *do* know how to play poker, right?"

"How to play, *and* how to win," I said with the kind of bravado I'd heard many a time from hunters and targets alike. As my father used to say, *When someone decides they need to slap you down, it's amazing how many times their weapon of choice is a secret that you came there hoping to learn.*

"Yeah, words are cheap," Yimm sneered. "Let's see your money."

I pulled a hundred-commark bill from my wallet and set it on the table. "So where is everyone?" I asked. "Out on a picnic or something?"

"Or something," Yimm said. "Floyd, it's your deal."

"Today's the day," Floyd said, an edge of frustration in his voice and face. He took the deck and did a couple more shuffles. "They're off doing the final setup."

"Really," I said, feeling my stomach tighten. So Nikki was about to earn her half-million commarks. "Shouldn't you be there?"

"Why?" Yimm retorted before Floyd could answer. "Mr. Cherno has his own people. They don't need him."

"I was just thinking that Mr. Gaheen might like a firsthand account of the event and aftermath," I said, looking back and forth between them, wishing fervently that Selene was here. Yimm knew something that Floyd and I didn't—that much I could read in his face and body language. Cherno was up to something that went beyond the assassination of a corrupt politician. "Since Floyd is one of Mr. Gaheen's right-hand men—"

"Mr. Gaheen doesn't need Floyd," Buckley put in. "He'll be right there watching the whole thing go down."

I stared at him. "Mr. Gaheen is *here*?"

"It's none of your business," Yimm cut in, throwing Buckley a quick glare. "Buckley, shut up. Floyd, deal the damn cards."

"He came in last night," Floyd said, staring hard at me. He'd caught the sudden change in my voice, I could see, and was wondering what had suddenly kicked me in the rear.

I took a careful breath, watching Yimm out of the corner of my eye. "Floyd, who hired Piper?" I asked. "Mr. Gaheen, or Mr. Cherno?"

"Mr. Gaheen," he said, still gazing at me. "Why?"

"And he knows about the portal Mr. Cherno has stashed away out there?"

"Of course."

"Do you know why Mr. Cherno needed it to be up and running before the job?"

A flicker of uncertainty touched Floyd's face. "No."

"I do," I said. "Deal the cards, and I'll tell you."

For a moment the room was quiet. Then, still watching me, Floyd pushed the deck toward me. I cut the cards and he dealt out five to each of us.

"Here's the thing," I said, picking up my cards. A pair of fives plus junk. "First of all, that's not Piper out there. That's an assassin who switched places with Piper after you dropped her off at the *Ruth*. Her name is Nicole Schlichting."

"Never heard of her," Yimm growled, just a little too quickly.

"I have," Floyd said, his throat suddenly tensing. "You're sure about that, Roarke?"

"I'm sure."

"Ridiculous," Yimm bit out. He was still holding his cards, but his fingers were squeezing them hard. He knew, and he knew I knew. The question was what he was going to do about it. "Mr. Gaheen hired an assassin named Piper. Everyone knows that."

"You're right, he did," I agreed, keeping Buckley in the corner of my eye. Yimm was clearly going to play it cool and keep the story going as long as he could. Buckley, on the other hand, looked like he could break at any moment. "Interesting thing about Nikki—we call her *Nikki*, you know. Anyway, Nikki has an interesting code of ethics that includes never taking a job against someone who's ever hired her."

I raised my eyebrows. "That's the key, really. Because Mr. Gaheen didn't hire her. He hired Piper. It was Mr. Cherno who hired—"

Abruptly Buckley dropped his cards and darted his right hand inside his jacket. Floyd tossed his own cards into the thug's face with one hand and dropped his other hand out of sight beneath the table. There was the sharp *crack* of a Skripka 4mm—

And Buckley collapsed face-first onto the table.

But Yimm was already in motion, shoving his chair backward hard enough to send it rolling nearly to the door. He leaped up and to his right, putting Buckley's slumped body between him and Floyd. "Freeze!" he snapped, yanking out his own gun and pointing it at Floyd. "Hands on the table." He threw me a glance, noted that I was still holding my cards with both hands visible, then turned back to Floyd. "You hear me?"

"I hear you," Floyd said coldly. His left hand was still above the table; now, moving slowly, he brought his empty right hand up to join it. "Is Roarke right? Is Mr. Gaheen Cherno's target?"

"Is he *Mr.* Cherno's target," Yimm corrected with a sort of oily maliciousness. "Come on, Floyd, don't be naïve. Gaheen's gone soft. You know it, I know it, everyone knows it. Mr. Draelon would never have let him rise as high as Mr. Varsi did. Neither of them would have been stupid enough to just hand everything over to him."

"Since neither of them is around anymore, I don't think their opinions matter much," Floyd countered.

"No, the only opinion that matters is Mr. Cherno's," Yimm agreed. He hissed between clenched teeth, scowling uncertainly. "See, here's the problem. Mr. Cherno told me to keep you two alive, that he still had a job for you. But that was before Roarke opened his fat mouth."

"I wouldn't do anything rash if I were you," I cautioned, lifting a hand warningly. "Mr. Cherno needs me to leave here with the tragic news of the accident that took Mr. Gaheen's life. Why else do you think he kept me around this long?"

"Yeah, that was the job, all right," Yimm growled. "But like I said, that was before you opened your mouth."

"It's supposed to look like an accident?" Floyd asked, frowning.

"Oh, it's going to be a dandy," I assured him, trying to run the odds. I was still holding my cards; Yimm was still holding his Skripka. My plasmic was still in its holster, while Floyd's Skripka was presumably on his lap—that was the only way he could have gotten to it in time to beat Buckley to the draw. All that put together left Yimm in complete control of the situation.

But he was standing behind Buckley, and the front of Buckley's chair was within reach of my own foot. If I could give the chair a hard enough kick to knock it back into Yimm, it might throw his aim off long enough for Floyd or me to get in a kill shot. "But like I said, Yimm, Mr. Cherno needs an unbiased observer like me to tell people about it," I continued, casually laying down my cards and resting my hands flat at the edge of the table. "Everyone else involved is one of Mr. Cherno's thugs. I'm the only one people will believe."

"You'd just flat-out lie about it?" Floyd demanded.

I shrugged. "Sorry, Floyd," I said. The table seemed heavy enough to provide the counterweight I needed for my move, but there was no way to know for sure until I tried it. "But I'm just a crockett, with a crockett's chronic financial trouble. I'm pretty sure Mr. Cherno can persuade me to tell the right story to the right people."

Yimm snorted. "Yeah, like Mr. Cherno's going to trust *you*," he said sarcastically. "You know what'd be a lot easier and a hell of a lot cheaper? Starting a few rumors and letting the gossips do the heavy lifting." His face cleared of the uncertainty and he turned his Skripka toward me. I shifted my hands to a grip on the edge of the table—

Abruptly, across the room to my right, the door jamb exploded in a banshee scream and a blazing shower of white-hot sparks.

I jerked, my mind freezing at the sudden and bizarre intrusion into our moment of truth and death. But Yimm wasn't so easily stunned. He spun toward the door, his gun tracking across the opening, his eyes trying to pierce the dazzling light show and see what was beyond it.

He was still watching and waiting when Floyd rolled his chair back a few centimeters, retrieved the Skripka from his lap, and put three 4mm slugs into Yimm's torso.

I tore my eyes away from the already fading spray as Yimm collapsed to the floor and lay still. "Let the gossips do *this* heavy lifting, you traitor," Floyd said coldly to the corpse as he stood up. "Come on, Roarke."

He started toward the door. "Yeah, coming," I said, watching the spark shower burn itself the rest of the way out. "What the hell was that?"

"Called a sparkler," Floyd said over his shoulder, pulling out his phone with his left hand and punching in a number. "Nice and discreet. No one even notices it until you need a distraction."

"It's very good at its job," I agreed, peering at the burned spot on the jamb as we passed. "Where did it come from?"

"Where do you think?" Floyd retorted. "My pocket. I put one by the door whenever I go into a room. If I don't use it, I take it off again when I leave. Remote trigger in my jacket cuff."

"On *every* door you go through?" I echoed, frowning. I'd never seen him do anything of the sort. "Since when?"

He gave me a pointed look. "Since Fidelio."

"Oh," I said. "Right."

Floyd muttered a curse and jammed the phone back in his pocket. "No connection," he said, picking up his pace and heading for the nearest staircase. "The center must be comm-blocked."

"Where Mr. Gaheen is right now?"

"Yeah, the Colonnade Center in Bachar Lune," Floyd said. "About an hour's flight from here." He gestured ahead. "I just hope there's still an aircar down there we can use."

"There was when I checked an hour ago," I told him. "*I just hope you can get it started.*"

"Don't worry about that," Floyd said firmly. "So what the hell is going on, anyway?"

"Like I said, a very clever plan," I said. "Mr. Gaheen hires Piper to take out Senator Gilles, so everyone in the organization who knows anything about the plan assumes it's Piper out in the darkness taking pot shots. I'm guessing that Mr. Gaheen will be chatting with Gilles, maybe even just walking past him, when the shot comes blasting in, barely missing the supposed target and regrettably taking out the wrong man."

"Mr. Gaheen," Floyd said, his forehead still furrowed with confusion as we reached the staircase and started down. "But it's *not* Piper out there. It's Schlichting."

"Right," I said. "According to Nikki, Piper is known more for quiet subtlety than total unerring accuracy, especially in a moving-target situation. A supposed misfire that kills Mr. Gaheen instead of Gilles will be chalked up to bad luck."

"Only it's *Schlichting* out there," Floyd repeated, still working it through. "And Schlichting never misses."

"She never misses," I agreed grimly. "And that's the problem Cherno had with his scheme. If anyone even suspects Schlichting pulled the trigger, the assumption that Senator Gilles was the true target goes straight out the window."

"And if they think Mr. Gaheen was the target, they'll start looking at Cherno."

"Exactly," I said. "Which is why a few hours from now Nikki will be seen on Meima, either by prominent upstanding citizens, the local badgemen, or both."

Floyd braked to a halt so suddenly he nearly lost his footing. "The *portal*?"

"You got it," I said. "The portal isn't just a convenient way to get from one planet to another. It's also the ultimate alibi machine."

For a pair of heartbeats Floyd stared at me. Then, abruptly, he turned and continued down the stairs, again picking up his pace. "The big meeting at Cherno's HQ on the Greater Southern Continent," he snarled over his shoulder. "It was scheduled for two weeks after Cherno first had me bring you here."

"Ah," I said as the final piece of the puzzle fell into place.

"Yes. If we'd been able to activate the portal when we first arrived, Cherno would have had you run the Piper/Schlichting drama to Kanaloa in time for that meeting. But when he couldn't make that work, he shifted his plans another month to the next time Mr. Gaheen would be here. Why exactly *is* he here, by the way?"

"Governor's dedication of the Colonnade Center," Floyd growled. "Mr. Gaheen has interests on Kanaloa, and also figured it would be a good cover for some quiet conversations."

"Very reasonable," I said. "Cherno probably didn't even have to suggest it to him. Of course, moving the date required the rest of us to tread water for a few weeks, but it was the best he could do."

"Yeah," Floyd said. "It would have taken a few more hours to get Schlichting here after the HQ meeting, but she'd still have shown up on Meima way before any ship could make the trip."

"Exactly," I said. "And if Selene and I hadn't found the other end in time for this one, he'd have postponed it until the next time Mr. Gaheen was in town."

"If there *was* a next time."

"There would be," I assured him. *There's always a second opportunity somewhere down the line,* Nikki had said, *and usually a third and a fourth.* "As long as Cherno had the portal and Nikki was on retainer, he could find another time and place."

We reached the bottom of the staircase and headed for the garage. "So let's make sure he doesn't get any more of them," Floyd said. He shot me a sideways look. "That is, if you're aboard."

"Mr. Gaheen was very nice to Selene and me once," I reminded him. "More importantly, I'd rather have him in charge of the organization than Cherno."

"Oh, Cherno will never be in charge," Floyd said softly. "Not for long, anyway. Trust me. Come on—let's get that damn aircar started."

CHAPTER TWENTY-FOUR

❖

Cherno's thugs had made sure the remaining aircar was locked down before they left their borrowed mansion. Between Floyd and me, it didn't stay locked down very long.

I didn't know if there were any speed limits in this part of Kanaloa. If there were, I was pretty sure Floyd broke all of them.

We'd passed over the outer edge of the city of Bachar Lune and were about ten minutes out from the Colonnade Center when a sudden thought belatedly struck me. The Center itself might be comm-locked to keep the assembled dignitaries' attention from wandering away from the organized festivities, but there was a chance that Nikki was outside that zone. I pulled up the number she'd called me from back on Niskea and punched it in.

I could hear the rhythmic buzz as the phone signaled. No answer. I disconnected and tried again. Still no answer. "I can do this as long as you can," I muttered under my breath, and keyed it again.

This time, on the ninth buzz, she answered. "If you called to try to talk me out of it, don't bother," she said.

I took a deep breath. "You don't have to do this, Nikki," I said, putting every gram of persuasion that I had into my voice. "Gaheen's a better man than Cherno. He deserves—"

"You think I don't know that?" Nikki cut me off.

I flinched. Even through a phone speaker the bitterness and

frustration practically reached out and slapped me in the face. "I just meant—"

"Trust me, I know way more about him than you do," Nikki said. "But I took the job. I accepted the contract. There's no way left for me to back out."

"Sure there is," I said. "You say you've changed your mind, you give back his money, and you call it even."

I heard her quiet sigh. "That's not how this works, Roarke," she said, her voice calmer but still on the edge of despairing. "You held my only chance to do that. Only you blew it."

I frowned. *I'd* held the only chance? What the hell was that supposed to mean?

"I suppose I can't blame you," Nikki continued. "But I took the contract. I have to do this."

"Nikki—"

"You won't see me again, Roarke," she said. "Say good-bye to Selene for me. I know you both hate me, but you still made me feel welcome aboard the *Ruth*. That takes a special sort of person."

"It's still not too late for me to stop you, Nikki," I said. "You said I could have done that once. Tell me how, and I'll do it now."

"You saved my life twice," she said. "I appreciate that. But this is the life you gave back to me. This is what I have to do."

"Damn it, Nikki—"

The phone went dead. I punched the number in three more times before I finally gave up.

"Well?" Floyd asked as I put the phone back into my pocket.

"It's like talking to a brick wall, if a brick wall had a ridiculous code of ethics," I told him, glaring across the lights of the city rolling past beneath us. "How much longer?"

"Two minutes," Floyd said. "I just hope I can get Mr. Gaheen or one of his people to let us in."

"Don't worry," I assured him grimly. "One way or another, we'll get in."

As my father used to say, *Persuading people to do what you want first requires you to find out why they don't want to do that. This will often involve loud voices or gunfire.*

In this case, the voices weren't loud at all. "I'm sorry, gentlemen," the chief door warden at the Center's main entrance said calmly. "If you don't have invitations, you can't come in."

"I'm one of Mr. Gaheen's men," Floyd said, trying to match the other's tone. "He sent word that he needed me here."

"Mr. Gaheen left us no such instructions," the warden said. His voice was still calm, but I could sense that it could go from quiet to loud at the snap of a finger. I could also sense that the gunfire my father had warned me about was also waiting in the wings.

"I understand," Floyd said. "But if you could send someone to ask him—"

"You're welcome to wait in your vehicle," the man said, still maintaining his civility. "If Mr. Gaheen happens to inquire about you, I'll be sure to tell him where you are."

Floyd turned to me, and I could see in his eyes that he was three beats away from hauling out his Skripka and opening fire on anyone and anything that stood between him and his endangered boss.

Which wouldn't be a *completely* insane idea. A sudden burst of gunfire would put everyone in the Center flat on the floor, which would surely ruin Nikki's timing and fire lines. Unfortunately, she was committed to this job, and she'd already told me that if she didn't succeed the first time she would keep trying until she did.

The more immediate downside, of course, being that such a move would probably get both Floyd and me killed.

Which left only one option.

I didn't want to do this. It was surely illegal, and could very well offer the same odds for my demise as a barrage of Floyd's 4mm slugs. But we needed to get in there, and this was the only card we had left to play.

Very literally.

"Enough," I bit out in the best official badgeman-style voice in my repertoire. "This is official Patth business. Mr. Floyd and I need to get in there, and we need to get in there *now*."

Mentally crossing my fingers, I pulled out Trent's Patth Expediter ID card and shoved it into the warden's face.

He stiffened to full military attention. "Yes, sir," he said crisply. He gave the backup crew loitering behind him a hand signal, and they moved out of our way. "Do you need me to send some people with you?"

"That won't be necessary," I said as Floyd broke from my side and hurried past the guards and through the entryway. "But stay alert," I added as I followed him through the door into the brightly lit ballroom beyond.

I'd noted once before that the whole planet was a convenient meeting place for the sector. That fact apparently made the opening of a new conference facility a bigger deal than it might have been elsewhere. The Colonnade Center's ballroom was packed with elegantly dressed humans and aliens, and the whole place was ablaze with glow and pomp and glitter. There were refreshment islands scattered throughout the room, each boasting a color-shifting spotlight blazing straight up like the end of a leprechaun's rainbow. Along a ninety-degree curve on the far side of the circular floor were a set of serving tables, with a similar arc of two- and four-person tables arrayed along the other two hundred seventy degrees. The lowest three meters of the ballroom's walls were made of intricately carved stone, at which point the stone gave way to crystalline glass that formed a dome above the whole room. Some clever trick of the dome's material or curvature allowed the starlight above to blaze through unfiltered without being dimmed or washed out by the city lights around us or even by the ballroom's own illumination.

Floyd was standing near the middle of the room when I caught up to him, methodically turning his head back and forth as he tried to locate his boss. "You see him?" he demanded. "You see him, Roarke? I don't see him."

"So let's run it backward," I suggested, turning my attention to the dome and the city beyond. "Nikki's new weapon is an Ausmacher missile-slug sniper rifle. Let's try to figure out where she'll be shooting it from."

"How the hell will that help?" Floyd gritted out. "She can see the whole room from anywhere out there."

"So we make sure she can't," I said, matching his same slow turn. As he'd said, there were several tall buildings out there, platforms from which someone with Nikki's skills could launch her attack. With the right style Ausmacher, in fact, she could theoretically hit her target from anywhere in the city that gave her the proper line of sight.

But the timing necessary to make Gaheen's murder look like an accident was going to be critical, and the farther out she was the more lag time between her squeezing the trigger and the missile reaching its target. A close building, then, something no more than a block or two away. One of the shorter buildings, maybe, where her subsequent retreat would be quicker.

"Does Mr. Gaheen wear body armor at things like this?" I asked Floyd as I did another slow rotation, this time focusing on the closer buildings.

"Yeah, but just a light shell," Floyd said. "Something that'll fit under formalwear—"

"There!" I snapped as something caught my eye. Not the lights of one of the taller buildings, but the total absence of lights in the more modest structure directly across the street from the Center.

The kind of blackness that would not only encourage a searching eye to skip past the building completely, but would also provide additional shadow for a hidden shooter.

"She's there," I said, turning to Floyd.

But he was no longer beside me. I craned my neck and saw him elbowing his way through the crowd toward one of the serving tables. Apparently, he'd finally spotted Gaheen.

I turned back toward the darkened building, looking around the ballroom. Lines of sight worked both ways, and there were a lot of glittering lights right in here with me. If I could get one of them turned toward Nikki's sniper nest, maybe I could blind her enough to make the shot impossible. All we would have to do then would be to get Gaheen out of here and try to make sure she didn't get a second shot at him.

The refreshment islands' spotlights weren't the brightest lights in the room, but they would be the easiest to turn around. I headed toward the nearest one, keeping an eye on the building.

I was nearly there when there was a single, soft flash from the middle of the darkened building. An instant later came an equally subdued *crack* of breaking crystal.

But there was nothing quiet or muted about the scream that erupted from across the room.

Earlier, Floyd had had to shove his way through a milling crowd of meandering partygoers. My trip was instead through a petrified forest of stunned and horrified witnesses to a murder.

Or maybe not. As I broke through the last circle of onlookers I saw there were two men in medic tunics kneeling over the body lying motionless on the floor. Their hands were red with Gaheen's blood, their clipped voices eerily loud in the silent room as they worked feverishly on the victim. Floyd was standing just behind one of the medics, as silent and motionless as Gaheen himself.

At one edge of the circle, I noted peripherally as I crossed the gap, was a white-haired man slumped on the floor, his face ashen as he clutched a small wet spot on the outside of his upper arm. Senator Gilles, probably, with a tiny flesh wound to show where Nikki's supposedly missed shot had scratched him.

I also noted with vague satisfaction that no one seemed to be paying the slightest bit of attention to him or his injury. Maybe he wasn't as big a fish in this pond as he thought he was.

I stopped at Floyd's side. "How is he?" I asked quietly.

"Still alive," Floyd said, his voice shimmering with anger and despair and hatred. "Don't know for how long."

"Are you two with him?" the medic we were standing beside asked as he finished connecting Gaheen to a compact artificial heart.

"Yes," Floyd said. "What can we do?"

"You can get back and give us room," the other medic said tartly. "Give it to them."

He pointed to a steel-clad data stick sitting in the blood beside Gaheen's phone and wallet. The medic we were standing behind picked it up and handed it over his shoulder toward us. "Here—it says to give it to his chief assistant in case of accident. Can you two do that?"

"Yes," Floyd said. He took the data stick, peered briefly at the small lettering on the side, and slid it into his pocket.

I glanced around the circle, stomach tensing as I spotted a couple of familiar faces. "Cherno's men are here," I murmured to Floyd. "Time to make ourselves scarce."

Floyd hesitated, then reluctantly nodded. "Service door behind the serving tables," he said. "Come on." With a final lingering look at Gaheen, he circled the medics and headed through the crowd on the other side of the circle. I kept an eye on the thugs I'd spotted, but they were making no move to follow.

But of course they didn't know that we'd figured out the truth. As far as they and Cherno were concerned, we were still dancing to his tune, off to tell the sad tale of Gaheen's tragic demise.

We were back in the aircar before Floyd spoke again. "Where to?" he asked.

"The mansion," I told him. "That's where Cherno has to bring

Nikki to make this scheme work. We have to make sure we get there first."

"Don't worry, we will," Floyd said grimly as he got the aircar up off the ground. "I just hope he doesn't bring his whole crowd with him."

"He won't," I assured him. "You may not have noticed, but we barely got out of there ahead of the badgemen. They'll have the place locked down for hours while they question everyone inside. No, Cherno and Nikki will be the only ones who'll be coming."

Floyd grunted. "Good."

We were burning the air over the city when another thought suddenly occurred to me. "By the way, did you leave a sparkler on the Colonnade Center door?"

"Yeah, but don't worry about it," Floyd said. "I've got more."

I figured Cherno and Nikki would be forty-five to sixty minutes behind us. In fact, I heard the sound of the trapdoor opening barely forty minutes after Floyd and I settled into concealment in the narrow space between the receiver module and the warehouse wall. Nikki, I guessed, had probably been driving.

I waited until the sound of their footsteps and tense conversation put them about midway between the trapdoor and the portal entrance. Then, tapping Floyd on the shoulder, I stepped out into view. "Hello, Nikki," I called calmly. "Mr. Cherno. Party end early?"

Nikki had dropped her long gun case on the ground and drawn her Jaundance 4mm before I finished my question. "Easy," she warned, her eyes above her veil steady on me, flicking briefly to Floyd as he joined me out in the open.

"Likewise," I said, showing her my empty hands and nudging Floyd to follow suit. "We're just here to talk."

"Well, we're not here to listen," Cherno bit out. In contrast to Nikki's eyes, his were blazing with anger and frustration as he jabbed a finger up toward me. "Kill them."

"No," Nikki said.

I hadn't yet seen Cherno truly surprised. The expression alone was worth everything we'd been through. "*What?*"

"Roarke hired me for a job," Nikki told him coolly. "Same deal as with you."

Cherno's eyes narrowed. "*What* job?"

"I don't know," she said, tapping her wrap. "He gave me a name in an envelope. I haven't looked at it."

"Why not?"

"He asked me not to."

Cherno shot me a confused look. "And you *took* a contract like that?"

Nikki didn't answer. Cherno muttered something vicious and shifted his pointing finger to Floyd. "Fine. At least kill *him*."

"Certainly," Nikki said. "I'll need the five hundred thousand up front."

"What the *hell*?" Cherno took a step toward her and grabbed for her gun. She countered with a similar step in the other direction, twitching the weapon out of his reach. "Give me that, you lousy—Hold it!" Cherno interrupted himself as Floyd crossed behind me and started circling toward Cherno's left. Abandoning his attempt to get Nikki's gun, Cherno jammed a hand warningly into his pocket. "Just hold it."

"Yes, hold it," Nikki agreed, shifting her aim toward Floyd. "You've put me in an awkward position, Roarke."

"Yes, I know," I said. "Sorry."

"I doubt it," Nikki said. "But I'm curious. When exactly did you sabotage my Ausmacher?"

"*Sabotage*?" Cherno bit out, his eyes still on Floyd.

"Sabotage that kept me from completing my job," Nikki said. Her voice and eyes were still calm, but I could sense the turmoil roiling beneath the surface.

Cherno snapped a look at her, then back to Floyd. "Are you saying he's still *alive*?"

"He was when we left," Nikki said. "I saw his fingers moving just before I closed down."

"And you just *left* him that way?" Cherno demanded. "Why the hell did you do *that*?"

"Come on, Cherno, be reasonable," I soothed. "How do you expect her to take another shot with all those people standing around gawking? Besides, you'd never have been able to pass that one off as a misfire. Actually, Nikki, it wasn't me who fiddled with your Ausmacher. I don't even know what he did to it."

"It was quite clever, really," she said. "Whoever did it knew I'd check the mechanism and rounds before the job and would certainly make sure the barrel was clear. So he put a thin coating of jellied snarling paste on the inside. Nothing I could see, and nothing my normal cleaning would clear out, but a layer that the missile had to dig through on its way out."

"Ah," I said, nodding understanding. "And since some of the paste clung to the tips of the stabilizing fins even after the missile left the barrel, there was an extra drag on it the whole way."

"Exactly," Nikki said. "Not much, but enough to slow it to the point where it wouldn't have enough momentum to fully penetrate Gaheen's body armor and the bone beneath it."

"So that's it?" Cherno demanded. "The great and terrifying Nicole Schlichting, who never misses and never fails, is just giving up?"

"Of course not," Nikki said. "Even with the snarling paste the round would have gotten most of the way through his sternum, so unless those medics were extraordinarily good he could still die. If he didn't..." She gave a small shrug. "I took your job, Cherno. I'll complete it."

"When?" Cherno countered, shifting his glare from Floyd to her.

"Never," Floyd said quietly. He reached casually into his jacket cuff—

And the edge of the trapdoor exploded in a scream and a blaze of sparks.

Cherno twisted his head to look. But Nikki knew better than be taken in by an obvious diversion. Even as Floyd snatched out his Skripka, she shifted her Jaundance toward him. The criminal enforcer versus the professional assassin, and in that frozen second I wondered distantly which of them would win the race.

Nikki.

The double boom blasted through the warehouse, briefly drowning out even the scream of Floyd's sparkler. To my left, out of the corner of my eye I saw a small cluster of sparks as Floyd's slug ricocheted off the portal's hull; to my right, I saw Floyd jerk violently as Nikki's 4mm slug slammed into his body. He twisted halfway around to his right and toppled backward onto the ground, his Skripka flying out of his hand and skittering to a stop a couple of meters closer to the trapdoor. Nikki shifted her gun warningly toward me; I raised my empty hands a couple of centimeters to remind her I was still not holding a weapon.

She and I were still facing each other in standoff mode when Cherno took a long step toward her, pulled his hand out of his pocket, and jammed a push knife into the inside of her forearm.

The attack was so unexpected that my brain never unfroze enough to grab for my plasmic. I just stood there, gawking like an idiot, as Cherno wrenched the Jaundance from Nikki's suddenly loosened grip and backed a quick step away from her. "You won't kill him?" he snarled. "Fine." He leveled the gun at me—

"Ah-ah-ah," I warned, holding up a finger. "Remember, your best shot at getting off Kanaloa is via the portal. And I'm the only one who can show you how to do that."

For a long and tense moment he stared at me, his eyes narrowed. I stared back, mentally crossing my fingers that Nikki hadn't told him how ridiculously simple it was. His eyes flicked to Nikki—"What about her?" he said. "*She* knows."

"You really think she's going to help you?" I countered. "Or Floyd? They both need medical attention, by the way."

Cherno's eyes shifted again, this time to Floyd, and I saw the crime boss's narrowed eyes widening briefly as he saw that Floyd's eyes were wide open and glaring in rage and pain as he held his left hand against his shoulder wound. "You didn't *kill* him?" he demanded.

"I only kill when it's a contracted job," Nikki said, her left hand similarly clutching her right arm around the grip of the embedded push knife.

"Or when it's personal," I added. "You want to tell him, Nikki, or should I?"

Cherno looked back at me. "Tell me what?"

Nikki remained silent. "Me, then," I confirmed. "It came from something she told Selene and me when she first came aboard the *Ruth*. She mentioned the death of Governor Ajagavakar of Golden Bough as a case study of how to botch an assassination. Ring any bells?"

There was a subtle shift in Cherno's face. He glanced at Nikki, turned back to me. "What, you think she gave a damn about a jerk like Ajagavakar?"

"Oh, I'm sure she didn't," I agreed. "Which was really the point. Of all the deaths in the Spiral, why bring up that one? So Selene and I did a little digging. Did you know that six hotel employees also died in that bomb of yours?"

I looked back at Nikki. "Which one of them was it?"

For a couple of seconds Nikki didn't speak. Then, she seemed to stir herself. "She was one of the cleaners," she said quietly. "My partner."

Cherno's breath caught in his throat. "Your *partner*?"

"Partner, spotter, recon expert," Nikki said. Her voice was still calm, but I felt a shiver run up my back. "Friend. There was a notice out on Ajagavakar, and I sent Amy to scout his hotel." She paused. "And you killed her."

"Not on purpose," Cherno insisted, an edge of nervousness creeping into his voice. Even with the only visible gun in the room firmly in his own hand, he'd also caught some chills from her voice. "He needed to die, and no one else was doing anything about it."

"Nikki was," I reminded him. "So was Piper, by the way. I assume Piper's the one who told you all this?"

"Yes," Nikki murmured. "On Balmoral, when we were switching places. I'd never heard how that went down, or who was responsible. Piper knew both."

For a moment no one spoke. Cherno possibly trying to find something conciliatory he could say, Nikki maybe working through the old memories, me waiting for the drama to work its way to a conclusion.

And so, naturally, that dead silence was the precise moment when the soft *thud* of an arriving passenger came softly from the receiver module.

CHAPTER TWENTY-FIVE

"Who's there?" Cherno snapped, swinging Nikki's gun toward the opening. "Show yourself. *Now!*"

"Don't shoot," Selene's voice came distantly. "I'm not armed. Please don't shoot."

Cherno shot me a look. "Show yourself," he called back. "If you're lying, I'll kill your partner."

There was another moment of stiff silence, and then Selene slipped into view from the module. "I'm not armed," she repeated, holding up her empty hands.

"Keep it that way," Cherno growled, twitching his head toward me. "Over by Roarke."

"Yes, sir," Selene said. She hurried across the floor toward me, her gait and stance the epitome of cringing fear and eagerness to please.

Only her pupils told a different story. Her appearance here was clearly part of a plan between her, McKell, and Ixil. All I had to do was play off her cues or otherwise figure it out...

"Floyd!" Selene gasped as she spotted him lying on the ground. "Are you all right?" Picking up speed, she hurried past me toward the injured man.

"Stop!" Cherno snapped.

Selene jerked to a halt midway between Floyd and me and

287

turned to face Cherno. "What happened?" she asked, pointing at Floyd. "Did you do this?"

"Roarke, tell your alien to shut up or she can find out personally what happened," Cherno snarled. "Schlichting...okay, fine, I accidentally scorched your friend. I still paid you half a million commarks for a job, which still means you can't kill me."

"I know that," Nikki said steadily.

"I'm so sorry we couldn't help you, Nikki," Selene said. "We just didn't realize in time what you needed from us."

"What are you talking about?" Cherno demanded, his eyes flicking between Selene and me.

I felt my heartbeat pick up. By moving past me toward Floyd the way she had, Selene had now put Cherno's back to the portal entrance and in perfect position for an ambush. McKell was on his way, or maybe was already in there waiting for the right moment to make his move. "She's talking about why Nikki let us see her face aboard the *Ruth*," I spoke up. "That's the key, Nikki, isn't it?"

Nikki didn't answer. "See, she was hoping we'd send her picture out to Bounty Hunter Central," I continued. Our job now was to keep Cherno's attention on us and away from the portal. "A scoop like that—the face of Nicole Schlichting herself!—would have gotten the image sent out to every major planet in the Spiral. With her anonymity gone, she'd have no choice but to return your money and back out of your contract."

"And *then* she could kill you," Selene added quietly.

"Problem is, we aren't in the hunter business anymore, so we didn't do that," I said. "Even so, she came damn close to getting her wish. Our boy Trent wanted her out of the way so he could interrogate me—God only knows why—and so he distributed a sketch of her to the local hunters in the Badlands on Niskea."

I looked at Nikki. "It took me awhile to figure out why you reacted so oddly when I showed you the sketch. It was good enough to be a problem, but not good enough for you to legitimately pull the ripcord on Cherno's job. In fact, you even said something about it not being very good."

Out of the corner of my eye I saw Selene's eyelashes suddenly fluttering. She'd picked up the incoming cavalry's scent. I took a small step toward her, pulling Cherno's attention a few degrees farther from the portal. "Like I said, I still don't know why Trent wanted to talk to me," I went on, raising my voice to cover the unavoidable *thump* when McKell hit the receiver module's inner hull. "My guess is that he was working for one of Sub-Director Nask's rivals and hoping to get something he could spin as dirt on Nask."

"But there wasn't anything, because there isn't anything," Selene said. She lifted her hands, pointing both index fingers at Cherno. "As you yourself certainly know."

And right on cue, our rescuer hopped out of the portal entrance.

Only it wasn't McKell, or Ixil.

It was Pix.

The little outrider hit the ground silently, dropping into a crouch, his head turned toward us as he took in the details of our face-off.

And then his bright eyes fell on Selene. Selene, and her twin fingers pointed straight at Cherno.

Pix leaped out of his crouch, charging silently toward his now confirmed target. I kept my eyes on Cherno, my brain spinning with a flash of anticipation as to what was about to happen. Pix leaped up behind Cherno—

And dug his long claws into the shoulder of the other's gun arm.

Cherno bellowed with surprise, pain, and fury, the gun he'd taken from Nikki going flying with the shock of the attack. He spun partway around toward me, his left hand trying to reach over his shoulder to get to the little animal now anchored agonizingly into skin and muscle. He got a partial grip on Pix's neck, probably hoping to either tear the creature loose or break its neck. Nikki stiffened, watching the battle but making no move to interfere.

And I knew what I had to do.

"Cherno!" I shouted, snatching my plasmic from its holster and lobbing it toward him. "Catch!"

Cherno was smart enough in his evil way, and if he'd been thinking straight he might have seen the trap. But he was in agony, his plan to take over Gaheen's organization had crumbled, and desperation had shoved out all attempts at rational thought. Abandoning his attempt to pull Pix off his arm, he reached up and plucked the arcing plasmic out of the air. He swiveled the weapon around, clearly intending to point it over his right arm and burn Pix off. He raised it up, trying to fine-tune the aim so that he would hit Pix and not his own arm.

And in that position, the plasmic was pointed at Nikki.

It was fast, it was precise, and it was efficient. One second she was standing still, Cherno's weapon pointed at her. The next second she'd pulled the push knife from her arm, reversed it as she took the two quick steps necessary to put her in range, and buried the blade in Cherno's chest.

For a moment he just stood there, the stunned amazement on his face quickly fading into the oblivion of death. "She can kill anyone in self-defense," I said quietly. "I assumed you knew that."

He didn't answer. He probably never even heard me.

A moment later his knees buckled and he fell to the ground.

Pix hopped off midway through his fall and went back into his crouch, probably awaiting further instructions. Nikki gazed down at the body another moment, then looked up at me. "You could have just shot him yourself, you know," she said.

"I didn't want to hurt Pix," I told her, nodding toward the outrider. "I also didn't want some future spectral profile analysis matching it to my plasmic. Besides, I figured you'd want to deal with him yourself."

"As long as he's dead," Nikki said. "What now—no," she interrupted herself, her eyes going suddenly odd. "You didn't." Wincing with the pain from her bleeding arm, she reached into her wrap and pulled out the envelope I'd given her. She tore it open, looked at the card inside, then looked back at me. "Robertine *Cherno*?"

I shrugged. "It seemed like a good idea at the time," I said. "Even without all the pieces, it was clear he was shady as hell. I figured he'd come to a bad end before this was over, and that he would probably have deserved it."

"And the million commarks was your insurance policy against him ordering me to kill you?"

"I was pretty sure that was somewhere on his list of things to do," I said. "To make his plot against Gaheen work, he'd have to eliminate anyone who had any of the pieces. Though he still hoped I could help spread his cover story before he fitted me for a shallow grave out there."

"Was that just a figure of speech?" Nikki asked. "Or is that what we're planning for him?"

"It's what *I'm* planning for him, anyway," I said. "You and Floyd need to head back to Meima for medical treatment. Selene, when are McKell and Ixil joining us?"

"They aren't," she said, a tense look coming into her pupils. "There's been some unexpected Iykam activity in the Trandosh area, and they needed to stay there to evaluate it and coordinate a response."

"Understood," I said. More understandable than any of the rest of them realized, actually. "Hopefully, it's nothing serious."

"I'm sure we'll find out." She lowered her voice. "I also came here to tell you that I found it."

An eerie feeling trickled through me. "You sure?"

"Yes."

"Okay." I took a deep breath. And that was going to make the rest of this whole thing a hell of a lot easier. Or, perhaps more accurately, a hell of a lot less impossible. "Can you help Nikki and Floyd through by yourself? I need to stay here and deal with Cherno before his men get back."

"Of course," Selene said. She could tell I wasn't being entirely honest with her, or was at least glossing over some of the details. But she also knew this wasn't the time and place to ask about it.

"That okay with you, Floyd? I added, walking over to him.

"Far as I'm concerned, you can put him in the mansion and set fire to it," Floyd gritted out. "Like Schlichting said, as long as he's dead."

"Okay, then." I reached down and took his arm. "I can at least help you into the portal. Selene, help Nikki."

"I'm fine," Nikki said, stepping across the room and retrieving her Jaundance. "I'm fine."

She headed to the portal, Selene close at hand in case she needed help, Pix scampering along behind them. I got Floyd's good arm over my shoulder and helped him through the opening, then walked him across the receiver module and into the launch module.

Along the way, I quietly relieved him of the data stick the medic had given him back in the Colonnade Center.

I waited until they were gone, then returned to the warehouse and retrieved my plasmic. I opened the trapdoor and listened for activity in the tunnel. There wasn't any. Closing the trapdoor again, I pulled out the data stick and held it to my lips. "Clear," I said. "Any time."

For a moment nothing happened. Then, across the warehouse, a point at the bottom of the wall burst into a shower of brilliant sparks, like Floyd's sparkler only a thousand times brighter. The blaze ran rapidly a couple of meters up the wall, went horizontal for another two meters, then turned again and ran to the bottom. The newly cut rectangle fell inward—

And Huginn and Muninn, still in their bloodstained medic uniforms, charged into the warehouse, heavy-duty Ryukind plasmics in hand.

"I *said* it was clear," I pointed out as they trotted to a halt, still looking around. "You don't need those things."

"We heard you," Huginn said. "We didn't necessarily believe you."

"Ah." I gestured up at the portal. "Well, here it is. I assume Sub-Director Nask has something waiting to haul it out of here?"

"He does," Huginn said. He looked up at the portal, then back at me, his expression that of someone waiting for a magician to do his presto. "Just like that?"

"Just like that," I said. "I assume Selene's mention of Iykam activity on Meima is the sub-director preparing to dig out the other half?"

"It is," Huginn said. "I trust Icarus won't try to interfere."

"I'll make sure they don't," I promised. "Provided you'll in turn allow them to withdraw unharmed."

"Peace begets peace," Huginn said. "An old Patth saying. If you don't shoot, neither will we."

"Seems reasonable," I said. "Speaking of shooting, how is Gaheen?"

"He was alive and stable when we turned him over to the local medics," Huginn said. "He should pull through."

"Good," I said. "I know he's a crime boss, but he's showing signs of mellowing in his old age. Besides which, I have a somewhat fragile connection with him that may prove useful in the future. I appreciate you keeping him alive."

"It was hardly a major priority," Huginn said with a shrug. "We needed to get you the tracker so we could find this place, and we knew that the scene of the attack was the first place you'd go. Saving his life was just a bonus."

"But there was also some professional pride involved," Muninn added. "We get a lot of training for our positions, you know."

"So I've seen," I said. "It also explains why the door warden was primed to honor my ID. You'd already pulled the Expediter wild card on him to get inside, hadn't you?"

"We had," Huginn said. "Speaking of which . . . ?" He held out his hand.

"Ah. Of course." Reaching into my jacket, I pulled out Trent's wallet. "The Expediter ID is behind the hunter license."

"Thank you." Huginn opened it, confirmed I was telling the truth, and tucked the wallet into his pocket. "By the way, Sub-Director Nask told me to remind you that his offer of an Expediter position was still open."

"Tell the sub-director I appreciate it," I said. "But right now, my time and talents are already spoken for. All right." I looked back at the portal. "I'll go through first and get McKell and whatever team he's assembled out of the way. Give me ten minutes, then you can follow for whatever coordination you need to do at that end. Oh, and you're in charge of body disposal. Agreed?"

"Agreed," Huginn said.

"And tell Sub-Director Nask I again wish him a speedy recovery." I turned and walked toward the portal entrance.

"Roarke?"

I turned back, the unpleasant thought flickering through my mind that Huginn had orders to shoot me and simply wanted me facing him when it happened. But his plasmic was back in its holster. "You were wondering earlier who Trent was working for," he said a bit hesitantly. "It turns out it wasn't another sub-director. It was the Director General himself."

I felt my mouth drop open. "The *Director General*? Seriously?"

He nodded. "After Sub-Director Nask's meeting with you on Fidelio, and then the portal hijacking, some questions were raised about possibly mixed loyalties. Trent's equipment was purged of any lingering Patth scent, then he was ordered to observe you and Selene and ask some questions." His lip twitched. "Though he never got to the second part."

"Not my doing," I assured him. "As for Sub-Director Nask, I've never seen him show anything but complete loyalty to the Patth. His small agreements with me have been focused exclusively in that direction."

"So he has said." A ghost of a smile touched Huginn's lips. "So also I've personally observed." He pointed to the portal towering over us. "You expressed interest in Sub-Director Nask's health. Your activities here will go a long way toward ensuring that that health continues."

"Thank you for letting me know," I said, nodding to him. "Remember: ten minutes."

I climbed into the receiver module and started across toward the other opening. Still, just because Nask was conniving purely on behalf of his people didn't mean his successes couldn't spread a few gains elsewhere. I'd already seen it happen a couple of times. Hopefully, I could find similar common ground with him in the future.

In the meantime, I needed to have a chat with McKell. And find out if my time and talents were indeed still spoken for.

McKell was waiting outside the Meima portal when I rolled my way through the receiver sphere opening. "That was fast," he commented as he gave me a hand out of the pit. It was night here, but I could see by the silhouetting of the nearby hills that there were at least two clusters of lights going nearby. "Selene told me you were going to bury Cherno's body."

"It's been dealt with," I said. "Selene told *me* you had an Iykam problem."

"Not yet, but it looks like we will soon," McKell said, looking around. "There are at least two groups gathering who are showing lights, and probably one or two others that aren't. I don't know where they're coming from—there's only one Patth ship on Meima, and it wouldn't normally carry this many of them."

"We have any resources on tap?"

"Right now, it's just you, me, Ixil, and Selene," McKell said grimly. "The admiral's got a line on an EarthGuard force in the region, and I'm told there's a ship somewhere on Meima that happens to be transporting a platoon of Royal Kalixiri commandos. But none of them can get here faster than a few hours or days. Until then, we're on our own."

"I assume there's a plan?" I asked.

McKell huffed out a breath. "Such as it is. Ixil's busy gathering all the explosives he can find so we can close off this end and bury the portal a little deeper. We decided that if the Patth are going to get it, we might as well make them work for it."

"Good plan," I said. "I have a better one. How much do you trust me?"

In the faint reflected glow of the distant lights, I saw his face stiffen. "Depends on the specific day," he said. "What did you have in mind?"

I braced myself. "We pull back," I said. "We skip the explosives, pull back, and let them have their portal back."

"We can't just—" McKell broke off. "What do you mean, *their* portal?"

"This is the other end of the portal Nask made off with on Fidelio," I told him. "No question about that—his scent was all over the Kanaloa end. Cherno somehow hijacked the Patth freighter that was carrying it. He killed a lot of Patth and Iykams in the process, I should add, and nearly killed Nask himself."

"All right," McKell said slowly. "I'm sorry about that. But if the Patth lost it, it should be considered fair game."

"You're not thinking it through," I said. "Try flipping it around: say that someone stole Firefall and it wound up in Patth hands. Wouldn't you assume the Patth had orchestrated the whole thing and go full-blown burned-ground on them? Especially if a whole bunch of Icarus Group people were killed along the way? *And* if Tera, say, ended up in critical condition?"

McKell hissed between his teeth. "*Do* they think we were involved?"

"I don't know," I said. "But if I were them, I would. The only way to convince them otherwise is to hand it back without fuss or argument."

McKell looked toward one of the lights. "Even that might not be enough."

"No, but it's pretty much all the proof we can offer," I said. "If we're willing to readily give up the profits from the hijacking, why would we have bothered going to all that trouble in the first place? I'm just thinking that if the Patth decide to play hardball, they can probably do a *very* thorough job of it."

"No *probably* about it," McKell conceded. "Seven years ago, when this whole thing started, the Kalixiri had to limp through a six-month Patth embargo before the Director General was convinced they didn't know where the *Icarus* had been stashed."

"So that's a qualified yes?"

"More a *damned if I like it* yes," McKell said sourly, pulling out his phone. "But it's still a yes." He punched in a number and held the phone to his ear. "Ixil? The plan's scratched. Yes, really, and I'll explain later. Have you heard from Selene?"

He listened briefly and focused on me. "He says she got Floyd and your assassin friend to the hospital and they're being patched up now. Floyd will have to be in an intensive care pod for a couple of days, but Piper should be out by morning."

I opened my mouth to remind him that the woman we'd brought back wasn't Piper. But I caught myself in time. There might be Patth or Iykam eavesdroppers out there, and McKell had obviously decided to maintain the cover story Nikki had established for herself.

And the possible presence of those same listeners meant I also needed to be careful about what I said next.

"Yes, I know," McKell continued into the phone. "But he'll just have to live with it. Don't worry—once Tera's convinced, he'll go along. Okay. I've got Roarke here. We'll meet you at the *Stormy Banks*."

"Make it the *Ruth*," I suggested. "I need to do some work on the ship before we can leave, and Selene and I can give you more details while I'm swapping out engine components."

McKell's eyes narrowed. But his voice, when he spoke, was just as casual as mine. "Fine, if that's easiest for you," he said. "Anyway, we need to get our stories straight before we talk to the admiral. Ixil? Meet us at the *Ruth*. And yes, Roarke's buying."

He hung up and put the phone away. "Okay, this is your party now, Roarke," he said, gesturing toward a runaround parked near the portal entrance. "After you."

I headed toward the vehicle, McKell scooping up a couple of bags of equipment along the way. His acceptance of my deal had loosened the hard knot in my stomach considerably, but it wasn't completely gone. I was still looking down the barrel of the admiral's fury for handing the portal back to Nask, and the fact that it was both ethical and inevitable wasn't likely to temper that anger significantly.

But if Selene had indeed found what she said she had...

I shook the doubts and fears away. We'd know soon enough. If she had, we were going to come out of this mess better than I'd ever hoped or expected.

And we would likely have opened a can of worms the likes of which the Spiral had never seen.

CHAPTER TWENTY-SIX

———— ◆◆◆ ————

Our little get-together took a bit longer to get organized than I'd expected.

First, McKell decided we should go to the hospital and see how Floyd and Nikki were doing. Floyd wasn't in great shape, but the news that Gaheen was alive and likely to pull through lifted his spirits considerably. His biggest concern was his need to get to a StarrComm center and send some messages to the rest of his organization's top people. The medics' biggest concern was his need to shut up, lie back in his pod, and heal.

He promised to contact me once he was well enough to leave the hospital. McKell wondered on our way out if that was a threat. I assured him it probably wasn't.

Nikki was already gone. I could understand that she'd want to keep a low profile, a goal that by definition required that she be seen by as few people for as little time as possible. Still, I would have liked to talk with her one last time before she disappeared.

Especially since she'd left an envelope for me containing the card with Cherno's name and the certified bank checks Nask had given me.

I toyed with the idea of going to the Trandosh ruins in a day or so and giving the money to whatever Patth was in charge, with instructions to return it to Nask. But on second thought I realized that would probably create more questions and trouble than even a million commarks was worth. Simpler to just hold onto the money until the next time Nask and I crossed paths.

That there would *be* a next time I personally had no doubt.

Given Nikki's interest in not seeing any of us again, I had no great interest in following up on her departure. McKell apparently did. We collected Selene, who'd parked herself near the emergency room entrance where she could monitor people going in and out, and headed to the Barcarolle spaceport to see if we could pick up the trail.

It was quickly apparent that Nikki had been there recently and had in fact gone right up to the gate. But for some inexplicable reason the gate was closed and locked. We reversed along the trail for a couple of hundred meters, but Selene was unable to find any place where Nikki's scent branched off. Our reluctant conclusion was that our quarry had passed a parked runaround along the way and then backtracked to it when she found she couldn't get into the spaceport.

Continuing the pursuit would now mean slogging through the city's runaround records. Given that Nikki was undoubtedly better at hiding and staying hidden than Selene and I—or even McKell— were at finding such people, it didn't seem worth the effort.

As my father used to say, *If you play hide-and-seek with a desperado, even if you win you're probably going to lose.*

My private assumption was that Nikki would go to the Patth to get a new face, as she had gone to them for her targeting implants. Something else to talk to Nask about the next time we met.

At first I'd thought that all these side trips were McKell's way of stalling off the unpleasant moment when he would have to call the admiral and tell him we'd handed the portal over to the Patth. It was only as we finally made our way back to the *Ruth* that I realized the delay was for another reason entirely. McKell wanted to make sure we stayed well clear of the Patth in the Trandosh ruins, and that any surveillance they had on us would confirm that, and let them set up their portal retrieval system in peace and without the threat of gunfire from either side.

McKell and I didn't always agree on methods, or sometimes even on goals. But when he finally came around he came around fully committed.

Selene was able to quickly confirm that no one had been

inside the *Ruth* during our absence. Even so, I had Ixil send Pix and Pax on a thorough search of the ship's ducts, nooks, and crannies, just to make absolutely certain someone hadn't managed to plant a camera or microphone. The last thing I wanted was a leak of the news I was about to present to them.

"Let me start at the beginning," I said when the outriders' search had been completed and we were all sitting around the dayroom table with drinks in our hands. "Or at least, my speculation as to the beginning. Shiroyama Island on Popanilla was a prison camp for Icari political prisoners. However it happened—prison break, rebel activity, full-blown Tsarist-style revolution—the prisoners got access to the Gemini portal and went to Fidelio. They scampered across the Erymant Temple grounds to the Janus portal—"

"The what?" Ixil interrupted.

"The Janus portal," I repeated. "That's what Nask calls it. Anyway, they went to the portal, got through to Meima, and tried to storm the Icari facility there."

"And during the attack they were shelled and destroyed," McKell said grimly.

"Actually, we don't know the final outcome of that battle," I pointed out. "Or whether the rebels lost the battle but went on to win the war. All we know for sure is that someone or a group of someones got to the Icarus portal and went through to Alpha, leaving the two portals keyed to each other.

"The question is *why*."

"If it was the rebels, the answer seems obvious," Ixil said. "They expected their comrades to follow them."

"To *Alpha*?" I countered. "A portal sitting in the middle of nowhere?"

"More like at the edge of nowhere," McKell corrected. "It *is* orbiting a habitable planet, after all."

"Anyone currently inhabiting it?"

"Not that we've been able to detect," McKell said. "But looking for lights on the surface is about all we've been able to do, so that's hardly definitive. More important, whatever its status now there could well have been a whole civilization living there all those thousands of years ago."

"But Alpha is floating in space," Selene pointed out. "They'd need a shuttle to get to the surface."

"Or a full-fledged starship to get out of the system," I agreed. "If I were a rebel who found myself in that position, I'd hightail it back to Meima and try for somewhere else."

"That might not have been possible," McKell said. "Earlier you said that Icarus and Alpha were keyed to each other, but that's not entirely true. Icarus *was* keyed to Alpha, but the Icarus address had to be manually fed back into Alpha's console to return."

"Perhaps they returned to Meima but were unable to shut off the Alpha preset," Ixil suggested. "Though that still raises the question of why they then didn't try to go somewhere else once they were in Alpha."

"Exactly," I said. "Which suggests they *couldn't* go elsewhere."

"Why not?" McKell asked, frowning. "If they knew how to get to Alpha, they should have at least known how to get back to Icarus."

"Unless the lack of such knowledge was why they left the link to Alpha open in the first place," I said. "Whether they were defenders or attackers, they were expecting someone—they *needed* someone—to join them."

"A friend?" Ixil asked. "A commander? Family?"

"No." I braced myself. This was it. "The people who were supposed to bring them the directory."

Ixil didn't react, but the outriders on his shoulders gave simultaneous twitches. McKell just continued to look like McKell. "What directory?" McKell asked carefully.

"You know what directory," I said. "The one that lists all the portals and their addresses. The one item anyone who'd gone to Alpha absolutely needed in order to get out again."

There was another silence. "I see where you're going with this," McKell said. "But there weren't any bodies in Alpha when we first arrived. Doesn't that mean they *did* get out again?"

"Not necessarily," Ixil said. "We've noted the portals have a certain degree of housekeeping programming. There's never been any dust or corrosion in any of them, and they seem to recycle and replenish the air as needed. Alpha might simply have purged the bodies or bones."

"And you think this directory is still on Meima?" McKell asked.

"Not just on Meima," I corrected. "Right here on the *Ruth*." I looked at Selene. "Selene?"

Silently, she stood up, her pupils a mix of hesitation and concern, and walked to the dayroom hatchway. I watched as she stepped through and headed aft down the corridor toward her cabin. Peripherally, I noted that McKell and Ixil were watching her just as closely as I was. "Where?" McKell asked quietly.

"Where I expected it to be," I said. "In a vault-type room just a little ways off the battle line between the defenders and the attackers. The team was presumably heading toward the Icarus and their rendezvous when the roof collapsed and killed all of them."

"And you got all this from the link to Alpha sitting open for a few thousand years?" Ixil asked.

I shrugged. "Sometimes I get flashes of insight. Sometimes they're even right."

"Yes," Ixil murmured. "Though in this case, I almost hope you're wrong."

I winced at the dread in his voice. "Because a directory will open up a galaxy-sized can of worms?"

"Because a prize like that is worth killing for," Ixil said bluntly. "Icarus was bad enough. This..." Again, the outriders on his shoulders twitched.

"Ixil's understating the case," McKell said soberly. "Icarus was worth murder. A portal directory is worth genocide."

"Maybe not," Selene said, reappearing in the dayroom hatchway. Clutched in her hands like a piece of thousand-year-old crystal was a rectangular object, about twenty centimeters by fifteen, wrapped in one of her shirts. "I didn't have a chance to tell you, Gregory, but—" She broke off. Crossing to us, she set the object down in the center of the table and sat back down. "See for yourselves."

I raised my eyebrows at McKell in silent question. He hesitated, then gave me a small shrug and gestured for me to continue. Taking a deep breath, I picked up the object—it was heavier than I'd expected—and carefully unwrapped it.

I found myself holding an old-style book about two centimeters thick. The binding was made of black metal, with a thin, slightly raised reinforcing bar wrapping around the front, spine, and back at the top and bottom edges. Between the bars was a wide hasp attached to the back cover that sealed onto the front to hold the book closed. The edges of the pages were a shimmering gold. I looked at Selene, again noting the nervousness in her pupils, my thoughts flashing back to what Ixil and McKell had just said about it being worth genocide.

But we were all allies here, I reminded myself firmly. Looking down at the book, I unfastened the hasp—it was held in place magnetically—and opened it.

The pages were flexible, but felt like thinner versions of the same metal as the binding. The first five pages contained close-spaced etched lines of alien script: some lines colored black, others colored red, the two seemingly randomly placed on the page. I focused on the letters, but they weren't even close to anything I was familiar with.

Starting with the sixth page, the format changed. Now, there were a few lines of the alien script on the on the left side of the left-hand page, with an ordered array of squares facing the words on the right-hand page. The squares were colored, also apparently randomly, in yellow or black.

The same colors as on the squares of a portal's destination readout panel.

I felt my heart sped up. I'd been right. There was indeed a portal directory, and Selene had found it.

I frowned. Or had she?

I flipped through another few pages. The script and color pattern changed, but the format remained the same.

And then I saw it, and my stomach tied itself into a knot.

This wasn't the portal directory I'd hoped for. It was, instead—

"Hell," McKell muttered, his expression that of a man who'd been handed a rare gem only to discover it was made of glass.

"Indeed," Ixil agreed.

I nodded heavily. Icarus destination displays, I belatedly remembered, were four rows of twenty squares. The pages here showed four rows of ten.

This wasn't a directory. It was *half* a directory.

"Which strongly suggests," I added, "that the ones who got through to Alpha had the other half."

For a few seconds no one spoke. "So that's it," McKell said at last. "Half a directory is like a draw at chess. Useless."

"Maybe not," Selene said hesitantly.

We all looked at her. "You think the other half's still here?" I asked.

"If it is, it's not near the spot where I found this," she said. "But I've been thinking. If you had half the address for the Icarus, Jordan, and you thought an enemy might have the other half, and you were trapped, what would you do?"

"I don't know," McKell said. "Guard it with my life, probably."

"But if you knew the enemy would simply kill you and still take it?"

"You'd do whatever you could to make sure that didn't happen," I said, watching Selene's pupils change from concern to dark horror. "If you could destroy it you would."

"It's a metal book with metal pages," McKell said. "Pretty hard to do without a plasma torch or industrial crusher."

"Then you'd have to send it someplace where they couldn't get it," I said. "Even if it killed you."

"There were no bodies in Alpha," Ixil murmured. "If they had no ships or shuttles...?"

"Are you suggesting they *jumped*?" McKell asked.

The outriders twitched again. "I can't think of a better way to make sure their half of the directory wasn't retrieved," Ixil said. "If it came to that..."

McKell exhaled a ragged breath. "If I couldn't get out of Alpha and there was no chance of rescue...yes, I probably would, too. It would certainly insure it was never retrieved."

"Maybe not," I said, running my fingers thoughtfully along the edge of the book. Selene had said it was made of something akin to portal metal. If the book was as indestructible as the portals themselves seemed to be..."If it survived the fall, it's probably still down there."

McKell and Ixil looked at each other. "If you're thinking what I think you're thinking," McKell warned, "no. Not a chance in hell."

"You sure?" I countered. "Selene can smell this stuff, remember. She found this under half a meter of dirt and stone."

"That was the Trandosh ruins," McKell said. "This is an entire planet. Huge difference."

"Granted," I said. "It might still be worth a shot." I looked at Selene. "What do you think?"

She gazed down at the book, her pupils shifting between anticipation, hope, and dread. "A bioprobe survey would help narrow the field," she said slowly. "But I don't know how we'd get a bioprobe in there."

"We'll figure it out," I said, eyeing the growing dread in her pupils. "Maybe bring a couple of them into Alpha in pieces and assemble them there. The important thing is that there are options."

McKell shook his head. "Personally, I think we'd have a better chance of finding a copy near some other portal."

"*If* we can find another portal," I warned. "And *if* the Patth don't find it first."

"Well, we're not going to solve any of this tonight," McKell said. He closed the book and resealed it, then picked it up. "First thing we have to do is tell the admiral that we lost the portal. If I'm suitably angry and mortified, and if the Patth retrieve the conversation, that should keep them off our backs while we smuggle this out of here."

"You could just leave it with us," I suggested. "The Patth would never suspect we would have something that valuable on the *Ruth*."

"Great idea," McKell said with a hint of sarcasm. "And if your friend Nask drops in for a chat?"

"He's not my friend," I said stiffly. "And even if he was, I doubt he'd stoop to searching the ship."

"Why not?" McKell countered. "They stoop to listening to private StarrComm messages. Sorry, but it goes with us. Ixil?"

"I agree," Ixil said. He stood up and produced a collapsible bag from a pocket. "Here—we don't want to steal Selene's shirt."

"Thanks," McKell said. He took the bag and carefully wrapped the directory inside. "We'll be in touch," he said as he and Ixil stood up. "Congratulations to you both. Excellent work all around."

"You're welcome," I said. "You might suggest to the admiral that when he's ready to shower us with praise he might want to sprinkle in a few extra commarks."

"Considering that he's just lost the new portal he was salivating over, I think we'll skip any mention of money *or* praise," McKell said dryly. "Fly safe. We'll be in touch."

"Thanks," I said standing up. "Come on, I'll see you out."

Selene was still sitting at the table when I returned, gazing into her cup. "Well, there goes the Spiral's only known list—partial list, anyway—of the Icari portals," I commented as I sat down across from her. "I assume you made a copy?"

"Of course," she said, still looking into her drink, her pupils looking distracted. "Do you really think we can find the other half?"

"No idea," I admitted. "But it's worth trying."

"Maybe in principle," she said. "But the mechanics and techniques will be a challenge."

"That's okay—the admiral lives for such things." I ducked my head to look more squarely into her lowered face. "Something else on your mind?"

Her pupils twitched in a wry expression. "Have I ever told you that you're nearly as good at reading me as I am you? And you humans have hardly any sense of smell at all."

"True," I said. "But we manage to muddle through. You want to talk about it?"

She lifted her cup, took a small sip. "I wasn't very polite to Nikki while she was aboard," she said. "I know you knew that. I think she did, too."

"One of the downsides of being a professional assassin," I pointed out. "A lot of the people you meet don't like you."

"It wasn't her," Selene said. "Not *just* her. It was just that she brought back memories..."

She took another drink, a longer one this time. "We have legends, Gregory, we of the Kadolians," she said. "Legends about where we came from, how we got to the Spiral, what it took to win our freedom."

"Sounds interesting," I said, keeping my voice neutral. Selene had never talked about her past before. "Which memories did Nikki bring back?"

"Those of the beings we once worked for," Selene said. "Another species, creatures who prized our talents for tracking and for trace-scent location and identification. They hired many of us to be scouts and analysts. Some of us became their version of bounty hunters." She paused, her pupils taking on a darker feel. "Some of us they made into assassins."

For a moment the word seemed to hang in the air between us. "I'm sorry," I managed into the silence. "I didn't...it must have been horrifying."

She shook her head. "Not to all of us. And that's the problem. You see, for many of us..." She took another drink. "We were good at it, Gregory. Good enough that many of us...they liked it."

"I see," I said, wincing at the banality of the words. "But that was a long time ago."

"I'm still of the Kadolians," she said. "I still have our strengths and impulses and weaknesses. I enjoy the hunt." She raised her eyes and troubled pupils to me. "Would I also learn to enjoy the kill?"

"That's not you," I said firmly. "You wouldn't go that direction."

"Are you sure?" she asked. "Because I'm not. If I was offered that job, against someone I believed deserved to die..." She closed her eyes. "I truly don't know."

I reached over and gently touched her hand. "I don't know what drives your people, Selene, or what would happen if you found yourself in that position. But there are two things I *do* know."

I held up a finger. "One: I trust you. I trust you with my life and the lives of everyone around me. Whatever situation we get into, whatever decisions you make, I will always back you up."

I held up a second finger. "And two: late at night, when you're hungry or tired or just finished with a case, is not the time to be thinking about things like this. So let's get to bed. Things always look different in the morning."

"I know," she said.

But she didn't, I could tell. Legends and memories were powerful influences in every culture. And even if the dark of night enhanced the emotions connected to them, emotions that would fade when the sun returned, the legends themselves were still there.

As my father used to say, *Just because you've convinced yourself there are no monsters in the darkened room doesn't mean you might not fall over a chair.*

The universe, I'd long since learned, was very good at setting up chairs in darkened rooms. So were the Patth.

Maybe the Kadolians were, too.

The End